We know they're out there.

The strange ones. The unsettling ones.
The ones who don't quite fit in.

Neighbors. Possibly even the one
right next door to you.

Could it be they're more than
just neighbors?
More than just odd?
More than just unsettling?

Could they be...

MORE MONSTERS NEXT DOOR?

3¢
003
BEAR GOBLIN

MORE MONSTERS NEXT DOOR

Edited by R.J. Carter

This is a work of fiction. All the characters and events portrayed in this book are fictitious, and any resemblance to real people is purely coincidental.

More Monsters Next Door © 2025 by Critical Blast Publishing. Individual copyrights to authors of these original works are as follows:

Byzantium © 2025 Mike Rusetsky
The Bitches of Arcadia © 2025 Ray Zacek
Not a House © 2025 Troy Riser
A Total Witch © 2025 Deborah Cardillo
Stoned © 2025 Kevin Hopson
Buryin' Mama © 2025 Lauren Stoker
What the Earth Remembers © 2025 Ikechukwu Henry
Pick His Bones Clean © 2025 Sirius
The Nick Victory Chronicles, Part 7: Now You See Me © 2025 Paul Barile
While She Was Away © 2025 William Couper
Turf War © 2025 Jen Poteet
Paradise Marsh © 2025 M.R. DeLuca
The New Neighbors © 2021 Lena Ng (previously published May 2021 by Page & Spine)
Your Reptoid Representative © 2025 Eldon Litchfield
The Inelegance of Space © 2025 Allister Nelson
The House That Crawled Away © 2025 Paul Lonardo
No One Would Even Care © 2025 LCW Allingham
Split Decision: A Sam Heller Investigation © 2025 Jacob Seinemeier
Let Them Rest © 2025 Eric Avedissian
A Night at Wolfe's Lake © 2025 Damascus Mincemeyer

All rights reserved. No part of this book may be reproduced in any form, including information storage and retrieval systems, without permission in writing from the publisher.

Critical Blast Publishing
624 Sunnyhill Drive
Belleville, IL 62223

Book Design, Typesetting, Cover Art & Interior Illustrations by George Peter Gatsis. © 2025 George Peter Gatsis. All Rights Reserved.

First Edition Dec 2025

0 9 8 7 6 5 4 3 2 1

ISBN: 978-1-967199-66-2

CONTENTS

Byzantium
Mike Rusetsky 1

The Bitches of Arcadia
Ray Zacek 31

Not A House
Troy Riser 57

A Total Witch
Deborah Cardillo 87

Stoned
Kevin Hopson 101

Buryin' Mama
Lauren Stoker 119

What the Earth Remembers
Ikechukwu Henry 133

Pick His Bones Clean
Sirius 159

The Nick Victory Chronicles, Part 7: Now You See Me
Paul Barile 175

While She Was Away
William Couper 189

Turf War
Jen Poteet 223

Paradise Marsh
M.R. DeLuca 231

The New Neighbors
Lena Ng 251

Your Reptoid Representative
Eldon Litchfield 261

The Inelegance of Space
Allister Nelson 275

The House That Crawled Away
Paul Lonardo 287

No One Would Even Care
LCW Allingham 305

Split Decision: A Sam Heller Investigation
Jacob Seinemeier 325

Let Them Rest
Eric Avedissian 365

A Night At Wolfe's Lake
Damascus Mincemeyer 387

36
USA
JOKUBAT

CRITICAL BLAST PUBLISHING
20¢
BYZANTIUM
APPROVED BY THE READING CODE AUTHORITY
Mike Rusetsky
CRITICAL BLAST PUBLISHING
THE NEW SHAPE OF HORROR

HEAD KNIVES 100% stainless steal daggers that launch from the top of your head and kill any conversation you find boring.

FISH BOWL FULL OF WORMS Are you tired of eating meat? Get yourself a bowl full of yummy worms and feel you are saving the planet.

SUPER SECRET BOOK SAFE The special camouflage feature activates, once placed on the book shelf. You'll never find it again.

DIGITAL PUZZLE T-SHIRT Get people's undivided attention when they get engrossed trying to solve the constantly changing puzzles.

DEFEAT BLACK MYSTIC ARTS KUNG-FU Tired of getting your ass kicked every Tuesday by Black Mystic Arts Kung-Fu fighters? CALL 666-HELP to enroll in self-defense training every Hellspawn should know to survive any dark alley encounter. Become a Ninth Circle Master of Judante!

RADIOACTIVE CANDY When you want to level up your personality and appear extra sweet to the people around you... and want to have a superpower over sugar... this candy's for you!

BOX OF LIVE BATS When you feel like a millionaire crime fighting hero and need to dress up your special cave, to give it that extra touch of atmosphere... a box of live bats is perfect for you. Food not included.

MONSTER VALUE STAMP THIS IS IT! CLIP THEM & COLLECT THEM ALL!

Mike Rusetsky is a Ukrainian-American author of horror, urban fantasy and speculative fiction. He started out as a playwright, with his original one-act productions Angel of Death and The Plight of Smitty earning critical praise. His recent publications include stories in anthologies by Outsider Publishing, Black Hare Press, Inkd Publishing, Storm Dragon Publishing, Wicked Shadow Press and the magazines Sometimes Hilarious Horror and Tales from the Crosstimbers. Mike is an active member of the Horror Writers Association. He lives in Columbus, Ohio with his beautiful wife and their spoiled Alaskan Malamute dog. mikerusetsky.com

All realtors promise the impossible, but mine actually delivered.

When Zoe and I first started looking, our real estate agent Maxine met us at every property with a wide grin and a high-pitched, "Hey, you two!" But as we walked the premises, each house slowly revealing its hidden flaws, Maxine's megawatt grin dimmed by degrees, her eyes correctly reading the disappointment on my and Zoe's faces.

The kitchen of this particular house was spacious and bright, but the roof showed signs of poorly patched wind damage. The two-car garage came equipped with a cool workbench for Zoe's woodcraft, but the HVAC system was fourteen years old and ready to go any minute. The house itself was acceptable, but the backyard lacked a privacy fence, which we needed for our dog. Always something rotten hiding beneath even the most lavish façade... sometimes literally.

I suppose it didn't help matters that my job as a Code Inspector for the City cursed me with a severely critical eye when it came to examining properties. Zoe joked about me "coming home with my hardhat on" when applying my inspection skills to each house, but what could I do?

And she was one to talk: during our very first walkthrough, she spotted a dilapidated tool shed behind the house which she immediately dubbed "the murder shed." I cackled when she pointed it out and asked what made it a murder shed as opposed to just a dusty old shed.

She merely shrugged and said, "It just looks like the perfect desolate spot to murder someone. Plus, the tools for dismemberment are already there."

I had to play along, and rebuked her in a showy stage whisper. "Not in front of Maxine, baby! She'll think we're looking to increase our body storage capacity."

Winking at our realtor, Zoe fake-whispered back, "If she wants her commission, she'll stay quiet about all the *bodies*." I couldn't help but snort with laughter.

"You'll have to excuse us, Maxine. We share a weird sense of humor."

She gave us a tight smile. "You guys are adorable. Never lose that spark between you. Believe me, it's hard to reignite once it goes out..."

Maxine stared off towards the wooden deck, clearly not thinking about real estate. It got a little awkward, but then she cleared her throat and refocused on us.

"Now, I can tell this place isn't really your style. What with the, uh, murder shed' and all. But if you have another half-hour to spare, I've got just the place for you."

And so it went. We spent almost four weeks looking at places, scouring damn near everything in the realtor database, and even more from Zillow. All the while Maxine's grin and greeting stayed bright as ever. "Hey, you two!"

Her parting words at every inevitably-disappointed showing were a variation on, "Don't sweat it, we'll find it soon!" and "You'll know the right place. It will speak to you!"

But would it? Zoe and I started to grow worried. Maybe our standards were too high? Our price range wasn't anything to sneeze at, but could our expectations use some adjustment? After all, a house was just a physical place. After six years of apartment hopping, we were ready to make the big investment; but it was so hard to give up the ethereal "dream home" we'd built in our minds. The dream seemed to dissipate each time we stepped into a pedestrian building with four walls and a hastily painted deck. To say nothing of the murder shed out back.

After nearly a month, Maxine's energy level was becoming difficult to sustain. But one day she announced that she had a truly special house for our perusal. It was an estate sale, which was odd because we'd expressly told her we weren't interested in deceased people's houses. Zoe was a nurse at Riverside Methodist, and she'd seen too much death. We'd walked through one early on in the process and it was a sad, cramped space, full of yellowing photos of family members and antique furniture that still retained the smell (and in one bed's case, the body indentation) of its recently departed owner.

"This one's not like other estate sales," Maxine assured us, trying to soothe our concerned expressions. "It's in a brand-new development, just built last year."

"Hold up a sec," I said. "You mean this house was built a year ago, and someone already died in it?"

She sighed, clearly hating my question. That's because realtors had to disclose any "decedent events" prior to a sale going through. I know my laws. Also, I live for the maudlin details.

"Not exactly," she replied. "The owner didn't die *in* the house. Technically, not even on the premises."

"I'm listening," Zoe said, and I sighed. Were we really entertaining the idea of visiting some dead guy's creepy house?

"He passed away peacefully, in an ambulance *en route* to Mount Carmel."

"There it is!" I said, feeling vindicated. "What happened? Did the ghosts in the house get him?"

"Eric!" Zoe hissed, elbowing me. "You're being rude."

I merely shrugged, staring down Maxine for a response.

"You could always do a quick walkthrough. It's not too far, I can even drive you."

Zoe and I exchanged a glance, a couple's telepathy message of "I'm cool with it if you are" passing between us. And really, what could it hurt, just to look?

#

"When did you say this was built?" I asked, as Maxine maneuvered her red Subaru through the neighborhood's gates. They were wrought iron and opened in the old-fashioned way: by swinging outwards, as opposed to the more common sliding style. They looked at least a hundred years old to me.

"Spring last year," she said. I made a sound of acknowledgment, unable to hide my surprise.

"Ooh, look!" Zoe said, pointing. "Is that a freakin' Venetian fountain?"

"Actually, yeah," Maxine said, a small smile playing on her lips. "The developer has shareholders who are big into antique furniture and architecture. They've amassed quite a collection of artifacts, and put some of the more impressive pieces on display. There are some walking paths here laid with pavers from the Greco-Roman times."

"You're shitting me!" I said, losing my composure. "Seriously? Is this for real?"

Zoe was silent, her brown eyes sweeping the scene as Maxine explained the backstory. An investment group that respected architecture in its many historic eras had been building small but visually distinct communities in suburbs along both coasts. This particular project, dubbed "Byzantium," was their first foray into the Midwest, and was inspired by the classical era. The houses here, although equipped with modern amenities, also reflected the imperial Roman theme in their exterior design. As we drifted past them, I could see how right she was: some of the homes were mansions propped up by columns of white-washed marble, others were more humble in scope, but still adhered to the assignment in their own ways. I even spotted one with a decorative aqueduct. Or was it functional?

"Okay, this is fascinating and all," Zoe said, and I braced myself. I could tell when true, unvarnished Zoe was about to come out. "But Maxine, you know our price range. This place doesn't just feel expensive—it feels *millionaire* expensive. Like, exploit-the-peasants-to-get-rich expensive."

"Yeah," I agreed. "We'd have to sell some vital organs to afford a mortgage here. Possibly *all* our organs."

"Oh, ye of little faith," Maxine sighed, and pulled into a driveway. It wasn't a circular one like a private roundabout out front, but a normal-looking, concrete slab driveway. "Don't you think I've got your back, after all this time? I snatched up this exclusive listing from a realtor friend. Technically it's not even on the market yet. You'd be the first to do a walkthrough. That is, unless you're not even remotely curious what it's like inside?"

I looked at the house she drove us to—far from a flashy McMansion or a faux Roman temple, it looked like a suburban Dutch Colonial. A few marble stone flourishes sculpted into the siding, in keeping with the theme, but it was a regular-presenting single family home. A dimensional shingle roof installed to building code. Two-car garage nestled into the side. Lush, manicured lawn.

"Damn it..." I said, my skepticism already waning, "I kinda want to check it out, babe."

Zoe broke into a smile. "Not if I check it out first!"

Maxine dangled the key fob towards us. "Want to Greco-Roman wrestle for it?"

#

I don't know why I expected the interior to feel like a museum (maybe Maxine's backstory still lingered in my mind), but we walked into a house that felt ready to be lived in. More than that: as soon as we crossed the threshold, it felt like home. It's cheesy to say, I know. But there was something about the bright, airy space of the foyer, the clean lines of the swirling-smoke flooring tiles, that didn't feel like I was a guest dropping by. It felt like I was coming home after a long day of visiting building sites.

I wasn't alone in my instant awe, as Zoe looked similarly stunned—and stayed uncharacteristically quiet—while she glided through the interior, absorbing the details. Maxine seemed to hold her breath too, probably due to our subdued reactions. She was used to us peppering her with jokes and comments, and I'm sure was steeling herself for the onslaught, but for once, we had nothing to say. Granite countertops, thick carpeting in the living areas, and plenty of sunlight streaming through the arched windows all spoke for themselves.

The backyard was another revelation: a cozy stone-paved patio with a built-in fire pit segued into soft, verdant grass that, to my apartment-dwelling mind, went on for ages before running into a tasteful privacy fence around the property. The yard was vast, the expanse of it only interrupted by a single upright object: a square stone-carved frame with two miniature columns bookending the indentation. A birdbath, maybe? It towered at least five feet tall, probably a Home Depot find made to look like an antique. I'd have to weed-trim around it, but that was a minor complaint. Overall, this yard would be an ideal place to entertain friends, and a safe playground for our sassy Labradoodle, C.S. Lewis. (His full name: Captain Sassypaws Lewis).

Zoe turned from the spacious yard to regard me, and I spotted a smile beginning to grow on her lips. It mirrored my own. Our couples' telepathy was perfectly in tune.

"Let's hear it. What's wrong with this one?" Maxine stepped out on the patio while saying this, then froze, clocking our idiot grins.

"It's perfect," I said, and squeezed Zoe's hand. "Magical, even."

"And no murder shed," my girlfriend cooed. "Yep, we'll take it!"

#

At Zoe's suggestion, I bought a nice pinot noir for Maxine's trouble. We gave it to her at the closing, after signing our lives away for two hours straight.

"Aw, guys. You didn't have to," she said, blushing but accepting the bottle.

"You earned it!" Zoe laughed. "Putting up with our crazy demands for a whole month. Thank you so much!"

"I hope the house is kind to you," Maxine said. "Told you the right one would speak to you, Eric!"

"I gotta say, I thought you were full of shit, but you were right," I said, earning an elbow in the ribs from Zoe. "It really is perfect, for our little family of three."

Maxine's eyebrows suddenly met, her face concerned. "You've registered your puppy with the HOA, haven't you? I just don't want any unexpected knocks on your door."

I nodded. "No problem. C.S. Lewis isn't on the forbidden breeds list, so he's in good standing."

Maxine's face brightened. "Fantastic! Well, it's time to celebrate the beginning of the rest of your lives!"

We cheesed at the camera that snapped our picture for the realtor's socials, us holding a comically oversized door key. I always rolled my eyes at my friends' photos in the same situation, but when it came to posing for my own, I didn't mind one bit. I guess it's a you-had-to-be-there thing. And we finally were.

We moved in that very weekend, despite our apartment lease still going for another month and a half. But double rent for almost two months was a small price to pay for living in a beautiful new community with a quirky visual vibe. Plus, no shared walls! We were in heaven.

C.S. Lewis took a full day to adjust to the move, sniffing out every corner of his new kingdom, at first with suspicion but eventually with the pride of ownership. It must've eased his nerves to have pissed on every blade of grass and stone paver in the backyard. The birdbath didn't escape his urine marks, either, its black stone darkened all the more.

Zoe got to set up her woodshop in the basement workspace. She was kind enough to share the area with my attempt at a home gym. I made my little nerd nook upstairs, in the fourth bedroom. It took hours to put up all my autographed musician posters and install the foam noise pads for my music studio. I wasn't the most popular neighbor in our apartment complex, even though I never owned a drum set. But guitars and keyboards? Oh yes. Finally, my hobby had room to grow—without ruining friendships with neighbors. Speaking of which …

The day after we moved in, a knock came at our door. This was odd, because we had a perfectly functioning doorbell. Zoe was in the basement, running her track saw with safety earplugs in, so I answered the door.

Before me stood a man about my dad's age, only better dressed. This fellow was a silver fox, wearing a brown sweater vest over a button-down shirt, and khakis with loafers to boot. Weirdly formal attire for a Saturday, but maybe he kept odd business hours?

"Um, hi there," I said, trying to look a bit more formal in my Punk-in-Drublic T-shirt and gym shorts. It's always a great idea to make a first impression while wearing music festival attire and reeking of sweat. In my defense, I had been puzzling together an Ikea dresser and wasn't expecting company.

"Good morning, you must be Eric Delgado," he said. Not a question, but a statement of fact.

"Guilty as charged. And who might—"

"My name is Jasper Auerbach. I live next door."

"Oh. Well, pleasure to meet you, Jasper." I went for a handshake, but he flinched at my gesture, so I put my sweaty paw away. Alright, then.

"You'll forgive my intrusion, but I saw your U-Haul, um, caravan the other day."

"That was us, me and my girlfriend Zoe. We're all good and moved in now. Hopefully we didn't leave any track marks on your lawn or anything?"

"Nothing like that," he reassured me. "I simply wanted to make a formal introduction and issue a welcome to the community. Byzantium can be a wonderful place for a new start."

"Oh, very cool. Thank you! We're pretty psyched to be here. First time homebuyers, so it's pretty surreal. Especially with all the old crap—I mean, the classic-themed stuff. It's— different, but very tasteful. You wanna pop in, Jasper? I've got some IPAs in the fridge..."

His pinched expression indicated that crossing my threshold was the last thing he wanted.

"Perhaps another time. I've got business to attend to."

"Of course," I nodded. "Business, yeah. What line of work are y—"

"If I can offer a suggestion," he interrupted. "A recommendation, really. Please keep a close eye on your... canine friend. The speed limit is seven miles an hour, but a small dog like yours could easily blend in with the road..."

He trailed off, as if beckoning me to imagine the tragic aftermath of letting my dog loose in the street. This made me like him even less than before. Who the hell did he think he was, talking down to me like that? Or was it a veiled threat?

"Our dog won't bother you, if that's what you mean," I managed, trying not to glare.

"Excellent," he nodded. "I'm sure you and your lovely wife—oh, my apologies, girlfriend— I'm sure you and your girlfriend will take great care of him, to the standards indicated by our homeowners' association. Of which I am the president, by the way."

My face must have betrayed my surprise, because he grinned a toothy, humorless grin. "That's right. I'll be available right next door... should you ever need me."

Okay, now that was a more definite contender for a threat. But why? We literally hadn't even done anything yet.

"Um, thank you, Jasper. Mr. Auerbach."

"Jasper is fine. Since you didn't ask, I will divulge that I am the *acting* president as of last month. My predecessor was the gentleman who first bought this place, and met his unfortunate end on the way to the hospital."

My jaw dropped at this information. The previous homeowner! This was starting to get uncomfortable. Why was Jasper being so damn smug about all this? Was it some kind of hubris-steeped power move? A veiled threat in case we should complain to someone? But what was there to complain about? I felt a tightening in my chest and swallowed a knot in my throat.

"I'm sorry about your friend, Jasper. It must have been a tragic loss, for you and the HOA both."

If he detected the sarcasm in my tone, he never showed it. "Thank you. Take care, Mister Delgado." He started to turn, then paused. "Actually, one last thing. Many of our residents use the services of a local landscaping company, Prodeus Lawn Care. You might want to consider them if they come calling."

After such a cold, bitchy visit, I was considering a swift kick to Jasper's pressed khakis, but by some miracle I abstained.

"Thanks for stopping by, Jasper!"

It was all I could do not to slam the door.

#

Zoe watched as I paced the living room, passionately summarizing the HOA president's visit. She was upsettingly calm throughout my narrative.

"Well? What do you think, babe?"

She shrugged. "What do you want me to say? That Jasper sounds rude as shit? He does. But Eric, we gotta play the long game here. We just moved in. It'll do no good to make enemies on day one. With our next-door neighbors, no less."

I exhaled an exasperated breath. "Really? So you're cool with him threatening our dog?"

She considered it. "Depending on his tone, he might just be a poor communicator. More of a policies-person than a people-person. Law and order above all else. That's probably why he's president of the HOA."

"*Acting* president. The guy who dropped dead in our home being the one he replaced."

Zoe moved towards me, putting a comforting hand on my back, then removing it immediately. "Eww, have you been working out? You're drenched in sweat!"

I laughed. "Thanks for the pep talk. Yeah, actually. I was in hour three of putting together that stupid dresser when Jasper came calling."

Zoe suggested we call it a day on the practical stuff, and I heartily agreed. She always had the more reasonable take on things. We spent that evening cuddled up on the couch, C.S. Lewis wedged happily between us. We ate Indian takeout and rooted for competitive glass-blowers on Netflix. It was a good night. But the newfound idyll wouldn't last long.

#

On Sunday morning, Zoe was out on the patio, painting some of her wooden pieces in her makeshift "open-air studio," when I suddenly heard her voice atop the basement stairs.

"Eric, you down there?"

I was mid-workout, blasting a Rancid playlist while shuffling disk weights off and on the barbell.

"Yeah, what's up?"

"I think I just saw your new bestie and his wife. They're... being weird outside."

That got my attention. I abandoned the weights (quite willingly, to be honest) and raced upstairs to see what she was talking about.

We stepped out on the patio, which allowed a nice view of our neighbors' yard. The Auerbachs had their own little Zen vibe going, with a tinkling water feature and even what looked like a lemon tree back there. Sure enough, I saw Jasper, along with a silver-haired lady roughly his age (wife was my guess). I shouted a friendly if sardonic "Howdy, neighbors!" but they both ignored me.

Zoe and I exchanged a look, and I shrugged. "Maybe they're hard of hearing? What the hell are they doing, anyway?"

Mr. and Mrs. Auerbach were up to something... unconventional. They kneeled directly on the grass side by side, their arms crossed in an accidental parody of the "Wakanda Forever" salute, and every fifteen seconds or so they would bend at the waist in a bowing motion. Asses up in the air, they stayed down for another quarter minute, then came back up in unison. This was a quiet and uncomplicated motion, but the sheer focus and dignity they put into the act was impressive. Especially considering what must have been elderly hardware they were working with, knees-and-joints-wise.

"Nimble," Zoe said. She must've been thinking the same thing.

"Is it like... yoga?" I asked, still trying to make sense of what I was seeing.

"Either that, or they're worshipping that little fountain," Zoe quipped.

I frowned. "Don't see any yoga mats, though. Weird..."

Zoe made an "I dunno" face at me, and we decided to leave well enough alone. I didn't need any more blackmail material for Jasper Auerbach to use against me, so I retreated back to my workout routine, leaving a bemused Zoe to continue painting her creations within spitting distance of the strange neighbor couple.

#

That afternoon, another loud knock came at our door. I started to suspect that no one around here knew how to use doorbell technology, but this time Zoe beat me to the entryway.

"Hello there!" she chirped to whoever was on the doorstep.

"Aft'noon, Miss," a male voice responded. Not Jasper. Higher pitched and more informal. Intrigued, I moved a little closer.

"I'm Rex, with Prodeus Lawn Care," he said. "Wonderin' if'n y'all need a little TLC for that yard."

I hip-checked Zoe, edging into the doorframe (a move I learned from C.S. Lewis). "Excuse me, hi. I heard you might come around asking, but we really don't need your services. I do my own lawn mowing and yardwork. Maybe others around here don't like getting their hands dirty, but I'm good with it."

The landscaping guy squinted up at me. A squat man in brown-green overalls, he didn't look dangerous, but something behind his hazel eyes under a sparse shock of unkempt hair seemed ominous. Despite his easy gap-toothed grin, there was something unkind about this man.

"Ya sure 'bout that?" he asked, holding me with that unsettling gaze. "'S no trouble, mister. I take real good care of the elements here. I know you got that... special feature and stone patio back there, and y'all's dog ain't been too kind to it."

Now it was Zoe's turn to frown. I felt her body tensing

up next to me. "Excuse me, Rex," she said. "I don't know who told you about our dog, but he's a very good boy. A model citizen, even."

"That right?"

"Yes sir. And we can mow around our own birdbath, thank you very much."

Zoe went to close the door, but I couldn't resist one last parting shot, sensing it might piss off Rex from Prodeus in just the right way.

"Besides, pal. I'm into the re-wilding method. Gonna plant native species and let them take over, so the bees can do their thing. So if this time next month it looks like a wild meadow back there, there's nothing you or anyone else can do about it."

The man gave a slow nod. If he was upset, he didn't show it. "Loud'n clear, pardner. Welp, you had your chance," he sighed, then ambled back towards his truck.

"Ridiculous," I said, closing the door.

Zoe nodded. "Where do they get off sending us this guy? I can't believe it. As soon as we own some property, everyone's trying to tell us what to do with it."

"Bottom line is, it's ours," I said.

C.S. Lewis came out to investigate the commotion. I scratched behind his ear and he leaned in, panting with pleasure.

"Don't worry, little dude. Your playground is safe from these horrible people."

#

That night, sleep didn't come easy. I stirred in bed, listening to the night outside our bedroom window. Wind gusts rising and falling, the occasional crazed birdcall. It didn't help that our house had noises of its own I was still adjusting to: settling floor creaks and plumbing whispering inside the walls. Granted, some of it could have been C.S. Lewis moving around downstairs.

Once I finally succumbed to sleep, I dreamt of C.S. Lewis digging vigorously in the backyard. I approached as he grunted under his breath, paws raking up the soil. He was digging right next to the stone birdbath, emitting a low growl as he worked.

"Whatcha up to, buddy?"

He ignored me, staying laser-focused on his goal. If anything, he even sped up, his paws flinging wet mud, fur getting caked in it.

"C'mon, Lewis. Let's go inside, before Mama Zoe wakes up and chews us both out. It's way past our bedtime."

A high-pitched whine came from his throat; it sounded worse than groomer dread. This was the soundtrack to obsession, a desperate yearning that couldn't be put into words. It chilled me to the bone.

"Hey, bud. We're done here, okay?"

I touched his hindquarters to get his attention, and he snapped around, snarling as if I was a stranger. Eyes wild, bared teeth glistening. I snatched my hand away, barely avoiding his teeth.

"Whoa, Lewis! It's just me, bud. Take it easy. Jesus."

He scowled at me, an expression I'd never seen clouding his eyes black, then his jaw relaxed and he turned away. Back to his task. I went to pet him again, then withdrew my hand. What if he actually connected this time? And what did he want with this old piece of junk? I was sure the only piss scent marking it was his own, as much as he'd watered the thing. I folded my arms, watching my dog as if in an altered state, feeling as alone, helpless and uncomfortable as only a dream can make you feel.

The alarm blared, and even before silencing it I knew this would not be a workday. I texted my boss about using PTO, then collapsed back on the pillow. The dream's effect lingered, and I stirred in a discomfort that was hard to articulate.

That morning, I fed C.S. Lewis—who was his normal, grinning, non-black-eyed self—and went out for a jog. The day off seemed like a good opportunity to check out our new neighborhood.

My run was a lollygagger's dream: some of these houses were truly resplendent in their outlandishness. I swear one of them was modeled on the Parthenon; I was more familiar with the replica in Nashville than the one in Greece, but still. The place was 90% pillars. I found myself chuckling at the absurdity of someone buttering toast or watching Sunday night football inside that monstrosity, when a red minivan almost plowed into me.

Tires squealed, the car skidded to a stop, and I felt the bumper lightly press into my thigh. If the driver had been any slower to react, my leg bones would've been crunched by this damn Subaru... I glared at the driver, only to see Maxine's terrified face looking back.

"Hey, you!" she smiled timidly.

We sat down inside in my recently furnished living room and I served her iced tea. Unsweetened for Maxine, Stevia'd for me. The near-accident behind us, I was happy to see a friendly face in my home.

"What do you mean? Did the guy actually threaten your dog?" she asked.

I hesitated. "Well, not exactly. But he mentioned the speed limit and what could happen to a dog running amok."

"As if Lewis would ever do that," she frowned, sipping her tea. Hearing his name, C.S. Lewis trundled over and plopped down at Maxine's feet.

"Exactly! Thank you. We trained him better than that."

She nodded, petting him idly, and I felt buoyed by her indignation on my behalf.

"What's Zoe think about all this?"

I shrugged. "She loves the place, we both do. I guess she's more determined to make peace with the locals. However... well, loco."

We shared a laugh. "You two are hilarious," she said. "Always going on about that murder shed." She shook her head, chuckling.

"But you came through for us!"

"Uh-huh, I sure did," she said, but the smile was losing its sheen. "Listen, Eric. I'm sure you're wondering why I stopped by like this."

I wasn't, but maybe I should've been? "I guess I thought you're on the prowl for another property in the great Byzantium community."

She gave a half-smile. "Not exactly."

"Okay."

"Have you done any... research since you closed on this house?"

"Research? You mean, aside from personally pissing off the HOA?"

"I mean, about some of what you've told me. It's shaping up to be a close-knit community here. And I wouldn't want you and Zoe to start feeling... left out. It's happened before, and I'd hate for that to be your experience."

I blinked, sipped my 'Teavia.' "I don't exactly get your meaning, Maxine."

She gnawed at her lip, a vacant stare in her blue eyes.

"The man who visited. The serviceman who does lawns."

"Rex, from Prodeus? What about him?"

"Did you give the company a quick Google? Be honest."

I set my glass on the coffee table. "Maybe. Just to leave them a shitty review, for trying to bully us into using their services."

"And?"

It's like she was waiting to hear something specific, and was patiently leading me to the right answers. I felt almost... entrapped by this line of questioning. But what could it be? Her business with us was over, she must've received her commission by now.

"I couldn't find it. Prodeus Lawn Care doesn't seem to have a web presence. No Google business listing or dedicated website, not even a Facebook page. *Nada.*"

She nodded, as if expecting this. But her question got my gears spinning.

"Wait a sec," I said, taking out my phone. "The search did give me a weird non-result."

"Oh?" she raised an eyebrow.

"Yeah, hold on..." I Googled 'Prodeus' again, and the results screen asked, "Did you mean *Proteus*?" It showed over 12,000 results for that word, all of them seemingly referring to a mythical being from ancient Greece. I looked up at Maxine and caught her eyes trained directly on me, watching intently.

"There's no Prodeus, but there is an old Greek god named Proteus, with a T." I told her this mostly to fill the silence spilling between us. It was starting to feel weird in here.

"Is that so?" she said, her eyes inscrutable. There was something in their brown depths that was unsettling, though, and I found myself barking an uncomfortable laugh.

"I mean, it's a typo, right? The local guy named his business after a Greek god but misspelled the damn thing."

"Did he, now?"

This was getting ridiculous. Why was she searching my face so thoroughly? Those hazel eyes of hers flecked with suspicion—wait a minute! Hazel? Weren't her eyes brown a minute ago?

Maxine sat there, still lightly petting C.S. Lewis's head with her manicured hand. Her fake nails were almost too long, bright-pink and sharpened to a point, like some young fashionista influencer. As I watched, they seemed to almost… grow. I looked up at her face, and found a yellow-eyed creature staring at me. Her long blonde mane was gone. Tufts of thinning, matted, dark hair poked through her wrinkled scalp now. Her nose had pressed in, nearly flush with her face now, and, improbably, coiled whiskers pushed out along her upper lip. Maxine was growing a mustache even as I watched, paralyzed on my loveseat cushion. In fact… she almost looked like a perverse copy of someone I couldn't quite place… a recent visitor, maybe?

"How— wha…" I started, but that's all I could get out.

C.S. Lewis stirred, sensing a change in the room. He looked up at Maxine—or at the thing that disguised itself as Maxine— when her talons (now filthy, gnarled foot-long things), pushed his head back down with force. He whimpered, disliking the sudden movement. She—*it*—held him in place, gazing at me all the while. Something liquid oozed from the cavities where human ears should have been. And there was a stink in the room… something briny, almost fishy.

"Did Wikipedia happen to mention what was Proteus' domain?" it croaked, as if a normal conversation could still be continued. The voice sounded gruff, like an old man under huge physical strain. Pretty sure there was also a gurgling noise underpinning it. I was still shocked to be conversing with an entirely new species, a waterlogged bladder of a thing wrapped in what appeared to be seaweed braids. The couch beneath it was visibly soaked through. As I took in all these details, my mind still reeled from hearing that *thing* use the word "Wikipedia." The incongruence was almost as jarring as its physical appearance.

"His domain... Ocean." I whispered. "Nature."

"Ah!" the thing said, satisfied. "And what powers does that mythical being wield?"

I glanced at C.S. Lewis, who was busy trying to wriggle his butt backwards, to slip out from the creature's grip. Good boy.

"Shape-shifting," I said aloud.

"Splendid!" the thing gurgled, sounding almost triumphant. It was pleased that I knew these details, which I was now understanding to be less mythological than biographical.

"Please don't hurt my dog," I said. I'm sure I sounded pathetic, but it's all I could think about right now. This *being* had trapped C.S. Lewis in a cage wrought of its claws, threatening to press them into his tender Labradoodle fur. I couldn't have that on my conscience.

"No chance! I may be a wish-granting deity," the thing admitted, "but you really should've done your homework, Eric. Because this situation doesn't meet the conditions under which I would grant you anything. In fact, I may have to take something of yours instead."

Its colorless glistening orb of a body began to swell outwards, spilling over the confines of the couch that was now useless to contain it. For the amount of moisture in my living room, my mouth had never been drier.

"What do you want from me?"

Proteus cracked a grin, fishstink escaping through the slit.

"What does any half-forgotten deity desire?" he asked. "Remembrance. Respectful remembrance," he added.

"Why don't you let my dog go and we can talk about it."

"Nice try, Eric. But I'm not bound by your wishful thinking, remember? You really should've read more of those search results. But I suppose you were too busy desecrating my aedicule to educate yourself."

"Desecrating your... what? I did no such thing."

"Lies!" he shrieked, his mouth enlarged, almost beneath the ceiling now. He was pulsing with a rage that filled his soap-bubble body with murky red clouds.

"I swear I didn't do anyth—"

"The aedicule built in my honor," Proteus thundered. "The Romans were copycats when they took over, talking a big game but copping the best practices from us Greeks. Renaming myself and my peers. But at least they honored tradition! Of this I approve."

I groaned. "The birdbath! It's some kind of altar, isn't it?"

"An aedicule, you piss-ant! And your awful dog urinated on it most disrespectfully."

"Okay. I get it now. I've been a poor steward of your stuff. But you're probably pissed this place even exists, right? Byzantium. Isn't it like, a mockery of your homeland? Western world's cheap replica of the real deal?"

He fell silent, watching me. "That assessment isn't entirely inaccurate," he allowed. "Your culture is trash and you know it."

"Can't argue with you there."

"Silence!"

I heard Lewis whimpering from somewhere beneath the bulbous bladder. Focus, I told myself. What the hell did that article say? This asshole is bound to grant someone a wish if… if what? But the god-thing kept speaking, making it difficult to recall anything.

"Who do you think preserved the artifacts throughout history? We old ones, we keep track of the remnants of our empire. Some of us watch and weep from a distance, but others… well, we get more hands-on."

With that, he began to roll towards me, easily traversing the coffee table between us, which sent Zoe's book of Frank Lloyd Wright designs swimming up its ugly belly. It floated inside him, only the outline visible through the translucent membrane of his skin.

I shrank in the loveseat, my fingers digging into the fabric tight enough to tear.

"I'm sorry!" I yelled. "We're a bunch of dicks, okay? We see something beautiful and we piss on it. I mean, look at our history. It's our damn nature, man."

The creature halted its approach, the whole pulsing mass of it inches away from my face. Droplets of condensation rolled down its body, evoking a glass pitcher of lemonade sweating on a hot day. I tasted salt on my lips.

"Your nature… needs to be corrected," Proteus boomed, and my dog gave a sharp yelp.

I dared a glance at the spot on the floor where he previously lay, but Lewis was no longer there. Just then, something large floated up within Proteus' body, and my heart sank at the sight. This disgusting creature had absorbed my dog, who was now floating inside it, paws akimbo and mouth barking soundlessly.

"Stop it! I'm the one you want!"

"That's what the previous resident thought. And he was also wrong."

I watched helplessly as air bubbles escaped from Lewis's snout. And then it came to me. The missing piece of trivia tumbled back into place. In order to get Proteus to do their bidding, one must …

As my dog flailed inside this leering monster, there was only one thing I could do. I pulled down my running shorts and aimed my manhood squarely at the deity.

"Hey Proteus! How do you like my *scroteus*?" I hollered, and released a hot streak of piss directly on his bulging belly. I got a little splash-back, but that's the price a hero has to pay.

Disgust crossed the god-thing's features. "Eww, what the fuck?! You gross little …"

I shrugged, my bladder nearly empty now. "Didn't see that coming, did ya?"

It reeled back, trying to wipe off my fresh urine. "No! You nasty little freak. What in the—" He caught himself then, his milky eyes alight with realization.

"That's right," I said, tucking my junk away. "I remembered."

"Son of a bitch," he sighed. "You got me."

I nodded. "In order to make Proteus grant your wish, you must catch him by surprise. Then his shape-shifting powers are useless to resist the mortal who outsmarted him."

He grimaced. "Well, that's one way to do it."

"My technique lacked finesse," I acknowledged. "But I was pressed for time. And now, here's my wish, you ugly bastard."

"I know, I'll free your damn dog," he said grumpily.

"Oh, that's a given. But it's not my main wish. Listen up, blobfish-fucker."

#

Zoe came back from her shift to find me washing vegetables in the kitchen sink.

"Are we not getting takeout tonight?" she asked, pecking my cheek in greeting.

"Nope! I'm in a cooking mood. Gonna pop these on the gas grill. Figure we should take advantage of our gorgeous backyard."

"That's surprising," she said, smiling at me.

"Yeah, I'm full of surprises today," I grinned back. "Oh, that reminds me: don't sit down on the living room furniture. I just deep-cleaned it. Same with Lewis, I had to give him a bath."

C.S. Lewis trotted up to Zoe, excitedly licking her extended hand.

"Hi, buddy! Oh, you smell soapy fresh! What's the occasion, Eric?"

I shrugged. "Just grateful to have a home we can enjoy together. Oh, and there's one more surprise outside."

She was intrigued enough to forego changing out of her scrubs before investigating.

We stepped onto the patio, and I heard Zoe emit a soft gasp.

"Are you serious? Babe, when did you find the time?"

"I had a little help," I admitted. "Like it?"

"Like it? I'm obsessed!"

She walked towards the new feature and circled its perimeter, admiring the craftwork. The water glistened in the

Koi pond, throwing gleeful light at us. The ancient aedicule towered in the center of the stone-bordered pond, a tasteful exclamation point surrounded by water.

"And who's this little guy?" she asked, pointing at the sole resident.

"That's our new pet, Proteus. He's a Mediterranean scorpionfish, and the noble guardian of our backyard."

Zoe beamed at me. "I can't believe you did all this. I love it! And Proteus will fit right in with our family."

"I'm sure he will," I smiled. "And if he doesn't, we can always toss him on that grill. Scorpionfish are a delicious staple of Greek cuisine. Right, Proteus?"

The spiky red fish swam in anxious circles.

Zoe chuckled, and Lewis gave an excited bark. We trailed back to the patio, taking our time and enjoying the smoky aroma of grilled vegetables. Holding Zoe's hand as Lewis weaved between us, I said a silent prayer of thanks for these simple blessings, to whatever gods were listening.

-(29)-

CRITICAL BLAST PUBLISHING
20¢
APPROVED BY THE READING CODE AUTHORITY
The Bitches of ARCADIA
Ray Zacek
HELL HATH NO FURY!

COCAINE FOR PETS When your pets become too excited during mating season and you don't want additional burden of feeding more pets, shot them up with some fine liquid snow and chill them out.

RENT AN ANGRY MIDGET! When you need to stop a Bully from harassing, or when you need to look like a decent human concerned for poor ugly monsters.

1to1 MODEL PIRATE SHIP! Some assembly required. Glue NOT included. Recommend a private Island cove as the staging areo.

HYPNO-ROBOT use the specia mind control eye harmonics to subdue the minds of your unwilling subjects. You'll never have to take ou the trash and everyone will worship you as if their life depends on it.

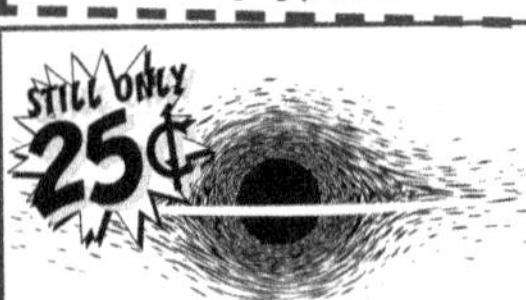

DIGITAL PUZZLE T-SHIRT Get people's undivided attention when they get engrossed trying to solve the constantly changing puzzles.

HOBO IN A BOX When your street is getting over-runned by homeless people and you need someone to speak their language and run them off to the next street down the block.

TRICK BLACK HOLE Get this special singularity and impress your friends by banishing them to other dimensions and realities.

EXPLODING DRINK Sit back and enjoy the highjinks as people unscrew their drink activating the chemical reaction, causing a foamy mess.

MAKE MINE MONSTERS!

Ray Zacek writes horror, crime/noir, dark fiction, satire, and whatever else percolates through his brain and can be translated via keyboard.. His work has been published by WonderBird Press, All Due Respect, Denver Horror Collective, Tule Fog Press, among others. His novel, Don't Be Cruel, published by Critical Blast, is available on Amazon. A retired federal officer and now full-time flaneur, he resides in Tampa, Florida.

Alice Taube died. Or rather, Alice's divine spirit was liberated from her physical body. Within a week, Alice's husband surrendered his spirit too and joined her in the sweet, mystical hereafter. Their bungalow on the suburban cul-de-sac of Arcadia Circle, like a vacant shell, remained unoccupied for weeks before it was sold and then demolished. Men operating heavy equipment shattered the peace and quiet, ripped off the grey shingle roof, knocked down walls, and shredded the old bungalow into splintered wood and a dustcloud chaos of concrete chunks, pipes, and tangled wire. With sadness Melanie Corvin observed this destruction. Worse transpired. The wrecking crew uprooted an ancient laurel oak that had graced the Taube front yard. Destroyed it! A virtual landmark with its twisting, gnarled, almost surreal limbs.

"That's monstrous!" Melanie said to her husband, Stanley. "I thought the old trees were protected."

"The city issues waivers," said Stan matter-of-factly, looking up from his desktop computer. "Somebody wanted the dirt but not the tree. Buildable fetches a lot of money."

Melanie sipped her chamomile tea. "Whoever builds a new house there, I don't like them already."

"Try not to prejudge," said Stan.

The lot remained vacant for weeks. Then signs popped up, permits were displayed, and construction commenced. A horrid house materialized in the leafy sanctuary of Arcadia Circle, among the tidy, dignified bungalows with dormer windows and pleasant verandahs. A modernist intrusion, a sinister pink cube with opaque windows.

"It's crass," said Melanie as she and the other women who lived on the cul-de-sac gathered for brunch, sipping cabernet sauvignon on Melanie's verandah, surrounded by blooming yellow hibiscus.

"Brutally ugly," said Betty Peregrine. A stout, wizened woman, she lived with her long-term partner Bruce Lejeune, both of them retired university professors.

"Hot pink is a silly color for a house," said Azalea Dubberly-Kite. She and her workaholic husband Fred Kite, an accountant, lived next door to Melanie. Azalea opened a second bottle of cabernet and refilled their glasses.

"Something we can all agree on," Melanie said, and they clinked their wine glasses together. They tippled.

Azalea, suddenly wistful, sighed. "I miss Alice."

They all did; the four of them had formed an intimate friendship, calling themselves the Bitches of Arcadia Circle, the name Alice Taube had conferred. Honey blonde Alice had been the youngest and the prettiest of their circle. Invoking her name now summoned regret like a cloud. "I'm gonna cry," Azalea sobbed.

"So should we all weep over Alice's passing?" asked Betty, as she helped herself liberally to more steak *tartare*. She chomped, swallowed, then spoke. "I *will* miss her youthful *joie de vivre* and the fragrance of jasmine with which she always adorned herself. But nevertheless, carry on we must."

"Carry on we must," Melanie affirmed.

Azalea wiped away the tears from her big, soft brown, sad bunny eyes. She raised her voice. "That's right! We got to keep a-going, we bitches of Arcadia Circle."

But who, wondered Melanie, *would be the new resident on their Circle?*

"The new owner is…" announced Stan the next morning, "*ta da!* Isabella Ciccolini!" At Melanie's bidding, he had clacked away at his keyboard researching the county property appraiser's database. Stan often worked from home, seated before his array of desktop computers like Captain Kirk at the helm of Starship Enterprise.

"What kind of name is Ciccolini?" said Melanie. Clad in her black power bra and leggings, she performed her daily yoga and stretched her long, supple legs while rhythmic oceanic sounds wafted from the Smart TV's speakers.

"Italian. Like Ciofeca." The Corvins owned a string of gourmet coffee shops called Ciofeca (cho-*feck*-a), catering to coffee snobs and university students. Their son Brendan worked part-time at one shop.

"Isabella Ciccolini, a single woman." Stan squinted at the screen. "Purchased from the Estate of Alice and Anakin J. Taube. Paid cash, a whopping amount."

Melanie gazed out the window at the pink atrocity on Arcadia Circle. "She tore down a perfectly fine old house."

"I can't find much else about her on the internet. A few past addresses and… well, well, well, she worked at a gentlemen's club called, get this, '4-Play.'"

"Isn't that charming?" said Melanie. She felt the satisfying post-yoga burn in her femoral muscles. She savored that sting.

"Interesting," said Stan, with a toothy grin.

She lasered him with a steely wifely gaze. "Don't be too interested."

Work on the pink house progressed. Pavers laid an intricate brick driveway and landscapers planted serried rows of sod. Then early on a Wednesday, a long and unwieldly moving van maneuvered around Arcadia Circle. Finally, Isabella Ciccolini herself appeared, with a roar of engine and screech of brakes, parking at the curb and emerging from a shiny orange Lamborghini. Tall, curvy, raven-haired, balanced on stiletto heels and wrapped tight in a red lambskin leather dress. Her ample breasts bulged.

"Oh, my!" said Azalea. She refilled her wineglass.

"My word," Betty said, casting a baleful gaze.

"What I expected," Melanie chimed in.

Betty hosted the monthly brunch, *frittatas* served by dutiful Bruce, who prided himself on his culinary skill. He'd then rinsed his whisk, tossed his apron, and withdrawn to his upstairs study, leaving the women convened on the verandah. The women of the Circle watched and eavesdropped attentively as Isabella Ciccolini strode about the property, inside and out, loud, and strident, waving her spidery hands shining with rings, supervising the movement of her furniture, and alternately hectoring, berating, and cajoling the movers in heavily accented English.

"You know what, ladies," said Azalea. "We really should go over there and introduce ourselves!" When Betty and Melanie greeted the idea coolly, Azalea went on. "No, really, we should! Y'all can be too darn harsh! We should give the girl the benefit of the doubt. That's only fair. Let's be neighborly. The least we can do. Who knows? Maybe she'll be the kind of gal we can take into our circle."

"Doubtful," murmured Betty, as she gobbled a croissant dripping with strawberry jam and licked her fingertips.

"Azalea is correct," said Melanie. "We're being too severe. Let's be civil."

Civil, yes. Formalities had to be observed. Courtesy often concealed the knife.

They agreed to call upon the new neighbor on Arcadia Circle, but Melanie didn't expect this to go well; she knew neither did Betty. But they went along to placate Azalea, who had a good heart, even if at times she was a bit dewy-eyed. Melanie also harbored a morbid curiosity to see Isabella

Ciccolini up close, like watching an awful movie on streaming TV only to critique its awfulness with satisfying bitchiness. Azalea scurried to her house, cut some roses from the garden, and wrapped them in paper. She summoned her beloved little dog and rejoined Betty and Melanie. They marched abreast across the cul-de-sac to the pink house; Azalea carrying the gift bouquet, Betty and Melanie on either side, talons temporarily retracted for the appearance of civility. The fluffy white dog traipsed behind them, slow and droopy. Betty glanced over her shoulder to spy Bruce at the upstairs window, with binoculars. As Melanie observed him with amusement, Betty gripped her cane and looked daggers. Bruce hastily retreated.

Isabella Ciccolini interrupted her scolding of the movers to stride toward them, breathless and more annoyed than cordial. "*Che cosa?* What?"

"Good morning," they said, and the women introduced themselves, pointed out each of their homes, and warmly welcomed Isabella to Arcadia Circle. "These are for you!" Azalea offered the roses.

"Nice." Isabella accepted the roses. "Is that your dog?" The feeble animal had plopped down on the new lawn.

"He's a Maltipoo," replied Azalea. "Poor Snowy! He's old and has eye problems and hip dysplasia."

"Don't let it piss or make shit on my lawn," said Isabella sharply. "If an animal is old and suffers, it should be put down."

"Oh, no!" Azalea scooped up and cuddled Snowy. Her lips curdled into a polite smile. "Do you have any pets?"

"No! Never! They need attention and Isabella only has attention for Isabella. Everything is for Isabella, and nothing is left over." She glowed, smiling enchantingly, almost in rapture with herself.

"I presume you are Italian." Betty swiftly cut in to change the subject.

"*Naturalamente*! From Sardinia, an island. Where sardines come from."

"Yes, I know of it."

"Most Americans don't!"

"I do not identity with 'most Americans,'" said Betty, as frosty as the white streaks in her helmet of grey hair. "I've traveled extensively, speak several languages, and taught university classes in anthropology. Folklore was my focus."

"Oh. That is very interesting," said Isabella, without even a miniscule trace of interest in her voice.

"Do you live alone?" said Melanie.

"Isabella likes living alone! Oh, I was married. He died. But don't be sorry! He died happy! Isabella knows how to please a man. He left me *molti soldi*. Money, money, money. Isabella likes money!" Bright-eyed for an instant with the thrill of lucre, she then shrugged. "I had him cremated. Funerals cost so much, cremation much less. I didn't keep the ashes. Only a little I rubbed on my body. His final request before he died. I scattered the rest. "But enough about him! How do you like my new house?" Before they could respond she continued. "Colorful, yes? I love color! My house makes the neighborhood more, how do you say, *vivace*. It is needed here with all these ugly old trees and boring old houses."

"We rather liked Arcadia Circle just as it was," said Betty.

"Now Isabella must ask you all to go. Sorry, busy-busy here, *cazzo pazzo*! Nice to meet you. *Ciao*, good-bye!"

She wheeled about and pounced on the movers who'd lumbered into the house carrying a bright, lime green leather sofa. She waved the bouquet at them like a wand. Rose petals flew.

"You don't like her, do you, Snowy?" Azalea patted the dog as the women recrossed the cul-de-sac. The ailing dog trembled in her arms.

"Well," said Melanie with finality. "We've met Isabella."

"That woman is dangerous," Betty announced abruptly, like an oracle delivering a blunt and troubling message, and hobbled home on her rosewood cane.

In the weeks that followed, the Bitches of Arcadia Circle ostracized Isabella Ciccolini, but they could not ignore her and the comings-and-goings at her house. A string of men visited: well-dressed men of middle age whose demeanor and vehicles suggested middle and upper incomes. Some were furtive, scanning the neighborhood suspiciously, but several strode boldly to her door. None arrived before eleven in the morning, and none remained past six in the evening, as if Isabella kept regular office hours.

When not entertaining male visitors, Isabella sunbathed in the briefest of bikinis, sometimes topless, on the balcony outside her second-storey bedroom. Equally jarring was the amplified music that emanated daily from the pink house. Lady Gaga, Bruno Mars, Bad Bunny, and an Italian rapper named Emanuele. But at night, noise was not an issue. The house of Isabella remained ominously silent and dark.

Night, as Betty had prophesied, was when the danger manifested.

Melanie stirred. Something woke her. Their bedroom was dark, the bed warm and cozy. The glowing digital clockface by the bed indicated 2 a.m. She heard Stan murmuring in distress. She felt him move—shaking, almost convulsive. Melanie switched on the bedside lamp. Beside her, the bed covers thrown off, Stan lay shuddering, his body jerking, his back arched. He groaned. A horrible, agonized, wretched groan. His mouth agape, gasping for air like a fish out of water. His swollen penis tented his pajamas. In panic, Melanie shook him awake. "Stan, Stan!" He woke with a start and sat up, wide-eyed, in shock, trembling. Melanie embraced him. Clung to him, desperately, as though if she failed to do so, he'd be irretrievably lost in some dark fissure.

"You had a nightmare. Are you alright?"

"I guess so." He grinned, a leer.

Melanie shivered. An uncanny chill suffused the bedroom. She sensed a presence, something lurking in the dark. Something malevolent. And not furtive, but bold, making its presence known. It lingered and then faded. Gone.

Stan got out of bed and switched on the overhead light.

Melanie shielded her eyes. "Where are you going?"

"I need to pee. And take a shower. I feel filthy."

Stan remained bleary-eyed and listless the next morning and postponed his usual Monday morning Ciofeca staff meetings. He shuffled about the house like a zombie in an open robe, boxer shorts and flapping flipflops. "I feel absolutely drained." He sniffled. "Must be some virus."

"You worry me," said Melanie. "You had *convulsions*."

"Oh, no, no, no. I'll be fine," Stan replied. "Tylenol, Vitamin C, and day or two of rest is all I need."

His dismissive attitude annoyed her. He became a grouchy zombie, slurping black coffee, complaining about his aches like a distraught child, and dribbling coffee on her immaculate kitchen tile. Melanie had ushered him to bed, and out of her way, when she heard an insistent ratatatat at the front door. She answered to find Azalea in the entry alcove, disheveled, distraught, and clutching a small bundle to her bosom.

"Omigod, Azzie, what is it?"

"Snowy's dead," said Azalea.

"Oh, poor thing, I'm so sorry!"

"Could Brendan take him to the vet for disposal? Fred left for work at the crack of dawn, like he always does, and I just can't. *I can't!*"

"Sure, Azalea," said Brendan who had emerged from his room in gym shorts and ragged Call of Duty t-shirt, his bright blue eyes full of sympathy. "I'll do that for you on my way to class."

"You're such a good, kind young man." Azalea sobbed. "Don't know what I'd do without my Brendan!"

Brendan often chauffeured Azalea, whose driver's license was revoked, to her doctor appointments or for groceries or other errands while Fred Kite was at work. Now Brendan took the dead dog wrapped in a quilt and gently placed it in the back of the Subaru Forester that had been his eighteenth birthday present. Azalea wept. Melanie hugged her and daubed her plump, tearstreaked cheeks with a Kleenex. While Brendan went to his room to shower and change clothes, Melanie brewed herbal tea and poured an ounce of cognac into Azalea's cup and then, at Azalea's pleading, added another pour of cognac. Medicinal, Azalea insisted, for her frayed nerves after the death of her beloved pet. They sat outside on the verandah in the coolness of the morning, and pleasant birdsong filled the air. But neither the coolness nor the birdsong consoled Azalea.

"I heard Snowy gasping in the middle of the night. It was horrible! It was like somebody was choking him! Oh girlfriend, it was weird! There was a sort of aura in the house. It was really nasty. And, no, I'm not imagining things!"

"I believe you," said Melanie.

Brendan had just driven off when the roar of the Lamborghini startled them and shushed the birdsong. With a screech of tires, Isabella careened out of Arcadia Circle as if in hot pursuit, leaving Melanie and Azalea astonished.

Two days later, night terrors struck Stan again. His convulsions shook the bed like a tremblor. Melanie bounced out of bed and hit the floor with a thud sure to leave bruises on her bottom and hip. The chill in the room gave her goosebumps. A sweet, suffocating odor hung in the air. Melanie almost gagged. Prone upon the bed, Stan muttered and moaned, the moans a weird, intense mingling of pleasure and pain. He spasmed. Melanie leaped back beside him.

"Stanley, wake up! Stan!" She switched on the bedside lamp.

"Huh?" He sat up in the arc of bright light, uncomprehending. "What?"

"You were dreaming again! Quick, before you forget, what were you dreaming?"

"I forgot already." Stan stared vacantly. "Nope. Nothing."

The chill in the room dissipated and only the faintest trace of the strange, musky odor lingered, a scent somehow familiar to Melanie, but her attention at the moment fixed on Stan. He shrugged. "Oh, I'm okay now," he said, nonchalant now. He glanced at the bright digital clock and gestured at the pale light seeping through the curtains. "It's dawn. I guess I'll get up."

"At this hour? Go back to sleep!"

Stan shuffled toward the bathroom, and stood in the threshold, a shadow in the harsh electric light. "I need coffee. Good coffee, not the bitter shit we brew at Ciofeca. Since I'm up and wide awake, might as well take advantage of it and get some work done."

"Don't be silly! Fred Kite isn't even up at this hour, and you know what an early bird he is. Quit this silliness now and come back to bed!"

"No, honestly, Mel, I'm perfectly okay." He shut the bathroom door. The lock clicked, to Melanie's dismay. In a few moments she heard the shower running. *Hot or cold?* she wondered.

Dressed, caffeinated, and fed, Stan insisted on going into work, but their son's car blocked the driveway. He roused Brendan, who stumbled out of his room, barefooted but still in the clothes he'd worn the day before. Father and son exchanged harsh words outside in the pale predawn light, but Melanie couldn't hear. Then Stan sped off, only a few minutes behind Fred Kite, and Brendan shambled back inside the house. He raided the fridge for OJ, gulped from the jug, replaced it in the fridge, and then steered unsteadily toward his bedroom. Melanie blocked his path.

"Hey," protested Brendan. "Do you mind?"

"Where were you last night?"

"Out," he said.

"Out where?"

"Just out." Uncharacteristically sullen and avoiding eye contact, his eyes were red-rimmed. *Was he hung over?* Melanie suspected so, although her son never drank to excess nor acted like this.

"What time did you get home?"

"I don't know. Late. Didn't want to wake you or Dad." Brendan sidestepped her and trod down the hall. He peeled off the polo shirt and dropped it unceremoniously in the hall hamper. Small red scratches streaked his muscular shoulders.

"How late?"

"I told you, I don't *know*!"

"Don't snap at me. I'm your mother and you live in my house!"

"Quit! Will you please just quit?" Brendan replied plaintively and retreated to his room, swinging the door shut. Melanie heard him plop into bed so hard she thought the bed might collapse.

The Bitches' brunch was cancelled that week; Betty and Bruce had gone to an academic conference out of town. Instead, Melanie and Azalea confabbed over coffee and almond croissants. Azalea doused her coffee with bourbon. Something distracted and bothered Azalea, and whatever it was, Melanie knew, would soon be blabbed.

"So," said Azalea, "is everything okey-dokey with you?"

"Well, no," Melanie admitted. With Snowy's recent demise, she hadn't wanted to bring up her own troubles.

"What's the matter, girlfriend?"

"Stan hasn't been sleeping well."

"Funny, neither has Fred!" And there it was.

"Nightmares?"

"Tell me about it!" Azalea replied with an eye roll. "Oh, I tell you, it's awful! Shakes like he has a seizure and cries out, and that's bad enough, but he sort of, well, let me put it out there plain and simple, Freddie jacks off. In his sleep, I mean. Not like deliberately. Is it the same with Stan?"

"I'm afraid so."

"I'm embarrassed as heck when our Guatemalan lady comes to clean and changes the sheets," said Azalea in a bouncing, bourbon thought stream. "What she must think! 'Course, she'd think it in Spanish, and I wouldn't understand a word. Ought to pay her more. Hope she's not deported, poor *chica*. That's downright weird that both Stan and Fred are having dreams like that."

"This is not coincidence," said Melanie. "Brendan has been acting strangely too."

"Oh, no!" Azalea adored Brendan like the son she never had; she and Fred had only an adult daughter, estranged now and living in another state.

"He's developed an odd sneer." Melanie imitated the nasty sneer, then knitted her brow. "There's something going on."

"Like what?" She looked at Melanie with her brown rabbit eyes, at once curious and apprehensive as if, confronted with a startling revelation, she might dash away. Melanie clasped Azalea's clammy hand and held it tight, binding her. *No running away, flibbertigibbet rabbit.*

"We both know."

"Do we? Oh, oh. Uh-huh. I feel you, girlfriend. Since you-know-who moved in. With her big Italian boobs and snazzy sports car."

From where they sat, through the bay window, they could see Isabella, across the cul-de-sac perched in a chaise lounge on her balcony, sunbathing topless again and painting her nails. Her long black hair flowed like a wave; a siren ensconced within a geometric pink shell. An Italo-Arab rapper warbled from a wireless speaker on the deck, discordant, strident, and execrable to their ears. Isabella was culpable for the ills that afflicted their men; an interloper, she pervaded Arcadia Circle like an evil vapor. Melanie and Azalea stared in meditative silence for several seconds. Finally, Azalea rattled her Wedgewood cup on its saucer and broke the spell.

"You know what?" she said. "We had better discuss this in full circle as soon as Betty is home!"

"We have to do something," said Melanie coldly.

"Oh, for sure, girlfriend!" Azalea nodded, splashing bourbon into her empty cup.

#

Thursday, Brendan missed lunch.

His usual routine consisted of community college classes in the morning, then lunch at home by noon. Melanie had made him a sandwich. But her son didn't appear. He had driven home; Melanie had heard his car while she did her yoga and listened to the soothing oceanic sounds. He hadn't entered the house. His Subaru remained in the driveway, but Brendan was nowhere to be found. *Where had he drifted to*? she wondered. A tiny nub of anxiety rubbed her heart. An hour elapsed. The nub grew. Another hour, the nub became a chunk with sharp edges. She texted Brendan. No answer.

"Don't worry about him," said Stan, oblivious at his desktop array, engrossed in sales figures and monitoring Forex, the S&P, and the Dow. "He'll be home eventually."

"Where did he go?"

Stan shrugged. "Maybe Azalea waylaid him for some task. Or he went to Betty and Bruce's house. He looks after the place when they're gone."

"It's unlike Brendan to vanish like that, without a word."

"You worry too much," said Stan. He looked haggard. Puffiness swelled under his pale blue eyes. He hadn't shaved. Didn't sleep well either and still woke up in the night and tramped to the bathroom.

"You don't look rested," said Melanie.

"Stop worrying about me." He picked at the remnants of tunafish on toast, like a seagull at the beach. Breadcrumbs and globs of mayo speckled his rumpled shirt.

"Darling," Melanie said. "You're a mess." She ushered him back to bed.

Melanie waited impatiently. She remained seated in the throne-like leather armchair in the living room, skimming magazines. An hour later, Brendan glided through the front door, grinning and looking as smug and satisfied as a wandering tomcat returning to its comfy shelter.

"Where did you go?" She startled him.

"Huh?"

"Where were you?"

"Out for a walk."

"A walk where?"

"Just around," said Brendan, annoyed.

"Just around is not a satisfactory answer." Her hard grey eyes zeroed in on Brendan. She could read her son's body language and calibrate his nervousness. His guilty glances avoided her gaze and that was telltale. "What are you not telling me?"

"If you must know," Brendan sneered, "I was at Isabella's. Don't give me that look. You don't like her but she's not a bad person. We talked. That's all, talked."

"About what?"

Brendan flopped on the couch. "Isabella grew up under a volcano in Sardinia. That's really cool. I moved some patio furniture for her. Put some chlorine in the spa. She made me lunch. Spicy spaghetti with olives, anchovies and red pepper. Wow. Delish. Never ate anything like it."

Brendan's smile failed to warm Melanie's frozen frown. "And that's all?"

"Yeah, that's all!"

But Melanie knew he was lying. Put adolescent male hormones with a woman *like that*, and... no, she would imagine no further. Melanie resolved to remain cool and collected, not reveal to her son how perturbed she was. But she had to be firm. Brendan had shambled into the danger zone. "This isn't the first time you were at her house. Don't try to tell me otherwise because *I know*. Listen to me! Do *not* go to her house again. She is *not* a good person."

"She was real nice to me," said Brendan with an adolescent smirk that exasperated and infuriated Melanie. "Isabella likes men. You and the other bitches don't want her in your circle, and I get that. She's not happy little Alice Taube."

"I forbid you!" Her anger swelled and sprouted wings. She wanted to pounce and throttle him.

Brendan laughed at her. "You're being a total fucking Karen!"

"Don't you dare talk to me like that!"

"Total fucking Karen! And Azalea's a fish and Betty's a fat, waddling snob and I am done talking to you. Leave me the fuck alone!" He slammed the door of his room.

#

"I was wondering when the two of you would put your heads together and concur with me that we have a serious problem on Arcadia Circle."

Betty Peregrine marched into the dining room of Melanie's home like a priestess, tapping her twisted rosewood cane as she proceeded to the brunch table and occupied the chair Melanie offered. Betty gulped black coffee and clawed at the macaroons on the table. "Now, tell me all about it. Spare me no details, however lurid, I *must* know."

First Azalea and then Melanie told her of their husbands' nightmares and strange waking behavior, their deterioration, the irritability and lack of concentration. Betty listened, magisterially impassive.

Azalea related, almost in tears, that Fred Kite had been chewed out like a rookie by a senior partner at the accounting firm for making egregious errors, and threatened with dismissal if he didn't straighten out.

Stanley Corvin, Melanie divulged, was on a similar downward trajectory and remained stubbornly in denial about it. "And there's worse. My son has been visiting her," putting a dread emphasis on *visiting*. Azalea gasped.

"I understand," said Betty gently.

"It's horrible!" Azalea lamented. "What do you think, Betty?"

"We have a monster in our midst," Betty replied. "A succubus. A demonic and malevolent creature. I sensed this strongly upon first meeting her, and I am rarely wrong about such matters."

Melanie nodded; she'd already suspected the same—more than suspected, was *convinced*—but wanted Betty, with her age, wisdom, and expertise in eldritch matters, to confirm her opinion.

Azalea gasped again, head bobbing in agreement, her worst fears confirmed too. She reached for more Prosecco.

"The succubus," Betty intoned, "is nocturnal, insidious, and seductive. She is insatiable. She has chosen Stanley and Fred and young Brendan."

"What about your Bruce?" said Melanie.

"Oh, Bruce is too old and debilitated to be of interest to a succubus, and I gave him a good talking-to when I caught him watching her. He is well trained, you know."

"What do we do?" Azalea wanted to know, hands fluttering.

"There's only one remedy," said Melanie. "Snakes."

The rosy color drained from Azalea's cheeks. "That's too extreme! Too hard! Let's not go *there*, girlfriend! We got hexes aplenty. We'll hex her, okay? Can't we bind her evil ass or put a freezer spell on her instead?"

Betty tut-tutted this protest. She clasped Azalea's hand. "No, my dear, I'm afraid Melanie is absolutely right. Apotropaic measures will simply not suffice."

"Say what? What does that mean and why won't it work?"

"Apotropaic, means to avert evil. No, my dear Azalea, evil encroaches too closely. Half measures will not do."

"Snakes it must be," Melanie reiterated like an invocation, feeling a frisson of excitement, and an instant of malice, at the mere sound of the word.

But performing the ritual and unleashing the deadly magic of the snakes required the full circle and Azalea remained faint-hearted. She fretted. Almost hyperventilated. Melanie and Betty planted her in a chair and stroked her hair to calm her. They chanted softly while Azalea babbled.

"Snakes are hard! They hurt! I have stretch marks from last time! Okay, that had to be done with Alice and Anakin because she was the chosen sacrifice and Anakin had to serve his goddess in the next world and we all agreed on that, but I don't want to do snakes again. Mel, you like summoning snakes a little too much. That's twisted. There has to be some other way."

"Don't be weak, Azalea. There *is* no other way," replied Melanie firmly. Betty clucked reproval at Azalea and then tapped urgently at the lunar calendar on her Tablet; a lustrous full moon would adorn the sky two nights hence and beneath that moon, carry on they must. Azalea regained her composure and breathed normally. She lifted her chin to face them. "Alright, carry on we must. Snakes it is. Let's do this thing, girlfriends!"

In two nights, the moon, the great and frightening female symbol, rendered Arcadia Circle pewter. At midnight, the Bitches met in Betty's house, the oldest and largest on the cul-de-sac. In Betty's house was a dedicated space, their spellcasting chamber. Incense burned, herbs too—mugwort, tannis root and blackthorn. Tendrils of smoke rose from the brass Tibetan censer. A window remained open, damask curtains pulled aside, to admit the moonlight. They shed their clothing and crouched, chanting, offering prayers to She of the Night, the Primeval Goddess and Creatrix, known by many names. Eurynome, Gaia, Kali, a thousand others, but all one and the same. To Her they offered prayers and attestation of wrath toward the interloper to their sacred circle. Close attention had to be paid to the incantations; Alice Taube had been exalted by her sacrifice, but the snake ritual against Isabella Ciccolini was entirely different—one of damnation.

Summoning snakes was as painful as birthgiving. The women shuddered, strained, and moaned until they were bright-eyed in holy trance. Their bodies contorted. Shapes emerged. From navel to labia, from thighs and folds of skin, the snakes materialized. Taking form, elongating, flesh wriggling. Three snakes combined into one of anaconda length and slithered out the open window. Across the lawn in the dark it glided, around the cul-de-sac in a loop, then over the newly planted sod to the pink cube.

The serpent found Isabella outside in the foaming spa. Alone, lounging, drinking Campari under soft lights while music played. Relaxed, oblivious, eyes half closed, humming along with the music. The serpent plunged into the water. Isabella shrieked but in an instant the serpent laced her body and pinched her neck to cut off any screams. It tightened its grip around limbs and torso, twisting, squeezing, twisting, flicking its black tongue. Isabella gasped. It held her beneath the foaming water. Until Isabella ceased struggling. Its task completed, the serpent released the limp body to float in the spa. Then it simply dissolved. Gone, vanished, leaving not a scale or scute behind. Across the cul-de-sac, the Bitches of Arcadia Circle adjourned, reverting to their diurnal bodies, and shaking off night magic like scurf.

"Well," Azalea sighed with relief as she tossed a balloon-like caftan over her head. Her core ached from the strain. "Glad that's over with! I'm hurting!"

"Oh, yes, so tiring," said Betty as she fitted pendulous breasts in a brassiere. She could not reach around; Azalea clasped the bra for her while Betty murmured, "But had to be done, my dears, however onerous. It had to be done."

"Had to be done," repeated Melanie, shimmying into black nylon shorts while she sat upon a toadstool-shaped ottoman. She glowed, in a post-ophidian languor, savoring the moment. Snakes were pure power. Better than sex.

"Our men ought to thank us for this," said Azalea, taking up her chalice of dark, scented wine. "We saved their happy asses! But they won't, and wouldn't even if we told them, which we never will."

"Matters not," Betty said gravely. "It matters only that we have restored balance to our little community. We shall be troubled no more by that dreadful succubus."

"Amen to that!" said Azalea and drained her chalice.

Two days later a police officer arrived late morning to conduct a welfare check, following up on an anonymous phone call. Melanie Corvin ceased watering plants to plant herself placidly in a rocker on her verandah and observe. The officer knocked on Isabella's front door. No answer. She knocked again—no answer. The diligent officer poked around, rapped on a window, peered inside, then scuttled around the back. Melanie waited, sipping iced herbal tea. Within minutes the screaming siren of an ambulance pierced the quiet cul-de-sac.

It was obvious that Isabella Ciccolini had drowned in her spa. The police officer had discovered her bloated body, glassy-eyed, decomposing, leaking fluids into the churning chlorinated spa. An accidental death, the medical examiner concluded. Drugs and alcohol involved. Tragic, how terribly tragic, her former neighbors said, masking their satisfaction.

Tranquility descended upon Arcadia Circle to the great relief of Melanie, Azalea, and Betty. Husbands slept well, undisturbed through the night. Brendan Corvin became once again the polite, dutiful son—minus the sneer, minus rebellion. The ugly pink house remained, of course, and over brunch the women speculated on its disposition.

"My Freddie thinks she probably didn't have a will," said Azalea. "And he says that leaves the place up for grabs."

" 'Intestate' is the proper legal word," Betty corrected. "In which case, if no next of kin can be located, and I doubt any exists because succubi are not known for family ties, the county government sells the house."

"And then we buy it," said Melanie. Betty and Azalea immediately voiced approval. Melanie added, "We should've done that after Alice and Anakin passed. That would have spared us the horrors of Isabella. This time, we're wiser. *We shall control who lives on the Circle.*"

"And that," declared Betty pompously, "is as it should be."

But their words had no sooner been spoken than Bruce, who had been napping upstairs, materialized in the doorway like a specter, gasping, his face purple. He collapsed. And with a final, foul exhalation, ceased breathing.

Brunch ended abruptly with a frantic call to 9-1-1.

#

Melanie and Azalea opened a bottle of Barolo from Betty's wine cabinet. They'd kept a vigil, offering prayers of solace and passage for distraught Betty and the now-departed Bruce. Betty, sedated, lay abed and they drank wine serenaded by Betty's stentorian snoring. Melanie closed the door gently.

"Poor old Bruce," said Azalea. "So sad he croaked. He was what? Eighty?"

"Seventy-seven," Melanie replied.

"I suppose it was for the best that he went kind of quick like that and didn't suffer." Azalea gulped her wine. "Didn't suffer *much*."

"You can go home if you want," said Melanie. "I'll stay with Betty."

"Oh, I don't mind. I'll stay too, sister. This couch is nice and comfy and I'm sleepy and too tipsy to get my sorrowful ass up and walk home." She kicked off her shoes and sprawled on the white satin of the Queen Anne sofa. Soon Azalea dozed off, snoring herself, but softly.

Melanie washed the wineglasses and deposited the empty wine bottle in the recycling bin, then retreated to the guest bedroom. A vintage clock ticked on the mantelpiece. Melanie, drowsy and fatigued, closed the door gently and lay on the soft duvet. In a few moments she slept.

But something prodded Melanie. A chill, like cold fingers flicking her face. She moaned. Half asleep, half awake. She could discern her surroundings with acuity like watching a movie in sharp focus, the camera panning: a cherrywood armoire, a vintage brass lamp, old sepia botanical prints on the wall. But Melanie could not move; her body remained unresponsive, her breathing shallow, and with a creeping fear she sensed a presence in the room, stalking her. A pervasive aroma, sweet, musky, and sultry.

Jasmine. Alice Taube's scent.

Can we talk? A whisper stabbing the darkness. Then ironic laughter. *It's time we talked, bitch to bitch.*

"No," Melanie murmured. Her fear assumed a wispy hovering female shape, a wraith that spoke in the voice of Alice Taube.

You summoned snakes and sacrificed your new neighbor for nothing. She was no more than a nuisance. I'm your succubus!

"Alice, don't! No, go away!"

No, I will stay on Arcadia Circle for a while. To seduce your men! You know why. Because you cheated me, Melanie.

"No, I did not! We chose lots!"

Don't lie to me! I know now. You fixed it so little Alice got the parchment that spelled her sacrifice. You and Betty and Azzie conspired against me. But I should thank you. You exalted me, you liberated me. From the flesh and from myself, from my mortal limitations. Sweet little Alice I am no more. I embraced the Darkness. I am the Darkness now! And I have become more powerful than you can imagine. None of you are strong enough to stop me.

"No, no—*nnnnnnnn!*" Melanie screamed, and pitched from the bed, flailing, wide awake now. But the shade of Alice Taube had departed, soaring into the night above Arcadia Circle, wicked and wild, and dancing under a waning gibbous moon.

CRITICAL BLAST PUBLISHING
20¢
NOT A HOUSE
Troy Riser
APPROVED BY THE READING CODE AUTHORITY
CRITICAL BLAST PUBLISHING
DEADLY CURB APPEAL

ATTENTION!
DEMONS!
VAMPIRES!
GHOULS!

NO MORE MONDAY NIGHTMARES!

ALL FOR $2.00

DEFEAT BLACK MYSTIC ARTS KUNG-FU Tired of getting your ass kicked every Tuesday by Black Mystic Arts Kung-Fu fighters? CALL 666-HELP to enroll in self-defense training every Hellspawn should know to survive any dark alley encounter. Become a Ninth Circle Master of Judante!

5¢

SNAKES IN A MAIL BOX Get these total mother-f$%Ken poisonous snakes and mail them with your get well gift cards.

LAST MAN ON EARTH HEARD A KNOCK AT THE DOOR!

ALL FOR $2.00

LEARN TO PLAY THE GUITAR! When you can't get a date for the weekend, rent a sexy Guitar Teacher to impress your friends and maybe you just might learn something too.

99¢

STICK IT TO YOUR ENEMIES! Real Voodoo Doll! Guaranteed Quality checked by the finest Witch Doctors! Send lock of hair and a SASE to DUDAT VOODOO, Box 9, Haiti.

SAVE $1.00

MONSTER VALUE STAMP
THIS IS IT!
CLIP THEM
& COLLECT
THEM ALL!

10¢

SUPER SHARP PIRATE SWORD When you want to capture the hearts and minds of the people around you, this sword will cut through the muscle and bone to get to the vital organs you need to sustain your hunger.

WELCOME MAT TRAP When you don't want people annoying you, a simple press of the button and the trap door will dispose of anyone who stands on it, while waiting for you to answer the door.

STILL ONLY 35¢

HYPNO-ROBOT use the special mind control eye harmonics to subdue the minds of your unwilling subjects. You'll never have to take out the trash and everyone will worship you as if their life depends on it.

Troy Riser is an award-winning writer and artist. His most recently accepted short story, "They Scream", will be appearing in Cirsova magazine's Spring 2026 issue. He is currently writing a novel (working title Target Girl), and swears he will finish it soon no matter what. Troy also likes drawing and painting angels, ravens, and monsters, and doesn't know what that says about him.

1

Winters are hard in Gary, Indiana. Some days frigid gusts of wind sweep off Lake Michigan and tear at the city like a feral thing, dropping temperatures to arctic levels, bringing storms, making the streets icy and treacherous and sometimes impassable, the only locals out in it those who *need to be*. The two DCS caseworkers, Shavon Bartholomay and Jerry Meeks, were in a county-owned Nissan Versa sedan heading east on Central a few blocks north of Marshalltown, and they were "*need to be*," responding to a call. Christmas coming, just a few weeks away, but neither Jerry nor Shavon were feeling it, that festive holiday glow. The Nissan's heater was going out and all they felt was the cold.

The street they were on was lined with ramshackle, single-story, two- and three-bedroom homes, many abandoned, with empty lot gaps in between like missing meth addict teeth. The row-upon-row desolated sameness of it still bothered Jerry even after three years in the field. His partner Shavon, who had grown up in Gary, chose not to notice. Shavon was immune.

Jerry and Shavon, Shavon driving, spent most of the drive in companionable silence. The two had been partnered at Lake County Department of Child Services for over a year and knew some at DCS saw them as an odd couple, Shavon a tall, long-boned woman in her early forties who still moved like the star college athlete she had once been, Jerry a stocky, prematurely balding, amiable man with an awkward comb-over and out-of-fashion brush mustache. But as different as they were, diametric opposites, the two had a groove. They were easy with each other.

Jerry broke the quiet. "Why can't we find this place? You grew up here. You know this town. *I* know this town. Shouldn't be this hard."

Shavon shared his frustration. They were running late. An anonymous caller had reported the sound of a crying baby coming from an abandoned house. Police would already be on the scene, waiting for them.

Not waiting long, Shavon thought. Gary cops were a cynical bunch, but even the most *jaded of them moved* when it came to kids. They would force entry without waiting for co-responders, which could be bad, depending.

Jerry gave up on the memory map in his head and tried using his GPS, but it didn't work, either. The feminine, British-accented voice on his cell kept intoning *Proceed to the route, Proceed to the route*, guiding them nowhere and getting on their nerves; rather, getting on Jerry's nerves but Jerry stoically didn't show it, a trait he'd picked up as a Navy corpsman in Afghanistan. His marines had needed him calm so Jerry had cultivated calm—or the outward appearance of it—until it became part of him, who he was.

"Finally," Shavon said, spotting a police cruiser parked just ahead. She pulled in behind it.

"Odd," Jerry said, peering intently at the display on his cell. "Odd how?"

"This shows up on the map as an empty lot. No house here."

"*Yes*, house here, Jerry." Shavon pointed at the small, boxy, aluminum-sided house to their immediate right, a plain concrete pad where an ordinary front porch would usually be, no awning above the door, its front yard a wild, unruly tangle of naked, thorny bushes and thatches of weeds poking through the snow. The front window was still intact, but their view of the interior was obscured by tattered, gauzy yellow curtains. Panels of siding were missing side and front, exposing silvery strips of insulation, two-by-four wall studs showing through beneath like the ribs of a dead animal.

Shavon went on, "Hundreds of abandoned buildings, Jerry. City lost track of this one."

"Entropy is a process, not an event," Jerry began, about to say more. Ordinarily, Shavon didn't mind when Jerry took off on nerdy tangents, but right now maybe a baby was in that house, crying in the cold. She cut him off.

"*Head in the game*, Jerry."

"Gotcha, boss, sorry. I'll stop now."

Since no officers were in sight, Shavon assumed Officers Latham and Neely had opted to go in—again, not a breach of protocol. Dispatch said a caller had heard a crying baby in that house. A crying baby could mean or be anything *but* a crying baby. It could be the yowling of feral cat, a passing addict's auditory hallucination, a false report, or nothing at all.

"This isn't good," Jerry said.

Shavon followed Jerry's gaze and saw what he meant. The house across the street, one not so rundown as others in this neighborhood, had a flashy, bright red, late model Chevrolet Camaro parked in its driveway, out front in full view.

Drug dealer dream car, Shavon thought. She looked for a gang tag and quickly found it, a GD gang sign spray-painted with a stencil to the side of the front door. Latham and Neely would've seen it, too.

"Dealers are not why we are here," she said, thinking out loud. "Latham and Neely know this."

"Shavon?" Jerry said.

Shavon didn't hear. She was finishing her thought. "Neely's young but Latham's eyes-on-the-prize. Child welfare takes priority."

"*Shavon?*" Jerry called again, this time with feeling.

A man approached them on the icy sidewalk, short and squat, bundled in a soiled orange parka, moving heavily, weaving slightly, whether drunk or high or old and careful, Shavon couldn't tell.

All the above, she thought.

As he came closer, Shavon got a read on his features. Late fifties, early sixties, she guessed, but the ages of addicts and alcoholics are hard to place since they don't so much age as disintegrate; his eyes were bleary and red, watery from the cold, the dark skin of his face etched with a deep web of lines like the craggy fissures in a rock.

"My dog!" the man cried out. "It got my dog!"

Shavon gave Jerry a quizzical look and mouthed the words *It got my dog?*

Jerry shrugged and shook his head. He turned to the old man and asked his name, his tone polite, just shy of obsequious. Street people almost always responded to courtesy. They got it so rarely.

"Douglas Banks," the man said. "Just 'Banks' is fine."

Jerry gave the man an encouraging smile. "Okay, Banks. An anonymous caller reported a disturbance at this address. They said it sounded like a crying baby coming from inside. Was it you who called it in?"

"No, not me," Banks said. "All I know about is Blue, my dog." He pointed to the house with a stubby forefinger. "You hear that, right? That's Blue in there. He's hurt."

Jerry and Shavon exchanged glances. Neither heard anything and both had been listening—not for a dog but for the crying child that had brought them to this place. Banks' head swiveled on his thick, fleshy turret of a neck as he looked from Jerry to Shavon. After a moment, their mutual confusion penetrated the alcoholic fog and he said, "But you don't hear Blue, do you? You think I'm imagining things, making stuff up. You think it's all in my head."

Shavon gave Banks a dismissive shrug. She had no patience with delusional drunks, not having it. She turned to Jerry. "We need to get on with this, look to the child."

"Eyes on the prize," Jerry said.

"Look," Banks said, "it's like I've been trying to tell you: there's something *not right* about this place." He pointed at the drug dealer's house across the way. "*Ask them bangers yonder*. They know."

Shavon said, "We're not asking those 'bangers yonder' anything, Mr. Banks."

Not like they'd talk to us anyways, she thought.

Shavon went on, "We do need to speak to those officers, though. You see them? They inside?"

"Didn't see no cops," Banks said, shaking his head. "I was out looking for Blue. That's when I heard him barking and carrying on—and I'm hearing him now, damn it, even if you don't!"

Shavon ignored Banks and turned to Jerry, who had anticipated her, as always. He was calling the office. While making the call, his ear to the phone, Jerry said, "What do we tell them?"

"Start with the missing officers."

"*Missing* is a strong word, Shavon."

Shavon granted the point. If they called it in now and the two missing cops showed up and not-missing, she and Jerry would look panicky and unprofessional. On the other hand, this was rapidly turning into a situation. If something bad had gone down here, their supervisor needed to know.

Shavon said, "Apprise Louise, Jerry. Tell her what we *do* know: two missing cops, possible drug op across the way, no endangered child we can hear."

"Roger that," Jerry said. He held his cell above eye level and did a 360-degree stutter-step pivot in place, squinting to see the signal bar. "We've lost signal," he said.

Shavon tried it herself, taking her cell from her purse and holding it up as Jerry had, getting the same result.

"Okay," she said, "We take a look around, see what we can find. Turn up anything or not, we head out, find a signal, and then call it in from there."

They approached the front and tried the door.

"Locked," Jerry said. "Force it?"

"Try knocking. Knocking works."

Jerry took off one of his gloves and rapped on the flimsy wooden door. No one answered.

"Let's check out back," Shavon said.

They were at the side of the house at the far corner when Jerry paused, then stopped. "Funny thing," he said.

"Talk to me, Jerry."

"Something I noticed but didn't register right away: no footprints out front. It snowed into the morning—not a lot, less than an inch, but no footprints by the door—other than ours, I mean."

"So Latham and Neely never made it to the door."

Jerry shook his head. "I don't know what to think, boss. I'm still weirded out by Blue, the imaginary dog."

"I hear that," Shavon said, "We try our luck out back. That don't work, we *didi mao* out of the AO."

"Sorry, we what?"

"An expression my father used," Shavon said. "He picked it up in Vietnam. In vet-speak it means 'Let's boogie on outta here.'"

"I like that," Jerry said. "Makes running away sound less Brave Sir Robin."

Shavon smiled, catching the reference, and then grew serious. "As a heads-up, running away is exactly what we do if we find ourselves in a situation. I know how you are, Jerry. No heroics, okay?"

"You sound like Nan," Jerry replied.

Nan was Jerry's wife, a perky, plump, bubbly blonde who worked as a pediatric nurse at St. Catherine's. Because of her job, Nan sometimes lapsed into baby-talk when speaking to grownups, but Shavon couldn't fault her for it. Shavon had done the same when her daughter Althea was a toddler.

They turned the corner, opened the gate to a rusty chain-link fence, and stepped into the backyard, the frozen, snowy ground crunching beneath their boots. In some vacant properties, Shavon could see evidence of once-happy homes, places where people had put in an effort: the remains of a rusty swing set for the kids, a few boards nailed onto the trunk of a maple that had been ladder to a treehouse, tomato stakes still standing where a garden had grown. But none of that here, nothing but bramble and scrub, with loose, snow-covered trash piled high against the back of the house, obscuring its degraded concrete block foundation and reaching almost as high as the windowsills.

Jerry knocked without result, same as the front. He put the flat of his hand against the back door, feeling for movement inside. Failing that, he tried the knob. No luck, locked. He glanced up at Shavon. She shook her head. Shavon trusted her instincts. Her instincts were telling her forcing this door and going inside would be a Very Bad Idea.

"Way outside our remit, Jerry."

"Technically, this house belongs to the city."

Shavon shook her head. "Technically this house doesn't exist. Empty lot, remember? Too many unknowns here."

"So, retreat and regroup?" Jerry said.

"What we do is help kids in trouble, Jerry. What we *don't* do is solve weird-ass Scooby Doo mysteries, so yes, retreat and regroup." Shavon caught his wide-eyed, startled look. "What?" she said. "What is it?"

"Gun," Jerry said matter-of-factly.

She followed his gaze and spotted it lying flat against the base of the house a few feet away, a pistol almost lost from sight in the trash and snow. Jerry strode over and picked it up by the butt with his thumb and forefinger.

"Not a Glock," Jerry said. "Baretta 92, civilian version of the M9, my primary in Afghanistan. No rust or wear, so not here long."

Shavon nodded, grasping the implications. Glock 17 generation 4 pistols were standard police issue in Lake County, not Barettas. She asked, "This a throwaway, you think? Our 'bangers yonder'?"

Jerry considered it and then shook his head. "If this were a throwaway, you'd think they'd throw it farther away than across the street."

"Loaded?"

Jerry expertly removed the magazine, conducted a quick visual inspection, and then slapped the mag home again with the heel of his palm. He gave Shavon another questioning look.

"Hold onto it," Shavon said.

"Think we'll need it?" Jerry asked, pocketing the piece in the front pocket of his poofy, thickly insulated winter coat. Shavon noticed Jerry's demeanor had changed. Jerry was wearing his game face, and she was glad to see it. She needed him sharp.

Shavon said, "I don't think we've got a problem a gun can solve, but there if we need it."

"There's more over here," Jerry said, gesturing at the trash piled against the house.

"More what? More guns?"

"More all kinds of crap," Jerry said, bending down and sifting through the rubbish heap. "Clothes, coins, buckles, random stuff...," he said, trailing off. He picked up a plastic child's baby doll, naked and forlorn, held it up for her to see, and then pulled the string. The doll started crying, a plaintive sound that carried over the wind. After it had finished playing, Jerry put the doll back in the pile, oddly gently.

"That our crying baby, you think?" Shavon said.

"Yeah, could be, maybe," Jerry replied. "No way to be sure." Jerry straightened, fished in his front coat pocket, and produced an electronic ignition key fob. He tossed it to Shavon, who effortlessly snatched it from the air and looked it over.

"The Camaro?" she said.

Jerry nodded. "Not something you'd throw away."

Jerry crouched down on his beefy haunches and went back to rummaging through the pile and then abruptly stopped, fixed in place for a long moment with his head at an angle and his hands on his knees as if deep in thought, turning over a problem.

"You find something else?"

"Not a thing," Jerry said. "We should go now, Shavon."

Jerry moved quickly, closing the distance between them in a few long, hurried steps, taking Shavon by the arm above the elbow, steering her away from the back of the house, and hustling her towards the street.

"The hell, Jerry?" Shavon said, stopping at the sidewalk, brushing his hand away. "What's wrong with you?"

"No time to explain," he said. "Let's just get to the car."

"Explain what, Jerry?" Waiting for him to respond, Shavon's focus shifted to the sidewalk and the street.

That old man, she thought.

"Where did Banks get to?" she asked. "He'd never leave Blue, real or not."

"Banks is gone, Shavon," Jerry said. "We can't worry about him right now. Right now, we need to move."

Shavon held up her hand. "Wait, you feel that?"

Jerry took a deep breath and nodded. "Yes, I feel that."

Shavon said, "I can feel it through my boots, like an earthquake, except Indiana doesn't *do* earthquakes."

"Shavon, you trust me?"

"I trust you, Jerry." She smiled. "You and me, we've been through it together."

"Okay, great," Jerry said. "I want you to walk with me to the car, Shavon. We get in the car, we start the car, and we *didi mao* the hell out of the AO. So please, Shavon, *let's get to the car.*"

Shavon studied Jerry's face and saw fear in there—real fear, mortal fear, and because fear is contagious, she started feeling it, too. "Fine," she said. "You're right, let's go. Nothing more we can do here."

2

The not-a-house took Jerry just as they reached the car. Shavon was opening the driver's side door when something like a rope (a whip?) shot out from the house (not a house) and snatched Jerry away as if he had been hooked off a vaudevillian stage, Jerry so shocked by the awful unreality of it he didn't cry out.

Acting on instinct, Shavon crouched for cover by the car at a whiplash-cracking sound she at first thought was a gunshot, a move that saved her because a second thick, cable-like tentacle came at her right after the first, coming so close overhead she could feel the rush of displaced air and hear the snap of its passing, followed by the shuddering thump and scrape as it retracted and slid off the roof of the Versa.

Purely reacting, Shavon was out and moving now, breaking into a sprint. She knew at that primal, primitive part of her brain not to run from predators in straight, predictable lines, so Shavon zigged and zagged, changing direction whenever she heard that awful cracking sound. Shavon chanced a glance over her shoulder and caught her first glimpse of the house / not a house—and even then that small, rational piece of her not filled with fight-or-flight panic understood what she was seeing wasn't its true form. What she saw instead was an act of translation, the closest her mind could come to its utterly alien actuality.

Giant rainbow-colored jellyfish was the visual impression it gave her, a pulsing, iridescent dome at its top, its cylindrical torso bristling with a forest of hundreds of writhing, nearly translucent tentacles. And weirdly, impossibly in her head Shavon could feel the nearly overwhelming mental and emotional presence of the monster as it cast off its psychic camouflage—not its thoughts because the thing didn't think as people think. It wasn't *people*. It was something *other*, so outside Shavon's frame of reference as to be indecipherable. Shavon couldn't read its thoughts, but she could, in a dim and limited way, sense its intentions. Its intentions were hostile, murderous. It meant to catch her, kill her, eat her.

I'm dead in the open, Shavon thought. She changed direction a third time and dashed straight for the drug house twenty-five yards away. Running was usually a joy for Shavon, one of her life's great pleasures. She had always reveled in the feeling of freedom it gave her and it was saving her now, a lifetime of training all coming down to this desperate hawk-on-a-rabbit chase in the snow.

The house / not a house almost had her at the parked Camaro. It had absorbed Shavon's pattern and adjusted, but because it telegraphed its intentions Shavon knew to go low and crawl under and through, rather than slide over the hood of the car. She scrambled the last few feet to the door, steeling herself to break it down only to find it unlocked (*lucky, lucky, lucky*, she thought), throwing herself across the threshold and onto the threadbare carpeted floor, back-kicking closed the heavy door behind her, expecting one or more tentacles to slam against the other side. But they didn't.

Limit of its reach, she thought.

Shavon stayed prone on the floor until the shock wore off and then slowly rose to her feet. Looking around, she saw the door looked new and reinforced. The windows were barred. It was warm inside, a fire going in the fireplace—not a real one, a fake, gas-fed fireplace, the kind turned on with a switch, the kind with ceramic logs unburning forever. Her aunt had owned one. Shavon hadn't liked it. She thought it cheesy. She liked things real.

Head in the game, she thought. *Jerry's gone and a shape-changing tentacled jellyfish monster the size of a house is waiting right outside.*

Not getting in, she thought, she *hoped*, and on the heels of that she pictured Jerry as she had last seen him, the shock on his face as the house / not a house drew him into itself. Shavon felt an onrush of grief coming on but held it back, shut it down.

"Save it for later," she said aloud. "Don't need it right now."

A cellphone rang as if on cue; not her cell because her cell was in her purse and her purse was in the Versa and the Versa was across the street, parked in front of a giant man-eating space jellyfish disguised as a house. The horrific absurdity of it threatened to swallow her up.

Shavon thought, *Nope, uh-uh*, as Jerry would say, not going down that rabbit hole. I am not crazy. This is happening. This is real. I will deal with it.

Shavon followed the phone's ring to a body in the kitchen, the gray-faced corpse of a young, once-handsome man in his early thirties, propped into a sitting position on the floor with his back against a dingy refrigerator. His eyes were open. It bothered her his eyes were open. The right hand of the corpse was missing, the stump shorn almost surgically clean above the wrist.

The hand that held the Baretta Jerry found, Shavon guessed. The hand Jerry saw in the rubbish heap.

Shavon saw the dead man had been trying to staunch the bleeding when he died, the thumb of his left hand caught up in the loop of a blood-soaked rag twisted into a torniquet a few inches above the stump, but too out of blood and time to cinch it tight. This had been recent, she guessed, the blood so fresh she could smell it. Shavon noticed too the clothes he wore—nice clothes, expensive clothes—Brooks Brothers shoes, Bottega Veneta slacks, Armani suit jacket, Oxford shirt without a tie—and figured she was looking at the owner of the shiny red Camaro out front.

Look at you, she thought.

A black nylon Nike gym bag was on the floor beside the body. Aside from bloodstains, it looked new, no signs of wear. The bag was bulging, and whatever was inside the bag was emitting an audible, intermittent hum, the sound more musical than mechanical, as if humming a nonsensical tune.

The still-ringing cell was on the kitchen table, almost lost in the clutter piled on it. Shavon glanced at caller ID. Jerry's phone. It was using Jerry's phone. Shavon picked up, half-suspecting what was coming.

Shavon darling, that you? Can we talk?

The thing was using the cell's text-to-voice functionality to communicate, speaking with the same feminine British voice she had heard earlier when she and Jerry sought directions. Shavon imagined the tip of one of those horrid tentacles poised above the keypad, texting. Imagining it made her shudder.

"Dead man in the kitchen," Shavon said. "Friend of yours?"

That would be Leon. Leon was very fast—like you, Shavon. Unlike you, not fast enough.

Shavon surveyed the kitchen. It had been converted to a meth lab, with propane tanks and big blue plastic barrels filling the space, lined against the walls and into the hallway leading to the bathroom and bedrooms, along with bags of powdered chemicals on the table, liquids in a row of tall plastic jars on the kitchen counter by the sink. But it seemed to her as if they hadn't been cooking meth for a while. The place was in disarray, trash everywhere: carboard pizza boxes, empty beer cans, moldering rags, discarded rubber gloves. Cloying chemical smells and the putrid stink of weeks-old garbage made the air nauseatingly fetid and hard to breathe. Shavon absently noted no sign of rats. *All this trash*, she thought, *there should be rats.*

It ate the rats, she thought. *Forget the rats.*

"Is Jerry alive?" Shavon asked the monster. She knew it would almost certainly lie but she asked anyway, holding onto that tiny sliver of hope.

Of course Jerry's alive. I need him, Shavon, because I need you.

"Show me he's alive," Shavon said. "Proof of life and we'll talk."

Come to the front window.

Taking the cell with her, Shavon returned to the living room, pulled back the curtain, and peered out. The house / not a house looked like a house again. Jerry was standing in front, swaying uncertainly, slack-jawed and dazed, but his eyes were open and aware. He was alive.

Wave, Jerry. Say hello! Hello!

Jerry knew or guessed Shavon was watching. She could read the movement of his lips. He was telling her to run, save herself.

Oh no, none of that now, Jerry, none of that!

One of the thing's tentacles, more substantial than the others she had seen, came out the maw of its front door like a giant amphibian tongue and snatched him back inside, a frog catching a fly.

"You want Leon's bag," Shavon said, turning away from the window.

Yes, Leon's bag—lying, thieving, sneaky little Leon. A piece of friendly advice, Shavon: Don't open the bag. What's in it bites.

Shavon said, "When the cops showed up, things were about to get loud. That's why you intervened. You don't want loud."

You know me so well, Shavon. We're like sisters.

"You tried covering it up, keeping up the pretense, but there wasn't enough time. You got sloppy."

What can I say? So easy here. I've grown complacent.

"You want whatever's in Leon's bag. You also want this place destroyed, all evidence with it, no loose ends."

You're very quick. I like that.

"Except Jerry and I *are* loose ends. Why would you leave us alive? Aren't you worried what we might say?"

What would you say? What could *you say? I know this world, Shavon. I've been around, ears to the ground, finger on the pulse. I listen. I watch. I take notes. No one would believe you.*

Shavon nodded to herself, imagining how this would play to anyone in authority—or even to family and friends. It was all so fantastically implausible. "A house monster," Shavon said aloud, "hiding in plain sight, taking people nobody'd miss."

You have no conception, little thing. I can cross vast oceans of space-time, mirror and multiply my being between the dimensional rifts and touch a thousand worlds. I do what I must. I do what I do out of love.

"Yeah, okay, not a monster," Shavon said, fearful of its sudden shift in tone. "After it's done, you let us go. That's the deal."

That's my girl. Welcome to the team.

Her end was simple: burn down the drug house, drop off the bag it wanted so much, grab Jerry, and go. The easy part was the first part since gangbanger meth labs want to blow up. It's what they do. Fire inspectors going through the ashes would never question the how and why of it.

Shavon looked down at the corpse. *Lying thieving Leon,* the monster had said. It had known this man by name. She recalled the exchange with Banks: Ask them bangers yonder, he had said. These gangsters knew about the house monster's presence in the neighborhood. They had some kind of arrangement with this thing, but then lying, thieving Leon got greedy.

The bag, she thought. *What's in the bag?*

Don't open the bag, the monster had said. It had been emphatic on that point. Its anxiety had been palpable.

"Oh, I'm definitely opening the bag," Shavon said aloud.

She walked back to Leon's body to reach it, stepping gingerly over and around the blood pooled on and around it, leaning over Leon and gripping the bag by its nylon handle, expecting it to be heavy but it wasn't. Whatever Leon had stolen wasn't made of gold. Bag in hand, Shavon crossed to the other side of the table, cleared a space, and set it down carefully. She noticed whatever was in the bag was no longer emitting that melodious humming sound, and took this as a good sign.

It bites, the monster had said.

Shavon thought of Jerry held captive, along with Latham and Neely, who she now knew were dead for sure. *So bite me, then,* she thought, and opened the bag.

Daddy's bowling ball Shavon thought when she saw the orb inside, an ebony sphere. She took it out and held it up. Her father had been in a company bowling league, his bowling ball a deep black with tiny flecks of gold as if floating just beneath the surface. The orb she held was like that, almost exactly like that, its black, opaque surface like a fine Japanese lacquer, giving her that same sense of unreachable depth.

Except Daddy's bowling ball didn't feel alive in the hand, she thought. *And maybe,* she thought, *this orb is like that monster out there and what I'm holding isn't what it really is.*

"I'm guessing not a bowling ball," she said aloud.

Shavon suddenly felt a new, jarring presence in her mind—not a brutal assault like that of the monster's, furiously savage and filled with vile intention. This stranger in her head was instead a probing, tentative presence, even shy.

It's reading me, Shavon thought. She could feel it back there, going through her memories like a curious tourist.

"YOU ARE NOT LEON!" its vaguely masculine machine voice boomed in her head, causing Shavon to recoil and grimace, so startled she almost dropped the thing.

"Too loud!" Shavon cried. "Turn it down!"

"ADJUSTING," it blared, making her wince again. After a moment, it said in a normal voice (*if a voice not mine in my head can be normal,* she thought), "You are not Leon. Where is Leon?"

Shavon didn't know if the orb she held could see or sense its surroundings but pointed it in the direction of the body. "Leon is dead," she said. "The monster killed him."

"Leon promised freedom," the orb said in her head. Previously, the inflection of its voice had been neutral, but its tone was different now. It sounded mournful.

So, not a machine, Shavon thought, at least not completely. *It knows sadness. It can feel.*

"Leon lied," Shavon replied. "Forget Leon. Who are you? What are you? Are you alive?"

"Define 'alive,'" it said, giving Shavon the distinct impression of boredom as if it had considered and then dismissed the question innumerable times. "My makers described me as a trans-temporal interpolation device." It sensed Shavon's confusion. "A possibility engine." It sensed even more confusion. "I detect timeline branch-points within a bounded probability matrix and plot solutions in alignment with command imperatives."

Shavon raised an eyebrow. "That thing out there your maker?"

"Not my maker," the orb replied. "Form follows function. It fed my makers to its young and made of me its slave."

Its young? Shavon thought, her mind balking at the implications.

After a moment, Shavon said, "So you see the future and feed it best possible moves, yeah? That way, it knows what's coming and adjusts for it. It never loses."

"I guide explorers," the orb said. "I show the way."

Shavon placed the orb on the table and pulled up a chair. Once seated, she bent forward at the waist, propping herself on her elbows until eye-level with it.

"Okay then, you and me, we need to fight this thing. Tell me how."

"You seek to kill it?"

Shavon thought of the doll in the trash heap. "That's the goal," she said.

"Survival is not always synonymous with victory," it warned.

"I get that," Shavon said. "Whatever it takes."

"Parameters established. Calculating," it said. "Done."

"Show me," Shavon said, and it showed her, projecting in her awareness a wireframe abstraction depicting a vast, tangled array of localized possible futures, each in a state of unrealized transposition and composed of dozens of shifting variables, the disparate threads converging and combining at the speed of time into a single, definitive *now*.

If Shavon bolted and ran and went to the authorities, the monster would be gone by the time they arrived. If Shavon kept her part of the deal, the monster would break the deal (it always broke the deal) and torture-murder-eat Shavon and Jerry both. Shavon saw it all, and at the end only one future emerged with the outcome they wanted, but it came with a catch. *Always a catch*, Shavon thought. The price paid to attain it would be nearly unbearably high.

"You have a choice," the orb told her.

"No, I don't," Shavon said. "You know I don't. How do we make it happen?"

Within its conceptual null-space, Shavon was subjected to a seemingly endless series of pass-fail A/B simulacra, where she tried and died over and over in bloody and painful myriad ways inside the mind of this alien machine until she found a way that worked. When it was over, Shavon came to in the here-and-now of the drug house meth lab. She saw by her watch only a few minutes had passed.

"I know what I need to do," Shavon said, more to herself than to the orb.

"I find myself afraid," the orb said. "Are you afraid, too?"

"I got no spit to swallow," Shavon confessed, "but hey, it's okay to be afraid. It's what you do, in spite of that fear, that makes you."

3

"Almost done here," Shavon told the monster when it called.

Good girl, Shavon. All over soon.

"You'll keep your end?" Shavon said.

The monster had learned emojis. It sent her a thumbs-up.

Shavon shouldered the bulging, bloodstained gym bag and grabbed one of the smaller propane tanks on her way out, pressing the button on the car ignition fob to pop the trunk of the Camaro outside. She needed to stay on the move, giving it no time to think and react.

Keep it guessing, she thought.

Outside, the sun had set but still had enough of a dusky glow in the sky so she could see. Moving quickly, Shavon stepped out, placed the propane tank inside the trunk, opening the valve and shoving it toward the back, above the gas tank, and then closing the lid. Leon's cellphone began ringing again. She ignored it, going to the driver's side, opening the door, gently placing the gym bag into the backseat, and sliding behind the wheel. The cell continued to ring. She closed the door and finally answered. She had gone off-script and knew it had seen her going off-script, but there was nothing for it.

I see this device has a visual function, little thing. This means you can watch while I skin Jerry alive and awake and screaming in agony for subjective eternity, begging for death and going insane from the pain. It'll be fun.

"I made a bomb," Shavon said.

A long pause ensued. Shavon could imagine it struggling to analyze this new paradigm on its own, without the orb.

You're bluffing, the monster said.

Shavon said, "You should never have left me alone in a kitchen filled with very nasty and volatile chemicals."

You cannot hope to hurt me, little thing. I am forever.

"'I am forever.' Listen at you, bitch," Shavon replied. "But yeah, okay, maybe you're right, maybe you are forever, but *I've got your subjective eternity* right here. I know your weak spot. I know your secret."

You know nothing, little thing. Try, you die. Jerry too.

Shavon said, "Nobody wants to die. Put Jerry out front, free and in one piece. Do that, give me Jerry, I give you what you want. Hurt him in any way or try to hurt me, I ram this pretty red car up your ugly monster ass."

It abruptly ended the call, and Shavon was grateful. She had known horrible people, too many to count, but those horrible people had been people and if she looked closely enough she could follow the causal chain that had made them that way. But this thing? Like dipping her hand into medical waste. Like vomit on her shoe. Oozing pus from an open wound. Squirming intestinal worms in a jar. Eyeless monkeys screaming in a lab and *Oh, sweet Jesus make it stop!*

It gets in your head, she thought.

The Camaro startled her when she started it. Leon's car was, Shavon guessed, far louder than it should've been (*custom work?*), but loud was fine. Shavon liked it loud. She was tempted to play music, go out with tunes, knowing Leon's sound system was sure to be the best money could buy, but resisted the impulse, dismissing it as childish. She didn't need the distraction.

Head in the game, Shavon.

Shavon stopped at the edge of the curb to pick up the pistol Jerry had dropped earlier when the thing had taken him. Based on her experiences inside the orb, Shavon knew to be especially careful here, and quick. If this thing was breaking the deal—and it always broke the deal—this was where it usually made its move, while the orb was within reach and she was out of the car, exposed and vulnerable.

Shavon stepped out, racked the slide of the Baretta, assumed the Weaver stance her father had taught her, and put a bullet through the wall of the house to the large propane tank she had lugged into the living room and stood next to the fake, gas-fed fireplace.

Shavon felt letdown by the fire. She had expected a raging conflagration like in the movies, but instead all she got was a muffled *whump*! followed by a growing orange glow visible through the curtain of the window by the door as the flames caught and spread. She guessed the fire would be a slow burn until it reached the kitchen, which triggered a twinge of regret. The orb was on the kitchen table where she had left it, surrounded by accelerants and combustibles. Even with its near-godlike conceptual abilities, the orb itself was easy to damage—or so it had told Shavon.

"Any outcome with myself intact ends in catastrophic failure. For this to work, I need to cease functioning, give it nowhere to go," the device had told her. "I wish it were otherwise."

"Me too," Shavon whispered, pocketing the pistol.

She got back in the car and drove slowly over the curb on the opposite side of the street, the big engine of the Camaro rumbling like a living thing. Shavon stopped the car a few yards short of the front door. Its porch light was on, and she wondered again at the thing's ability to shape its form even down to the wires and lights. Not long after, but forever for Shavon, Jerry came out, staggering a little as he made his way to the car and slid his bulk heavily inside.

"Hundreds of them, Shavon," Jerry said, his round, moon face sickly pale from shock, his voice a dull monotone, his gaze fixed in a thousand-yard stare. "Its *children*, all around me in the dark, chittering in my head—they were in my head like this thing gets in your head and they're all down there, Shavon, down there *waiting to be born*. This thing gives birth, they'll eat the world."

Shavon nodded. "I know, Jerry."

"You know?"

"I know, so I made a bomb."

"You made a bomb?" Jerry said, his head coming up as if jolted awake. He scrutinized her profile, noting her set, determined expression. He knew that expression. "Right, you made a bomb," Jerry went on, the same way he would say, 'You baked a cake,' as if Shavon building a bomb was the most natural act in the world, something she did, part of her day.

"We're sitting in it," Shavon said.

Jerry thought it through. He had a quick mind and saw where this was going and how it would end. He didn't argue alternatives. Instead, Jerry simply said, "No other way?"

Shavon shook her head regretfully. "It's the only play this thing can't see coming. Monsters don't *get* sacrifice, Jerry." Shavon allowed herself a quick, small smile, as if remembering a joke. "They have no conception."

Jerry gave a small sigh. "It'll be hard for Nan, but I'm cool with it, weird as it sounds to say it out loud. Too dumb to be scared, I guess. What do you need from me?"

Shavon continued to look straight ahead at the silent, seething house / not a house. She sensed it watching her closely in turn and could feel the rancid, gut-churning flavors of its madness emanating from it in a chaotic, writhing, maggoty gestalt. Hatred came off it in waves. And hunger. It was always hungry. Its hunger defined it.

So many mouths to feed, Shavon thought.

Without taking her eyes from it, Shavon said, "Reach behind you and open that gym bag in the backseat. Yank that 550-cord until you hear a click. That click is the Piezo igniter I stripped from the fake fireplace back at the drug house. It sets off the ether. The ether sets off the propane. The propane blows the tank. Tank's nearly full." Shavon squared her shoulders, bracing herself for what was coming. "Boom should be big enough."

Jerry said, "That's some real Rube Goldberg shit right there, Shavon." He sniffed the air. He could smell the propane filling the interior. "I won't ask how you knew how to do this."

"Practice," Shavon said. She didn't elaborate.

The monster loomed, and Jerry and Shavon could feel its gibbering rage bearing down with a withering intensity, making Shavon's head hurt and her nose bleed. Jerry fell back in his seat as if pushed, his eyes squeezed shut from pain of his own. The house / not a house had finally figured it out, figured *them* out. It knew.

"We should hurry," Jerry said. He started to reach across to fasten his seat belt but caught himself, shook his head wearily, and gave a short, rueful bark of a laugh.

Shavon said, "I can't stop thinking about that sad little toy that brought us here."

"The doll, you mean? The kid it belonged to?" Jerry said.

Shavon nodded. "Yes, the little girl."

Jerry twisted in his seat, reached in the bag, jerked the looped nylon 550-cord, and thought of his wife.

At the sound of the igniter's click, Shavon floored the Camaro, making the tires squeal and the big engine roar. As the Camaro caught traction and leapt forward, Shavon cried out with a roar of her own, primal and savage, letting go the pent-up fear, disgust, and dread she had been holding back as her world flared bright white and silent.

I am forever, the house / not a house had bragged to Shavon, but found in the end it wasn't forever and instead ceased to be, its raving mad-god consciousness flung screeching with hatred and rage into the inky blackness of the void, its tentacled, stalk-like corporeal form caught up and consumed by the rising fireball of a crack-of-doom explosion, its thousand voracious, insatiable, immolating young screaming as they burned, its womb a tomb.

3¢
USA
AMAROKIE
105

CRITICAL BLAST PUBLISHING
20¢
A TOTAL WITCH
Deborah Cardillo
APPROVED BY THE READING CODE AUTHORITY
CRITICAL BLAST PUBLISHING
NO ONE SURVIVES... THE HOA!

HUMAN MASK When you need to walk among the humans, without being singled out as a monster. Get this mask in black, white or polka-dot, to blend right in!

SUPER SHARP PIRATE SWORD When you want to capture the hearts and minds of the people around you, this sword will cut through the muscle and bone to get to the vital organs you need to sustain your hunger.

SUPER SECRET BOOK SAFE The special camouflage feature activates, once placed on the book shelf. You'll never find it again.

MAKE MINE MONSTERS!

HELIUM GAS & BALLOON SET Get away from the day to day grind of your boring life and steal a whole house while the owners are away.

BOX OF LIVE BATS When you feel like a millionaire crime fighting hero and need to dress up your special cave, to give it that extra touch of atmosphere... a box of live bats is perfect for you. Food not included.

LEARN TO PLAY THE GUITAR! When you can't get a date for the weekend, rent a sexy Guitar Teacher to impress your friends and maybe you just might learn something too.

RADIOACTIVE CANDY When you want to level up your personality and appear extra sweet to the people around you... and want to have a superpower over sugar... this candy's for you!

HEAD KNIVES 100% stainless steal daggers that launch from the top of your head and kill any conversation you find boring.

RENT AN ANGRY MIDGET! When you need to stop a Bully from harassing, or when you need to look like a decent human concerned for poor ugly monsters.

Deborah Cardillo has been published in the horror anthology Along Harrowed Trails from Timber Ghost Press, and will have a story included in the upcoming anthology The Twelve Knights of Christmas from Button Hall Publishing.

"Someone's bought the Weavers' house,"

says Dad, looking out the window. The old Weaver place has been for sale for practically forever and slowly falling apart the whole time. Joyce, the president of the HOA, is always mad because the Weavers' lawyers pay all her fines rather than fix anything up. Now a guy in a suit is putting a little SOLD! sign on top of the FOR SALE sign.

Mom comes over and leans against Dad. "It'll be contractors and noise for weeks fixing it up."

But instead of people coming and working, a truck comes and starts unloading furniture the very next day. Heavy furniture with dark wood and purple fabric and carved with lion's feet and stuff. And that night, a lady shows up. She's old and wearing a tall black hat with a point. She's got green skin.

"Dad, is she a witch?" I ask.

"I guess she is," he says, and picks up my little sister, who puts her face in his neck. Mom takes my hand. I'm pretty grown-up, because I'm ten, but I let Mom hold my hand in case she's scared. And maybe I'm glad she's holding it too.

Nothing too interesting happens for a few weeks. Her green face peeks out her window sometimes. At night, the shadow of her pointed hat makes an arrow on her lawn. We get used to seeing her.

Then she comes knocking at the back door. Her yard and ours don't have a fence between and she comes to the kitchen door like a mom in a black and white TV show. Dad opens the kitchen door and places himself in the middle of it. His hand is close to the baseball bat he keeps against the wall.

"Yes?"

"Sorry to bother you." Her voice is exactly what you expect, both high and crackly, like she was gonna cackle any second. She has an accent, but it's hard to tell where from. "I am Hilda. I just moved in next door. Just wanted to say 'Hi.' I have brought you gingerbread."

She holds a plate stacked high with dark squares of cake. Mom, my sister, and me, sitting at the kitchen table, lean into the smell. Buttery and spicy. The deep, dark undertone of molasses. So good. My mouth turns into a well of saliva.

"That's very nice of you," Dad says uncertainly, "but I'm not sure..."

Mom stands up. "How sweet. Thank you so much." She sweeps past Dad and takes the plate of gingerbread from Hilda. "It smells delicious. Come in. Share it with us. I'll make coffee. Or tea if you prefer."

"Tea would be just lovely," Hilda says.

Dad gives Mom a weird look, but he steps away from the baseball bat and lets Hilda in. Hilda smells of herbs and pine and dirt. Not dirty. Good, clean dirt, if that makes any sense. She smells like I figure a forest smells. But here she is in our neighborhood, far away from any but the sickliest trees that are all cut back hard to HOA standards so they don't touch anybody else's property.

Mom makes tea and pours milk for me and my sister. She doles out the pieces of gingerbread on the fancy dessert plates with the gold along the edge. She gives me and my sister funny looks when Hilda can't see. My sister grabs her fork, but I get what Mom is trying to say. I catch my sister's elbow under the table. We all try to act normal, except my little sister who stares, waiting for Hilda to take the first bite. And she does.

"Not too bad if I do say so myself," says Hilda and cackles for real.

"It looks amazing," says Mom and picks up her fork, which lets us know we can eat it. Hilda wouldn't eat it if it's poison or magicked. I let go of my sister and she takes such a big hunk it barely stays on the fork. I take a little at first. It's so delicious I gobble it in as big chunks as my sister does.

Soon Hilda and Mom are talking about baking things, then Dad offers to take a look at the leak in Hilda's sprinkler system.

Me and my sister have seconds. I'd have thirds if Mom didn't catch me.

"Did you make the gingerbread for a house?" my sister asks suddenly. "To catch kids?"

"I'm so sorry," Mom says, embarrassed.

"Oh, it's all right. Children are curious," says Hilda, smiling. Her teeth are pointy, where they aren't missing. "No, sweetheart. My cousin had a house made of gingerbread, but it was the hard kind, like for gingerbread men. She had to move when it fell apart after the first heavy rain. You have never seen such a mess."

My sister keeps going. "You're not trying to make us fat to eat us?"

"Tonya, that's enough," Mom says.

"No. I do not eat children. I do not eat any kind of people. Or pets. A child asked me that once. I eat all the same kinds of things you do. Mostly."

That "mostly" seemed like it was saying a lot on its own, but it didn't matter. As long as she doesn't eat people, dogs, or cats then it's fine. I make another play for a third piece of gingerbread and Mom lets me, probably to show Hilda we appreciate her, after Tonya was rude.

"I am sorry," Mom says again.

"No, dearie. It is fine. That is why I came over. To sort out any questions you might have. I wanted us to start with a nice clean slate and for you to know you are safe. Witches are not common, and people usually worry."

Now Dad's cheeks go hot. "Well, thank you for that, ma'am."

Hilda looks at the baseball bat for a second. Then she nods. "You're welcome," she says, and pats his hand. Her nails are long, sharp, and black. She doesn't touch Dad's skin with them.

After Hilda leaves, Mom says, "Well, wasn't that nice?"

After a second, Dad smiles, looking a little confused but happy. "Yes. It was."

"I hope she comes back with more gingerbread," I say, and try for a fourth piece.

"Don't you dare," says Mom. She laughs like she's kidding, but she isn't. I leave it. It just means more later.

That night is the first full moon since Hilda moved in and is when the really witchy stuff starts. At moonrise, a swarm of bats swell from Hilda's chimney.

"Well, that explains why she came over to make nice," Dad grumbles.

"They're sort of pretty," Mom says. "Like a plume of smoke and a flock of starlings had a baby."

Dad harumphs. "A baby made of bats."

Me and Tonya are glued to the window, watching the cloud of bats twist and swarm in front of the low-hanging, orange moon.

"I learned about bats in school," I offer. "They eat mosquitos and other bugs. They're cool."

"They're cool," Tonya echoes. Sometimes she isn't a complete pest.

"Mosquitos have been rough this summer." Dad steps up next to us and looks out the window for a while. "It is pretty. Okay."

Tonya hugs his legs.

Soon, the bats disperse into the night on their bug hunt.

#

Tonya and me wait for the school bus. It's four days since the bats first danced in the moonlight. Even though the moon is on the wane, they're still swarming every night so far.

"Hey." Tonya tugs on my hand. Because she is little and restless, I have to hold her hand while we wait. I hate it, but she tattled on me the very first time I didn't do it, and I couldn't use the PlayStation for a whole week. "What's that?"

She points at Hilda's mailbox, a plain white one. There is a bright yellow envelope decorated with pictures of pink rosebuds attached to the side of the mailbox—that blue tape that's not supposed to pull off your paint sticks the envelope on. It clashes with the yellow and pink. It's a letter from Joyce, the HOA president.

"Oh no," I say.

"Oh no!" Tonya says, because I did, not because she knows what the Joyce's special complaining stationery looks like.

Last year, Dad put a birdbath in our backyard, and we got a letter just like that taped to our mailbox. You couldn't even see the birdbath from the street. But it was against the rules and Dad had to take it down. He said bad words the whole time. Our pretty birdbath is still sitting in the garage.

"Hilda's in trouble." It makes me sad.

"Oh no," says my sister, and this time she means it.

#

When we get home after school, Hilda and Mom are in the kitchen. The yellow and pink envelope with the blue tape is on the table between them. Mom's reading the matching yellow and pink letter. Hilda's pointy hat is on the floor by her feet. Her white hair is in a tidy, braided bun, which I didn't expect. A pie is next to the envelope on the table. A few slices are cut out and it oozes blood red juice into the dish.

"But they are not pets," Hilda wails.

"The HOA has rules about how many pets you can have. And Joyce says if they're pets, you have too many," Mom says, slow, like she'd said it a few times already, "But she goes on to say that if they're not pets, they're vermin."

"Bats are not vermin."

"Bats eat mosquitos," I say, to show her we're home, but also to show off to Hilda. I'm angling for some pie.

Hilda gives me a weak, snaggle-toothed smile. "That is right. They provide a service. They make the neighborhood better."

"I agree," Mom says. "The bats provide a service, and I think they're very beautiful too. But either as pets or as wild animals, they are against HOA rules. She says the HOA will fine you if they're not gone in two days, and that she'll call the animal control services to get them exterminated if they're not gone in a week."

"Exterminated? She wouldn't!" Hilda says, bloodshot eyes widening in shock.

"Bet she would," I say, sidling toward the pie. "Mr. Lewis's little dog Boris used to get out sometimes. Never hurt anybody, just sniffed around. Joyce called the dog catcher and said Boris was a menace."

"But Dave Lewis is so nice," says Hilda. "What happened?"

Mom pats Hilda's warty hand. "We got poor Boris back from animal control, but he was almost put down. Now he only gets supervised time in the yard, in case he tries to wriggle under the gate."

Hilda sighs. Her shoulders slump. "I see how it is. All right." She breathes deep and puts on a smile just like the kind Mom puts on before Grandma comes over, except with pointier teeth. "Why don't you ask your mother if I can give you some pie?"

#

No bats make swirling shadows in front of the moon that night or the next.

There are still no bats on the third night, but balls of dim green and purple light float in Hilda's yard. They aren't even as bright as the light from Mom's phone when she plays Wordle in the dark next to Tonya's bed, trying to get my sister to sleep.

The lights drift around like giant, slow fireflies, flickering gloomily. We all stand at the window. They are just as nice to watch as the bats. Relaxing. Tonya even falls asleep in Dad's lap after a while. She can barely sleep even in bed some nights, which is how Mom got so good at Wordle. If you look long enough at the lights, you can see that they kinda have faces, with dark spots for eyes and a triangle nose, like a skull. But they're not scary. Because Hilda makes gingerbread and cherry pie and is scared about her bats being safe and is a nice old lady, even if she is a witch.

"It's nice having Hilda next door, isn't it?" I whisper so I don't wake up Tonya.

Dad smiles and musses my hair. "Yeah." He whispers too. "It actually is."

#

That Saturday morning, Hilda comes over. She has two yellow and pink letters from the HOA now. And a platter of pumpkin scones with a little bowl of butter.

"What has Joyce done now?" Dad asks, frowning, but also grabbing a scone. "Is it about the lights?"

Hilda puts the food down on the table. I slip in and grab two scones. I butter them and the scent of sweetness fills my nose. Honey butter! After a look from Mom, I give one scone to Tonya.

Hilda hands Dad the letters. "She sent another letter about pets and when I told her the will-o-wisps were not alive, she sent another about Christmas? I don't understand."

Dad reads the letters. "Okay. The HOA has rules about Christmas lights. They can only be hung after Thanksgiving, and have to come down by January 5th. And you have to turn them off before 10 every night."

"The will-o-wisps are not Christmas lights!" Hilda says, nearly in tears she's so mad.

"Yeah, but it's all colored lights outdoors. We wanted to hang lights last Halloween and she made us take them down."

Mom pats Hilda's back. "I'm sorry."

"Joyce is the worst," I say, and reach for another scone. Mom nods and I grab it.

"She is," Hilda agrees.

There are no will-o-wisps that night. Tonya cries and says she'll never sleep again.

#

Two days later, when Tonya and me are waiting for the school bus again, a big truck delivers a black cauldron. It is so big and heavy, two guys have to haul it into Hilda's house. And they are working hard.

"Is it a birdbath?" Tonya asks. "Like the one Dad had to put away?" She did remember.

"I don't think so," I say. The guys turn it on its side to fit it through the door.

"A bathtub?"

"Maybe." But witches don't take baths in cauldrons. They use cauldrons for witch stuff.

There are no lights and no bats that night. No anything witchy at all.

Mom sighs. "Joyce wins again."

"That woman always wins," Dad grumbles.

"It was a very nice bird bath," Mom says, touching his arm. "And I loved it while it was up."

Dad hugs her.

#

In the morning, billows of white smoke climb out of Hilda's chimney—funny for spring, but not against the rules. The breeze pulls it across our yard. It's not smoke at all, it's steam. It smells like Hilda smells, like pine and soil, like herbs and cut grass. Not a delicious smell, like Hilda's baking, but a good smell, like wild places and freedom. Like playing in mud and rolling in leaves and coming home with sticks in your hair because you had so much fun. Mom stands on the front steps instead of watching us at the bus stop through the window while she puts on lipstick to go to work. She tilts her head up and breathes deep. Even Tonya is happy and calm, not shifting from foot to foot or dragging on my hand.

The next day, the steam smells like spices. The best cookies ever. Dark and delicious with cinnamon and vanilla and maple. Me and Tonya are almost drooling while we wait for the bus. Dad comes out and stands with Mom instead of rushing around in a panic looking for his computer bag for work.

The day after that is water. Cool places and wet stone. We stand together as a family, Tonya up on Dad's shoulder, and wait for the school bus together.

"Hilda is the best," says Tonya, putting her chin on Dad's head.

#

On Saturday morning, I'm up early to play on the PlayStation before Dad wants to watch sports. Outside, Joyce passes by, her yellow dress bright in the morning sun. The light also makes the silver in her dark hair bright, almost pretty. She stops and looks at our lawn. She takes a tiny tape measure out of her purse. Bending down, she measures our grass to see if we need to mow. She smiles, because Dad mowed Thursday night after work. But then she sees the dandelion.

I asked Dad not to cut that dandelion, so it will make a fluffy seed head and Tonya can blow on it and make a wish. Joyce takes a picture of it with her phone. Under my breath, I call her words I'm not supposed to say. Joyce isn't taking a picture because it's a nice yellow flower. She's taking a picture to show to Dad and complain about weeds.

I wish I could go and yell at her to leave Tonya's dandelion alone, but it would probably get me in trouble. So I dig for more gold in my game instead.

Hilda comes over in the afternoon. She has a big metal bowl with a plastic cover tucked under her arm, and I'm excited to know what she brought this time. But I'm sad too because she has two more yellow envelopes. One is rippled and the ink is smeared from getting wet.

"It's not about the smells, is it?" Dad asks. He looks sad. The scents of the steam from Hilda's house made the week better for all of us.

"Well, yes and no," says Hilda. She puts the big bowl on the table. "She did write me a letter about it. Said I was producing noxious odors based on lifestyle choices. I wrote her back asking her to come over for tea so we could discuss it. She wrote back saying she would. And she did, this morning."

Hilda peels the plastic lid off the big bowl.

"I have turned her into a frog."

A big green frog sits in a shallow pool of water at the bottom of the metal bowl.

"Huh," says Dad, grinning. "Well, she still has to live somewhere. I guess I should bring out that bird bath after all."

CRITICAL BLAST PUBLISHING
20¢
STONED
Kevin Hopson
APPROVED BY THE READING CODE AUTHORITY
GETTING TO KNOW HER WAS HARD

SHOP BY WEJAA BOARD

STICK IT TO YOUR ENEMIES! Real Voodoo Doll! Guaranteed Quality checked by the finest Witch Doctors! Send lock of hair and a SASE to DUDAT VOODOO, Box 9, Haiti.

HEAD KNIVES 100% stainless steal daggers that launch from the top of your head and kill any conversation you find boring.

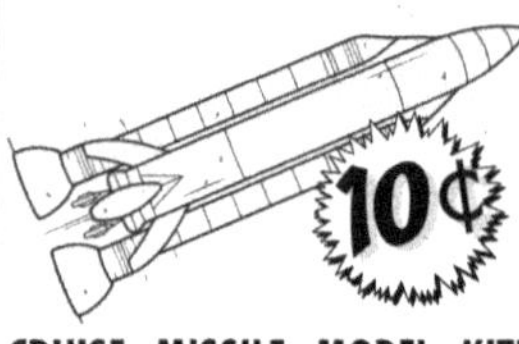

CRUISE MISSILE MODEL KIT! When you need to deliver a message across the country. Optional payload BATS IN A BOX sold separately.

BOX OF LIVE BATS When you feel like a millionaire crime fighting hero and need to dress up your special cave, to give it that extra touch of atmosphere... a box of live bats is perfect for you. Food not included.

RADIOACTIVE CANDY When you want to level up your personality and appear extra sweet to the people around you... and want to have a superpower over sugar... this candy's for you!

HUMAN MASK When you need to walk among the humans, without being singled out as a monster. Get this mask in black, white or polka-dot, to blend right in!

SNAKES IN A MAIL BOX Get these total mother-f$%Ken poisonous snakes and mail them with your get well gift cards.

EXPLODING DRINK Sit back and enjoy the highjinks as people unscrew their drink activating the chemical reaction, causing a foamy mess.

BOW AND ARROW KIT! When you need to go into battle on Tuesdays and don't know what weapon to take with you.

Kevin Hopson's work has appeared in a variety of anthologies, magazines, and e-zines, and he enjoys writing in multiple genres.

Todd craned his neck, trying to catch a peek of the fenced-in backyard from the street. He didn't want to draw attention, but he didn't want to be guilty of trespassing either.

"What the hell are you doing?"

Todd spun around, and a thirty-something man with dark hair stared back at him.

"Bryce," Todd said. "How are you?"

Bryce shrugged. "I'm fine. But you didn't answer my question."

Todd let out a breath. "Just trying to get a better look at Selina's garden."

Bryce arched an eyebrow. "Okay," he said with a hint of sarcasm. "And why would you be doing that?"

Todd debated whether to answer truthfully. If he did, he would probably sound like a lunatic. Then again, most people in the neighborhood already had that impression of him.

"I know this is going to sound crazy," Todd said, "but—"

"Hold on," Bryce interrupted. "Let me just stop you right there. If this is another one of your ridiculous theories about a neighbor, maybe you shouldn't tell me."

But Todd wanted to be a good neighbor, and that included warning others of potential dangers in the community.

"Just hear me out," Todd finally said.

Bryce huffed. "Fine."

"I noticed a life-sized statue in Selina's garden a couple of weeks ago, and it looked just like Hank Tillman."

"Didn't he move away a few months ago?"

"Yeah."

"So, what are you saying?"

Todd hesitated. The next words out of his mouth were going to be difficult for Bryce to fathom. "That he didn't move away. Selina turned him to stone."

Bryce's eyes narrowed, then his shoulders bobbed from laughter. "Seriously?"

Todd didn't answer.

"You're telling me that she's some sort of modern-day Medusa?" Bryce said.

"I don't know. Maybe."

"But I've looked at her and haven't turned to stone."

"Same with me, but maybe something else triggers it."

Bryce shook his head. "How'd you even get a good look at the statue?"

"I noticed it from the street, so I walked up to her fence and inspected it. But she caught me snooping, which is why I'm standing here instead."

"Maybe she's an artist, and the statue just happens to resemble Hank."

Bryce made a decent point, and Todd couldn't deny the possibility.

"I don't believe this theory of yours for a second," Bryce said, "but I like you well enough, which is why I'm going to make a suggestion."

"What's that?"

"Talk to Katie."

Todd's brow furrowed. "Clint's daughter?"

"Yeah. I've heard she's very knowledgeable about these things. Monsters. Aliens. Cryptids. You get the gist. The two of you would probably get along great. If nothing else, she can at least humor you."

"Huh. I had no idea. Isn't she still in high school?"

"Uh-huh. I think she's a senior now."

"And she knows all about this type of stuff?"

"That's what Clint says. He doesn't care for it, but it's one of her passions."

Todd deliberated. He'd definitely have to talk to Katie. "Thanks, Bryce."

"No problem." He winked an eye and grinned. "That's what neighbors are for."

#

Todd put a finger to the doorbell and pressed it, a muffled chiming noise immediately following. When the door opened, a hulking figure stood before him. Clint Baker was six-foot-five and close to two hundred and fifty pounds. His reddish-brown hair was parted to one side, and a bushy beard sprouted from his face.

"Hey, Clint," Todd said.

"Morning," Clint grunted.

Todd wiped a bead of sweat from his brow and choked down his anxiety. "I was wondering if I could talk to Katie."

"Katie?"

"Yeah."

"What do you need to talk to her for?"

Todd could understand Clint's apprehension. Todd didn't know Clint well, and he knew Katie even less.

"My niece," Todd managed to spit out. "She has a school project. They have to pick a monster in Greek mythology and write about it, but she's having a hard time with it." Todd paused. "Bryce said Katie may be able to help. I hear she's quite knowledgeable on the subject."

Clint pursed his lips, and a pang of doubt washed over Todd. He couldn't tell if Clint was buying his well-rehearsed lie or not.

"Why is she having a hard time with it?" Clint asked. "A Google search will give her all of the information she needs."

It was a legitimate point, and Todd had half expected Clint's response.

"They have cheap Wi-Fi," Todd said. "It's always on the fritz."

"Then go to the library."

Jesus. This guy wasn't going to make it easy.

"Fair enough," Todd said, "but she was hoping to talk to Katie about it. Kind of like an interview or something. It would set her project apart from the rest of the kids'."

Clint sighed. "Just so you know, I don't exactly approve of Katie's interest in these types of things. But she's a good student and I just want her to be happy, so I bear it." He let out a breath. "If she can help your niece, I suppose I'm okay with it."

Todd grinned. "Thanks."

"I'll pass along your request and get back to you."

Todd's grin quickly faded. "But I was hoping to talk to Katie myself."

Clint raised an eyebrow. "And why's that? You have a thing for teenage girls or something?"

"What? No. I just thought it would be the polite thing to do. Plus, I was one of those horror geeks growing up, and I still am to some extent. So, I'd love to pick her brain as well."

Clint just gawked at him, and Todd was close to throwing in the towel.

"Give me a minute," Clint said.

Clint closed the door, and that's when Todd realized he'd been sweating profusely. His armpits were wet with perspiration.

The door opened a couple of minutes later, and Katie appeared. She had her mother's dark hair and blue eyes.

"Hi, Mr. Stevenson." She stepped onto the front porch, closing the door behind her. "My dad said I might be able to help with your niece's project. It sounds interesting."

Todd combed a nervous hand through his hair. "Actually, I'm the one who needs the help."

"Huh?"

"I'm just going to come out with it," Todd said. "I think Selina Murphy can turn people to stone, and I need your help proving it."

A chuckle escaped Katie's lips. When she realized Todd was being serious, she cleared her throat. "Okay. Why do you think that?"

Todd presented his case to her, and Katie listened without saying a word.

"Hmm," she finally said.

"What?"

"There's probably a reasonable explanation for what you saw, but I'm still intrigued. So, you're telling me that Selina is some sort of Gorgon?"

"A what?"

"A Gorgon. They're female monsters in Greek mythology. They're known for their snake hair and their ability to turn anyone who looks at them to stone."

Todd shrugged. "I guess."

"But Selina doesn't have snakes for hair, and I've never turned to stone when looking at her."

Todd pondered. "I know, but you have to admit that her dreadlocks kind of resemble snakes. And maybe something else triggers the spell."

"Maybe."

Todd exhaled. "So, will you help me?"

Katie mulled it over. "I don't know much about Selina. She keeps to herself and rarely talks to people."

"I agree, but maybe she's like that for a reason. If Selina *is* turning people to stone, she'd want to live a private life and stay out of the spotlight, right?"

Katie nodded. "It makes sense. But it still doesn't mean much. A lot of people are introverts." She met Todd's gaze. "But I'd be willing to offer my services. For a price."

"How much?"

"Fifty dollars a day."

"What?"

"That's my going rate."

"So, you've helped other people with problems like this?"

"A few."

"Have any of their claims been legit?" Todd asked.

"No, but at least I debunked their theories."

Todd was starting to have second thoughts, and Katie seemed to notice.

"Look," she said. "I'd be willing to waive my daily fee on one condition."

"And what's that?"

"I have another mystery I've been looking into. It's a personal one. If you help me, I'll help you."

Todd pondered. "Okay. It's a deal."

#

Todd stood in the front yard of the old Leary place and stared at the house. It was ten o'clock in the evening, and the summer sun had set over an hour ago. Despite the darkness, the heavy air weighed on him. Todd glided a hand along his forehead, wiping a drop of sweat from it.

The house used to belong to an elderly man named Frank, but most of the kids in the neighborhood called him Old Man Leary. He died from natural causes several weeks ago, but Katie swore she'd seen Frank wandering the streets at night ever since. She also said a second-floor light would come on at night without explanation.

Katie stood on the front porch and glanced over her shoulder at Todd. The driveway was devoid of any cars, and the house was covered in shadows, the glow of a nearby street light the only source of illumination.

"You just want me to stand here?" Todd whispered.

Katie nodded. "I'm going to ring the doorbell. Tell me if you see a light come on upstairs."

Since the front porch was covered, Katie couldn't see the second-floor windows from where she was positioned.

"Okay," Todd said.

Katie had agreed to go along with Todd's story, telling her father she would be happy to help Todd's niece. But that wouldn't justify why Todd, a forty-year-old bachelor, was hanging out with Katie in the middle of the night. If anyone saw them together, he'd have a lot of explaining to do.

Todd swallowed and scanned his surroundings, failing to notice any prying eyes. Then again, he couldn't see much.

"Here we go," Katie said, putting a finger to the doorbell.

Todd tilted his head back and watched. A few seconds later, the room directly above the porch lit up.

"I see a light," he hissed.

Katie backed away from the door and descended the steps, sidling up to Todd.

"Is someone else living here?" Todd asked.

"Not that I know of," Katie replied.

"Then what are you suggesting? That Frank is still alive? Or his ghost haunts this place?"

"He could be a zombie or a ghoul, too."

It was Todd's turn to be skeptical. "Really?"

Katie shrugged.

A creaking noise stole his attention, and the silhouette of a figure appeared in the doorway.

"What the—" Todd couldn't finish his thought.

"Who's out there?" a man's voice said.

Todd hadn't known Frank well, but he'd crossed paths with him on several occasions, even chatting with Frank from time to time. The strange thing is that the man's voice resembled Frank's almost to a T.

The porch light flipped on, the man's face coming into view. Even from afar, Todd recognized that face.

His mouth hung agape. "It can't be," Todd stuttered. "Frank?" he said aloud.

"Mr. Leary?" Katie chimed in.

"No," the man said. "I'm Gabriel. His cousin. Who are you?"

Katie approached the front door, but Todd hesitated. Curiosity eventually got the better of him, and Todd hurried to catch up. He climbed the steps and stood next to Katie, still amazed at the sight in front of him.

"You sound and look just like him," Todd said. When Gabriel didn't reply, Todd elaborated. "Frank, I mean."

Gabriel's lips stretched into a grin. "His sister used to tell me that all of the time. God rest her soul."

"Are you living here now?" Katie asked.

Gabriel shook his head. "No. I'm the executor of Frank's will, so I'm just staying here until I carry out his final wishes. I'll be putting the house up for sale soon."

"I see," Todd said. "That makes sense." Katie had clammed up, so Todd took the initiative. "Well, we're sorry to have bothered you, Gabriel. Thanks for your time, and please accept our condolences."

"Thank you. You two have a good evening."

Gabriel closed the door, and Todd gawked at Katie.

"Looks like another bust," Todd said.

"Which doesn't bode well for you," she said with a sly smile.

"Whatever. A deal is a deal. I helped you. Now it's time to return the favor."

#

"This is your plan?" Todd said, walking beside Katie. It was a Sunday morning, and the summer heat was already getting to him. "We're just going to bang on Selina's door and hope she comes clean?"

"No," Katie replied, her pace failing to slow. "We're not going to be that obvious. We both agree that she's a private person, so we're probably not going to witness anything out of the ordinary in public. But I'm not going to do anything illegal either, so breaking and entering isn't an option. The only choice is to confront her."

Todd threw his arms up. "Well, if that's the case, I could have done this without you. What help are you going to be to me?"

"You might be surprised."

They were nearing Selina's house, and Todd spotted a woman in the distance. She'd just gotten out of her car and was making haste as she walked the brick pathway to the house.

"Hey," Todd said. "That's Selina."

"Selina," Katie shouted, waving a hand at her.

Selina looked their way but didn't stop. In fact, she picked up her pace and quickly disappeared into the house.

"That was kind of rude of her," Todd said.

"Maybe she's in a hurry."

"That's obvious enough. But why?"

Todd followed on Katie's heels as they approached Selina's house. The lawn looked like it needed a good mowing, and there was little color to the yard. No flowers. No plants. Just a few generic bushes that had seen better days.

Selina lived in a brick, ranch-style house, but it was a cookie-cutter house. Todd had seen plenty of others in their neighborhood just like it. Katie climbed the steps to the front door, Todd remaining at her side.

Katie glanced at him. "You want to do the honors?"

"You really think she's going to answer the door? She couldn't get in the house fast enough after seeing us."

"There's only one way to find out."

Todd shook his head.

"Fine," Katie said. "I'll do it."

She put her index finger to the doorbell and pressed it, but Todd didn't hear any kind of chime or dinging noise.

"Did you press it hard enough?" he asked.

"Of course, I did," she huffed. "But I'll do it again if it makes you happy."

Katie pushed the button a second time but the result was the same.

"Maybe it's broken," Todd said.

"Then I'll have to knock."

Katie put a knuckle to the door and gently tapped it.

"She's not going to hear that," Todd said. "You need to give it a good bang."

"It was loud enough. I don't want to be an obnoxious neighbor and kick down her door."

"Really? I barely heard it, and I'm standing right next to the door."

"Then you must have a hearing problem. In fact—"

"Please stop," a woman interrupted.

When Todd turned to look, Selina stood in the doorway. She had chocolate-colored skin, hazel eyes, and dreadlocks that came down to her shoulders.

"Hi, Selina," Katie said.

Selina's eyes narrowed. "Kathy?"

"Katie," she clarified.

"Right. Sorry." She looked at Todd. "And you're—"

Selina couldn't conjure up a name, so Todd let her off the hook.

"Todd," he finally said.

Selina nodded. "Todd. Right." She pursed her lips, and Todd and Katie stood there in awkward silence.

"Uh," Todd stuttered, attempting to break the silence but failing miserably at it.

"We were just talking about you," Katie said. "Nothing bad. It's just that we rarely see you around. You're kind of a mystery to us, so we thought we'd be neighborly and pay you a visit."

"I see," Selina said.

Todd's heart pounded up into his throat. He took a deep breath, hoping to calm his nerves.

Selina turned to him. "Are you okay?" She immediately put a hand to her mouth, wanting to take it back.

"Yeah," Todd lied. "I'm fine."

And that's when the strangest sensation washed over him. Todd's body tingled from head to toe. When he tried to speak, his lips and tongue wouldn't budge. Though his vision was fine and he could still hear the sound of his own breath, Todd couldn't will his other muscles to move.

Katie's eyes bulged. "Todd?"

"I'm sorry," Selina said. "It's my fault."

"What's your fault? And what's going on with him?"

"He's in a state of suspended animation."

"What?" Katie swallowed, taking a moment to compose herself. "Is he okay? Can he even breathe?"

"Yeah. He can breathe and still has all of his senses. He just can't speak or move for the most part."

"This is crazy." Katie took a much-needed breath. "So, it's true. You really can turn people to stone."

"Where did you hear that?" Selina covered her mouth with the palm of her hand. "Damn it. I did it again."

"Did what again?"

"Nothing. Forget it."

Katie's brow furrowed. "Anyway, Todd's been suspicious of you. He's the one who came to me about all of this."

"As you can see, he hasn't turned to stone."

"But he's frozen."

"Like I said, he's in a state of suspended animation. It's not the same."

"But how?"

"If I ask someone a question and they don't answer truthfully, the spell takes hold. It doesn't happen as often as you'd think. People can lie in my presence. It's only when I ask them a question that the spell works."

Katie shook her head in disbelief. "This is unreal. How do you break the spell?"

"By touch."

Selina took a step forward and rested a hand on Todd's shoulder. A huge puff of air escaped his lips. He could breathe deeper now and managed to spit out a few words.

"I knew it," he gasped. "You're Medusa!"

Selina's shoulders bobbed from laughter. "Hardly. I'm just an ordinary person who's had to live with this curse my entire life."

"A curse?" he asked, still panting.

"Maybe not an actual curse, but close enough. I inherited it from my mother. She was a witch."

"Wow," Katie said. "You're a real-life witch?"

"No," Selina insisted. "I refuse to practice witchcraft. I don't want any part of that life. Unfortunately, I have no control over genetics, so there's only so much I can do about my affliction."

"It doesn't seem like an affliction to me," Todd said, his breathing steadier now. "It seems more like a gift."

Selina exhaled. "Then you should try going through life with a perpetual fear of talking to people. I've been an outcast all of my life as a result of it. People think I'm stuck up or shy, but I'm just trying to protect them. I try to avoid asking questions, but sometimes they slip out, which you learned the hard way." She paused. "Anyway, it's a no-win situation. If I stay the course, people will call me a bitch. If I tell them the truth, they'll call me a freak."

Todd understood where Selina was coming from, but he didn't completely agree with her.

"I don't think you're a bitch or a freak," he said.

"Same here," Katie chimed in.

"And we give you our word," Todd said. "Your secret is safe with us."

He glanced at Katie, and she offered an approving nod.

Selina managed a smile. "I appreciate that."

"I have a question for you, though," Todd said.

"Okay."

"What about Hank?"

"Hank?"

"Hank Tillman."

"He moved away during the winter."

"Yeah, but I swear I saw a stone statue of him in your garden recently."

Selina chuckled. "I never thought about it, but it does look a little like Hank." She pondered. "I see where you're going with this. You thought I turned Hank to stone. But that statue isn't made of stone. It's plastic. And it definitely isn't Hank. It's Walter."

"Who?"

"Walter. I found the statue at a flea market and decided to name him. Being that I'm alone most of the time, I sometimes catch myself talking to him. I hate to admit it, but it's true."

"It's nothing to be ashamed of," Katie said. "And maybe we can change that. You being alone all of the time," she elaborated. "If you're up to having a new friend that is."

"Make that two new friends," Todd said.

Selina beamed. "I'd like that. More than you can imagine."

CRITICAL BLAST PUBLISHING
20¢
APPROVED BY THE READING CODE AUTHORITY
CRITICAL BLAST PUBLISHING
Buryin' MAMA
LAUREN STOKER
GONE... BUT NOT FORGOTTEN!

75¢

WELCOME MAT TRAP When you don't want people annoying you, a simple press of the button and the trap door will dispose of anyone who stands on it, while waiting for you to answer the door.

15¢

HYPNO-ROBOT use the special mind control eye harmonics to subdue the minds of your unwilling subjects. You'll never have to take out the trash and everyone will worship you as if their life depends on it.

ALL FOR **$2.99**

BECOME A PIRATE IN ONE WEEK! Learn to talk and kill like a Pirate. Optional hand and leg amputation. Pirate Ship sold separately. Arrrrrr.

MONSTER VALUE STAMP
THIS IS IT! CLIP THEM & COLLECT THEM ALL!

HEAD KNIVES 100% stainless steal daggers that launch from the top of your head and kill any conversation you find boring.

SAVE **$100**

RENT AN ANGRY WOLF! When you need to rip apart your competition, or when you need to look like a decent human concerned for dogs or something, something.

LAST MAN ON EARTH HEARD A KNOCK AT THE DOOR!

LAUREN STOKER's short stories and non-fiction have been published in the U.S., Canada, the U.K., and Australia. Lauren has also published three books of (mostly comic) satire, including BLOOD WILL OUT (With the Proper Solvent) and THE POTATOES OF DEFIANCE. She lives in New England with her cat (and Chief Shreditor) Sam. For links to her publications see: www.LaurenHStoker.com.

Before he died, Jeb Finch made two requests of his sons, Dwayne and Caleb, and made them promise to honor them. "Number one: Don't sell the farm, unless you really got to. Two: But if you got to, dig Mama up from the ol' cow pasture down in the lower 40 and take her with you. Jest git a big enough rig so she don't tumble out. Oh, and crank that ol' coffin lid down real tight. Don't want nobody to see that stake in her heart, nor the pitchfork neither." He reckoned that would spook the deal right then and there, if the realtor saw.

#

Jebediah Finch was a sensible man in all things and had thought long and hard about the problem of Emeline and how she went. She'd been his wife for nearly 30 years, so he knew her inside and out. Which meant that he was pretty damned sure of what he had to expect after he himself passed. There'd be a snowball's chance in Hell that she'd allow him to rest easy, after what he did to her. But it had got to be done. Weren't no way around it. It's what you do with them bloodsuckers.

'Course, his sweet Emmie wasn't always a bloodsucker. The bloodsucking thing was a sad development that came one night as they were easing into their late middle age. When they'd first met, she had swept Jeb right off his dusty, cowboy boots. She'd been a right pretty lil' thing, and smart, too, especially when it came to running the farm. Emmie'd been the best wife a man like Jeb coulda wished for; she'd been his solid partner in life, as well as in business. They'd enjoyed a good and loving marriage for donkey's years, even after she sorta blimped out, the way a lotta farm women who are good cooks tend to do after a while. Hell, he'd put on a bunch of pounds himself, but neither of them cared nor complained. They jogged along together, comfortable as a pair of old bedroom slippers, had them a couple of sons, and their farm prospered. Sure, they got a few grey hairs along the way, but that's only to be expected.

Everything was just fine, or so Jeb reckoned, until that city slicker with the pointy black boots and pointy black hairline came along. Outa nowhere, he drove right up their long drive from the state highway about twilight, askin' if there was some place nearby he could rest for the night. Said he was a travelin' salesman and had got lost on his route.

Naturally, Emeline, bein' the kind-hearted woman she was, told him he could stay the night with them. Caleb could give up his room and bunk in with Dwayne.

Well, one night turned into three, turned into a week, then another. When Jeb enquired how soon Mr. Slick would be leaving, Emmie shushed him and told him she hoped not any time soon. Said the man was polite and clean, and helped her out no end in the kitchen.

Jeb wasn't sure what the dude was sellin' but it was clear Emmie'd bought it and it wasn't vacuum cleaners or encyclopedias. And damned if the varmint didn't sweep her off her feet, with his sweet-talkin' and poetry and such. His funny accent musta been icin' on the cake to her, exotic and foreign. He sure wasn't from around those parts, that was for damned certain. Sounded like he'd swallowed a wad of hairballs and was tryin' to cough 'em back up.

Since the dude was stayin' on a spell, Jeb asked Emmie couldn't their visitor help out on the farm? Jeb pointed out he could sure use an extra pair of hands, and 'twas only fair, what with the dude's free room and board.

But that was a no-go. Emmie made it clear that a body like Hans (that was the dude's name), so refined and a scholar to boot, couldn't be expected to git cow manure and such on him. Jeb couldn't see what difference that should make and said so. But all Jeb got for his honesty was an apron tossed at him with Emmie's invitation to make his own lunch. She told him she had better things to do.

"Like what?" Jeb called after her, as she flounced out of the kitchen.

"Like reading my novel. Or maybe just watching what *I* feel like on the TV for once!"

"But, honey, you don't watch daytime TV!"

"Well, maybe it's time I started. Ethel next door's always talkin' about those fancy cooking shows she watches."

"Your cookin's fine jest the way it is," he cajoled.

"Don't mean I shouldn't be allowed to improve myself, if I want to," she retorted. And that was that.

The rascal slept all day, too. When Jeb asked about *that*, Emmie told him their guest had given up his sales job and was takin' a night course, studyin' to be a fleabottomist. Something to do with takin' folks' blood. In a hospital, Jeb assumed.

Then Emmie started coming on all dreamy and absent-minded. Took to wearin' a scarf around her neck. Hans had probably put the notion in her head that scarves were the latest fashion statement, even in the sweltering August heat.

Sometimes the dude left at nighttime, driving out onto the highway in his fancy, black Chrysler. Then Jeb would catch Emmie gazing out the kitchen window over the dark, dusty fields, sighing to herself. It got so that when he came in for his mid-day dinner, there'd be nothing laid on the table yet. He tried to be patient, but a man who's bustin' his butt from dawn to dusk, out in the fields and tending to his beasts, needs his belly filled, guest or not.

Then Emmie started wastin' away. The woman lost at least 30 lbs., just by mid-September, and had no energy at all. Down to about 250, she was still a big girl, but now she was hollow-eyed and white as a sheet—all over. Bedroom slippers didn't even fit her anymore. Took to sleepin' downstairs in the den, she tossed and turned so much, she said. On their lumpy, plaid sofa bed, for cryin' out loud!

Jeb was a pretty sound sleeper, normally, but one night his stomach was bothering him so he went downstairs to their bathroom. When he came out, he thought he'd just peek in on Emmie, he was that worried about her lately. To his astonishment, the den's window was wide open, even though the October temperature was down to the 40's and, as he crept up to the sofa bed, somethin' flew out the window. Looked like a big, black bird or a bat. Closin' the window, Jeb turned to his wife. She lay on her back, still and quiet in a spreading pool of blood, right beneath her neck. He saw the two puncture wounds and knew the truth at last. Holding her, he cried out, "Emeline! My old darlin'. Are you gone? Dear Jesus, don't let her be gone!"

But she was. And Mr. Slick's black Chrysler was gone, too.

Heart-sore and wet-cheeked, Jeb woke his boys up and told them, "Boys, your mama's gone."

"What you mean, 'she's gone,' Daddy? She take off on us?" Dwayne demanded.

"No, son. She's passed and is resting with Jesus now." And they commenced to cryin' and carryin' on.

"What in Sam Hill happened to Mama, Daddy?" Caleb cried.

Jeb broke it to them as best he could. "Sons, you'll probably not believe me, but I'm pretty sure that city man was a vampire."

"A *vampire*?! they chorused, wide-eyed in disbelief.

"Ain't no such thing!" Caleb challenged.

Jeb raised a flat palm. "Jest hear me out. When I went downstairs and walked in to check on her, I found the window wide open, and some ol' bat-like thing flapped out it when I come in."

They shook their heads. Papa was losin' it. Then Jeb led them to the den and showed them the puncture wounds on their mama's throat. They started bawlin' harder, pleadin' with her to wake up and tremblin' at the shock.

"Mighten that be somebody's ol' dog, one that's gone mean or rabid?" Caleb asked.

"Son, what kinda dog you know of that sucks blood?" Jeb replied. "And leaves his dinner otherwise untouched," he muttered. They all knew even a rabid coyote wouldn't have left without at least an arm to tide him over.

"Lordy, Lordy!" Caleb wrung his hands. "What we gonna do, Daddy? And what we gonna tell the neighbors?"

"Whatever we do, we cain't jest leave her here," Dwayne chimed in. "We gotta bury her proper."

"I know, son. But let's jest wait a bit. I'll turn off the heat in here. Temperature's cold enough now she won't spoil. I wanna see if that sumabitch comes back for a re-fill. Maybe he don't know he's drunk her dry. Even so, there's still the three of us left. If he does come back, I'm gonna be ready for him." *And,* he thought, *I'll be ready for her, if she's not forever dead.*

The boys shuddered and clutched their throats, pulling up the collars of their PJs.

"You boys make sure you keep your windows closed and locked, front and back doors, too. Promise me, okay?"

They'd never bothered before out there, among honest farming folk and so far from town, to lock up, even at night.

"Yessir, we will. But, Daddy, if the guy comes back, how you gonna catch him?"

"Don't you worry about that. I'll be waitin' up for him and I got me a plan. Dwayne, fetch me that silver champagne bucket your grandma gave your mama and me as a wedding present." That fool present would finally find a good use.

"All right, if you want me to, Daddy," Dwayne said, his face a picture of bewilderment. And off he trotted to the dining room.

When he came back, Dwayne handed the bucket to Jeb. "What you gonna do with that? We ain't got no champagne. And, anyhow, this don't seem like any time to celebrate."

"Only thing I'm fixin' to celebrate is sendin' that sumabitch straight to Hell. With this here bucket, I'm gonna fabricate me a cure, a way to keep everbody safe."

With those cryptic words, he pulled on his boots and tugged on his barn coat and heavy farm gloves, then marched off with the champagne bucket to the forge in the barn, admonishing his sons to lock up behind him.

Half the night he worked the bellows and melted down the silver bucket, then dipped the tines of his pitchfork he'd sanded smooth and clean into the molten metal. Then he plunged the pitchfork in the horse trough. Bessie and Nellie May were startled by the sizzle and whinnied anxiously. "Don't worry, old girls. I'm jest makin' something to git rid of a pest, a big, bad one."

Then he found an old fence post behind the barn, cut it down shorter and sharpened it to a fine point.

'Round about 3:00 a.m., he finally cooled and closed down the forge, then brought the pitchfork back to the house, making sure first to close and bar the barn doors. Livestock would be easy pickings to bloodsuckers, otherwise.

Figuring the vampire was full for the night and most likely miles away, Jeb went to bed but kept his coat on, just in case, with the pitchfork next to his bed. The fence post he stowed in the den.

After that, it felt like the house itself was mourning: still and sorrowful and a little cold. The leaves of the big old oaks in front withered and turned brown, then dropped their sad cargo on the ground. Even the cows and chickens seemed mopey. It was the worst in the mornings when they'd no longer wake to the good smells of eggs and bacon frying, sometimes pancakes with maple syrup. They missed Emeline's cooking, that was for sure, and her sweet ways too, before she changed. They'd have to learn how to feed themselves from here on out. Jeb predicted a whole lot of TV dinners.

For several anxious days that felt like an eternity, nothing happened, and they were worried they'd soon have to scramble and do something about Mama. She wouldn't keep forever, even in that cold room. And critters would likely set up house inside the closed-off den—squirrels and raccoons and Jeb didn't know what all.

As he waited, Jeb found himself wondering if, once they buried her, Emmie could somehow rise up out of a grave. And come back for them? Surely not. Or did two tons of earth not matter to an undead spirit? He didn't want to take *any* chances.

On the fifth day about midnight, Jeb heard the crunch of tires on the drive, a smooth-running engine shut off, and a car door quietly close. He was ready.

By and by, there came a fluttering at the window of the den where Emmie's body lay. Expecting this, in the dark Jeb had tiptoed into the den and silently eased up the window all the way, keeping his rough, calloused fingers hidden by the heavy side curtain. He'd left a candle burning each night to illuminate the monster's bait. A blue ribbon in her blond hair, Emeline was cleaned up and wearing her laciest nightgown that Jeb had tenderly dressed her in. In the candlelight, you couldn't tell that she wasn't asleep or playing possum, waiting for her gentleman caller.

Black, web-like wings swooped in. The creature landed on the arm of the sofa bed. As Jeb watched, eyes bugging out, from behind the curtain, the thing transformed into Hans, complete with pointy boots and hairline, and an honest-to-God cape. With red satin lining, for Chrissake. *Well,* Jeb amended, *not actually for* His *divine sake. More like that horny bastard roasting sinners in God's Basement.*

Hans bent over Emeline, nuzzling her throat and crooning sweet nothings to her in German, or some such outlandish language. Easing the window closed again, behind the curtain Jeb gripped his pitchfork. Abruptly, Hans stood up, realizing dearest Emmie was stone cold, and not from the arctic air flowing through the open window. Foiled, his red eyes flashed with fury.

"Vas ist dis? Zumeone hass been schlurping from her alzo?"

Jeb lurched forward with his pitchfork, tines facing out. "Hands off my wife, Hans! You killed my Emmie! You jest drained her dry and now you're gonna die!"

Hans raised a black eyebrow and sneered. "A pitchfork? Zeriously? I am used to zees things, you know. Zey haff no effect on me. Und garlic is chust good seasoning. I vill go elsewhere to dine." He swirled his cape and made for the window.

"I don't think so!" Jeb lunged for the vampire, plunging the silver-tipped tines all the way through Hans's arrogant body. There was a screech, a sizzle, and a stinking whisp of smoke. Jeb looked down with a grim smile as the pitchfork toppled at last off the vampire, its silver tines red with smoking blood. Hans lay on the rug, a pool of ash.

"Well, there ya go, ashhole!" Jeb crowed.

At which point Emeline's undead eyes flew open and she shot up out of the bed, "Jeb, what have you done? You killed my Hans!" She tossed the covers aside and made for him. But he had something ready for her, too, if it came to it, and held it out, point toward her breastbone.

His voice quavered. "You better stay back, Emmie!"

Slowly she advanced, ignoring him, a snarl twisting her face. "Jebediah Finch, I put up with you and your boring, hick ways for years, and when I finally find a man who cares for me and treats me like a lady, like someone with a brain, not just a skillet, you go and kill him! I'll get you for that!"

"Ah, honey, he didn't love you. *I* do. He jest wanted supper." Jeb began backing up, reaching for the door. Still, she came on.

"Emeline, I told you to stay back! Look, honey, you didn't understand what you were doin'. And I forgive you and I don't want to do this, but I will, by God, if I have to! I've got our sons to think of."

"Oh, suddenly you're the tough, manly man now, are you?" she sneered and reached her meaty, farm-hardened hand toward his throat.

Jeb shut his eyes and plunged the sharpened stake in her heart. Emeline fell back on the bed gasping. "Well, *damn*! I never reckoned you had it in you, Jeb. Figures. First time you ever serve *me* a stake, ain't no eggs nor potatoes to go with it. And now you've ruined my best nightgown!"

With a hiss she fell back, once again mortal. Once again dead.

Unlike Hans, Emmie didn't turn to ash. Too recently undead, Jeb supposed. But what with the putrid pile of ash Hans had left and Emeline's blood on the carpet, Jeb knew he was gonna have to rent one of them Stanley Steamers from the Safeway.

#

Jeb, Dwayne and Caleb buried Emeline and her bloodsucking lover a couple of days later. They'd needed to build a deeper coffin to accommodate Emmie, the ashes, the stake through her heart, and the pitchfork. No sense leaving evidence lying around.

The service was private—just the family and closed-casket.

The Chrysler Jeb sold to the local, used-car lot. Said it had been dumped on his land a while and he couldn't locate the owner. After the police couldn't find any record of the car's registration, no one questioned it. The money went a ways towards repairing the barn and buying a new combine.

#

So Jeb, now 80, was extracting deathbed promises from his sons. Even though he'd stopped smoking when he was 23, the docs told him it was the cigarettes that got him. Jeb couldn't help wondering, though, if his lungs had been poisoned instead by inhaling the unholy ashes of his wife's lover. Payback from Hell, he reckoned.

Jeb still missed Emmie and hoped once he got to the other side, she'd listen to reason and forgive him. But he wouldn't hold his breath for that.

CRITICAL BLAST PUBLISHING
20¢
APPROVED BY THE READING CODE AUTHORITY
What the EARTH REMEMBERS
Ikechukwu Henry
CRITICAL BLAST PUBLISHING
...THE SPIRIT NEVER FORGETS!

STICK IT TO YOUR ENEMIES! Real Voodoo Doll! Guaranteed Quality checked by the finest Witch Doctors! Send lock of hair and a SASE to DUDAT VOODOO, Box 9, Haiti.

READING IS 20 TO LIFE!

ATTENTION!
DEMONS! VAMPIRES! GHOULS!

LIVE TO SEE WEDNESDAY!

DEFEAT BLACK MYSTIC ARTS KUNG-FU Tired of getting your ass kicked every Tuesday by Black Mystic Arts Kung-Fu fighters? CALL 666-HELP to enroll in self-defense training every Hellspawn should know to survive any dark alley encounter. Become a Ninth Circle Master of Judante!

BOW AND ARROW KIT! When you need to go into battle on Tuesdays and don't know what weapon to take with you.

HUMAN MASK When you need to walk among the humans, without being singled out as a monster. Get this mask in black, white or polka-dot, to blend right in!

THIS IS IT! CLIP THEM & COLLECT THEM ALL!

EXPLODING DRINK Sit back and enjoy the highjinks as people unscrew their drink activating the chemical reaction, causing a foamy mess.

HOBO IN A BOX When your street is getting over-runned by homeless people and you need someone to speak their language and run them off to the next street down the block.

Ikechukwu Henry is an Igbo Nigerian writer whose writings tackle the issues of environmental and climatic crises, family dynamics, queerness and speculative otherworldliness. He was fifth place in Christian Speculative Fiction Prize, Shortlisted for The Oriire Folktale Prize and has stories published in, but not limited to, Brittle Paper, The Kalahari Review, Lampblack Magazine and others. When not writing, he can be found searching for the next magazine to submit to.

The air hung heavy in Nkwerre that day, thick with humidity and the coppery tang of wet earth. A low rumble of a generator in the distance vibrated softly through the floor, mingling with the scent of woodsmoke that drifted in from the neighbor's compound, threading itself into the cluttered silence of Chike's pottery studio. Inside, the only light came from a rectangular window, its dusty panes muting the sun's glow into a jaundiced wash across the cement floor.

Chike sat hunched on a low stool, his knees splayed on either side of the wheel, his bare feet planted on the cool floor. A sweat-drenched cloth clung to his shoulder, forgotten there, while in front of him sat a lump of clay so dull and unyielding it may as well have been stone. He had kneaded it, moistened it, even cursed under his breath at it, but it refused to respond. It just sat there—a silent, mocking mass that resisted the rhythm of his hands, the vision in his head, the need in his chest.

His breath rasped out slow and shallow. He had been in this same position for three hours, longer if he counted the days before. Nothing came. Not a single vessel, not a bowl or a vase or a mask. Nothing worth firing. His fingers itched with the memory of form, the feel of shaping something with curve and life, but it had vanished. Inspiration had withered somewhere between expectation and exhaustion.

He leaned back slowly, stretching his spine until his neck cracked softly, and let his gaze drift to the open window. The view framed the shared compound yard, where two houses faced each other with a patch of coarse grass and red soil between them. His own house, inherited from his father, mirrored the newer bungalow that had remained unoccupied for months. Until last week.

That was when the woman arrived.

He saw her now, for the first time really, sweeping the veranda across the yard. Her body moved slowly, each stroke of the broom measured, silent, as though she were moving inside a world separate from his own. The broom's bristles scraped the concrete gently, barely audible over the whine of a nearby inverter. Her wrapper clung to her hips like it had been wrapped, not by her hands but by the wind. Her shoulders were broad, her arms sinewy with age and something older than age. Her skin was the dark of wet loam and looked smooth even in the failing light. She didn't pause, didn't look up, didn't seem to notice him watching.

Chike squinted, unsure why the sight of her twisted something uneasy in his chest. She didn't seem threatening— just silent. Maybe too silent. Her eyes, though he couldn't quite see them, seemed like the sort of eyes that never blinked. He sat frozen for a minute longer, not thinking, not shaping, just watching her sweep a path that needed no sweeping.

The sun dropped lower. Long shadows stretched from the compound walls like quiet fingers. Chike stood abruptly, wiping his hands on a rag that had already given up trying to stay clean. He muttered something—maybe a prayer, maybe a curse—and turned his back on the window.

That night, he didn't eat. He couldn't. The weight in his chest hadn't shifted. His fingers ached not from work but from the absence of it. Sleep came in fits, shallow and gray.

When he awoke the next morning, it was with no plan or hope. Only habit. He pushed open the door of the studio while rubbing sleep from his eyes and froze.

The light streaming through the high window was golden and soft, the kind of morning light that usually made everything look harmless. But something was different. He felt it immediately—not in the air, not in the smell, but in his body. In his bones. The clay on the wheel was not the same lump from yesterday.

It looked identical. But when his fingers brushed it, the feeling jolted him. It was warm. Not from the sun, but something deeper. It was supple, pliant. It responded to his touch—not just yielding, but guiding. Like the clay itself wanted to become something.

He didn't think. He sat, wet his hands, and let them press into the mass. It rose easily under his palms, a tall cylinder that leaned and curved, shaped itself as though listening to the spaces between his thoughts. Every twist of his wrist, every pinch, every lift brought a whisper of form he had never envisioned but instantly recognized. It was no longer Chike shaping the clay. He was merely translating what was already there.

By noon, seven pots stood along the drying bench. By three, there were twelve. Each one unique. Each one startling. Some curved with the gentle grace of calabashes, others jagged and sharp-edged like the old war masks kept in shrines. He ran his hands over their surfaces, feeling lines he didn't remember carving, patterns that shimmered faintly in the afternoon light. Spirals and weaves that seemed etched in motion.

His heart beat like he'd been running. Sweat soaked his shirt, but he didn't feel tired. He felt awake in a way he hadn't in years. This was what he had been missing. This was the breath that had abandoned him. Recognition. Legacy. Art.

Evening came. The generator kicked on again, rattling somewhere two houses down. He moved through the studio like a man anointed, arranging the pots, cleaning his tools, touching each creation once more.

And then he heard it.

A sound so quiet it could have been imagined. A wet, rhythmic thump. It came and went, like the gentle tap of water dripping onto fabric. He paused, rag in hand, brow furrowed. He looked toward the studio door. Nothing. He looked at the window. No rain. He stepped closer to the drying bench.

There.

The largest pot, one with a jagged ridge twisting around its neck like a thorned vine, pulsed faintly. The spiral on its side shifted, just slightly, as if settling into place.

Chike stared. The air was suddenly still. The clay's surface glistened, not with moisture, but with something slicker, like skin caught under sweat. He pressed a hand to the pot. It was warm. A soft sound rose—too low to be language, but too deliberate to be wind.

He pulled back.

No more sound came. The pot stood quiet. Still. Beautiful. Harmless.

He turned away. Walked slowly back to the stool and sat down. His limbs felt heavy now, like the adrenaline was draining and leaving something hollow behind.

Across the yard, the light on Ijeoma's porch flickered to life. She sat motionless in her plastic chair, her face cast in orange shadow. She didn't move. But Chike had the unshakable sense that she was looking directly into his window.

He didn't sleep well that night either. But the clay would be waiting in the morning. And something deep inside him wanted to touch it again.

#

The sun hung overhead like a suspended blade, its heat slicing down through the moist air, thickening the atmosphere until breath itself felt like an effort. Nkwerre groaned beneath it. The hum of generators pulsed through the neighborhood like an arrhythmic heart, broken only by the occasional bark of a restless dog or the hollow clang of a distant metal basin. In the shared compound yard, the earth had begun to crack in places, not from drought but from something older, something that churned beneath the soil with slow, silent insistence.

Chike hadn't left the studio in nearly forty-eight hours. The kitchen in his house remained untouched, the pot of yam he had boiled on the first morning still sitting by the sink, its contents gray and stiff with abandonment. The only nourishment he seemed to take now came from the clay itself—and from the attention his creations were drawing.

The first pictures had gone online the day after he shaped them. He had taken them without thinking, not bothering to clean the studio or arrange the lighting. He snapped the shots quickly, his hands still stained with red earth, then uploaded them to his artist's page with the caption: "New works. For Owerri showing." Within hours, the messages began. First comments, then private inquiries, then bulk orders. One collector from Abuja offered to buy four of the pieces outright, without haggling. A gallery in Enugu requested a solo exhibition. A former client who had stopped commissioning him two years ago begged for a new piece.

Chike had never received this kind of attention, not even during the height of his father's acclaim. It should have thrilled him. It did. At first.

Now, as he crouched in the center of his studio, sweat pouring from his face and shoulders, his arms trembling from the effort of shaping his thirteenth pot in two days, the thrill had curdled. The euphoria had bloated into something rancid. His eyes burned. His breath came in short, sharp pulls. He hadn't eaten. He hadn't slept. He couldn't stop.

Every time he paused, the studio became unbearable. The silence was no longer empty; it pressed into him like a presence. The pots—twenty-three of them now—lined the studio's edges. Each one stared at him with carved expressions that hadn't been intentional, with contours that seemed to shift when he wasn't looking directly. Some curled into themselves like they were sleeping. Others leaned outward, as if reaching. They weren't alive, not in any human sense, but they didn't feel still either.

And worse, when he left them too long, they began to fade.

He had noticed it first that morning. The spirals on the first pot he'd made, the one that had seemed to shimmer in the light, had dulled. The glaze hadn't cracked, but the color receded. The edges lost definition. The shape sagged ever so slightly, as if it had grown tired of holding itself upright. He had panicked and immediately turned back to the wheel. Within minutes of his hands working fresh clay, the pot brightened again.

That had terrified him. He had tried not to admit it aloud, even to himself. But the clay wanted him. Needed him.

His shirt was soaked through, plastered to his back. His fingers had begun to split at the joints, little cracks blooming near his knuckles, sore and weeping. But he kept going. The wheel spun. His feet pressed the pedal harder.

When he finally stopped, it wasn't out of exhaustion; it was because his hands seized. He tried to close them and couldn't. They had locked into half-curled claws. He cursed under his breath and staggered up from the stool. The whole studio seemed to pitch slightly as he stood. He had to grip the wall to steady himself.

Clay still clung to his wrists like it didn't want to let go. He scraped some off on the edge of the workbench and stumbled outside into the glare of the midday sun.

The backyard was quiet. The red earth shimmered under the heat. He moved toward the clay pit, the shallow hole his father had dug years ago. It had always produced the best red clay in the compound—sticky, rich, perfect for throwing. But lately, the texture had changed. Even the color.

He crouched at the edge of the pit, looked down. The surface of the mud seemed undisturbed. He lowered his hand toward it and paused. Something stirred beneath. Not visibly. But in his fingers. In his chest. A warning. Or a greeting.

He pressed his palm into the soil. It should have resisted slightly, should have taken effort to dig into. Instead, his hand sank with unnatural ease, up to the wrist, as if the earth had parted for him. But it wasn't loose mud. It was… clutching. The pressure around his hand wasn't passive. It felt like it was pulling.

Chike yanked his hand back, stumbling as he did. The clay clung to his arm in thick strands, reluctant to release. He stared at the pit, heart hammering. Then, as if pulled by instinct, his eyes drifted to the other side of the yard.

She was there.

Ijeoma sat on her porch, her back straight, her legs crossed neatly beneath her wrapper. Her broom lay beside her, untouched. Her eyes were on him, calm and unreadable. Her face didn't move, didn't twitch. She simply watched.

He tried to look away. Failed.

There was something about her presence—quiet but impossible to ignore. She hadn't spoken since she arrived. He had heard no sound from her compound except the occasional creak of her door, the sweep of her broom, the sound of a chair shifting. He didn't even know how he knew her name. It had never been spoken between them. But it echoed in his head now, sharp and clear.

Ijeoma.

He didn't wave. Didn't speak. He turned back into the studio, the air inside somehow thicker now, as though the pots had breathed it in while he was gone.

He paused near the large vase—the one with the thick neck and the unnatural lip near the base. It had begun to change. A long hairline crack had appeared, forming a slight opening near its bottom edge. At first glance, it could be dismissed as an accident. Firing flaw. But Chike crouched. Looked closer.

The crack curved. Just a little. The lip of it pulled inward. Its interior was darker than it should have been, like looking into a throat.

He leaned closer, hand outstretched, but stopped before touching it. A sound came from inside. Barely audible. A dry, shuffling whisper. Like leaves blown across dry tile.

Then it came again, clearer.

"Chike."

He jerked back. The voice had been faint, impossibly so, but familiar. It didn't sound malevolent. It sounded curious. Inviting.

He stared at the pot. The surface shimmered slightly in the afternoon light, the patterns moving, not like paint or glaze, but like skin under breath.

He backed away slowly, step by step, until his back hit the studio wall. He didn't run. He didn't speak. He just stood there, breathing in shallow gasps, watching as the room around him shifted from a studio into something else. A sanctuary. A trap. A womb.

Outside, the generator coughed. A bird took flight from a rooftop and vanished into the white-hot sky. And somewhere beneath his feet, the earth exhaled.

The sky that evening sat swollen and heavy over Nkwerre, pressed low enough to feel like it was breathing on the rooftops. Dark clouds rolled across the sky in silence, gathering not in haste but with a slow, methodical promise. The first warning came as a stillness—no wind, no bird calls, not even the distant throb of a generator. It was the kind of silence that existed before rupture. It wrapped the town in anticipation, in waiting, like something vast and invisible crouched above, watching.

In Chike's compound, the only light came from his studio window. A lantern burned low on the floor near his wheel, casting long shadows that crawled up the walls and across the ceiling like ink poured in water. The generator had died hours ago. The electricity hadn't returned. He didn't notice anymore. Not fully.

Inside, the air was thick with clay dust and something else—something denser than humidity, something heavy that filled his lungs each time he breathed. His shirt clung to his chest, damp with sweat, the collar gaping. His hands trembled even when they rested on his lap. The skin on his palms had darkened, not just from clay, but from hours of soaking in it. The grooves of his fingerprints had deepened, the flesh along his knuckles swollen and cracked. But he no longer felt pain. Only a pulsing throb in his wrists, like the studio itself had begun syncing to his heartbeat.

The pots were no longer just objects in the room. They were presences. They sat along the walls, motionless but alert, their surfaces rippling ever so slightly when the lantern flickered. The larger ones now leaned forward by imperceptible degrees. One had shifted position during the night. He had seen it move—not dramatically, not obviously, but he remembered placing it near the door. Now it sat to the left of the window. A relocation that had happened without sound or cause.

And they whispered. Not all at once. Not constantly. But in turns, like a conversation that waited for him to turn his head before continuing. Each whisper was soft, delicate, never urgent. They didn't demand. They suggested.

Keep going.

Don't stop now.

You're close.

They spoke in the voices of encouragement, but each syllable curled beneath his skin and stayed there, like wet ash.

The newest pot, still wet, stood in the center of the room. Unlike the others, this one bore no pattern, no decorative swirls or embellishments. Its surface was smooth, still, blank like untouched skin. But it breathed. He could see it rise and fall, ever so slightly, as if something just under the surface was sleeping lightly. Its mouth—a wide, open rim—faced the ceiling like a flower seeking the storm. Chike watched it. He hadn't touched it in hours. Yet it remained damp. As if it didn't want to dry.

He rose from his stool slowly, his body moving like an old machine unsure of its parts. His shoulders felt too large. His arms too long. The room tilted, not from dizziness, but from something deeper, a sense that he was no longer fully grounded to the space. He crossed the floor, avoiding the edges of the room where the other pots sat like watching figures. He walked to the bench, reached beneath it, and pulled out the small, iron hammer he used to chip dried glaze.

It was cold in his hand, and heavier than he remembered. The weight reassured him. Made things feel real again. Not sacred. Not cursed. Just breakable.

He turned and faced the first pot he had made after Ijeoma's arrival. The one with the spiral ridges, the first to whisper. It stood tall, its contours perfect. Too perfect. He stepped closer, hammer raised. His breath came fast. His fingers tightened on the handle.

Then, the pot moved.

Not violently. Not even clearly. But it shifted. The spiral along its side unwound a little, just enough to reveal something beneath—an eye. Not a literal one, not with iris or pupil, but a concave dimple that gazed. That acknowledged.

"Chike," it whispered again.

And he froze. Because this time, it wasn't a suggestion. It was a promise.

The pot shimmered. Not from light, but from within. Its surface became slick, wet. And in the swirl of its glaze, images bloomed—his face on magazine covers, gallery openings in Lagos, international showcases. He saw a studio bigger than his father's ever was, apprentices hanging on his every word, his name spoken with reverence. He saw the citywide billboard: *CHIKE MADUKA — VESSELS OF LIFE.*

His grip on the hammer loosened.

The pot leaned forward slightly. Its mouth widened just a little.

You were nothing before us.

We made you.

Let us make you more.

He took a step back, suddenly aware of how dry his throat was, how shallow his breath had become. The promises shimmered again—fame, mastery, legacy. His father, stern and proud, placing a hand on his shoulder. His mother, alive again, smiling, holding one of his pots with joy in her eyes.

He raised the hammer again.

Lightning split the sky outside. The sudden burst lit the compound with a blinding flash. The thunder followed, loud enough to shake the window panes. The lantern flickered violently, then died.

And in the doorway, framed by the pulsing light from the storm, stood Ijeoma.

She wasn't the same woman he had seen before. She was taller now—not just in height, but in presence. Her frame seemed to hold the air around her. Her wrapper trailed behind her like living roots. Her eyes were deep, not dark. Deep. Like looking into the bottom of a well carved before memory. She stepped into the room, bare feet soundless on the concrete.

The whispering stopped. The pots began to tremble. Not aggressively. Not like they wanted to attack. They shuddered like frightened things. Chike watched as the spirals on their bodies began to twist in reverse, pulling in on themselves. The breathing slowed. The warmth began to leave the room.

Ijeoma raised her hand. Not toward him. Toward them. And they responded. The pot nearest to her cracked. A thin fissure formed down its side. A groan sounded from within it—not pain, but protest. It began to split further, and a thin trickle of mud seeped from the break, pooling at its base. The spiral patterns froze mid-turn.

She moved slowly from one vessel to another. At each one, she placed a single hand. No chant. No gesture of force. Just presence. And at each touch, the life drained away. Not violently. Not cruelly. But with finality.

Chike stood frozen, hammer in hand, his breath silent. The pots didn't look at him now. They watched her.

The room filled with the scent of earth. Not wet clay. Not kiln-burned ash. But deep earth, the kind turned by ancient rivers, the scent of forests buried beneath cities. It was the scent of something returning home.

When she reached the large pot—the blank one, the final one—she paused. Her hand hovered above it. For a moment, Chike thought she wouldn't touch it. That she would leave it to him.

But then, she did.

Her palm met its surface. It pulsed once beneath her touch. A breath. A death rattle. Then it crumbled. Not shattered. Crumbled. Into dust. Thick, red, wet. Like meat returned to soil.

She turned to him.

Her face wasn't angry. Nor cold. It was tired. Ancient sadness pooled in her gaze. Her lips didn't move. But he felt the apology. Not for what she had done. But for what he had almost become.

She stepped past him without a word, without a sound, and walked into the storm.

Rain came hard and sudden, drumming against the roof like a thousand fists. The wind howled into the compound, lifting dust and dead leaves. Her figure vanished into it, swallowed by water and night.

Chike stood alone in the studio. The hammer still heavy in his hand. Around him, the pots were just pots again. Beautiful. Empty. Lifeless. Cold.

The silence returned, real this time. The kind of silence that comes after something sacred has left. The rain fell like it was trying to erase the world.

Water crashed onto the compound's corrugated rooftops in deafening sheets, pouring over the edges in thick streams that pooled quickly along the red earth. The compound itself had become a basin, the walkway between the houses swallowed beneath a shallow flood, its muddy current gliding over stones, leaves, and clay runoff. Thunder rolled in long, low bursts that sounded too heavy to be sky-born, and lightning split the darkness in jagged intervals, revealing the soaked, blurred outlines of trees and walls for a heartbeat before plunging everything back into shadow.

Inside the studio, Chike stood motionless.

His ears rang with silence, not the absence of sound, but the deep silence that followed rupture. The lantern at his feet was long dead. A streak of rain slithered down the inside of the windowpane. Every corner of the room was drenched in shadow, but he could still see them. The pots. Dozens of them. Their forms remained, but their spirits had fled.

The studio no longer breathed.

The hammer, still gripped in his hand, had grown heavier with each second that passed. It was not just a tool now. It was a weight. A symbol. A reminder of how close he had come to giving himself completely to something he didn't understand. And even worse—something he had nearly welcomed.

He took a slow step forward.

The floor scraped faintly under his bare feet, the concrete damp with humidity and something else. He passed the shattered remnants of the final pot—the one Ijeoma had touched last. Its dust had melted in the storm air, forming a dark smear on the ground. It looked like blood but smelled like soil, clean and final.

He lowered the hammer to the floor beside it and knelt. His hand hovered over the dust, fingers twitching involuntarily, unsure whether to touch or recoil. It no longer pulsed. It no longer whispered. The thing inside it, whatever it was, was gone. Not banished—reclaimed.

The air had changed.

It was lighter now. Not in temperature or pressure, but in presence. The claustrophobic sense of being watched, measured, needed—it had disappeared with Ijeoma. The studio was his again. Or at least, it had returned to something closer to itself. A place of making. Not of feeding.

He rose unsteadily and crossed to the drying bench. He picked up one of the older pieces—the second or third pot he had shaped after the inspiration returned. It felt wrong in his hands now. Not because it was haunted. Because it was empty. Beautiful, but no longer alive. The ridges were still elegant, the surface still smooth, but the thing that had made it unforgettable—the movement, the breathing silence—was gone.

He turned it in his hands slowly. Then set it down.

Another followed. And another. Each one he touched felt cold. Weightless in the wrong way. They were his, now. Entirely his. And it terrified him how much less they felt because of that.

He moved like a man performing a ritual, touching each vessel, one by one. Some had dried completely. Others, still moist, had begun to harden. He should have felt relief. He should have celebrated. But all he could feel was the quiet ache of something important that had just slipped through his fingers.

He had his art back. His hands were his again. His studio was silent. And the clay was once again just clay.

But what had it cost?

Outside, the rain slowed a bit to a steady rhythm. A cool breeze drifted in through the open window. The wind no longer carried dread. No longer whispered. It was just wind. Chike walked slowly to the door and pushed it open.

The compound was soaked. Water pooled around the roots of the pawpaw trees near the fence. The clay pit at the far edge was nearly overflowing, its sides collapsing slightly under the weight of the storm. And across the yard, Ijeoma's house stood dark. Quiet. The front door was shut. Her chair was gone.

He took a step out, bare feet sinking slightly into the wet earth, and stared at her porch.

She had returned to her house after the studio. But somehow, he knew she wasn't inside anymore. Something older than logic told him that she had passed through the threshold once more—through whatever veil had thinned when she arrived. Her presence had been temporary. A ripple. A mercy. Or a warning.

He whispered her name once. "Ijeoma." Just to hear it aloud. It disappeared into the night without an echo.

And then, like a man returning to a life he had forgotten was his, he turned back toward the studio.

He spent the rest of the night cleaning.

He washed the tools, scrubbing dried glaze and clay from their handles. He stacked the now-ordinary pots gently in the corner, careful not to break them. He swept the floor, pushing the remains of the crumbled vessel into a small pile and wrapping it in an old cloth. He didn't throw it out. He placed it in a sealed bucket, covered it, and slid it beneath the bench. Not because he feared it. But because something in him couldn't bring himself to discard it.

At dawn, the rain stopped.

The studio smelled of clean air and wet soil. Outside, the sky brightened slowly, not with the brilliance of triumph, but with the soft, gray light of aftermath.

Chike stood in the center of the room, his palms open, his breathing even. He looked at the wheel. Then at the clay slab in the corner. It sat untouched, mute. No warmth. No pulse.

He walked over, tore a piece off, and placed it on the wheel.

He began to work. Slowly. Clumsily. The clay resisted. His muscles remembered the old rhythm, but the ease was gone. Every turn took effort. Every curve faltered. He frowned. Pressed harder. Tried again.

The pot that emerged was imperfect. Asymmetrical. A little slouched at the rim. The surface plain.

But it was his.

He sat back. Looked at it. Then at his hands.

They were shaking.

He raised them slowly, watching the light catch the calluses, the cracks, the grooves where the clay had lived. They looked too thin now. Too human. But they were his. No longer guided by something else. No longer possessed.

He wasn't sure if that was victory or punishment.

The door creaked open behind him with the morning breeze. Light spilled across the floor. The pots remained still in their corner. Nothing moved. Nothing whispered.

He rose and walked to one of the shelves. He placed the imperfect pot beside the others.

It didn't breathe. It didn't shimmer. But it was real.

He stood there a long time, in the silence of a space returned, in the presence of his craft once again humbled, once again mortal.

Chike stayed in the studio.

He didn't reach for the clay right away. He didn't check his messages. He didn't respond to the growing buzz of orders that still pinged through his silent phone.

He simply stood there. Free. Alone. Whole. Chike stepped back from the shelf, looked at his hands one last time, and waited to feel them turn to clay. But nothing happened.

Only the silence remained. And for the first time in days, he allowed himself to wonder whether being whole was worth what he had lost.

The storm had passed, but it had left the world hollow.

Rain still dripped steadily from the roof's overhang, tracing silent lines along the walls of the studio where the thunder had once echoed like war drums. The smell of wet earth was no longer suffocating—it was clean now, rich and oddly cold. In the dim light filtering in through the open door, the air no longer carried the breath of other things. There was no presence anymore. The studio had been exorcised.

Chike stood in the center of it all, surrounded by the remains of his miracle.

The hammer he had clutched so tightly was still on the floor, forgotten. The pots around him were still upright, still intact, but without the shimmer, the swell, the living silence they once held. They were clay again. Only clay. Beautiful in form, yes, but ordinary in soul. They no longer pulsed or whispered or shifted when he turned his back. They no longer fed on his breath.

But neither did they need him anymore.

He moved slowly, his feet sticking slightly to the damp floor as he walked to the shelf near the window. The space beneath the bench still held the cloth bundle—the crumbled remains of the last pot. He bent down, reached with tentative fingers, and drew it toward him.

As the cloth fell away, he expected nothing. But inside the bundle, beneath the broken clay and sticky red dust, something small and dark nestled in the folds like a seed buried in fertile ground. He picked it up carefully and turned it over in his hand.

It was a carved token, no larger than his thumb. Smooth, cold iron. Its shape was subtle, worn by time, but unmistakable. A woman's figure—arms to the side, hips wide, feet buried in a circular base. No eyes. No mouth. Just a face smoothed to abstraction. But around her neck, an etching remained sharp: concentric spirals—not unlike the ones that had marked his pots. She was not beautiful. She was not delicate. She was ancient. Earth-bound. Watching.

He stared at it for a long time, unmoving.

Then a memory rose from nowhere.

He was seven, kneeling in his grandmother's garden while she weeded barefoot in the soil. She had told him not to touch a clay lid resting on top of a jar by the yam barn. When he asked why, she said it wasn't for food. It was for keeping Ala out of the house.

"The earth swallows what belongs to it," she had said, not looking up. "And sometimes, it lets something slip through. Just to remind you whose mouth you're living on."

Back then, he had laughed. He had thought it was nonsense. His mother had scolded him that evening for mocking sacred things.

He stared at the iron figurine again. His chest felt hollow in a different way now. Not out of fear—but recognition.

She hadn't come to him. She had come for the clay.

Not to curse him. Not to teach him. Simply to exist near him. That was enough. A god's silence was still thunder.

He placed the figurine on the table next to the first pot he had made. It looked wrong beside it, too real, too old. The pot had been beautiful when it pulsed. Now it looked like a replica of itself.

He touched it lightly. It was cool, matte. The pattern had lost its depth. The ridges were ridges now—not breathing lines but just decoration. He pressed harder, half-hoping it would react.

It didn't.

And in that moment, he realized he had been left with the gift of forgetting. Ijeọma hadn't tried to teach him a lesson. She hadn't punished him. She had simply walked back into the rain and taken with her the terrible blessing she had never meant to give.

He finished cleaning in silence.

He scrubbed the glaze buckets, rinsed the brushes, and swept the fine dust into a tray. As he lifted the rag from the last pile near the door, something underneath caught his eye—a scrap of cloth, folded tight and damp. Not his. He crouched, peeled it back, and found a note wrapped in palm leaf fiber. The paper was too clean, too perfect to have come from anywhere local.

The note read only a name:

"Ijeọma"

And below it, a single symbol etched in charcoal: a circle, half-buried in a square. The same symbol his grandmother used to mark the shrine wall on New Yam Festival mornings.

He stood up, feeling the room tilt slightly again—not from exhaustion this time, but clarity. A kind of spiritual vertigo.

He needed to see someone. Someone older.

Although it was still dawn, he left the compound and walked barefoot through the now-silent town. The streets were still wet, the red earth bleeding through the cracks in the tarmac. He passed the Anglican church, the empty stalls at Nkwerre Market, and turned into the old quarter where the houses were smaller and the silence was thicker. At the far end of a moss-covered wall, he knocked on a narrow iron gate.

Mama Agụnwa answered after the third knock.

She was his father's cousin. Nearly blind. A woman of few words and long silences. She had been the last to wash his grandmother's body before burial, the last to speak aloud to the family spirits.

She let him in without question.

He sat on the mat across from her, iron figurine in hand, and began to speak. He told her about the neighbor. About the pots. About the whispers. About the silence. He didn't hide anything. Not even his shame.

She didn't interrupt. Her clouded eyes fixed on his hands the whole time.

When he finished, she leaned forward, took the figurine, turned it once in her knotted fingers, and nodded once.

"Ala," she said. Her voice was like branches pressing against tin. "You hosted her. You worked on her soil. The earth moved to remind you who it belongs to."

Chike stared at her. "Why would she choose me?"

She raised her eyes slowly. "She doesn't choose. She returns. Where her name is no longer spoken, she walks. And where hands shape the clay without thanks, she waits."

Silence followed. Heavy. Sacred.

Chike lowered his head. "I destroyed what she gave."

"No," she said. "You survived it."

He sat in the silence for a long time. When he finally rose to leave, she handed the figurine back to him.

"Keep it near the pit," she said. "Not for worship. For memory."

He returned to the compound at midmorning. The studio was dry now. Bright. The pots were lined up neatly, cold but still malleable to the touch, perfect in a hollow way. He took the smallest one—a simple bowl—and placed it on the wheel. He tore off a chunk of untouched clay, wet it, pressed it down.

It resisted. It always had. That was how he knew it was real.

He began to turn the wheel slowly, his fingers shaping the curve. There were no whispers this time. No visions. No rhythm but his own. His hands were clumsy again. The bowl collapsed slightly under his left thumb.

He smiled. He placed the figurine on the sill above the wheel, just beside the window. It faced outward. Toward the earth. Toward her house.

She would not return.

He knew that now. And yet he kept his hands moving. Chike pressed the clay again, steady now. And though the pot took no breath, and the walls did not speak, he shaped it anyway—aware, humbled, and watched.

He had his art back. And for the first time, he knew what it cost to lose it.

He was alone. But he was no longer ignorant. The earth had spoken once. That was enough.

CRITICAL BLAST PUBLISHING
20¢
APPROVED BY THE READING CODE
Pick His Bones Clean
Sirius
TERROR FROM THE DEEP!

STICK IT TO YOUR ENEMIES! Real Voodoo Doll! Guaranteed Quality checked by the finest Witch Doctors! Send lock of hair and a SASE to DUDAT VOODOO, Box 9, Haiti.

SNAKES IN A MAIL BOX Get these total mother-f$%Ken poisonous snakes and mail them with your get well gift cards.

LEARN TO PLAY THE GUITAR! When you can't get a date for the weekend, rent a sexy Guitar Teacher to impress your friends and maybe you just might learn something too.

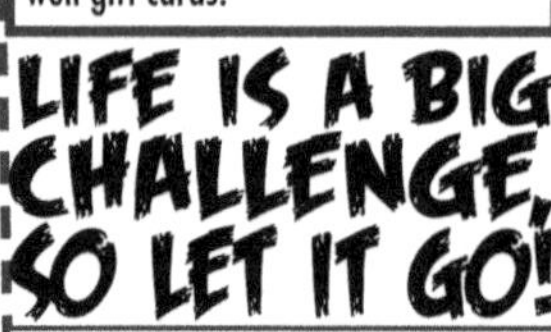

FISH BOWL FULL OF WORMS Are you tired of eating meat? Get yourself a bowl full of yummy worms and feel you are saving the planet.

WELCOME MAT TRAP When you don't want people annoying you, a simple press of the button and the trap door will dispose of anyone who stands on it, while waiting for you to answer the door.

1to1 MODEL PIRATE SHIP! Some assembly required. Glue NOT included. Recommend a private Island cove as the staging areo.

RENT AN ANGRY WOLF! When you need to rip apart your competition, or when you need to look like a decent human concerned for dogs or something, something.

HEAD KNIVES 100% stainless steal daggers that launch from the top of your head and kill any conversation you find boring.

BECOME A PIRATE IN ONE WEEK! Learn to talk and kill like a Pirate. Optional hand and leg amputation. Pirate Ship sold separately. Arrrrrr.

Sirius is the author of Howling Devil in the Sticks, which was selected for Critical Blast Publishing's The Monsters Next Door anthology.

A hurricane tearing through Pickbait, Florida, snapped a magnolia tree in half and dropped it right onto Ford's trailer. It sheared off a whole corner of the roof and sent several shingles flying. He went looking for them the next morning, but he was only able to find one wedged into the muddy bank of the marsh. The rest were lost to the four winds, which he was sure would go over well with the insurance company.

The entirety of Crowned Magnolia Park was in shambles. Some had it worse than others, and Ford's situation couldn't quite be counted amongst the worst. His home was still *there*, after all, which was more than he could say for a neighbor down the street whose trailer had slid back a whole seven inches. The one next to him, thank God, was just fine. Only a few magnolia leaves from Ford's tree had landed in that neighbor's yard, and so his relief was tinged with just a hint of bitterness.

"Did you hear there's another one coming up the coast?" The neighbor's screen door slammed shut following the sound of his voice. Ford looked up from the yellow pages of the phonebook clenched in his hands. A whole column of tree removal services, and not one of them with hours listed for a Sunday.

"Another hurricane?" Ford glanced over at the crumpled tree branches smashed against the side of his house. "Christ."

"I'll say," his neighbor's voice was creeping closer. When Ford turned his head again, he nearly knocked his nose against the taller man's chest.

"S-Sorry," Ford stammered, reeling back to try and avoid stepping on his neighbor's feet. They had never *really* spoken. For the past five years, Ford left for work at 8 a.m. and didn't get home until 6 or 7 o'clock, depending on whether he stopped to grab dinner. On weekends, he liked to go deep sea fishing, or camping, or really anything that involved getting out of the house. His neighbor was seldom out—and on the rare occasion he could be spotted, it was usually pitch-black outside, and he was usually standing on the bank digging his toes into the mud.

Ford had to admire him, though. Because clearly, that man wasn't afraid of *anything*. Not gators, not snakes, not hollering rednecks in expensive speedboats.

"When's it supposed to hit?" Ford asked, trying to keep the conversation going. His neighbor was too tall to be handsome, because in Ford's mind, you could either be six feet tall *or* a looker, but it wasn't fair to be both. However, that didn't mean he wasn't plenty distracting, with his sleek tied-back black hair and his silvery eyes like dimes.

"Sometime tonight or early tomorrow morning," the neighbor said. His pale eyes slid up and down the side of Ford's house, surveying the damage. "Do you have somewhere to go?"

"No," Ford said. "My parents moved to Nevada last year and my grandparents are all dead."

"Rough deal," the neighbor rubbed his chin. "Well, I'm by myself. You can sleep on my couch, if you want to. I don't know if you'll want to risk weathering another storm with a hole in your roof the size of a Ferris wheel."

"It's not *that* bad," Ford glanced over his shoulder once again. He could tape down a tarp over hole, sure, and clear as much of the tree away on his own as possible before the next storm hit. But who knew how much good that would do? The worst of the damage just happened to be over his bedroom. He'd be sleeping on a couch either way.

"Up to you," his neighbor shrugged. "But I have some

smoked trout I don't mind sharing, either."

"Well, if that's the case," Ford finally gave in and smiled. "Just let me grab a few things. I'll be right over."

#

Ford didn't bother gathering up too much, just his toothbrush and a change of clothes. Anything else was only a few feet away if he *really* needed it before the storm hit. And he hoped to be well asleep by the time the next hurricane started blowing its way through.

The wind was already starting to pick up by the time he walked over to the neighbor's house. Strands of his short blond curls whipped around and stung the sides of his face. When he opened the screen door, the wind nearly took it out of his hand. He had to grip the aluminum handle to drag it shut and then hold it for a second to make sure that it was really closed.

"I wasn't trying to rip off your door, I swear," he said. From somewhere in the house, his neighbor laughed.

"I believe you," his neighbor said. Ford dropped his bag onto the tweed couch and then shoved his hands into his pockets. He crept sheepishly towards the kitchen, drawn to its yellow light like a moth.

"I know this is awkward," Ford said. "But I don't think I've ever actually introduced myself properly. My name is Ford Richardson."

"I'm Beck," his neighbor replied. "Beck Fisher." He was standing by the stove, and when he saw Ford, he raised his spatula and gestured at the table. "Have a seat. Dinner is almost ready."

"Are you sure I can't help you with anything?" Even as he asked, Ford obediently pulled out an aluminum-framed chair and took his seat.

"Not a thing," Beck flipped the spatula mid-air and then caught it. "I've been going all day. I love this weather."

Ford raised an eyebrow but didn't question it. Outside, the wind howled against the sides of the trailer, strong enough to make the windows rattle. "It's the only downside of living so close to the beach, for me," he said, trying to keep up conversation. "I prefer a nice clear, sunny day, myself. Better for fishing."

"Oh, no," Beck's smile widened. From Ford's angle it looked unnatural, like the corners were curling up towards his ears. "That's where you're wrong. The best fishing is done in a storm. Have you ever been out a boat when it's raining?"

"No," Ford admitted. "I think I'd choose life, any day."

Beck laughed, although the sound was more a gurgle, like he had a throat full of water. "I'll take you out, one day," he said. "There's nothing like it."

Ford sucked on his teeth and tried not to appear as uncomfortable as he was starting to feel. He shifted in his seat and looked across the table at the dishes and salad bowl that were already set out. "What did you say you were making?" He tried to change the subject. "Smoked trout?"

"Just warming it up," Beck said. "I already smoked it the other day, and I've been saving it." He turned around with cast-iron pan in hand and set it down on top of a quilted potholder. "The only thing I expect to see on your plate at the end of the night is a pile of bones."

Ford tried to take a deep breath, but he couldn't *quite* get one all the way down. It got stuck in his chest and made him feel a little lightheaded. Beck's silver gaze was penetrating, and the longer he was stuck in its path, the more nothing seemed to matter. Ford's fingers started to tingle, but he didn't notice they were numb until he dropped his fork.

He bent over in his chair to pick the utensil up off the floor, and when he sat up again, Beck was on the other side of the table, and their eye contact was broken. Ford could breathe again, but now all he wanted to do was leave.

The battering wind and the sudden onslaught of rain, like a thousand hand-sized rocks being hurled at the roof, told him that legging-it was not really a possibility.

If that was the case, he might as well eat.

The prongs of his fork bit into the smoked fish without any resistance. His mouth had already started watering just from the smell, but he didn't realize how *hungry* he was until he took his first bite. He hated to admit it, but the fish was damn good. It melted on his tongue and tickled every tastebud with that rich woodsmoke flavor.

Beck placed his fingertips together and smiled at Ford from across the table. He hadn't touched the fish himself; he seemed to be too enraptured in enjoying his guest.

He was weird, for sure, but *weird* wasn't really a crime. Ford took another bite and then popped the tab on a cold Cola from the fridge.

"I don't know what to say, Beck," Ford finally told him. "You know your way around a catch."

"I like to think so," Beck set his hand on his chest humbly and flashed his teeth in a grin. "Thank you, kindly."

#

A nasty clap of thunder pulled Ford out of a dead sleep. He groaned and rested his hand against the back of his neck, using his other hand to grab his chin so he could pop out the kink that had formed on Beck's couch. It wasn't the worst thing he had ever slept on, but it could have stood a few improvements. He tried to look around, but the living room was pitch-black even though he'd left a lamp on. Given that, he could only assume that the power was out.

Ford waited for the span of a heartbeat for the next bolt of lightning that he knew would surely follow, but it didn't come. There was another boom, and he realized it wasn't thunder at all—but the screen door slamming in the wind. The rain was coming down so hard that it slanted sideways and streamed through the mesh, hurling itself with enough velocity that it misted him in the face.

"Beck?" he called out. Ford tossed his blanket to the side and jumped to his feet, still only half-awake. "Beck! I think your power's out!"

There was no answer. Ford moved towards the door, stepping carefully and keeping his arms out in front of him in case he slipped in a puddle. When he finally reached the screen, he grabbed hold of its handle and slammed it closed. He flicked the little latch on the side with his thumb, but it was broken. He sighed and dragged his hand down his face. All he could think was *of course.*

A flash of light caught his eye and drew his attention back towards the yard. It was gone in an instant, and for a moment all he could see were the vague shapes of leaf litter and neighborhood junk being thrown around the yard.

Then the light flashed again. This time, he saw it clearly by the low pier that jutted out over the marsh. It was a fluorescent green—a perfect circle—and it pulsed underneath the surface of the water like a heartbeat.

One, two, three flashes, and then it was gone. Before it disappeared again, Ford caught sight of two very human hands gripping the side of the pier.

"Have you ever been out on a boat when it's raining?" Beck's words flashed through his head and Ford's stomach dropped. His neighbor wasn't *that* much of an idiot, right? The man wouldn't have gone out in the middle of a hurricane to try and catch fish in a swamp...

Right?

"Beck!" Ford called out again, hoping that he was wrong and that he had just seen a gator, or something else. Again, there was no answer, but the green light appeared again, this time hovering around the end of the pier. There was *definitely* something moving with it. If Beck was underwater, he was going to be carried out of reach within a matter of seconds.

Ford wasn't wearing shoes or pants. He was just in his boxers and a white cotton T-shirt, but he still tore out of the house without a second thought. He raced down the front porch steps, slipping on the wet wood and having to fling himself to the ground to keep from falling on his face. He pushed himself back onto his feet and kept going. The wind buffeted him at every angle and the hard, fast rain blinded him, but he kept running until his bare toes left slick grass and hit mud. He stopped at the edge of the bank and squinted, shielding his eyes with one cupped hand, as if *that* was going to make a difference.

"Beck, are you out here?" His voice was lost to the wind. Ford kept moving, searching for the pulsing green light. He stubbed his big toe against the edge of the pier and his nail split in half past the quick. He shredded his pain through his teeth and kept going, hobbling now across the dangerously slick planks. And, of course, there was no railing on either side.

He looked for any signs that Beck had gone out—a capsized speedboat, a fishing pole—anything. On the best and clearest of days, the water was green and murky. In the hurricane, it was like a sea of ink. Beck would be *lucky* if a gator didn't grab him before Ford could.

"I'm going to kill you!" Ford got down on his knees and started crawling towards the edge of the pier, slamming his hands against the slats each time before moving forward just so he didn't accidentally go too far. "You're an idiot, if you're out here!"

The green light came back. This time, it was halfway underneath the pier, and he could see it through the spaces in the boards. Ford leaned over the side to get a closer look, holding out one hand while using the other to keep gripping the pier for dear life. "Beck?" The wind stole his desperate words again.

The fluorescent green rippled, and a face emerged from its center. It looked a lot like Beck, except the cheekbones were far too hollow, and the sunken eyes were not silver. Instead, they were entirely black, with barely a prick of white in the center to catch the glowing light.

Whatever it was, the face smiled at him, showing off a mouthful of teeth like razors.

Ford choked on his own spit and reeled. He nearly lost his balance and his life flashed before his eyes, but he was able to use his grip on the pier to pull himself back. The face was still there, staring up at him, while something else rippled underneath the water.

This time, it looked like a gator tail—thick and dark green—except it boasted fins bigger than county fair quilts that dragged across the surface of the water and swirled underneath the pier.

Ford couldn't even force his mouth closed. He began to crawl backwards, all the while keeping his eyes on the fading green light and the ghoulish face in its center. He didn't want to look at it anymore, but he didn't want to lose sight of it, either. The rain pelting the water made *everything* look like it was moving.

And as badly as he wanted to believe this was all a dream, he couldn't focus on anything except getting back inside the house.

The face-like-Beck's tilted so that more of its head broke the surface of the water. Two pale, webbed hands with hooked, milky nails grabbed onto the side of the pier and the creature started to follow him, using the pier to pull itself along, one hand after the other, still grinning.

"Beck!" It opened its mouth and shrieked, but the voice itself was a distorted mockery of Ford's own panic. "Beck!"

"Oh my god," Ford's stomach lurched. He wanted to throw up. "Oh my god, oh my god…!" He couldn't crawl back fast enough. The bank still seemed so far away. And once he reached it, what then? Would this thing follow him, dragging itself all the way into the mud?

"Oh my god!" The creature screamed like it was dying. "Oh my god! Beck!"

Someone else had to hear it. *Someone* had to come help him, right? Ford's foot finally hit the mud, and he dropped to his belly, rolling off the planks and onto more-or-less solid ground so he could scramble away that much faster.

The creature stopped at the edge of the mud bank. It stared at him, its head half-submerged until most of what Ford could see was its buried, pinprick eyes.

Ford swallowed hard past the lump in his throat and stood up. His whole front was coated in mud, but he didn't care. The wind tried its best to knock him off his feet, but he dug in his heels to keep himself steady.

"Ford?" It was Beck's voice, clear as a bell over the howling wind. "Ford? What are you doing out here?"

Ford didn't want to take his eyes off the creature, but it didn't look like it was going to come onto shore, either. He dared to glance around, looking for his neighbor.

"Beck!" He called out. "I'm right here!"

"Ford, there's so many fish!" He couldn't pinpoint the source of Beck's voice, but it seemed to be coming from the bushes near the pier. "I told you there's nothing like a storm!"

Ford ground his teeth in frustration. "Beck, I need you to get back here!" He looked back towards the water, but he couldn't see the creature's eyes anymore. His heart kicked up and slammed into his ribs. "There's something out there—it's got to be a gator, or—I don't know! Get back here!"

"Okay, okay!" Beck called back. "Come help me get these fish! They'll be great for breakfast!"

"Your power is out! You're not cooking anything!" Ford waved his arms. "We're in the middle of a goddamn hurricane!"

"Wait, what is that?" Beck's voice climbed. "What is that in the water?"

"Oh, shit—" Ford darted forward, diving towards the bushes. He grabbed shrubs by the handful and moved them aside, looking every which way, desperately, for a sign of Beck. "Don't go near it! I don't know what it is!"

"It looks like me!" Beck's voice trembled, cracking with fear on the last note. "Why does it look like me?"

"Do not go near it!" Ford screamed. He slipped on the mud and fell backward, knocking his head against a root. Pain shot through his skull and he groaned, rolling over onto his stomach where a stick jabbed him in the gut, making him curl into a ball.

Ford looked up. There was so much water in his eyes that he could barely see a thing. He could tell he was on the edge of the bank, however. There was foamy, churning water lapping at his knee.

Ford blinked, trying to get some of the rain out of his eyes. He raised his grimy hand and wiped it across his face, but he only succeeded in pushing dirt into his tear ducts.

"Look at you," Beck said. Despite the wind, his voice was now clear as a bell. Ford squinted through the fuzziness. He could just make out his neighbor's features, that pale face and dark hair, leaning over him.

"I hit my head," Ford said. "Can you help me up?"

Beck didn't move. "Your blood is in the water," he said. "That's not good."

"Beck," Ford's voice broke. "Help me."

His vision cleared enough to where he could make out more of his neighbor's face. Beck was smiling down at him—the wide, uncanny grin full of impossibly sharp teeth.

He thought that Beck was standing, but in truth, he was just holding himself up on the edge of the bank. Behind him, the water rippled and churned, and those sail-like fins skimmed the top of the water.

"I'm sorry, Ford," Beck said to him. "I eat every catch down to the bones."

Ford tried to move, but he couldn't. He was caught in that gaze again, and he hadn't even realized it. Beck's eyes were back to being silver, and the only feeling Ford still had was a slight tingling in his fingertips and toes. He tried to speak, to make one last plea, but the only sound he could manage was a whimper.

Beck threw his head forward and stretched his mouth open until it was nothing more than a black, wet tunnel that eclipsed Ford's vision.

In the end, Ford was grateful for the numbness, because he didn't feel a thing.

-(173)-

3¢
SMIRKWHISPER

CRITICAL BLAST PUBLISHING
20¢
APPROVED BY THE READING CODE AUTHORITY
THE NICK VICTORY
CHRONICLES
PART SEVEN: Now You See Me
Paul Barile
CRITICAL BLAST PUBLISHING
THE CASE OF THE PEEK-A-BOO SUSPECT!

HELIUM GAS & BALLOON SET Get away from the day to day grind of your boring life and steal a whole house while the owners are away.

SUPER SECRET BOOK SAFE The special camouflage feature activates, once placed on the book shelf. You'll never find it again.

CRUISE MISSILE MODEL KIT! When you need to deliver a message across the country. Optional payload BATS IN A BOX sold separately.

BOW AND ARROW KIT! When you need to go into battle on Tuesdays and don't know what weapon to take with you.

HOBO IN A BOX When your street is getting over-runned by homeless people and you need someone to speak their language and run them off to the next street down the block.

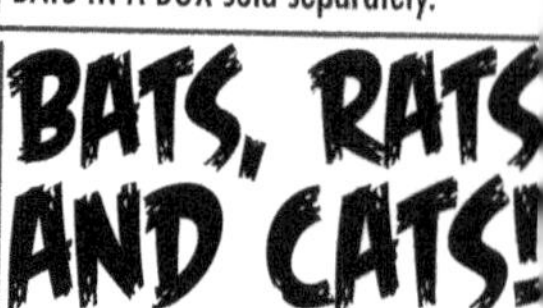

DIGITAL PUZZLE T-SHIRT Get people's undivided attention when they get engrossed trying to solve the constantly changing puzzles.

RENT AN ANGRY MIDGET! When you need to stop a Bully from harassing, or when you need to look like a decent human concerned for poor ugly monsters.

FISH BOWL FULL OF WORMS Are you tired of eating meat? Get yourself a bowl full of yummy worms and feel you are saving the planet.

EXPLODING DRINK Sit back and enjoy the highjinks as people unscrew their drink activating the chemical reaction, causing a foamy mess.

BOX OF LIVE BATS When you feel like a millionaire crime fighting hero and need to dress up your special cave, to give it that extra touch of atmosphere... a box of live bats is perfect for you. Food not included.

TRICK BLACK HOLE Get this special singularity and impress your friends by banishing them to other dimensions and realities.

Paul Barile is an award winning filmmaker (The Gospel According to Pork Chop) and the self-proclaimed King of Coloring Books. His true passion, though, is writing pulp fiction. He will be wrapping his M.A. spring 2026.

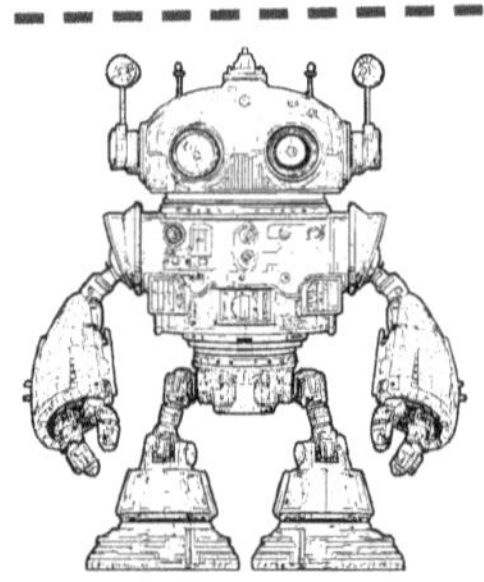

By the time Sabre's body ragdolled back to the pavement, the red T-bird had vanished around the corner leaving me holding the broken body of my best friend. I hate Mondays.

The nurses at the hospital seemed as happy to see my mug as anyone these days, maybe more because they were chatting me up about the strange things happening on their floor. I'm not sure how they figured out who I was, but there's no bad attention, even when your best friend is bandaged ass-to-elbow and they're feeding him with a straw.

I sipped thick coffee out of a porcelain mug and let the nurses take turns chirping about this and that, but it all sounded cuckoo to me. I was born at night, but it wasn't last night. These stories just didn't hold water. I listened and nodded and agreed, but there wasn't anything that was going to make me leave Sabre's side. Not even the tall, slender drink of water with the perfect gams.

"I don't know how to explain it, Mr. Victory," she said. "Things are just ... Things just aren't natural."

"What things, Miss ..."

"Brandy," she said. "Brandy *with a 'y.'* I'm respectable."

"Okay, Brandy-with-a-y, what's happening?"

Before she could answer, a large cup of ice chips got up from the food tray table and floated right past us and out the door. I looked at Brandy who was wide-eyed looking back at me.

"You saw that?"

"Saw what?" I asked.

"Come on, Mr. Victory, you didn't see that cup of ice just get up and float out of here?"

There was no way I was agreeing with her on this. The looney bin is two floors up and I got plans for the weekend. I'm playing it cool and not admitting to seeing anything.

"You didn't see *anything*?"

I didn't like lying to the dame, but I gotta keep an eye on my buddy. I can't go off half-cocked chasing a glass of ice chips through the hospital. I'll just get him another cup. They gotta have plenty of cups and plenty of ice. It's a hospital, for the love of Pete.

I set my new fedora on the back of the chair and headed out in search of a new cup of ice. Not a floating cup—just a good old-fashioned cup of ice chips. When I got to the ice machine, there was a gaggle of candy stripers chatting and pointing back at me. I'm a simple kind, but I had to admit to liking the attention.

"Are you Nicky Victory?" the one with the baby-doll face chirped.

"Nick Victory, but yes, I am he... or him."

"Are you here to look into the things that are happening in room 4261?"

The other girls watched quietly as if the baby-doll face was their mouthpiece.

"I'm here for my friend, Sabre. Sabre Bratcher."

"What kind of name is that?" she pressed. "It sounds exotic."

"He's from the far away land of Melrose Park."

"Wow," she sighed. "I'm Peaches."

"Nice to meet you, Peaches. I gotta get back to my friend."

I grabbed my ice and headed back to the room. I hated Sabre being here. Seeing him all busted up like that was tough. Tougher for him, but it wasn't easy for me either.

Brandy was still there tending to Sabre when I strolled back in with his ice. She took the cup and started feeding him. He smiled a little, but I could tell the smile hurt him. Trouble was, Brandy was the kind of skirt that could make a guy smile—even if he's busted up and wrapped in plaster. I smiled at his smile as I reached for my brim, which wasn't where I left it.

"Brandy, did you happen to see a blue fedora? I put it on the back of the chair here when I went for the ice."

"I haven't seen it, Nick," she said. She turned her attention back to Sabre.

"It was brand new," I said. "Didn't even have the Vitalis stains yet. You didn't see it?"

"Sorry, no."

As we were yammering about my hat, the newspaper floated out the door. I looked at the paper and then I looked at Brandy. By the time I looked back to the paper, it was floating down the hall. She was as white as Minnesota in December. I was still pissed about the hat.

"Aren't you going to go after it?" she piped.

"The paper or the hat?"

"Either. Aren't you curious? Even a little bit?"

"I guess I am," I said.

I poked my melon out the door to see if there was anything going on that I needed to know about. To my right was Peaches and her gaggle. To my left was the ordinary assortment of civilians shuffling back and forth with no clue about a missing fedora or a floating newspaper.

"Well, go ahead, Nicky."

"Don't rush me."

I've never been yellow. I like to refer to myself as cautious. I looked back at Sabre. He'd have run out there with all his flags flying and found that newspaper. He was always doing that type of thing. I took one step, then another. I walked down the hall, sticking to the orange stripe in the tile.

It only took one room for me to find my fedora. Seeing my *brand-new* fedora sitting on that food tray table, gave me a quick shot of juice. I stormed the room and grabbed my hat. As I turned to leave, I heard a voice.

"My dear man, unhand my fedora," the voice said.

"This is mine, *pal*," I said, even though I didn't see who I was talking to.

"I'm right here," the voice said.

"Where?"

"Right in front of you."

"Listen, *sport*, you can keep the paper, but I'm taking the hat back and that's final."

"Are you sure it's yours?"

I still couldn't see whoever I was talking to. I was just happy to grab my lid and beat it out of there. I sensed someone else in the room, but I couldn't see anyone and I only believe in what I can see with my own two peepers.

"It's mine," I said.

With that I was gone.

"Did you get the paper?" Brandy asked when I came back into the room.

"The hinkiest thing," I started. "I heard this voice, but there was no one there. I mean I heard him—heck I argued with him—but I never did see him."

"So, you don't have the paper."

"No. No, I don't."

Brandy hotfooted out of the room and pulled a U-turn into the room next door. I forgot about Sabre for a minute and followed her.

"Mr. Griffin," she said to the man lying there in the bed.

I never saw anything like this in my life. The guy was

wrapped in Ace bandages from head to toe. He was wearing a pair of aviator glasses, but there was not one piece of guy exposed. He was wearing a ratty fedora on the top of his head.

"Good day, Brandy," he said.

"Do you need anything, Mr. Griffin?"

"Please, Brandy, I insist you call me *Jack*."

That voice was familiar, but I never knew anyone wrapped up like a mummy. I stood and watched as Brandy flitted like a moth to a flame. Only thing was, with no face, I couldn't tell if he was smiling or not. If a dame like Brandy was paying that much attention to me, it surely would have stretched out the bandages.

"Do you need anything, Jack?" she repeated.

"Who's your friend?" he asked nodding toward me.

"This is Nick Victory," she said. "His friend is in the next room."

"Hello, Nick Victory. I'm Jack Griffin," Griffin said. "That's a sharp fedora."

"Yours is..."

"Grey," Griffin said, sparing me the awkward need to comment on his brim. "It's old and it's a little beat up, but it has seen me through more than my first two wives."

Two wives. Some guys have all the luck.

"It was nice to meet you, Mr. Griffin. I gotta get back to my friend. Good luck with the healing."

"Oh, call me *Jack*," he responded.

"Well, Jack, best of luck."

I walked out of the room and back to Sabre's room. I couldn't believe, after all he's been through, they'd put old Sabre in a room next to some kind of a mummy. Sabre deserves so much more. I figured I'd find the sawbones and have them move Sabre to nice quiet room with no Universal monsters next door.

"Poor man," Peaches said, as she walked in pushing a cart with magazines, candy bars and cigarettes.

"He's a good man," I said. "The best."

"You know him?" She seemed genuinely shocked.

"He's my best friend."

"Oh, I was talking about Mr. Griffin. He's been through so much. Did you see all those bandages?"

"I did."

"He was in a horrific fire and he's burned up real bad."

"You don't say," I said, rubbing my chin like Jimmy Stewart.

"*Real* bad."

She left a catalog for *Goods and Services* on the bedside table next to Sabre. Someone had spilled coffee on the catalog, obscuring one of the letters in the title. Then she left, taking the air out of the room with her.

I sat down intending to read the paper, when I remembered the paper was gone. So I grabbed the catalog and began flipping through it. I had one eye on the book and one eye on Sabre. Sleep was beginning to overwhelm me like a cheap suite in a nice hotel.

When I woke up, the fedora *and* the catalog were gone and the newspaper was back. I jumped up out of that creaky chair and headed out the door, only to bump into Brandy. Bumping into Brandy is its own experience, but I had to find my hat.

"Hey, Nicky," she said.

"Hey, Brandy."

"Did you lose something?"

"My hat is gone again."

I brushed past her into Griffin's room. There on the food tray table—next to the catalog—was my hat. Griffin was not in his bed. I didn't care about him. I just wanted my hat back. As

I grabbed the hat and made for the door, I saw the bandages in a small pile at the foot of the bed. They were clean as a nun's conscience. There was no way they'd been covering burns. I ran out of the room looking for Brandy.

I found her at the nurses' desk checking charts and quaffing black coffee out of a little cup that read *World's Greatest Nurse* on the side of it. She looked over the rim at me and smiled enough to encourage me to chat her up about this Griffin character.

"He's got a rare condition that makes his skin sensitive. That's why he wears those bandages. They're planning on running a battery of tests on him to see if there is anything they can do for him."

"Are you saying there was no fire?"

"Not to my knowledge."

"He's covered in bandages, but he's not bleeding or anything?"

"No, he's not bleeding or anything."

At just that moment I saw the ratty grey fedora float past the nurses' station and step onto the elevator. By the time I got to the door, it hushed closed and began its descent. I scratched my head. There was no way a fedora—ratty or not—floats out of a room and down the hall and no one notices.

"I didn't see anything," Brandy said.

The red light above Sabre's door was more important than the hat. I followed Brandy into the room to make sure my friend was okay. She clicked off the call light and began to check him from stem to stern. All points considered, he seemed okay, but I'm no doctor.

"Jack," he whispered.

Brandy looked at me and I looked at her and by the time we looked back at Sabre, he was sawing wood again. We wouldn't be getting much more out of him any time soon.

I sat down and started rifling through my mental rolodex for all of the Jacks we knew. It would've been better if the skel's name was a little more unique; there are a lot of Jacks in this town. It wasn't Jack Spriggins—he's in the hoosegow for stalking. It wasn't the Jack who chased the Jill down the hill—they ended up in Bayonne with a mess of rug rats. It wasn't Jack Horner—he was running a bakery in Chicago. He really is a good guy.

It was then I saw *my* brim floating by again. I looked at Brandy who was still leaning over Sabre, but her head was turned and she was looking out the door with the most mystified look on her face. She looked at me and then back to the door. The hat was long gone by then, but she couldn't look away. It seemed like she was waiting for the hat to return.

"Okay," she whispered. "I saw it that time."

"Me, too."

"What are we going to do?"

"You're going to make sure to take care of Sabre. I'm going to go see what's happening."

I walked into the room next door and there was Jack Griffin wrapping the last of the bandages around his hand... or where his hand should have been. There was nothing but air. The thing of it was, with a few deft moves, the wrapping became a hand. He turned, startled. I was as startled as he was, but he was not handling it well.

"What gives, Jack?" I asked.

"It's just a hat," Jack responded, trying to gather himself.

"Not the hat, Jack. I am talking about you. I saw you wrapping something that wasn't there."

"I can assure you it's there. Don't trust everything you see or don't see."

"I don't trust much, and I trust *you* even less."

"Things aren't always what they appear."

"They rarely are, so why don't you enlighten me?" I was getting edgy.

"Clearly, I'm not here because of some fire."

"Clearly. And the skin condition?"

"I imagine I would need normal skin to have a skin condition," he said with a rueful chuckle.

"My patience is running thin, Jack."

"You probably won't believe me if I tell you," he said. He pulled on his aviator glasses.

"You're probably right," I said.

Just then Brandy showed up in the doorway and Jack saw his chance. He grabbed his ratty fedora and ran out the door, pushing past Brandy and heading for the staircase. He wasn't waiting for the elevator this time. He opened the heavy metal door and disappeared down the stairwell, with me in hot pursuit. I was right behind him, following that nasty fedora, with the Ace bandages trailing behind him like the streamers at parade for one. We busted through the doors out onto Route 66 and he bolted toward the hot dog stand just east of us.

He made a hard left at the corner and disappeared for a minute so I kicked it up a notch. I felt like Jesse Owens in tan Oxfords. When I got to the bakery, I banged another hard left and my Oxfords got tangled up in the Ace bandages. I windmilled for a minute, but caught myself before I spilled. I looked up and there was the ratty fedora bobbing in the air taunting me with every bob.

I got back to the hospital to check on my old chum and was surprised to see Peaches feeding him ice chips. I could almost make out his devilish grin under the bandages. He was in good hands. I thought I might go find Brandy and pitch some woo.

Brandy was back at the nurses' station filling out forms on a clipboard and nibbling on the end of her pen. I stood there and watched for a moment. Dolls like Brandy don't come along every day. Even a guy like me knows to stand back and burn the image of her into my brain.

Finally, I screwed up my courage and walked to where she was standing. She didn't look up right away. Maybe she was burning my image into her brain.

"Oh, you're back?"

I guess her brain remained burnless.

"Yeah, I don't know what happened. One minute we were running down the street and the next minute there's a pile of bandages and I'm watching that old hat sail out of sight."

"I'm sorry. I was just looking at Jack's record to see if I could why he was here in the first place."

"It's the chemical compound."

"Wow, Nicky. You know about chemical compounds? I'm impressed. I'm a bit of a sapiosexual."

"Can you do that before marriage?" I asked.

"She means she likes smart guys—legit smart guys," the voice repeated.

"Griffin?"

"One and the same."

"Why, I oughta…"

"No hard feelings, *dick*," he said.

"Wait. Is he *back*?" Brandy asked.

"He is."

"In the flesh… sort of…"

"All right, funny guy, what gives?"

"I'm here to see my old friend, Doctor Kemp. He wants to know what it is that makes me, well… me."

"I know Dr. Kemp. He's brilliant."

"He is. He's the closest thing I have to a friend and I trust he will learn from my success and failures and then give me my life back."

My brain caught a red light and everyone else was on green. I was still stuck on this sapiosexual thing and how it affected Brandy's lady parts, and now I'm talking to a legit invisible man. She didn't even notice me anymore. I watched her moving in the direction the voice was coming from. I moved away, almost imperceptibly.

"Don't be scared, *pally*," he said. "It ain't catchy."

"Nah, I need to get back to my friend. You all have a good night."

I headed back to the room where I could at least be happy for Sabre. Something good might come out of all of this for him. I sat in the creaky chair and listened to Peaches singing Connie Francis softly to Sabre.

I dozed for a moment and when I woke, my hat was still gone. I wouldn't have expected anything different after a day like this. There was a small tug on the old ticker when I thought about Brandy-with-a-y, but I knew nursing old Sabre back to health was going to be my occupation until he was well and ready to get back on his feet.

My friend needs me and I'm not going to disappear now.

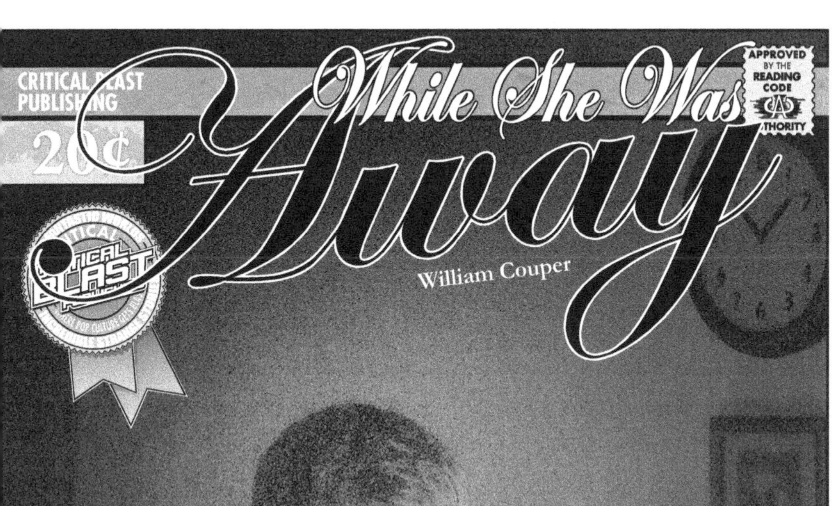

CRITICAL BLAST PUBLISHING
20¢
APPROVED BY THE READING CODE AUTHORITY
While She Was Away
William Couper
HOARDING HORROR IN THE HOUSE

SHOP BY MOB DISCOUNT SERVICE

ATTENTION!

DEMONS!
VAMPIRES!
GHOULS!

SURVIVE TUESDAYS "YOU" DAYS!

DEFEAT BLACK MYSTIC ARTS KUNG-FU Tired of getting your ass kicked every Tuesday by Black Mystic Arts Kung-Fu fighters? CALL 666-HELP to enroll in self-defense training every Hellspawn should know to survive any dark alley encounter. Become a Ninth Circle Master of Judante!

HYPNO-ROBOT use the special mind control eye harmonics to subdue the minds of your unwilling subjects. You'll never have to take out the trash and everyone will worship you as if their life depends on it.

MONSTER VALUE STAMP THIS IS IT! CLIP THEM & COLLECT THEM ALL!

HELIUM GAS & BALLOON SET Get away from the day to day grind of your boring life and steal a whole house while the owners are away.

YOU ARE NOT THE THING!

SNAKES IN A MAIL BOX Get these total mother-f$%Ken poisonous snakes and mail them with your get well gift cards.

FISH BOWL FULL OF WORMS Are you tired of eating meat? Get yourself a bowl full of yummy worms and feel you are saving the planet.

RADIOACTIVE CANDY When you want to level up your personality and appear extra sweet to the people around you... and want to have a superpower over sugar... this candy's for you!

BOX OF LIVE BATS When you feel like a millionaire crime fighting hero and need to dress up your special cave, to give it that extra touch of atmosphere... a box of live bats is perfect for you. Food not included.

William Couper is a working class writer from Scotland whose work has appeared in various print and online publications including, Cosmic Horror Monthly, Penumbric Speculative Fiction Magazine, and Black Sheep Magazine.

Movement broke into his doze. Blearily, he focused on the man tottering along the street. The clock said it was ten past one in the morning. He would have closed his eyes and hoped the drunk didn't look in his direction, if it weren't for something further along the street, high over the man's head. Two glittering red points in the deep shadow above the downward-pointing cone of illumination from a streetlight.

Rory was in his car, swaddled in the duvet, seat as far back as it would go, almost horizontal. It wasn't a comfortable place to sleep, but it was much better than being in the house on his own. He wanted to minimise how often he did this because it would get back to Jane and he didn't want to have the discussion again.

The points moved as though leaping, until a large silhouette formed around them. A lamppost swayed a little when the bulk of the unseen thing landed, but if he hadn't been following, he might have thought it was the wind. The man was unaware and stumbled along, muttering incomprehensibly.

He slipped off the pavement and staggered into the road. Somehow, he managed to stay upright, despite a hazardous few seconds when one leg flailed at hip height. In confusion, the man looked around again, unsure of how he got onto the road. He laughed when he pieced it together and remounted the pavement. The thing on the lamppost nearest the man stopped as though uncertain.

Rory was tempted to open the car door and warn the man, but he didn't want to put himself in danger. He watched with growing terrified fascination.

The stalking thing dropped, and Rory was treated to a bizarre sight. At first, he thought it was a shaved gorilla. Its skin was pale and coloured orange from the amber streetlight.

There was no hair on the thing's body, and he could see, with unwanted clarity, huge and ugly genitals. Its arms were long, a third longer than the body that was over seven feet tall. Two large, mobile ears sprouted from the side of the face to the top of head. The face was fierce, with huge eyes and a canine nose, down to a wide mouth, dispelling the idea of a great ape. From this distance he couldn't see the thing's teeth. He could see the long, black claws curving from each digit as they reached for the man.

Despite watching, he almost missed what happened next. The man's head was wrapped in the creature's powerful hand and it lifted him up the lamppost in one smooth movement. The lampposts shuddered more as it leapt away into the darkness. Mutterings were cut off without a scream. Rory was left with the impression of a stiffening body as though hit with a metal pole.

For a long time, Rory stared at the spot the man had last occupied. It had happened so fast that his eyes created an outline of the man for a disconcerting length of time. After a while he was looking into the darkness.

He lay back down and huddled under the duvet.

#

Brendan slumped out of bed, unable to stay there any longer. He looked at his phone and found he had slept for an hour. The dreams had stopped at last. It was too late to attempt to sleep again, he had to get ready for work.

The dreams had kept him awake since after twelve. Whenever he fell asleep, he would be launched out of the slumber a short time later, with terrible images clinging to the inside of his mind. The images would fade in the moments of gasping terror as he mentally scrambled to recall he was at home, in bed. The worst occurrence was after one, when he screamed as he emerged from his third short attempt to sleep. His heart felt like it was about to implode, and he feared for his safety, but a quick survey of his bedroom told him he was safe. Though it peaked then, the nightmares continued until dawn.

The weird, creeping feeling of danger settled onto his shoulders and he carried it into the shower with him. He hoped he could shrug it off as the day went on, but he felt it would still be with him when he got back home.

#

"You sound exhausted, Rory," Jane said.

"I didn't sleep very well last night," he said.

"That's obvious. What's wrong? Miss me too much?"

He laughed, as was expected, but he didn't deny it.

"Where are you now?" he said.

"Somewhere near Cardiff. Some shitty chain hotel. At least I know what I can expect in one of these places."

"You're still not over the place in Weymouth, are you?"

"The cleaning was a joke, and the 'continental breakfast' was a few stale rolls, a wrinkly apple and tea I'm sure someone scooped out of a toilet."

"At least it was only for one night."

"Have you ever slept in a dirty hotel for a night? It's horrible. I think I slept all of two hours. It's really hard to sleep when you keep expecting something to crawl over your face."

Try sleeping after seeing a man plucked off the street, he thought. He had decided not to tell anyone about what he had seen last night. No one would believe him, as, after all, he had trouble believing it himself. Jane would be too tempted to patronise him if he told her, and then would come the worry. He didn't have the capacity to deal with either reaction.

Had he seen it at all? That was the question he had been asking all night long. There was a good chance he'd dreamt it and woke, with the duvet pressed against his ears and a horrific tableau conjured by his subconscious branded behind his eyes. It was such an outlandish thing to see, the reality eroded after an hour. At four, when he got back home, the idea of some huge ape-thing abducting a man from the street seemed idiotic and he felt stupid for allowing it to stop him sleeping the whole night.

"At least you're in a cleaner place now," he said and paused. "You *are* in a cleaner place now?"

"Oh, yeah. I would be whatever happened, I'm not going to spend three days in a place like the one in Weymouth. I would have moved hotels and put it on the company's account."

"You're going to have words with someone."

"Oh, yes. Adam is going to be hearing a lot about that hotel. He'd better hope he's booked decent places for the rest of this trip."

"The other conferences are in bigger places…"

"You've been to plenty of crappy hotels in big cities."

"Adam had better be smart enough to have booked you into good accommodation."

"That's adorable, always thinking of other people."

"I'm the real humanitarian."

"What have you got planned today?"

He clenched his jaw, because they both knew the answer, and she knew the question annoyed him.

"Scouring the job sites for a while and then I need to go and pick up some bread and coffee."

"Droughts don't last forever, Roar. There's something waiting out there for you."

"There are such things as deserts, Jane."

"That doesn't apply here." Someone muttered in the background. "Fine. Got it. I have to go. This keynote is important. I'll speak to you later. Love you."

"Love you, too. Bye."

"Bye," her voice was distracted, and the word was cut off.

He was left with the afterbuzz in his ear, even when he took the phone away. He didn't begrudge her going away on the business trip, he couldn't afford to begrudge it, since he had been fired from his last job, it was their only source of income. It was a good income, but it was stretched a bit to cover them both. If he had a job, they would be back to the way they had been. He wouldn't have to scrape for things to do at home while Jane was gone. He wouldn't feel so isolated and uncomfortable in his own home at night while Jane was away, that he felt the need to sneak to his car and sleep several streets away. Despite now being sure he had dreamt the man's abduction he didn't think he could bring himself to do it again. Not during this trip.

As he had said to Jane, he went to the PC and started his depressing search through job sites.

#

He felt deflated when he left the flat. Another round of emails requesting applications or the emails being applications themselves, and not an ounce of hope in any of them. Getting away from the computer was a blessing.

A look at the car. It was tempting to hop in, but he would be back home quicker, with the computer sitting in the office waiting and judging, the collection of electronic parts imbued with his failure and resenting him for it. No matter where he was in the house, he would feel like it was staring at him. Away from the house he could put it out of his mind to a degree, at least he wouldn't be compelled to sit at it.

Some exercise would do him good. He might start trudging after a short time, but at least it was movement. Better than being at home, isolated. Outside, he was still on his own, but being surrounded by other people, even if he did not know them, held a small amount of comfort.

He passed the bit of waste ground he had parked the car in last night. A few people walked along under the lampposts, unconcerned and unaware. While he couldn't dismiss his unsettled feeling, he could dismiss the reality of what he saw.

The rest of his walk was taken up with thoughts of what Jane was doing on her trip and whether he should visit his friend Martin.

In the town centre, he revelled in the huge number of people around him. The place wasn't a bustling metropolis, but there was enough of a crowd to make him feel both anonymous and involved.

By the time he had gone around the crowded supermarket and left, he was tired. So much of his days were made up of feeling tired, even though most days he slept until mid-morning. Having nothing to do sapped his reserves more than a weeks' worth of twelve hour shifts ever had.

After finishing his small shop, he saw Finn Allen, his next-door neighbour, outside the supermarket. Rory had pitied Finn for a long time. The man had lost his wife almost fifteen years ago and his mental state had been shattered. Rory had only met Yvette once, but she had seemed nice. Finn had seemed strange even then and he had deteriorated, as though his wife was the one mooring keeping him tied to reality. There had been numerous visits from family, healthcare workers, and social workers over the years, but they were unable or unwilling to help him.

"Hey, Finn. How's it going?" Rory said to him.

Finn twitched, as though he hadn't noticed Rory and stared at him. He inched a bit too close for Rory's comfort, and the constant smell of damp paper, musty clothes, and aged sweat he carried clogged Rory's nostrils. Rory took half a step back for his own benefit and hoped Finn wouldn't take offence. Finn was too preoccupied with something else to notice or comment.

"Locking your door doesn't work, you know," Finn said.

"Why is that?" Rory said, unsure of what else he could do. He didn't want to upset Finn and cause a scene.

"I don't know," Finn was thoughtful. "I was walking through my house one night, and there it was, large as life."

"What was?"

It was Finn's turn to frown. Even though it seemed he wasn't listening to Rory, the question had penetrated, and he was confused. Rory regretted asking the simple question. Finn struggled to pin down an answer, his eyes darted from side to side, as though he were reading a ledger and his mouth would open ready to reply, but nothing would come out and he went back to rapidly reading an invisible document.

"It's something," he said, uncertain. "Curled up like a big dog. And there's the smell."

Rory was surprised by this, as he was aware of the kinds of things Finn had crammed into his house. Any smell strong enough to punch its way through the thick haze that must fill his home had to be pungent. On some warm days, when Finn left his door open, Jane would complain of the smell wafting through their garden. Damp, rot, mustiness, and faeces.

"Has an animal got into your house?" Rory said. "If there has, you might need to phone someone."

Finn jolted. "No. That's okay. It's nothing. I can deal with it. Don't you worry, Rory. I can get on top of it."

With a flurry of gestures, Finn trotted into the supermarket. Rory wondered if he should phone someone when he got home. For all the worries he'd had for Finn's mental health over the years, he had never thought he might need to be taken into care. He was in his late fifties, and it wouldn't be long before the struggle with taking care of himself became too much.

He decided he wouldn't, but he noted to keep an eye on his neighbour. He hoped it wasn't the beginning of a severe deterioration. He made his slow way back home.

#

Brendan jumped up out of bed and ran to the toilet. His heaving stomach almost emptied before he got to the bowl. A painful spasm brought up the sandwich he'd eaten before bed. He stayed there, groaning for several minutes until he was sure nothing else was going to happen.

The image from his dream was so clear and so disgusting, that it had activated his inability to cope with blood. Even remembering the torn-open corpse made him queasy, though not enough to cause another bout of vomiting.

Where could that have come from? He avoided horror films, true crime, or real-life medical documentation, as it all made him too uncomfortable. It was the reason he hadn't been able to attend the births of his two children.

He sat on the floor, with his legs out in front of him and got his breath back. The acidic tang lingered in his throat and the back of his nose. It would make him more comfortable if he could swirl at least a little water around his mouth and blow his nose, but for the moment he had no energy. His legs and arms felt too shaky.

He used the time to consider how such an extreme image could have been conjured from his mind. He had never had a dream like that before. The rare times he'd had nightmares, they were filled with crushing sensations of being hunted or that his children were sick or dead, nothing so graphic as a mutilated body.

The splayed flesh had been so butchered he didn't even know if it was a human body. He didn't know why it mattered so much to him, but it did. There was no way to be certain, the dream image had come and gone like smoke, he now had trouble holding onto it even as he concentrated.

It was going to be another odd day at work, as he would be preoccupied again by his night-time mind.

At last, he felt confident enough to stand and his legs were solid as ever. He stared at himself in the mirror, nothing too unusual, perhaps the skin under his eyes was darker than normal. Some shadows under the eyes were to be expected after two nights of interrupted sleep.

Once he had got the worst of the aftereffects of vomiting under control he plodded back to his bedroom. As he was about to get back into bed, he stopped with the corner of his duvet bunched up in his fist.

He turned towards the window. A shuddering, electric sensation started in the top of his skull and trickled down the sides of his head, his neck, and dispersed through his body. It was a horrible sensation and it got stronger as he edged to the window, yet he couldn't stop himself from going.

With the buzzing feeling came the certainty there was something out there, perhaps not far away. It was dangerous and terrible. He couldn't say what it was, but he knew, in the same way he could curl his fingers or feel his tongue move in his mouth, that it was real.

He pulled open the curtain. The orange illumination from the streetlight poured in, the window was about ten feet away from it. He was hit with the ugly realisation that the awareness of the thing became stronger.

It couldn't be real. What he was sensing was so inhuman and incomprehensible that it had to be his imagination. Imagination had always been a vestigial thing for him and so had become uninteresting as he grew up. He much preferred tangible things.

Once his eyes were used to the glare, he looked along the quiet street. Parked cars and bushes ruffled by the slight wind were the only things he saw. Nothing else moved. He had heard foxes screaming a few nights ago, but there was nothing now.

The only noise was what was going on inside his head. A clamour for attention he refused to believe but couldn't ignore. His arms wouldn't move; he couldn't make his legs take him back to bed and his eyes would close only to blink. He stared out into the night, helpless against this unwelcome episode. He resisted the description that wanted to impose itself. *Invasion.* This couldn't be an invasion, outside influences inserting thoughts in the minds of others was impossible.

He whipped his arms up and gripped the curtains. The effort to perform the simple task was immense and closing the curtains proved to be almost beyond him. When the curtains were closed again, he felt the thoughts ebb, their power drained away. As he had after vomiting, he spent several minutes gathering himself while the last toxic vestiges of the thoughts fluttered away.

Glad that it was so close, with his legs unable to support him anymore, he fell into bed again.

#

"Do you know if they've found that guy yet?" Martin Sinclair said and pulled out a newspaper from the day before. He pointed at the photo on the front page.

Rory stopped with his cup of coffee an inch off the table and stared at his friend. It had been a few weeks since he had seen Martin and his wife Laura, and he thought it would be a good antidote to his loneliness and general discomfort.

Martin's question didn't help with the discomfort and made a small coil of fear form around his brain. He tried to hide it, but Laura frowned at him.

"What's wrong, Rory? You look like someone threw white paint in your face. If you're going to be sick, you know where the toilet is," she said, with a smile.

"It's okay. I've been a bit under the weather recently. Who was this guy?" Rory said.

"You need to be more up on the news, pal. He's a local guy. Name's…" Martin stopped and screwed his face up.

"Tony Underwood," Laura said and shook her head.

"Yeah, him. He vanished after being at the pub a couple of nights ago. There's CCTV shots of him leaving and coming out this way, but he didn't turn up for work the next day. His family was on TV appealing for him to come back and for anyone who might have seen him to come forward," Martin said.

The strength in Rory's arm vanished in a moment and the cup dropped to the table. An inch or so higher and it would have smashed, as it was coffee sloshed across the table. He stood up and almost collided with Laura, as they both reached for the roll of kitchen paper.

"Sorry!" he said.

"It's fine, Rory. You sit down," Laura said and looked at him with concern.

"Did you know this guy?" Martin said.

Rory didn't answer. He stared ahead, his fear-addled brain swirled and bubbled. The air in his lungs felt inadequate. All idea of where he was fell away.

"Rory, man. You're making me nervous," Martin said.

Rory remembered where he was and who he was with and blinked at Martin in confusion.

"What's going on?" Laura said as she mopped up the mess.

"I...um," Rory said. He wondered if he should tell them — if he should tell anyone. It was as though a deeper part of his mind took over and the words pushed out from him. "You cannot tell Jane any of this. Especially you, Laura. What I'm going to tell you has to stay in this room."

"For goodness' sake, Rory. Just spit it out. We won't tell Jane a thing," Martin said.

For her part, Laura shrugged and looked confused.

"I was sleeping in my car a couple of nights ago," Rory said.

"Oh man, this again," Martin said.

"Yeah, but that's not what's important here. Will you let me finish?" In response Martin put his hands up in mock surrender. "I woke up at about one in the morning. Can't say why, but I did. There was this drunk guy stumbling along the street. Totally fucked up. Then I saw something. Now, look, this was probably a dream and a coincidence."

"You saw this guy? You have to tell the police," Martin said.

"Martin, mate. You're going to find out why I can't do that. I saw something. Something on top of the lampposts."

"The lampposts? Are you going to tell us he was abducted by aliens?" Laura said.

"No. This was one thing. A big creature that stood on top of the lampposts," Rory said. "And it was watching this guy. It jumped along those lampposts like a big monkey and dropped down and snatched him right off the street."

"What was it?" Martin said, a slight smile on his face.

"I don't have a damn clue. It might have been a gorilla, but its face was all messed-up and it was bald."

"A bald gorilla thing? I think you were dreaming," Laura said.

"That's what I've been trying to convince myself of, but I can't get the image of this weird thing just grabbing this guy and disappearing with him out of my head. It could have been a dream, but it was so vivid, and it's stayed with me for days. Usually, I can barely remember dreams a couple of hours after I've woken up," Rory said.

"I'm usually like that too, but there's that one that just sticks with me. Last year I had one where Laura died. Scared the shit out of me, I can tell you. Oh, and there was the one with the toilet. I wouldn't worry about it," Martin said.

"This is the longest trip she's taken, isn't it?" Laura said.

"Yeah. She's been away two weeks and there's supposed to be two more. At least the first couple were in the UK, but the last week and a half she's going to be in Germany."

"Those long trips weren't so bad when you were working, were they?"

"No. It was still a pain, but I had something to distract me."

"What took you so long to come round then?" Martin said. "Our door's always open, mate."

"Thanks, man. I just don't want to be a bother to you," Rory said.

"You're one of our best friends, Rory, you're not a bother, we love having you here," Laura said. "Now we're going to worry more when you're not here."

"You shouldn't. I'll be fine."

"You know you haven't given us much reason to believe that, honey?"

Rory laughed. "I like to complicate things."

"I wish you wouldn't, mate. Why don't you come around on Saturday and we can have something a bit stronger than coffee?" Martin said.

"I think I could use that. Thanks," Rory said.

#

He hadn't drunk anything stronger than a black coffee, but he felt a bit woozy when he stepped out of the car. It was late, the air was cool, and he felt good. It was amazing how being with good people had such a rejuvenating effect. Martin and Laura had insisted on him staying for dinner and that had turned into watching an old film on DVD. And another. Saturday night was going to be good.

The cool late-night air seemed to enhance the warm glow he carried with him. A slight ruffle of a chilly breeze tousled his hair as it whistled past. He smiled.

He felt his smile snap out of existence when he looked up. The bulky thing came into view at the end of the street and moved with the same feline ease he recalled from before. It looked freer now, as it swung under the lights. Long, powerful arms moved with surety and the hands hooked the bars with natural ease. The pointed head thrust forward, intent on its destination.

It flashed through the light and into the darkness, out of sight in a handful of seconds.

All good, secure feelings were gone, and he stood, afraid it might come back. Somehow, he didn't believe standing still would be a defence, but his body would do nothing else. His mind became a blankness of terrible thoughts, a whiteout of panic.

With as much care and slowness as he could muster, he closed the car door and winced at the echo. He expected to see the thing, propelled by those arms, reappear, now intent on him.

The thought of those fingers wrapping around his skull and being yanked off the street spurred him into action. With stiff-legged speed, he rushed to the front door, while fishing for his keys. His trembling hands made the task beyond him. It was only when he stopped on the doorstep that he was able to achieve the simple goal. As he fought with the keys, he tensed, expected to be taken.

He refused to turn, terrified of seeing those red-reflecting eyes a few feet away.

There was no relief when he inserted the key and turned it. Even when he swung the door open and he fell into the house, he was terrified of being snatched away. He was shocked to find there was nothing out there as he closed the door. He stood gasping in the foyer as though he had sprinted from Martin and Laura's. He engaged all the locks and waited for over an hour before going to bed.

#

The face was undeniably familiar, yet Brendan had never met the man in the picture. He stared at the newspaper article and tried not to panic at this second time seeing the man. When he had seen the man's face the first time, it had been contorted in unbelievable terror and shock, a far cry from the contented happiness conveyed in the photo.

The man had disappeared around the time Brendan had dreamt about him. His name was Arthur Venik, and he had gone out to buy something for his pregnant wife late at night. His car had been found this morning, the door lying open, abandoned, and the few items of shopping on the passenger's seat. Brendan recognised the car, too. There were no signs of a struggle, and he knew why.

He remembered the huge, pale hand holding the man's skull as though it were the size of a ping-pong ball. The most disturbing thing about the vision was that the hand and arm seemed to be Brendan's, yet he couldn't control what was happening. He was powerless to stop the man being carried away as whatever Brendan occupied leapt away at an impossible height.

"Hey, Bren, you falling asleep again?" Steve Eppings said and made Brendan jump.

"Jesus, man. I was miles away."

"No kidding. You holding something good?"

"How stupid do you think I am, Steve? You know the security guards would be full of anything I brought in by now."

"And you would be out of a job."

"And I would be out of a job. I still haven't managed a full night's sleep in weeks."

"Maybe you should see a doctor."

Brendan had considered that but stopped short. What would he say? He wasn't willing to admit he was having strange dreams and even stranger feelings when he was awake in the middle of the night. He had told no one he worked with about what was happening. Even Steve, whom he considered a friend, would have thought he was insane if he told him. There was no one he could tell.

"Maybe," he said. "I'll have to find time for it first."

"We have a couple of hours a week to do other stuff. They aren't complete slave drivers."

"Their generosity knows no bounds."

"Seriously, mate. If you can get some help, you should go for it. You look like you're going to drop."

"My ex-wife would love that."

"I bet she wouldn't like the child support payments to dry up."

Brendan shrugged. "You have to take the rough with the smooth."

Steve laughed and wandered off, leaving Brendan to stare at the picture of a man he couldn't have known the fate of, yet he did.

#

Rory was surprised to see Brendan come out of the health centre, and even more surprised at the look he gave him.

They had worked together for five years before Rory lost his job. Rory never understood how the decision was made to keep one of them on, while letting the other go. He and Brendan had started in the place a few months apart, and now Brendan was still working there.

The look of polite friendliness flashed across Brendan's face and was immediately replaced by something else.

Brendan walked up to Rory, examining his face.

"Hey, Brendan. How are you doing?" Rory said, even as he leaned away.

Brendan said nothing and kept up his scrutiny of Rory. At first Brendan seemed angry, but his expression opened up into wonder, even excitement. This disturbed Rory even more, because he knew what Brendan was looking for.

"You've seen it," Brendan said, confirming Rory's certainty.

"I don't know what you're talking about, Brendan. I have to get home,' Rory said and made to walk away.

He felt the thrill of desperation, like a snap of static, in Brendan's hand as it closed on his arm. He tried to pull away, but Brendan wouldn't let go, his fingers felt like steel. Rory became aware of how much taller and bigger Brendan was. The directness of his gaze sapped his strength and ignited his curiosity.

"Fine. I've seen something weird and scary. I saw it take Tony Underwood a couple of weeks ago," Rory said, defeated.

"We have to talk," Brendan said. "Come on."

Rory allowed himself to be dragged to the nearest pub. It was before twelve, so the place was quiet. Brendan insisted that Rory sit, while he went to the bar. A few minutes later he sat across from Rory with two glasses of soft drinks.

"I have to get back to work. If they smell booze on my breath I'll be out on my arse," Brendan said.

"They gave you time off to go to the doctor? I'm surprised."

"I'm not. I fucked up an entire batch the other day because I haven't slept. I think Paul thought it was a better idea to let me out for a couple of hours than have me wreck another load of merchandise."

"That prick's still there? I didn't think he could think that far ahead."

"Oh, he can't. The manager probably made him do it."

"That sounds much more likely." Rory took a sip of the drink and said, "When did you see this thing? Actually, how did you know I'd seen it?"

Brendan gave a bitter laugh and let out a long breath.

"I would say you probably won't believe me. You've seen it, so there's a good chance you will. You still might think I'm off my fucking nut," he said.

"Let's hear what you have to say before I make a judgement."

"I can sense it right now, you know."

"You know where it is?"

"It's nothing that precise. I can feel it's out there." Brendan waved towards the pub door. "It's sleeping, or dormant, or whatever, right now. It's like when you have a cold, and your ears are blocked. As much as you try to clear it or ignore it, it's always there."

"That's weird and I can see why you're a bit cagey about talking about it."

"It's not even the best part. It's how it started. The reason I haven't been able to sleep for weeks is that I can see through its eyes while I'm sleeping, like I'm in its head. I get snippets of it moving, attacking people."

"So, you've seen where it goes."

"No. I told you — snippets. Like it broadcasts when it's at its most...I don't know...wound up? After it hunts someone and gets them, it just fades. But I do see other things."

"Like what?"

"Memories. I think. If they *are* memories, this thing is old. Like I've seen it running across rooftops in ancient Egypt, maybe even older. It's been in Medieval China, Renaissance Italy, and places I don't even know."

"What would a thing that's thousands of years old want with this shitty place?"

"The same thing it's always wanted. Feeding grounds. I don't know if it's unique, but it took a long time to understand what it actually feeds on."

"What does it feed on?"

"Blood."

"Wait. It's really fucking old, it drinks blood, and does it sleep during the day?"

"Yeah. Everything I've seen has been at night."

"You know what you're describing, right?"

"I *know* it's a vampire. These legends have to start somewhere."

"Yeah, but it's usually some poor bastard's got a weird disease or people are misunderstanding something we think is simple. It's not some freaky creature that looks like a cross between a gorilla and a wolf."

"Is that what it looks like? I've only ever seen the arms."

"Be glad that's all you've seen."

"I'm not. I've seen the worst of what it's done."

"This has been a giggle, mate, but I have to get going."

Rory downed the rest of his drink and stood up. Brendan held out his hand in panic.

"Wait! What are we going to do about it?" he said.

"Do? What are we supposed to do?'

"We can work out were it sleeps during the day and kill it."

"No, mate. I've seen enough of what it can do. I'll just avoid going out at night and hope it goes away again."

"How long is that going to be? We're the only ones who know about it and I want to be able to sleep."

"Take whatever pills the doctor gave you and wait. You said it moves around."

"That could take months or years. Something that old is going to be patient."

"Maybe you should take its lead. I'll see you around."

Rory walked away before Brendan could reach across and grab him or launch into another tirade. As he was walking out into the street, he cast a last look at Brendan. The man looked deflated, lonely, and afraid. Rory could be sympathetic, but he didn't have the stamina or strength to afford the resources that it would require to help Brendan.

He walked into the street and was glad of the sun.

#

Brendan woke from the doze with a start. He always woke up with a start these days. There was an image in his mind, and he stumbled from the sofa to the PC.

A few minutes of searching and he found what he was looking for.

He realised after Rory left the pub that he should have told him he had been creating a map of all the places he had seen in his visions. The idea had come to him in the last few days. He had compiled all the places he had seen the vampire attack people.

It still felt strange thinking of it with that name. He realised he had known it but had danced around the term in his own mind for weeks. When Rory said it out loud it gave Brendan the bravery to accept it. With all the crazy things he had witnessed recently it seemed like resisting the easy description wasn't a sensible thing to do.

This new flash, this new image looked familiar, even without the use of the map, which made his search easier.

It was the first time he had seen a contemporary interior. A dark place, that the vampire's eyes made easier to see. Piles of magazines, some so old and mouldy that they slumped at alarming angles. There was what seemed to be a wall of plastic bags on one side and a drift of jar lids on the other side. The glimpse through a dim and dirty window of a distinctive gable.

After his first blush of elation, he became alarmed at how close this location was. A few streets away, within short walking distance, in fact.

It was dark outside. He drummed his fingers on the desk, knowing he had already made his decision and was impatient.

#

Rory was in the kitchen, staring into the fridge, knowing he was going to heat the cannelloni ready meal he had bought that day. It was well after eleven and he had already eaten most of a roast chicken for dinner. He had taken the container out of the fridge when he saw movement in the street.

A tall, heavy figure made its way along the pavement and stopped outside Finn's house. He was sure it couldn't be who he thought it was, that would be too much of a coincidence. When the figure switched on the torch and went down the side his neighbour's house, it was revealed to be Brendan.

"What are you doing, you crazy fucker?" Rory whispered.

He was fearful of the answer.

As Rory watched, the container in his hand forgotten, Brendan played the torch beam around the side of Finn's house and stopped on the door. Brendan reached for the door and pushed it open, revealing a dark interior.

While Brendan was occupied with shining the torch inside Finn's litter-crammed house, the vampire appeared on the roof. A surge of terror and shock made Rory drop the container. He took a step towards the window and stopped. Again, he feared what would happen if he were to shout a warning. He didn't know how safe he was from the thing, even in his house.

He watched as the vampire slunk from the roof and onto the wall, clinging on by a means he couldn't work out. Stretched out, the creature was enormous. While its toes touched near the peak of the roof, the tips of its claws were inches away from the top of the door.

With a fluid movement, it slithered down the wall and dropped onto the ground, next to Brendan.

Rory expected Brendan to scream, but he gaped up at the thing towering over him. Those huge, red eyes blazed in the torchlight. For the first time Rory saw its teeth, a row of long, neat, transparent needles.

For a long time, the man and the vampire locked stares, neither moved. A dim hope sprang in Rory that the thing would let Brendan go, even though Brendan showed no indication of trying to escape.

With maddening slowness, the vampire brought up its hands. Its fingers were half as long as Brendan's arms and the scything claws the length of his hands. Those fingers closed around Brendan's jaw, cradling his head, and distorting his face. Still Brendan didn't struggle or make a sound.

Rory became aware of the thumping in his ears. His chest was full to bursting and a thin trickle of tears escaped his eyes. Shame gnawed at the fear in his mind. He'd left Brendan to this, his cowardice hurt and made him feel smaller than he already did.

The vampire lifted Brendan up by the head. At last, the torch fell from Brendan's dangling hand and smashed. For a moment Rory was left staring at the shadows of a huge ape-thing holding a limp mannequin. The slashes of light from the street were enough to show him what happened next.

With the care of a parent cradling their newborn, the vampire carried Brendan through the open doorway, ducking to get through. It passed into shadow and was blocked from sight when it closed the door.

Rory stood, mesmerised, and horrified. He wiped his eyes and looked at the time. The sense of worthlessness and mortification had hardened, pushing back the fear and helping to form a plan. He wasn't going to go into Finn's house while it was dark.

If Brendan was right this thing had killed thousands of people over the centuries and it would kill even more while here. This was his chance to put a stop to it and make himself safer. To make up for not helping Brendan when he needed it.

He ran upstairs, into the spare bedroom. The old chair had been there for months, Jane had said she wanted rid of it numerous times. He was never so glad of his laziness.

The chair was broken but still too solid for him. He got the largest hammer they had and smashed off one of the legs. One end was a mass of splinters and while it would hurt wasn't practical for what he wanted.

He hoped this would work.

Woodworking wasn't something he had ever excelled at. It took him two hours, a broken carving knife and almost slashing his hand with two different chisels to get something resembling a decent point.

He waited in the kitchen, perched on a tall stool, watching Finn's door. Makeshift stake and hammer held in his hands, resting on his legs. For a while, he worried he would nod off, but the jittering energy in his body didn't allow even the hint of sleep.

An hour after sunrise he hopped down and went out of the back door. A few people moved through the street, going to work or exercising in the bright, early morning sunshine. None of them aware of the terrible danger that lurked within Finn's house, a few hundred feet away from them.

As he stood outside the back door, he heard his phone sing from the counter where he had left it. Jane's ringtone. He was tempted to go back and answer, but he decided he would make an excuse when she phoned again later.

At Finn's door, he stopped. It was slightly ajar. How long since he had last seen Finn? The day outside the supermarket and now the thing Finn had said made sense now. He crunched through the broken glass of Brendan's torch.

He pushed the door open with the head of the hammer. The foul smell rushed out in a thick wave and he coughed. He waited. No sounds of movement, Finn didn't call a question.

A minute to prepare himself and he walked into the dark, stinking kitchen. The floor was sticky with spilled food. Containers of all kinds were a field of trip hazards. More containers and things he could not recognise were piled to the ceiling. There were two conspicuously clear areas: the cooker and the sink. A single clean pot sat on the cooker and the sink was empty. A pile leaned close to the gas stove, a fire hazard to offset the strange neatness.

With great care, Rory picked his way along the narrow passage through the kitchen. Out of the kitchen were two directions, one led to the living room and the other to the stairs with their clutter of piled rubbish that looked like a series of ugly traps.

He decided to explore the living room. Columns of eclectic items reached the roof. In the middle of it all was a single larger clearing in which was a slumped armchair, an ancient, dark, portable CRT television and Finn. He sat straight up in the seat, unmoving.

"Finn?" Rory said and got no response.

Approaching slowly, partly out of reverence and partly to be sure he didn't stand on something that would make him roll over ankle, Rory saw Finn's eyes were open. The old man's skin was grey, and his eye sockets were dark. Flies marched across his face without a response. Rory almost jumped when Finn blinked.

"Finn. Come on, you need to get out," Rory said.

All Finn did was continue his shallow breathing. Rory, fearing he would regret it, shook Finn's shoulder. The man's head wobbled a little, but he didn't acknowledge anything had happened.

"It'll be okay, mate. I've got something to do and then I'll be back," Rory said, unconvinced Finn even heard him.

Going up the stairs presented the exact challenge he thought it would. Objects slipped under his feet, and unstable piles tumbled at him. He used the home-made stake to steady his ascent. He should have taken a torch. The windows were so filthy there wasn't enough light breaking through to see properly.

It felt like a miracle when he got to the top of the stairs without falling all the way to the bottom. There was even less light up here. Closed doors compounded with the dirt-clogged windows to create a realm of deep shadow.

As he had expected this proved to be his greatest challenge. So close to the thing, all but trapped upstairs by years of accumulated and neglected crap, his resolve started to waver. All the faith he'd built up in his plan, that felt unshakable after a sleepless night showed its true weakness. He wasn't a hero, he was just an unemployed fool who should have known better than to come in here. This display of will wasn't him at all, and now he was faced with two horrible options: go down the hazard-strewn stairs or push through the stinking first floor of Finn's house.

Indecision held him there like being snagged in a fishing net. He struggled and rethought, until he made the decision to go on, foolish or not.

He groped along one of the walls of rubbish, hoping there was a space for a light switch. No such luck. The air up here was damp and there was another stench the general stink couldn't cover. It could only be the smell of rotting corpses — the smell Finn spoke of. The flies up here were bolder, flying at him in droves.

A few steps to the side and he found a door. He pushed it open and the force of the smell of faeces made him vomit onto a nearby pile. The bathroom was cluttered, the bath and sink were unusable, and the piles crowded in on the toilet.

Even though the meagre light from the window was welcome, he was tempted to close the door to shut the disgusting smell away. He wanted the light more and he couldn't vomit any more.

The next door he opened offered him a wall of rubbish a few feet away. There was a passage through to the left. The windows in here were both filthy and blocked by more piles. The smell of rotting flesh was intense, and the crazed flies offered a palpable barrier.

He pushed through, stumbling and half-blind. He was afraid of falling, unsure of what disgusting stuff he would fall into.

The passage turned into the room, and he found there was a makeshift wall partitioning the middle. A pile of jar lids had fallen across the floor and there was a faded wall of plastic bags. Five bodies were strewn around the floor. All were wrinkled, and dried, while four were naked, all seethed with flies. He only recognised Brendan by his clothes, he was diminished, nothing more than a leather-robed skeleton. A glistening U-shaped series of wounds marred the corpse's neck. In the middle of the floor, lying on its side on a bed of stolen clothes was the vampire.

He stood next to the body of Brendan, regarding the creature. Even after every time he had seen it, he hadn't been prepared for how huge it was. Under the smooth, pale skin was ropy, powerful muscle. It was still, even more still than poor Finn downstairs. There wasn't even the hint of low breathing, and its large ears didn't twitch at his presence. It was unaffected by the masses of flies crawling across its body.

This close to the vampire, he paused again. Whatever passed for his bravery turned to liquid again. He looked back. There was still time and room to escape, but his conscience now bloomed, a flowering of obligation joined with his shame to make him act.

Rory couldn't ignore the flies and was spurred to move by the unpleasant feeling of hundreds of tiny legs skittering across his skin. A cloud erupted from him when he strode up to the vampire.

Its long arms were up around its head, exposing its side and chest. He felt his own chest and found his heart with ease.

Swiping flies away, he bent over the vampire. Quick glances at its face showed it remained asleep, dormant, or whatever it was. The large eyes were fixed shut. There was no reaction when he put the tip of his homemade stake against its chest where he guessed the heart should be. The skin was leathery and tough, and it took some effort to make a dent in it with the wood. His hand shook in time with his thundering heart, and he screwed his eyes shut to steady his nerves. His hands still shuddered.

He drew the hammer back and slammed it into the stake. The point of the stake pierced the skin an inch.

The thing moved. He was thrown across the room and crashed through the wall of plastic bags and bounced off another pile, closer to the actual wall. A band of pain encircled his ribs. He gasped and writhed on the floor. Points of red flashed in his vision in unison with each agonised breath.

He rolled onto his back and found the vampire looming over him. He cast around, hoping the stake was close by or that he was lying in the sun. He could see neither the stake nor a window.

Furious red eyes bored into him. They were so old and knowing. The weight of them stopped him from crying out or struggling, even as it leaned down and pierced his skin with its innumerable teeth.

#

Jane was only a little annoyed that Rory hadn't answered the phone. He was probably still asleep and not heard it. It was still before nine, after all. He would appreciate the surprise of her returning early. He wouldn't appreciate Laura for phoning and telling her about what he had been doing. She needed to think of something to help him cope with his situation.

"Rory!" she called when she walked in.

No answer.

"Rory! It's your wife! Time to wake up those lazy bones!"

Nothing. She left her luggage at the door and went upstairs. She ignored the open spare room door and went into their bedroom. Empty.

She decided to investigate the spare room. The chair he should have got rid off months ago was there, broken and surrounded by shards of wood, two chisels, and the carving knife twisted beyond use. She retreated, nursing a lot of questions.

"Rory! I'm getting really worried now!"

She hurried downstairs and after checking the living room and kitchen, found the back door open. Rory's phone was on the kitchen counter, with her missed call on full display.

Before she went out into the back garden, she knew Finn's door was open. The smell was too familiar. She looked around the garden and found no sign of Rory.

When she looked up, she saw Finn at his door. His skin was grey and his eyes sunken to the point his face looked like a skull. He looked at her without expression, which didn't change when she smiled at him.

"Hey, Finn," she managed to say. "You haven't seen Rory, have you?"

Instead of answering, Finn closed the door, leaving Jane in the garden, alone.

William Couper

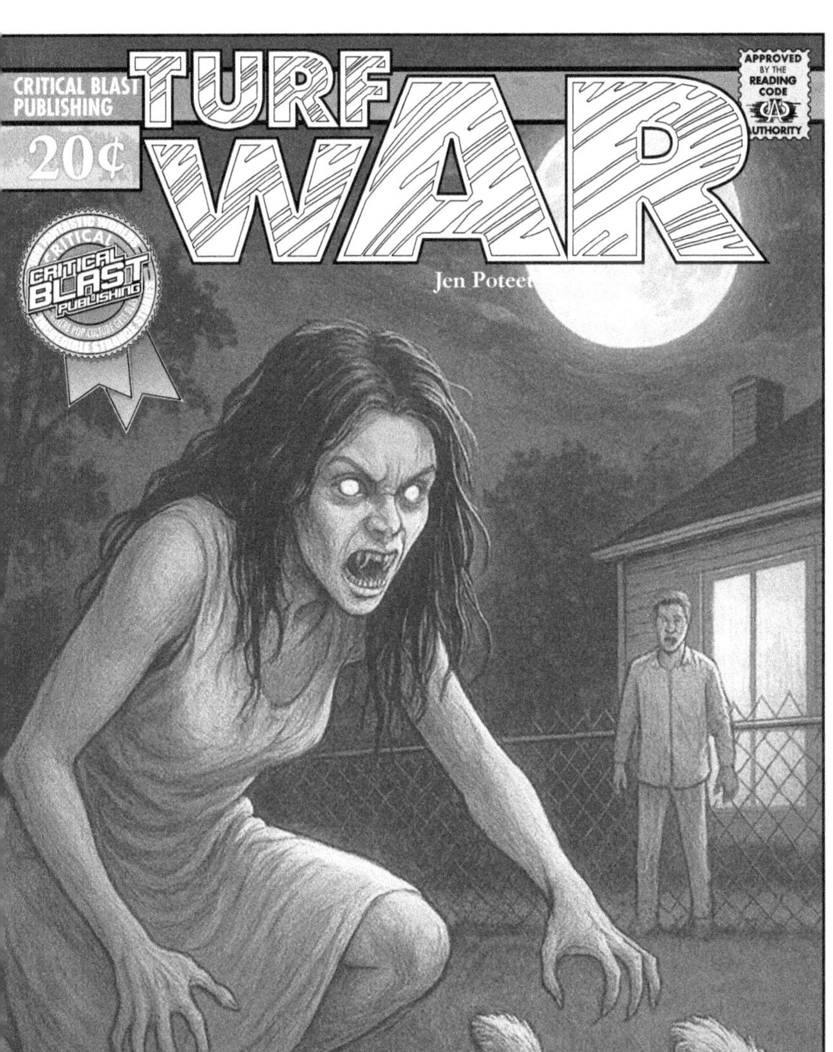

CRITICAL BLAST PUBLISHING
20¢
TURF WAR
Jen Poteet
APPROVED BY THE READING CODE AUTHORITY
CRITICAL BLAST PUBLISHING
TERRITORIAL BEASTS!

 SHOP BY KARATE KICK

HEAD KNIVES 100% stainless steal daggers that launch from the top of your head and kill any conversation you find boring.

FISH BOWL FULL OF WORMS Are you tired of eating meat? Get yourself a bowl full of yummy worms and feel you are saving the planet.

SUPER SECRET BOOK SAFE The special camouflage feature activates, once placed on the book shelf. You'll never find it again.

IT'S JUST A TUESDAY!

DIGITAL PUZZLE T-SHIRT Get people's undivided attention when they get engrossed trying to solve the constantly changing puzzles.

MONSTER VALUE STAMP
THIS IS IT! CLIP THEM & COLLECT THEM ALL!

DEFEAT BLACK MYSTIC ARTS KUNG-FU Tired of getting your ass kicked every Tuesday by Black Mystic Arts Kung-Fu fighters? CALL 666-HELP to enroll in self-defense training every Hellspawn should know to survive any dark alley encounter. Become a Ninth Circle Master of Judante!

RENT AN ANGRY WOLF! When you need to rip apart your competition, or when you need to look like a decent human concerned for dogs or something, something.

BOX OF LIVE BATS When you feel like a millionaire crime fighting hero and need to dress up your special cave, to give it that extra touch of atmosphere... a box of live bats is perfect for you. Food not included.

Jen Poteet has been romanticizing monsters since the 80's when she started watching the Double Creature Feature after her Saturday morning cartoons. She's never been afraid of the dark, instead has found herself more curious of what lurks there. She currently dwells in the foothills of the Blue Ridge mountains with her family, her home is practically an unofficial pet rescue and spends most of her time creating. Jen Poteet currently has four published works, appeared in multiple anthologies and online journals in no specific genre because she just loves words.

In a quiet community just outside of the suburban sprawl, birdsong fills the tree lines streets, dotted with upper middle-class single-family homes. On Saturday mornings, Lilith starts her day with an oat milk espresso macchiato made from a polished appliance perched on her gleaming granite countertop. She then breaks her fast with Sashimi style slivers of calf's liver, all the while admiring her floral landscaping and compiling a mental to-do list.

Her meal finished and waterproof clogs adorned, she slips a pair of designer gardening gloves over her spa manicure. Lilith then grabs a pair of pruning shears, before exiting the mud room door. With her heightened sense of smell, she easily avoids the logs of fecal matter littered along the edges of her peonies. Her hackles instantly raise with fury. The shears in her grip bend as she sees red. With deep breaths she attempts to use a coping skill her therapist taught her to help with her bouts of anger. But this is something Dr. Stu doesn't understand. This is an act of war.

In the midst of calming her imminent freak out, Lilith almost misses Thor and Zeus walking their human down the sidewalk. The Cane Corsos skid to a halt, sensing her ire. They crouch down and lower their giant brindle heads in submission.

"It's ok boys." She assures them and pulls out a few slivers of dried beef from her pocket. The dogs perk up with her praise and wag their tails.

Peter thought it was strange how his giant dogs acted like giant sissies around his neighbor. Even weirder was that the woman had pockets full of meat. His dogs seemed to like her just fine, though she kind of gave him the heebie-jeebies. He guessed she was somewhere middle aged, but probably has had some surgical help, because her skin is as smooth as a porcelain doll. The fact that she never smiles probably helps keep wrinkles away too.

"The Labradoodle at 4297 defecated in my flowers again." His neighbor's voice has an edge to it that makes the hair on his arms raise. Zeus and Thor whine.

"Aren't you President of the HOA? Can't you fine him?" The woman nagged him about a pink flamingo he stuck by his patio last summer, surely she can nag anyone to obedience.

Lilith's eyes flare. "My complaints are falling on deaf ears."

A shiver runs down Peter's spine as his fight or flight instincts kick in. "Well good luck with that!" He squeaks out before scampering off. Lucky for him she can control her prey drive and was too preoccupied with her current predicament to be enticed by a chase.

She could just break the dog's neck and be done with it she muses, however she would most likely be a suspect as many times she has breached the subject of doing something about this menace. The board was not amused when she suggested euthanasia. There is one avenue Lilith hasn't ventured. If she can't get through doing it the human way, she has no other choice but to follow her animal instincts. She isn't a puppy, and this isn't the first time she has dealt with unwanted attention. She just needed to send a reminder who the Alpha in this territory is

#

Chris wakes to the sound of his dog in an absolute uproar. He follows the clamor of furious barking to the kitchen, to look out his sliding glass door. He rubs the sleep from his eyes, to be sure he's not going crazy, before looking out again. There is a woman in his yard. The moonlight shines down on her, illuminating the white skin of her legs and bare ass as she holds the hem of her pale nightgown up to take a shit in his grass. He wonders if the edible he ate last night is still in his system, but as she turns to inspect her mess, he realizes he recognizes her pinched face.

It's the snobby bitch who keeps complaining about his dog. He opens the door, and Studmuffin leaps out in a flurry of brown fur and teeth. Chris follows, ready to confront the lunatic for trespassing, amongst other things. If she gets bitten, it's her own damn fault.

Before the dog can spring, Lilith has it in her clutches. She could easily rip the thing in half but then she would have to kill the human too, and that is not a mess she wants to deal with. She loves her house. She loves this neighborhood. She will not be scared away by some male who needs to learn its place.

The Labradoodle, unfortunately named Studmuffin, understands his grave mistake when the wolf's teeth are at his throat. He whines. He lowers his eyes. Anything to appeal to the Alpha.

Chris is horrorstruck. *Is she going to eat my dog? What the fuck is happening?*

When Lilith's low growl reaches his ears, his body reacts and he loses control of his bladder. As it leaks through the fabric of his pajamas, the acrid smell tickles her nostrils, reminding her that he is there. She releases the dog, who instantly rolls over to show his belly and subservience. Lilith then stalks closer to the human. His body trembles with fear, the scent of it heavy in the night air. Saliva drips from her mouth. Her jaw has distended, the change so close now, but she can keep it at bay with the moon only half full. Two weeks from now she will have no control, shedding her skin like a jacket. She knows her eyes glow as she looks directly into the human's, his pupils blown so wide they are completely black. "Tell anyone about this and I'll rip out both of your throats for real." Her voice is a thing of nightmares, deep and raspy. The beast inside of her is tearing to get out and feast on their entrails. She bares her teeth one last time.

Chris has never been so scared in his life. At the sight of the monster before him his body becomes overwhelmed with fear, he blacks out and crumbles to a pile on his lawn.

With a prim sniff, Lilith walks on bare feet back to her Dutch Colonial, satisfied the turf war was won. Delighted at this, and the night being young, she finds herself in the mood for a little snack. She takes a detour to the patch of trees adjacent to the neighborhood and goes for a hunt, her neighbors completely unaware that it could be their flesh she devoured instead of the wild hare she finds. Well... most of them of unaware.

Jen Poteet

CRITICAL BLAST PUBLISHING
20¢
Paradise Marsh
M.R. DeLuca
APPROVED BY THE READING CODE AUTHORITY
CRITICAL BLAST PUBLISHING
DELLA'S PAST LIES IN THE MUD

COCAINE FOR PETS When your pets become too excited during mating season and you don't want additional burden of feeding more pets, shot them up with some fine liquid snow and chill them out.

HEAD KNIVES 100% stainless steal daggers that launch from the top of your head and kill any conversation you find boring.

HYPNO-ROBOT use the special mind control eye harmonics to subdue the minds of your unwilling subjects. You'll never have to take out the trash and everyone will worship you as if their life depends on it.

1to1 MODEL PIRATE SHIP! Some assembly required. Glue NOT included. Recommend a private Island cove as the staging areo.

DIGITAL PUZZLE T-SHIRT Get people's undivided attention when they get engrossed trying to solve the constantly changing puzzles.

HOBO IN A BOX When your street is getting over-runned by homeless people and you need someone to speak their language and run them off to the next street down the block.

BECOME A PIRATE IN ONE WEEK! Learn to talk and kill like a Pirate. Optional hand and leg amputation. Pirate Ship sold separately. Arrrrr.

MAKE MINE MONSTERS!

LEARN TO PLAY THE GUITAR! When you can't get a date for the weekend, rent a sexy Guitar Teacher to impress your friends and maybe you just might learn something too.

M.R. DeLuca began storytelling at a young age and now has more than ten publishing credits across genres such as mystery, science fiction, horror, and humor. When not writing, she enjoys reading, needlepointing, and searching for the ultimate whoopie pie recipe. Visit her at mrdelucawriter.blogspot.com.

A sickly-looking woman knocked on the cottage's front door with one hand and balanced a covered dish in the other. "Hi, I'm Della Trowler. I just moved into the area yesterday and wanted to introduce myself."

A matronly woman answered and frowned slightly before audibly sniffing the air. Her features softened as she smiled. "I haven't had a whiff of that famous peach cobbler in years, but I'd know it anywhere. You must be Ginnie Trowler's daughter, all grown up. I'm Helen Ward, a friend of your Granny, heaven rest her soul. Please, come in."

"Actually, if you don't mind, I'd rather talk out here. Truth be told, I've just spent the past five months trapped indoors by cold and snow and could use some fresh air."

"That 'fresh air' you smell is pluff mud. It's the confluence of everything in the marsh— grasses, critters, fish. Anything and everything that's dead as a doornail and decomposing. Some outsiders complain it smells like rotten eggs, salt water, and spoiled seafood mixed together, but most of us are used to it, or downright like it."

Della cocked her head thoughtfully. "It doesn't smell bad to me. If anything, it's familiar and comforting, though I don't really remember ever smelling it before. I even don't remember ever being in South Carolina."

She chuckled. "If that isn't proof you come from around these parts, I don't know what is. Let me bring the food inside and I'll bring out something to drink. We can sit on the porch for a spell and chat. Now you set yourself down. I'll be back in a jiff."   She took the dessert and retreated into the clean but clearly antebellum cottage.

Della settled into an old wicker chair that was sturdier, and more comfortable, than it looked. She used the opportunity to take in the view, something she hadn't done much since she'd arrived.

What the marsh before her lacked for in trees, it made up for in plenty of grasses, wildlife, and mud. She didn't know any of the grass names—scientific, regional, or otherwise—but she could tell there were many kinds. They were tall, short, bright green, grayish green, yellow green—name the green and it was probably there. They swayed gently as the breeze blew or when the muddy waters from which they rose rippled with the tease of unseen animals underneath the surface. They grew in tight, thick clumps, making it impossible to see through them. What could be seen easily, though, were egrets and other birds wading through the shallower waters, every so often diving for crabs and oysters; sometimes they were successful, sometimes not. She couldn't decide which animal she was rooting for, or if she should morally even take sides.

And the mud... The pluff mud was everywhere, and made its presence known not just from its salty putrid smell but the unsightly brown lumps that dotted the wetland. It mounded above the waterline in places, browning the immediate area. A few feet away there would be clearer, or at least bluer, water, as well as graceful willow-like grasses and robust animals doing whatever they needed to do to survive. But from the little ecology she knew, she understood that nutrients in mud were fundamental to water-based ecosystems, and everything in the marsh would die without it. It was still mind-boggling how much beauty sprung from such ugliness.

She also couldn't help but think that for such a tranquil, picturesque place, it was very much alive and competitive.

Right when she resolved herself to the idea that the older woman wasn't returning and that it was time to head home, Mrs. Ward exited the house with a tray of drinks in her hands, and sat down on a nearby chair, leaving the screen door to bounce closed behind her.

"Mrs. Ward—"

"Ah-ah-ah, I'll stop you there. That was what everyone called my mother-in-law, and don't make an enemy of me off the bat by likening me to her! You'll do just fine with Miss Helen."

Miss Helen placed the tray of drinks on the table and took one, motioning for Della to do the same. She complied and took a sip. It was delicious. "This is delicious. Is it sweet tea, Miss Helen?"

"Yes, and probably the only thing I can make from scratch that's halfway worth consuming."

Della didn't know the woman well enough to say any platitudes that sounded sincere, so she opted not to say anything at all. They briefly sat in an awkward silence, just rocking in the two side-by-side wicker rocking chairs.

Miss Helen exhaled heartily. "We haven't seen you since you were small enough to hide in oyster grass. You look... different. And I didn't see you move in, neither." She grimaced. "I usually know everything that goes on around the marsh."

Della retired the glass to the tray. "I came in pretty stealthily, in all honesty. I didn't arrive in the Lowcountry until twilight, and I didn't use a moving van or anything like that. Everything I have fit in a suitcase and a couple of bags. As you know, Granny's—well, now my house—is off the main road to boot. It'd be more surprising if you did see me."

"Makes sense, I reckon." She took another sip and pursed her lips. "How are your parents?"

"Mom and Dad died a few years back of idiopathic illnesses. You know, when they can't name what's wrong and it becomes the old 'doctors are idiots who don't know the pathology' thing? I think I've inherited that from them, unfortunately. I feel like I'm wasting away, aimless and weak. I can't even keep a job for long because I've battled unnamed health problems since I was little—" She stopped herself. "I'm so, so sorry, Miss Helen. We just met and I shouldn't be unloading on you like this."

Miss Helen placed her smooth hand over Della's free one. "Sugar, your Granny was a pillar of this community, a model citizen, and my dearest, oldest friend. And you are her only grandchild. If lending you my ear helps you in even the smallest way, it is my privilege to do just that."

The sentiments were as sweet as the tea, but something troubled Della. It was the woman's hand. If she was friends for a long time with her own grandmother, who just died at 108, shouldn't it be wrinkled? She averted her eyes quickly, though, when Miss Helen caught her staring.

"So how did you come to know about your Granny's house?" the older woman prompted. "I recollect when you and your mama and daddy lived with her in that big old house. But you were too young to remember, and your parents never would've told you."

Interesting that she knew enough about her parents to know that. A gift and curse of small towns, she guessed. "Granny's lawyer contacted me to say she died and, because my parents were already gone, I'd inherited her house. I immediately decided to pack up and leave. Nothing and nobody was keeping me in Utah.

"So I quit my dead-end job I was about to lose anyway for too many absences, loaded up my junker, praying that it'd last the trip, and drove cross-country. I picked up the keys from the lawyer and came straight here."

"Was his name Percival Higgins?"

"Yes."

"Percy has an office in Charleston and a satellite office here, though he's been spending most of his time here lately since he's semi-retired. He's lived here his whole life, too. He's good people."

Della couldn't tell if Miss Helen meant that he was good people because he lived in the area his whole life, or if those were two separate statements. She didn't want to ask.

"But I will have to talk to him. I know he took an oath to uphold the law and keep clients' confidences, but nevertheless he should've warned us that a potential outsider was coming in."

Della shifted uncomfortably. She wanted to change the subject, desperately. "To my knowledge, you're my closest neighbor, which is why you're my first stop on my self-introductory tour. Is everyone spread so far apart? Like with Granny's place, I barely could see your cottage until I was practically on top of it."

The woman nodded wisely. "Our houses in this part of the region are set back farther from the road than most others. We like our privacy here. And though we don't have many trees, the ten-foot common cattails also help keep us hidden away from prying eyes."

She sipped some more sweet tea and looked Della straight in the eye. Her shrewd glean was unnerving. "So, level with me, Della, darling. Are you plan on staying, selling...?"

"I wouldn't sell." A rent-free place to live while she tried figuring out her life? She would hold onto it, for at least a while.

"That's good. Doubt you'd get much for it even if you tried. Almost nobody moves in, in part because almost nobody moves out.

"You can have a good life here, if you embrace it. The people, the marsh, the lifestyle. I never understood why your parents left it all behind. Scratch that, I do, but I don't. Does that make sense, hon? You know what, just ignore an old woman's ramblings.

"Since you're staying, let's get you acquainted with the area. Or rather, reacquainted."

"Are we visiting other folks? I have more cobblers at home." Della had made six that morning, having woken up unusually rested and energized, which was especially surprising after driving ten hours a day for four days straight.

"We'll see about that later. I'm referring to the four-mile boardwalk stretching across the marsh. I don't think you've seen it yet, as it's down a ways. It starts here and ends at the small public beach one town over. We invariably see the occasional stray tourist who takes the walk as a fitness challenge, but for the most part it's a quiet and pleasant way to see what makes the marsh so special to the people around here."

Della bit her lip. "I'm not sure I'm well enough to traverse one mile, let alone four."

"We'll only go as far as you think you're able. Come, you'll see. I'm not taking no for an answer."

Miss Helen effortlessly rose and opened the screen door and then the front door. She called into the house, "Norm, I'm going out into the marsh for a bit! Going to show the Trowler girl around. She came back yesterday."

"Trowler? Haven't heard that name in years! I'm skinning fish right now so I'll meet her properly at the next boil, if she's still around." He paused. "And Helen, keep an eye out for Saturday! It'll be here before you know it."

"Will do!" She turned to Della. "Let's go, hon. Follow me."

The two women strolled in silence as they followed the edge of the marsh. When a long, narrow boardwalk finally came into view, Miss Helen gestured to it and said, "There it is."

Della did not want to go on it. It was worn and eroded, and she couldn't even see the end, which disappeared into the distance. "Is it safe? It looks really, really... used."

"Used and old," she replied proudly. "I like to think of it as a metaphor for our marsh—if you take care of it, it'll last for the ages." She took the first step and, although the boards creaked under her feet, she walked with confidence.

Reluctantly, Della followed.

The first stretch of boardwalk had barely a three-foot railing. When they moved too close to the walk's edge, the tips of the smooth cordgrass that sprang up tall from the marsh below would tickle their feet. Every once in a while Miss Helen would stop and point out an osprey, a fiddler crab, even a small alligator. She spoke about the harmony and energy that pervaded the area, and acted as it were perfectly natural to be nary six feet from many creatures that wouldn't hesitate to attack or even eat them if given the chance.

The farther along they walked, the calmer Della became. With each step she was invigorated all the more. It no longer mattered that the boardwalk seemed endless; she felt like she could keep walking forever.

She said, "I can see why you say Granny was so involved. She must have truly loved it here. I'm not sure why my parents never returned, or why they left in the first place."

Miss Helen exhaled as a shadow passed over her face. It was so brief that if Della had blinked she would have missed it. "It's complicated. As is most of life, I guess."

"They never spoke about living in the Lowcountry, and I wouldn't have known about my grandmother or her house if I hadn't received the letter from Mr. Higgins. I figure something really, really bad must have happened here. Do you perhaps know what that was?" Della said the last part hyper-casually.

Miss Helen laughed mirthlessly. "You need to spend some time with Norm, because that is some fishing you're doing right now. And I will tell you, but let's walk a bit more first."

Della was so further awash in serenity and potency that, by the time the railing abruptly stopped, she wasn't even nervous. In the middle of a marsh, sauntering down barely seven-foot-wide wooden planks, with strange animals and foliage all around, and miles of boardwalk open on both sides before her; and here she was, feeling as strong as she ever had. It was incredible.

She didn't realize she had walked so far ahead until Miss Helen finally spoke again, interrupting her thoughts. The voice came from behind her, so she turned around to see the older woman with her hands open and pressed together. "Della, stop. I can't do this. I see how you are now, how your whole demeanor and even complexion just changed with this short walk on the marsh. You need to know the truth. We need to talk."

"Excuse me?" Della had to reorient her frame of mind to try to make sense of what she just heard.

The woman sighed. "Your parents, they had a, a crisis of conscience. That's why they left our colony."

Della was now dizzy with confusion, and planted herself firmly in the middle of the walk, lest she listed sideways headfirst into the marsh. "What bothered them? And did you say 'colony'?"

"Your mama and daddy, may they rest in peace, would disagree with me, for sure. But I think you need to know your heritage." Her eyes softened, as did her voice. "Land sakes, I can't believe they went to their graves without telling you.

"See, I fully blame your parents on this. If they had just told you when you were young like everyone else does, you'd be used to it by now and wouldn't find what I'm about to tell you strange. But no, instead they whisk you away and deny you your birthright."

"Miss Helen, I have no idea what you're talking about."

"Everyone who lives around the marsh— We're like the cordgrasses: tough, hard to uproot, and we stick together. For the most part, anyway.

"This marsh is a special place. It is harsh and doesn't seem fair all the time, and but it survives and thrives because we allow it to. And in turn, it takes care of us. We are its keepers, and we take this job very seriously."

Della tried to keep her face as placid as possible, but her warbled voice betrayed her nerves. "All right. I believe you."

The woman glared. "No, you don't. And don't look at me like I'm serving you barbecue without any sauce. What I say is not crazy, though you may think so." She visibly steeled herself. "It is our responsibility, our duty to do whatever it takes to keep this marsh alive and well. Why? It's because I was born from this pluff mud. Your grandmother was born from this pluff mud. Your parents were born from this pluff mud. *You* were born from this pluff mud."

Della stared at the older woman.

"Maybe I'm getting a little too poetic. I'll spell it out plainly." She didn't blink. "We are alive only by the grace of this marsh, and its pluff mud and its grasses and its animals and everything else it gives to us. Our people are marsh people. We are a distinct, unique, proud race of people. Sweetie, everyone here is a Marshian."

Della nearly burst out laughing, but thought twice when she noted the grave demeanor Mrs. Ward retained. "A 'Marshian'? That's a real term?"

"Yes. Some say Marshites, but it doesn't matter what you call us." She shrugged. "There're a lot of us out there, and we have many cousins too, though almost nobody strays from their respective bodies of water. Some are from swamps or bayous or bogs or mires. We're not all of the same species, but we're similar enough."

Now Della was sick to her stomach. "Are you telling me that I'm not really human?"

"Your parents were so stubborn. They died pretending to be purely human. We might be descended from them, but we certainly don't have the same needs. We are completely intertwined with the health of this marsh. If it declines, or we move too far away from it to regularly drink its water and eat its food, we become ill. That's why your parents were ailing and died young, and why you are sickly, too. You've been feeling better since you came back here, haven't you? Probably drank some water last night, brushed your teeth with it, too?

Breathed in the salty air? You're already less pale than when we started this walk."

The gears shifted in Della's mind. Could that be why she felt like she was on death's door for as long as memory served her? Could it all be cured by moving to the marsh?

The woman didn't need to say a word. "I say your thoughts playing out on her face. It's all making sense now, isn't it?" said Miss Helen, relaxed and with a small smile. "Yes, the marsh gives us not just nutrients, though. It gives us life! Vitality! Vim and vigor! Our people usually live ninety-plus years, and healthy ones, too. That's because of the symbiotic relationship we have with our marsh."

Della was becoming a believer. If she helped take care of the marsh, it would help take care of her, and she certainly felt that she needed to be taken care of. The promise of health was just too tantalizing to walk away from. If she did, she'd be instead walking toward an early grave, like her parents. "So what is it that I'd have to do? How do I, we, take care of the marsh?"

"We feed it."

"That sounds alright. What do we feed it?"

"People."

Della instinctually took a step backwards. "I'm sorry, did you just say people?"

"Yes, because it needs large amounts of organic matter and there are only so many large animals here. There aren't that many gators, you'll be happy to know. Oh, don't worry! I don't mean us! Marshians are never fed to the marsh until after their deaths or unless they misbehave, as in do something that can harm the marsh or other Marshians. There's not many of us to begin with, anyway. It's usually strangers, sweetie. People expect tourists to get lost in marshlands like this, so their vanishings fly under the radar. In fact, it'd be weirder if they didn't disappear at all.

"We make it a point to feed the marsh on the regular. At midnight on the days of each seasonal solstice, we hold a Lowcountry boil for our marsh community. It's a big hullabaloo, with plenty of lookouts, and that's when we take the chosen sacrifice into the deepest thickets of seven-foot sawgrasses, or a deep trough of pluff mud, and give the corpse to the marsh. Then we boil some marsh water, pluck some grasses, catch some fish and shellfish, and reward ourselves with a good-old fashioned boil, where we each are reinforced with a heaping dose of life-extending, age-slowing marsh goodness into our bodies. To prove it, do I look 97 to you?"

Della's jaw dropped. "More like 67! Wow." She wondered. "Is there a reason it has to be at midnight, and do you always use tourists?"

"I don't know who came up with the schedule, but we've always used it and it seems to work. And you don't want the littlest kids there, anyway. It's dark and crowded and they don't have the sense not to fall headfirst into a gator's mouth, if you know what I mean.

"If anyone else comes along in the interim times, like businesspeople looking to develop land, or beachgoers who decide to trek across the whole walk and stumble upon our area and stay too long, then the marsh just gets fed more often. It doesn't hurt it. And sometimes we don't need to kill the humans first, if we're lucky enough to catch them off-guard and shove them into the pluff mud. It's like quicksand, you know, so they'll either suffocate to death or the gators will get them and when the marsh feeds on the gators, the cycle continues."

"So, you're saying when you give life to the marsh, the marsh gives life to you?" Life was sounding really good to Della, because hers had been a struggle for so long.

"Which is the point, I mean. The marsh is both life-giving and life-taking. It's dependent on us, and we're dependent on it."

"So what happens if you can't find someone in time for the quarterly boil?"

"That's never happened before. There's always a tourist even in the off-season, or prospective developers snooping into land and property rights in hopes of building over the marsh."

"Do you take turns, um, capturing?"

Miss Helen smiled. "Taking notes, I see. There is no one designated person, so it's more like a team effort. Anyone who wants to join in the selection process can."

Della quieted. She had one final question before she wholeheartedly committed to this new life. "So why did my parents leave?"

Miss Helen looked down at her feet briefly before regaining her confidence. "We're not total isolationists. We graduate from school, we work in Charleston, and we have some, albeit limited, interactions with non-Marshians on a regular basis.

"One day some of us brought in a man we killed on the beach. He was a surfer, but the Marshians who made the selection hadn't recognized him as a local, so they figured him for a tourist. Turns out he was an old high school friend of your parents. Nice guy, they said, and they'd seen him in Charleston not long before. He had recently seen some movie and was taking up surfing, so they had told him of a nice quiet beach where he could practice, not thinking anyone here would mistake him for a visitor.

"We tend to keep track of our non-Marshian neighbors to avoid them and the ensuing press circus and investigations that could eventually descend on us. His disappearance caused a commotion in the region for a while, and was a close call for us, but it really affected your parents. They blamed themselves, and the marsh, and us for his death. So while most were at the boil, in the dead of night they fled your Granny's house, stole you away from us, and left forever. And they knew it would kill them, but didn't care. Their grief, their guilt, was too strong.

"It broke your Granny's heart, but they never returned. She loved them, and you, and I think that's why she willed you her home instead of to another Marshian. She wanted to give you the option of returning to your roots."

"I want to come back." The words flew out of her mouth before she could even think them. It was inexplicable, but every fiber of her being cried out to stay, even after learning what she had to do in order for that to happen. "I want to be a true Marshian."

Miss Helen stepped forward and gave the younger woman a quick, firm hug.

"I'm so glad you passed the test! You don't know how much I really, truly am! I knew I had to do my duty, but I was hoping for the off-chance that your time in the outside world wouldn't have irreversibly corrupted you, that if you'd come back, you would want to stay and be part of us. Oh joy! You being Henry and Ginnie's daughter and all, and your Granny's sole grandchild, it would've broken my heart if you'd said you want to leave or sell. I would've had to serve you up to the marsh!"

Della swallowed hard. Now the suggestion to take a casual walk along the marsh made sense: an isolated boardwalk, a hip-high railing on some stretches and no barrier in others, Miss Helen walking behind her for a while.

"Don't take it personally. It's nothing you did. Your parents threw us all for a loop, that's all. They were the only ones in recent memory who'd have ever left. So after that, we just all collectively decided not to let the same mistake happen twice. If anyone else tried to leave for the outside world, we couldn't risk them letting others know about our paradise, though admittedly the chances of anyone believing them would be small. And if anyone had the misfortune to wander here or try moving into our area without our approval, well, they were a liability, too."

"I just want to mention again, I am going to live here and be a part of the Marshian colony. I'm not going anywhere." Della genuinely wanted to stay, but she figured it wouldn't hurt to reiterate that fact again.

"Praise the marsh, you're finally home! Everyone else will be thrilled, too, when I introduce you at the Saturday boil." Miss Helen beamed like a proud mother at her prodigal daughter. "And you'll be healthy as a horse in no time at all."

Any vestigial hesitation melted away. "So I'll get better quickly?"

Miss Helen grasped Della's hands. "You should, honey, you should. Drink plenty of water in the meantime. I'll have Norm send over some fish, and don't fret, the next solstice is this weekend." She laughed softly. "You've arrived just in time. It's like you were called."

Della was, morbidly, curious. "So, do you have, um, someone picked out yet?"

"Not yet. We tend to get them fresh, usually the week of. With the beach and the boardwalk there're usually good pickings. Dusk and dawn are best because there are fewer witnesses."

Duly noted. "Am I too much of a novice to help?"

Miss Helen grinned. "No, no, of course not. We love enthusiasm for the community, and the marsh, of course. Think of it as your initiation, too."

Della looked out at the marsh. A peace settled over her as she surveyed the grasses and mud piles that shrouded countless bodies. She could empathize with her parents on an intellectual level, but she couldn't fully understand why they'd given up everything for someone who wasn't even a Marshian. Life was never fair; it was a zero-sum game. Someone had to win, and someone had to lose, and if she had her druthers, the latter wouldn't be her. If there was a good opportunity that presented itself to her, she'd take it gladly. "I think I'm going to be happy here."

Miss Helen slid her arm into her new protégé's and carefully turned herself and Della around. The two walked blissfully down the boardwalk and back toward the shore. "Now, let's talk logistics. I know it'll be your first time helping with the choice, but there are little tips and tricks you need to know for picking out a nice juicy one..."

-(249)-

CRITICAL BLAST PUBLISHING
20¢
The New NEIGHBORS
Lena Ng
APPROVED BY THE READING CODE AUTHORITY
CRITICAL BLAST PUBLISHING
THEY'RE OUT OF THIS WORLD!

DEFEAT BLACK MYSTIC ARTS KUNG-FU Tired of getting your ass kicked every Tuesday by Black Mystic Arts Kung-Fu fighters? CALL 666-HELP to enroll in self-defense training every Hellspawn should know to survive any dark alley encounter. Become a Ninth Circle Master of Judante!

SNAKES IN A MAIL BOX Get these total mother-f$%Ken poisonous snakes and mail them with your get well gift cards.

STICK IT TO YOUR ENEMIES! Real Voodoo Doll! Guaranteed Quality checked by the finest Witch Doctors! Send lock of hair and a SASE to DUDAT VOODOO, Box 9, Haiti.

SUPER SECRET BOOK SAFE The special camouflage feature activates, once placed on the book shelf. You'll never find it again.

SUPER SHARP PIRATE SWORD When you want to capture the hearts and minds of the people around you, this sword will cut through the muscle and bone to get to the vital organs you need to sustain your hunger.

WELCOME MAT TRAP When you don't want people annoying you, a simple press of the button and the trap door will dispose of anyone who stands on it, while waiting for you to answer the door.

RENT ANGRY MONSTERS! When you need to stop a Bully from harassing, or when you need to look like a decent human concerned for poor ugly monsters.

Lena Ng roams the dimensions of Toronto, Canada, and is a monster-hunting member of the Horror Writers Association. She has curiosities published in weighty tomes including Amazing Stories and Flame Tree's Asian Ghost Stories and Weird Horror Stories. "Under an Autumn Moon" is her short story collection.

"Don't open the door," said Mabel, as she peered through the lace curtains at the strangely gelatinous form on the porch. It stood a little over six feet tall and gave off a serenely pulsing, phosphorescent glow. At its feet was a green puddle of slime which dripped off one side of the porch and started to turn the grass yellow. "I think it's the Jehovah's again."

"Don't be ridiculous," Harold, her husband replied, scratching the hairy bit of belly that escaped from his yellowed undershirt. Despite the length of their marriage, he still wondered at how Mabel was able to get up every morning without getting lost in the bathroom. "That thing's got two heads." He started down for the basement. "I'm gonna get the gun."

When Harold returned, he opened the rickety screen door with shotgun at the ready.

The two-headed creature moved its mouths in twin approximations of a smile. "Greetings, Earthlings, we're your new neighbours. I'm Klaxon and here is my brother..." he nodded toward his other head, "...Klang." He tapped a tentacle on the porch as Harold's stare stretched out. "Aren't you going to invite us in for hydration? We come bearing gifts."

Harold glanced at the tentacles which bore no gifts. The twin smiles grew wider which did nothing to put Harold at ease. "Get off my porch."

"Now, now, dear." Mabel patted her hair curlers. "They're just trying to be friendly. And they've come all the way from"— she looked at the two green, blob-like faces—"wherever they've come from. We want to be good neighbours. Remember old Mrs. Jessop? You couldn't wait 'til that woman died. We don't want something like that to happen again."

Harold didn't lower the weapon. The silence seemed to draw out over the horizon into the glooming twilight. Finally, he gestured with the gun to one of the white, plastic chairs. "We'll sit outside."

The new neighbours slimed their way across the porch. It took awhile as the human hosts stood frozen. "Relax, human male...it's male, isn't it?" Klaxon asked.

Harold answered with a glare.

"We mean you no offence if you are nonbinary. We ourselves are nontrinary." Klaxon waggled a tentacle in what he thought was a soothing gesture. "You may put down your primitive weapon. If we had wanted to obliterate you, we would have done so by now." He fitted his form into the seating receptacle.

Slowly, Harold took his finger off the trigger and propped the gun against the plastic porch table. "What is it that you want?"

"Just wanted to introduce ourselves, neighbour to neighbour. Your names are..."

Harold spoke over crossed arms resting on his protuberant belly. "Harold. This is my wife, Mabel."

Klaxon put out a tentacle which Mabel gingerly shook. Each round, quarter-sized sucker disengaged with a gentle pop. "We hope to clear up any misgivings before they arise. We've read how humans fear what they don't understand. Practice our Earth skills, try to fit in." The tentacles' suckers opened and shut rhythmically. "No worries, Earthlings, we have extensively studied your culture..."

"By watching decades upon decades of television..." his brother finished.

"So we are familiar with your social rituals." Klaxon continued. "We know how suspicious humans are of aliens, extraterrestrial or otherwise. Don't worry, we're not here to probe you—"

"—Or eat you—"

"Klang and I understand consumables should be unmoving..."

"With the exception of cats."

"*Sshhhhh*, Klang." Klaxon gave a quick shake of his jelly-like head. "Haha, just a little joke. We know cats – and humans—are strictly off limits as consumables." The table wobbled against his mass. "We are only here for academic purposes. Not because we destroyed our own planet with the overconsumption of fossil fuels, thus altering its climate to an intolerable temperature which forced some of us to look for resources on other planets, then upon our return, unwittingly unleashed a terrible virus upon the rest of the population—"

"Definitely not," Klang added.

"No," Klaxon said, "we're here strictly for curiosity and research, just in case we need to preserve your species once it heads for the brink of extinction..."

"Which we hope is not anytime soon," said Klang, "since we haven't seen Hamilton yet."

Mabel brought out some glasses of water. She set down one glass in front of Klaxon, paused, then decided to set another down in front of Klang. The alien wound a tentacle around the glass, and then slowly doused it over its skin. "Ah, delicious hydration. Keeps the slime in working order."

Harold slapped a mosquito with a meaty hand. "So where are you from exactly?"

Klaxon waved a tentacle in the general direction of the sky.

As Klaxon conversed with Harold, Klang turned his attention to Mabel. "What about your offspring? How many revolutions of the Earth are they?"

Mabel pursed her thin lips. "Excuse me?"

"You know, around your puny sun?"

"They're twenty-seven and twenty-four years old, if that's what you're asking."

Klang raised his brow ridges in delight. "And what flavours are they?"

Klaxon bent a tentacle to elbow his brother. "We understand we are not to ask what flavours children come in. We know you do not devour your weak ones."

Klang looked disappointed. "You wouldn't happen to know the whereabouts of any delicious cats, do you?"

Klaxon clamped a tentacle over Klang's mouthpart. "We do not eat cats nor humans nor harvest their planet for resources because we can't get our act together back home. How many times do I have to tell you?" Klaxon spoke around Klang's head to Mabel. "Anyway, if we eat anything off limits, please be sure to advise us."

Klang reached into the depths of his globules and pulled out something that started squirming under the green slime. "We have brought you a gift from our planet." He squeegeed off some of the slime from the glass container. "Don't mind the plasma coating. It is only there for preservation." He placed it on the table. "Apply directly to the forehead," he added helpfully at the neighbours who seemed to have been hit by a freeze-ray.

Mabel made a face. Klang stretched his neck to examine it more closely. He blinked his three eyes an inch away from her expression. "That looks like fear. Am I right? Fear, isn't it?" he asked, turning his head towards his brother.

"Earthlings are so difficult to read," agreed Klaxon. "Where we're from, it's pretty simple. When we're purple, we're afraid, and we squirt an ink jet and disappear from our enemies. When we're angry, our skin turns red. Then we start obliterating." He fanned out his tentacles. "Now, how can we make you feel more comfortable?"

Harold flinched at the round mouth and rows of teeth that was suctioned onto the glass container's side. "First, you can put that away." The jar disappeared back into the amorphic entity. Harold pulled at his stubbled, double chin. "Now that the kids aren't here, we'll be needing some help around the house. New neighbours generally mow their neighbour's lawns for the first year. As a sign of neighbourly good faith. They also help with watering the garden, cleaning the eavestroughs, power washing the siding..."

Klaxon nodded sagely. "I see. To trim the herbaceous vegetation on your property is a sign of law and order?"

"Something like that. As well, Mabel needs a weekly ride to her doctor's appointment."

Klaxon tapped opposing tentacles together. "If she is somehow defective, you can always get a new one."

Harold hesitated a moment before sneaking a glance at Mabel and her curlers. "Doesn't work that way here."

Klaxon leaned forward and rested part of his blob on the table. He spoke in a conspiratorial whisper. "On our planet, the female dies after she lays her eggs. Then we get a new one. Can we be of assistance?"

Harold grunted. "I think I'll be ok."

"She'll have fresh slime and extra curly tentacles..."

"Ummm, no."

"You don't know what you're missing." Klaxon looked disappointed. "So, after these tests, we'll be accepted into your neighbourhood?"

"On a trial basis. How good are you guys at repairing roofs?"

Klaxon's head gave a quiet slosh as he thought over the question. "I've repaired a Bonegrinder 4000 before. Remember that, Klang?"

The phosphorescent green on Klang's face glowed a little brighter. "How could I forget? When that Habozorian got stuck and all those limbs were flailing around..." Laughter burbled in small bubbles alongside his gills. "Good times."

Klaxon emitted his own bubbles before turning back to Harold. "Now for some getting-to-know-you questions. Which sport's team do you empathise with? What's your favourite fish? Have you mastered time travel? Have you signed any contracts with extraterrestrial creatures for exploitations of your rare earth minerals? And, most importantly, do you think we will fit in? Be honest." The slime started to sizzle the plastic in anticipation.

Mabel lent a woman's scrutinizing eye to her guests. "Well..." she said, "you could start off by wearing pants."

"What do you think, Klang? Need we get these so-called pants?"

"Let's not rush into things, Klaxon. What other species on this planet wears pants?"

"My brother does have a point, Mabel. Maybe it is you who doesn't need pants."

Harold shook his head. "No, on Earth, pants are almost a necessity. Helps to keep out the cold. You have so many things to learn. Maybe you'd better write this down."

After another glass of hydration and much shaking of tentacles, bowing, head bobbing, and waving, the new neighbours headed back next door. They fixed some snacks, settled onto their couch, and turned on the television.

"Do you think Harold was being truthful about mowing his lawn and pants-wearing? I've heard humans can be a deceptive bunch," said Klang, as he started on his second cat.

Klaxon shrugged what could have been shoulders and reached for his own cat. "When on Earth…"

CRITICAL BLAST PUBLISHING
20¢
APPROVED BY THE READING CODE AUTHORITY
YOUR REPTOID REPRESENTATIVE
Elon Litchfield
DOUGLAS FOR MAYOR
SNAKES IN POLITICS!

HUMAN MASK When you need to walk among the humans, without being singled out as a monster. Get this mask in black, white or polka-dot, to blend right in!

SUPER SHARP PIRATE SWORD When you want to capture the hearts and minds of the people around you, this sword will cut through the muscle and bone to get to the vital organs you need to sustain your hunger.

SUPER SECRET BOOK SAFE The special camouflage feature activates, once placed on the book shelf. You'll never find it again.

COCAINE FOR PETS When your pets become too excited during mating season and you don't want additional burden of feeding more pets, shot them up with some fine liquid snow and chill them out.

LAST MAN ON EARTH HEARD A KNOCK AT THE DOOR!

HELIUM GAS & BALLOON SET Get away from the day to day grind of your boring life and steal a whole house while the owners are away.

BOX OF LIVE BATS When you feel like a millionaire crime fighting hero and need to dress up your special cave, to give it that extra touch of atmosphere... a box of live bats is perfect for you. Food not included.

RADIOACTIVE CANDY When you want to level up your personality and appear extra sweet to the people around you... and want to have a superpower over sugar... this candy's for you!

HEAD KNIVES 100% stainless steal daggers that launch from the top of your head and kill any conversation you find boring.

EXPLODING DRINK Sit back and enjoy the highjinks as people unscrew their drink activating the chemical reaction, causing a foamy mess.

Elon Litchfield lives in North Carolina with a mixed-species family of small mammalian carnivores. He writes a little science-fiction, a bit of fantasy, some humor, and a lot of horror. While he appreciates Godzilla, Tyrannosaurus Rex, and green iguanas, he is not himself a reptoid, and no one can prove otherwise.

Nancy Rodriguez walked into David Douglas's office ready to explode.

Douglas was dead even with John Ford in the polls.

The pressure was on. Everyone expected her to have the perfect answer to the crisis. For the voters, the choice seemed a no-brainer since business was good, unemployment was low, crime was down and the program to address the homeless situation was taking off. The city flourished. But there were outrageous groups voicing other concerns, ones involving a specialized perception of the preservation of history and heritage mixed with a seasoning of internet-spawned hidden agenda conspiracies.

Nancy was the spinmeister of Douglas's court, the illusionist in charge of combating the conjured phantasms of John Ford and his constituents. And when the problems came from their own staff, she was the campaign's exorcist.

And a newbie.

Apprenticed to the master Josh Hunter at the start of Douglas's campaign, the man suddenly retired due to health concerns. All his responsibilities fell on her, and she had hit the ground running.

It was a strain on everything in her life; her romantic relationship, her family, her health, even her cat.

But she was committed. Dedicated. There to the end. Not some rat to abandon the ship.

Douglas looked at her. "I'm planning to reveal something. Something that will affect the election."

It doesn't matter what it is, she thought.

Douglas released a long sigh. "And it will come as a shock to everyone."

Nancy almost smiled. Although still new to the chess game of politics, the master Josh Hunter had been her tutor. Unless her boss committed outright murder or some other shocking crime, nothing couldn't be handled.

"Nancy, I'm a reptoid."

She gave up. Everything was hopeless.

If the opponent held weird conspiracy beliefs it was one thing, but when the person you're fighting for went all *non compos mentis* it was different. It wasn't covered in her political campaign grimoire.

Douglas stood up, not imposing since the man wore colorful bowties and ill-fitting suits over his lean five-foot three-inch frame. She recalled that Hunter had remarked it helped create an image of humbleness and honesty.

"Please listen, I can prove what I'm saying. But I need you to be calm. Accepting."

She held up her hand. "Sir, I'm familiar with Icke's influence on the conspiracy circuit with the whole UFO alien race world domination thing, but I can't help you if you have similar delusions. This goes beyond Ford's usual range of kooky conspiracy proclamations. There's real world issues and then this nutso-bozo crazy bull-bull-bull-" Nancy took in a deep breath, the word needed to be said. "*Bullshit* that makes the process nothing more than a psycho-circus play. My experience is in dealing with actual campaign issues. Not this hysterical stupid crazy-" She took a deep breath. "S-s-shit."

Nancy was sure she was fired.

Her boss gave her a slim smile. "Nancy, look at me."

She did.

The candidate held up his right hand, snaped his fingers, and his features melted away.

The David Douglas that Nancy knew now had pale green scales all over his face and hands, his hazel eyes transformed into bright yellow, and round pupils became thin black slits. The lips were almost nonexistent, but her boss still had on the pinstriped gray suit and goofy brightly colored bowtie.

"This is me, Nancy. The real me. I'm not from outer space. I'm not part of a grand conspiracy to take over the world. I don't eat people. Those like me aren't planning on subjugating humans to become a slave race. I am intelligent part of this planet, just like monkeys, whales, elephants, crows, and humans. One of its children. I think people need to know."

Nancy retreated into a memory from a leadership seminar a few years back. It was called You Go, You! (which sounded suspiciously like the title of an anime show she watched as a child) lead by the motivational speaker guru Skip Wendel. Skip looked like a dehydrated Eddie Deezen, but his words and conviction possessed an inspirational power that rattled the psyche. He taught the GCF Method of handling a crisis, Ground, Center, and Focus.

She took in a deep breath, in through the nose, out through the mouth, then visualized her feet taking root into the ground. Her mind's eye now a microscope, narrowing on the situation at hand.

"Sir, this is an . . . interesting development. I can . . . I can . . .."

Nothing. Nothing came to mind. GCF be damned.

"So, you're a lizard," she said.

"Well, a reptoid. Although some of us prefer saurian. Like your ancestors came from primates, my people evolved from reptiles. We-."

"I thought dinosaurs became birds," she said, surprised that her brain managed to jump into analytical mode, but realized it was a subconscious attempt to escape the conversation. "Never mind, go on."

Her boss held up both hands while shaking his head. "Nope, good question. Not dinosaurs, but reptiles. There is a difference. Nancy, this is who I am. But because of that British ex-soccer player, now turned paranoia guru, I'm supposedly part of a global conspiracy established to overthrow humanity."

"Sir, why come out with this? This will shock everyone, especially your supporters."

Douglas made a noise that Nancy couldn't determine was a sigh or a hiss. "The reptoid conspiracy is one of the more bizarre ones out there. If I come forward, expose myself, demonstrating that I will disclose everything about me, then surely the other accusations of Ford will be dismissed. Think of it like this, I just told everyone I'm a reptoid, so why would I hide being part of some Deep State cult or grand plot to subjugate humanity or working to steal money or whatever? I just admitted to being a reptile person."

Nancy had to admit there was a logic to his reasoning, but only if the recipient was a rational person. Voters were not rational people; their reasoning was as fluid as quicksilver.

"Why couldn't you just have an affair like normal politicians?" She was whining but didn't care. "Or be closeted gay. Gay is really big now."

"Uh, well, I'm not married, so can't have an affair. Anything newsworthy would be more like a casual hook-up." Her boss presented Nancy with Jazz Hands. "Hey, look at me. I was with a woman. Or guy. I like sex. Shocking."

"W-w-what, what do you want from me?" Nancy's reality was in flux. She thought her question sounded like it came from a victim of a crime, but it was because she didn't know how to approach this problem. Someone confessing to being a member of a hidden race of reptile beings...?

David Douglas sat down and held his lipless face in his hands. Nancy felt herself grounded. It was an all too human gesture of despair.

The reptoid spoke.

"I've been working for years to make this city a better place for everyone. And I believe I've done some good. But rather than embrace the idea that we're all in the same boat, there are those who want to make it a competition. Us or them. Our way or the highway. And those motivated by personal greed, whether that be financial or egotistical or both, capitalize on that to further their own needs."

Davis stood up. His slit pupil eyes narrowed on her. "Nancy, are you scared of me?"

Nancy gulped. "Well, yes. I admit I am."

"We are scary, Nancy. And you know why? Because we're just like you."

He pointed at her. She just then noticed that his scaly hands only had four fingers.

"Some of us are nice, some not. We make the same errors in judgement, the same stupid mistakes, and therefore are no different from humans. Only in realizing our own limitations and faults are we in any way superior, and that's because we've been around longer than you have. We are scary because we are capable of the same wonderous things and the same terrible things. We share the same tragedies."

Douglas walked around the desk to stand before her. She caught a slight musky odor she associated with visiting the reptile house at the zoo. "Nancy, I'm the same candidate. My position on the issues hasn't changed. The only thing that has changed is that you know I'm a reptoid. My skin is actually scales, but I work for the people. All people. Even those that don't like me. Just that simple."

He adjusted his bowtie. Nancy focused on the four fingered hands manipulating the tie, not sure why she found it fascinating. "Will you please still work for me? I need you."

Nancy pursed her lips. Why was she here? What was her purpose? Her goal? Whether reptoid or human, did she believe in her client?

"The first thing we'll do is this..."

#

"Guess we need to be sure we have our umbrellas ready for Monday. And now back to Peter Carr for the latest in the political arena."

"Thanks Colin! And now, the news on what's happening on the election front. Ford and Douglas are neck-in-neck two days before the election, but Douglas does have a slight lead. Voter turnout is at an all-time high. This is democracy in action. Ford has declared the election fraudulent stating that if he doesn't win then there must have been due to some clandestine effort, because there is no way he could possibly lose otherwise.

"David Douglas will be going live in a few moments with a final election statement. We'll be covering that live when it...wait, it's now. Douglas has come out early and is ready to address the people. We now go live to David Douglas's announcement."

#

"Good evening, ladies and gentlemen, everyone. I stand before you a humble public servant wishing to serve you further in developing a better society for everyone. A society of fairness, of justice, a society focused on the common good.

"That sounds like a lot of political hooey. I realize it does. But there are some of us who believe in it. That our efforts are to construct a better society and not just in it to line our pockets or push personal agendas.

"My opponent would have you believe that I'm some sort of creep involved in grand conspiracies focused on demeaning and exploiting you. That is simply not true. And I want to prove that to you, by showing you something unexpected. I will reveal a secret about myself, and in hope doing so with show that I'm a man of the people, all people.

"It will come as a shock. And you will need a few seconds to adjust, to take in what you will see, but it is just me."

Douglas held up his right hand, then snapped his fingers.

#

"Peter Carr here. I don't know what's going on with Douglas's statement. If we're just patient, then . . . oh my fucking God what the damn shitting Hell oh shit oh shit . . .."

#

"This is me. I'm a reptoid.

"We were here before you. When your ancestors were living in trees and afraid to walk the ground we lived in colonies around the planet. But there was a terrible disease that decimated us. Those that survived interacted with you, which led us to be incorporated into your cultures, your legends. We are in your histories, folktales, and myths. You've feared us. Revered us. Destroyed us. Called us supernatural and less than natural. Made us into demons and gods. Even aliens. But we were born of this earth just like you. We embrace the same rights. We believe in the same justice.

"We are not the cause of your woes. We all create the world in which we live.

"Have you ever felt alone? You're a good, decent person, just wanting to live your life. To have a job and maybe a few friends and maybe even a small circle you could call a family. You just want to feel safe. Secure. But you're demographically speaking not 100 percent normal. There are some who say you shouldn't exist. That everything would be better if you didn't. That if you went away somehow existence would be a paradise because your mere presence caused the fundamental problems of the world.

"That is the philosophy of bullshit. And it's propaganda.

"Take X out of the equation and Y becomes perfect? That is not reality. We are all people. No matter what demographic you like to put others in, it is all under the label of people. Somebody has something negative to say about somebody else, and it's all because of fear. Well, no more fear. I stand before you as the ultimate representation of something different. I'm a reptoid. But I live my life as you do. I worry about bills. I want to find a mate. I don't want to cause pain. I don't want to cause suffering. I have no idea what I'm going to do this weekend. I just want to live my life.

"And if you're one of those who think there is a grand conspiracy to control everything, why would I come forward? If I had the power, why would I need to expose myself? With a wave of my hand the election would be set in my favor. But I'm not in charge, you are. There is no world covering cabal controlling everything. No Deep State. No hidden boogeyman. Our problems are caused by our own actions, and our own inactions. I reveal myself this evening to simply say, we all want the same thing.

"If you're looking for this fabricated element, this mythic puzzle piece, that if uncovered, if removed, would make the world right, that's laziness. We all must work. And work together. To make our world better. Forge our society into a better one. I expose myself to you, plainly show you what and who I am, in the hope of that effort.

"My name is David Douglas, running for reelection, hoping to serve you and our whole community.

"And I hope you approve of this message."

#

The news reports flooded in.

"I'm not a reptile person, but my Grandma was, and she took care of me when my parents couldn't and wouldn't . . .."

"I'm a reptoid and an American citizen. I served in Afghanistan for--."

"I married a reptoid, and we have a beautiful half-reptoid son. I want him to grow up in a world--."

"Ahh! Lizard people! Ahh!"

"Back at the Battle of the Bulge, a reptoid saved my life. I found that out after he carried me to safety after a German attack. He had been wounded dragging me away. He died later under enemy gunfire, but I'll never forget--."

"I know for sure one of them ate my Pekingese..."

#

Nancy poked Douglas harshly in the ribs. He had fallen asleep while watching the tally still in reptoid form. He batted her hand away, struggling to sit up and seemingly embarrassed that he was snoozing.

"Wake up, sir. You won," she said.

"I won?"

"Yes sir, you're not dreaming."

He held up a hand for a high-five, or in this case a high-four-five.

Nancy hesitated. Then thought skin was skin, whether hairy or scaly. She returned it.

Nancy felt lighter than air. Everything had worked out.

It had been a bit of a gamble, but then in politics everything was.

Most of what Douglas said was improvised; he admitted to her later that he became nervous, but he followed her guidelines and pulled it off.

Ford issued a generic statement of defeat. She had expected him to raise the flag of war due to the election results, but the man simply withdrew. It was mysterious.

Douglas's reveal caused a social media avalanche. Thousands of news shows flooded the airwaves with personal reptoid stories and Facebook exploded with reptoid groups.

Celebrities were coming out.

Reptoid was trending.

All was a tornado display of social awareness.

Her cell blared a text notification. It was a message from the party HQ. Not the local, but THE party HQ. It was a straightforward question.

Is David Douglas interested in a run for the Presidency?

She knew Douglas. Meek but not weak and focused on the "little guy." He had the insane viewpoint that justice meant justice for everyone, and basic rights existed for all people. He was not beholden to big business and held fast to his core beliefs. In respect to Evolutionary Politics, he should have died out. Douglas just didn't have the proper survival skills for the established political environment a politician needed for the big prize. Such a choice would be career suicide.

But rather than him having to adapt to the environment, maybe the environment needed to adapt to him.

She replied.

Mr. Douglas is interested in serving the American people as President. Please direct all questions and concerns to me.

She would talk to David later.

CRITICAL BLAST PUBLISHING
APPROVED BY THE READING CODE AUTHORITY
20¢
the inelegance of SPACE
Allister Nelson
CRITICAL BLAST PUBLISHING
A MATCH MADE IN SPACE

HEAD KNIVES 100% stainless steal daggers that launch from the top of your head and kill any conversation you find boring.

RENT AN ANGRY MIDGET! When you need to stop a Bully from harassing, or when you need to look like a decent human concerned for poor ugly monsters.

RENT ANGRY MONSTERS! When you need to stop a Bully from harassing, or when you need to look like a decent human concerned for poor ugly monsters.

SUPER SECRET BOOK SAFE The special camouflage feature activates, once placed on the book shelf. You'll never find it again.

HUMAN MASK When you need to walk among the humans, without being singled out as a monster. Get this mask in black, white or polka-dot, to blend right in!

READING IS 20 TO LIFE!

BOX OF LIVE BATS When you feel like a millionaire crime fighting hero and need to dress up your special cave, to give it that extra touch of atmosphere... a box of live bats is perfect for you. Food not included.

SNAKES IN A MAIL BOX Get these total mother-f$%Ken poisonous snakes and mail them with your get well gift cards.

EXPLODING DRINK Sit back and enjoy the highjinks as people unscrew their drink activating the chemical reaction, causing a foamy mess.

WELCOME MAT TRAP When you don't want people annoying you, a simple press of the button and the trap door will dispose of anyone who stands on it, while waiting for you to answer the door.

Allister Nelson is a Pushcart Prize-nominated author whose work has appeared in The British Fantasy Society, Apex Magazine, ILLUMEN, Renewable Energy World, The National Science Foundation, Luna Station Quarterly, Prismatica Press, Coffin Bell, etc. Her work has been curated by Kevin J. Anderson and nominated for Poland's top fantasy prize.

It was not, shall we say, typical of the D.C. suburbs for a healthy-looking, strapping young alien to crash-land his hotrod spaceship on my estate's front lawn.

"Ari, this is private property," I said drily, whiskey on the rocks in hand as I peered out the back porch at my manicured McLean lawn. "It was a hard day on the Hill. I don't know if I'm up to dealing with anymore pointed 'illegal alien' diatribes just because we support Dreamers. Lord knows the Republican media are grueling me, the other Democrats, and of course, my Senator."

Ahriman – hooded gold eyes, tan sandalwood skin, long ringlets of brownish black hair – smelled of attar. As usual, my trespasser was shirtless, fixing his junkyard midlife-crisis ship in some type of reflective metallic blue cyberpunk pants better befitting disco, not an astronaut.

He simply gave me a thumbs up. "Sorry, Carole, just a moment. Not like I had a choice where 'Cygna' landed. Amesha Spenta hit me *right* in the metallic ball sack – of course, metaphorically speaking."

I sipped my whiskey and sighed. "The upkeep here is difficult, and you always hit the bushes. This is a $53 million dollar property that I got in a divorce settlement from the old D.C. football team owner, after all. I need to take an Ibuprofen and go to bed."

Ahriman threw up his hands, then noetically magicked a black leather jacket to appease me, silver lamellar shirt under it. He knew how I felt about youth exposing their midriffs.

The scent of attar and lilies *reeked.* "Sure, Carole. You know this happens sometimes. Your property is right below the warp-hole of the Pleaides. I never *meant* to crash here, but I appreciate you keeping it a secret. And Carole, dear, you could stand to be, well, a bit more relaxed. You have a stick up your ass tonight."

I eyed his tasteless blue metallic pants. He was carrying a, shall we say, heavy space gun. "Look, Ari. You might be able to solve that."

Ahriman lit a cig. "By what? Writing your Tinder profile last crash didn't reel in many eligible suitors. And the old guy who lived here, whatshisface, *Brad* is more your type. I'm not sure getting a master of arcane sciences, laser guns, and alien machinery to write a Capital staffer's bachelor bait trawls will capture the right audience of men for you."

"Hmm." I adjusted my pencil skirt. "But you got me so many dates last time, dear. And Ari, couldn't you magick a new dress for me, in return for destroying my favorite rhododendrons?" I curled my upper lip, disappointed as thoughts of my last dalliance with a man salted my memory.

"A dress? I could, sure," Ahriman smiled, relenting. We were old acquaintances, after all.

I smiled serenely. "The last one I wore to the First Lady's dog birthday cocktail was *fabulous*, and I met this really great guy in it. Too bad he had the yacht accident in Old Town."

Ahriman jerry-rigged his space cruiser to an impromptu loading dock he had built by my azaleas a few months ago. Eyesore, it was, all silver and lasers. "How old are you, Carole?"

"52 and fancy. But don't tell the boys that. I like to pretend I'm 43. That's what the Botox and facelift is for. I like to keep my face airtight, like a cruiser."

"You are eternally a maiden to me, Carole – incapable of sentient thought, more Procrustean ooze. You know, my dear old hostess, I think you'd do better with a man your age, old friend." He magicked a Corona from my fridge, spaceship engine jetting blue halonic fuel.

"Hmm, well, you see, Ari I like young men. They don't have the gray tendrils of death and anger in them. Millennials and Gen Zer's come with less baggage."

Ahriman leaned against the hood of his ship, his skintight suit reeling up to reveal dusky abs. I couldn't help but imagine – no, Carole. Don't let the menopause heat get to you!

Ahriman spoke languidly, pleased as pudding with himself: "Hmm, well, I'm older than the Big Bang, so I get it. I too delight in tender young things like Jahi the Space Whore, my wife. But to me, dear Carole, you are not even cellular. Just RNA floating in a celestial vat, a speck of nothing. Not even sentient yet. I couldn't even call you spawn. Fleshy waterbag, maybe. And that's only out of *respect*."

"Thanks Ari, you always have a way with words. It's nice you think I'm still young... wish *Brad* had felt the same way before he banged the Washington Commander's cheer squad and his secretarial staff." I turned on the inviting porch light and opened the glass sliding door. "Hey, come inside, Ari - you can at least *look* over my dating profile. Say if the new haircut I got in my profile pic is okay. If my joke answers and "Ideal Date" section gives younger gentlemen any sparks. I just don't know what to write about myself these days..."

"Huh. You need my help? I'm flattered..." Ahriman magicked away the Corona, licked his bottom lip, and stretched like a desert cat, his gold eyes shimmering. "Hmm, well, Amesha Spenta is reconvening on Planet Nibiru right now with the Rebel Federation, so I guess I have time to kill. My meeting with my brother Aeshma Daeva and my wife, Jahi the Space Whore, isn't for another warp hour."

Ahriman and I found ourselves eating a garden salad, fresh from my *own* garden, with a new recipe for dill sauce we tried out. He made it for me from scratch as I soaked my callused heels in some Epsom salts and warm water – walking from the Capitol South metro station to the office and all over Capitol "Hell's" stomping grounds in dress code-required high heels was a *surefire* way to get sore feet, and misaligned toes.

Ahriman rubbed my feet, then fed me some salad with a silver fork. He was doting on me – oh, the darling youth! Though... supposedly *I* was the young one here, considering he was an alien warlord.

"It's good, your produce and my salad craftsmanship" Ahriman said as he cleaned up our plates and massaged my back. "Okay, alright, Carole. I'll write the profile again."

Afterwards, we kissed, made love as usual, and tended to our own inner gardens.

#

Ahriman's profile had worked, for a bit. He had written some Persian whirling dervish poetry – Rumi, he said, whoever *that* was – rehashes, to make me sound like I read love poetry and was literate beyond legal files. Then, Ari had finagled my favorite ice cream flavor – pistachio – into a quip about men's dress shoes, and how I'd like to kiss a man with his shoes *off*.

Ahriman met me for coffee at Northside Social on Tuesday after we worked all day – me on the latest Senatorial bill, him on his spaceship clunker

Ahriman stirred his cappuccino, pensive, gold eyes hooded with malaise: "So, how'd the latest string go, Carole? And is Brad giving you shit? My ship is in the shitter."

"Why did you call me, Ari? I told you to never call me. The psionic waves you emit on my iPhone always freezes it. Text next time, *dear*."

"Hmm, well, I tried to fly the ship, right, but the engine gave out – halfway through launch, *fuck me, Carole*. I unfortunately crash-landed in Dyke Marsh. I, uh, need to couch surf again."

"Not my yard this time?"

My sometimes Alien Loverboy winced, then checked his ether watch. "No, the warp to the Pleiades had a dakini maiden army guarding it, and the Peri traders weren't far behind. Amesha Spenta is up my *ass* lately, Carole." Ahriman sipped his coffee, jittery – the drink black, *black* like his combat boots. A bead of dark liquid clung to his lip, the liquid hot and sinuous. He was shaking. I held his hand, making soothing noises, and squeezed it. Tears of blood formed in his stressed eyes, silvery-indigo, and his eye membranes nictated like a Siamese cat.

I smiled gently: "No couch needed, Ari. You deserve a proper rest. I'll fix up a guest room."

"Thanks, old friend." Ahriman smiled, squeezing my hand back, then gulped down the cappuccino. "Aaah. Say, why don't you have kitchen staff, Carole? Robotic scullery maids? Slaves to roast space ox and spill their vittles to divine the war? Wait, you wage no wars. Except against Republicans. Whatever those are."

"Yes, Ari. Yes. See, I'm private. Brad always fucked the maids."

\#

"It's late, Ari. What are you doing watching TV?"

"Jahi the Space Whore called. She's cheating on me," Ahriman sobbed, his oud-fragrant, oiled curls buried in the pillows, looking like a wounded lion. "I fucking *knew* it."

I swallowed my quip of how Jahi, the Space Whore, always, well, prostituted herself to Amesha Spenta like clockwork on Tuesdays.

"Well at least turn something better on than Anakin Skywalker reruns," I said kindly, my motherly instinct kicking in, though I had never been blessed with little ones of my own – infertility was a curse, you know, but I liked to mother the youth in my life, and mentor young interns. Ahriman drew out that same maternal streak.

"He's a bit relatable, Carole. This Anakin child. Talented at war. Dark-edged. Set against on all sides. No luck in love."

"Murdering his one and only true love – his wife Padmé?"

"Oh, I'd love too!" Ahriman howled, suddenly slamming my old duct-taped together remote onto the couch and turning into his dragonic lion form, bat-winged with scorpion tail stalking my halls, like I had once seen on a museum exhibition at the Met about Zoroastrianism.

"Fuck women!" the Beast of Ahriman growled.

"Well, good night, try to get some rest. And not *all* women are heartbreakers, Ari."

Done raging, he fell asleep, a pile of claw, scorpion appendages, lion fur, and fangs. His void tentacles writhed, dripping poison onto my midcentury modern sofa.

I plumped the pillow, then dusted Cheeto crumbles off the blanked Ahriman's beast form snoozed fretfully under as I cleaned up his mess. The Corona had spilled some yellow drops of beer, and his lime was half-chewed. "Typical man blues. At least he's faithful, unlike Brad, the absolute *ass*," I sighed, fixing my steel bob in the mirror.

I looked back: a mature, elegant, stunning woman – the doctors made sure the nip-tuck did the base work, and the hairdresser put the final touches on my Capitol Hill armor. "I'm sure to steal a heart at the First Lady's dog Baptism tomorrow."

I opened today's mail, tired from a long day as Media Officer for the Senator. "Hmm, what's this? Carole Derringer and... 'plus one' to Baxter the Dog's Baptism? *I need a date?*"

#

Ahriman looked a bit out of place in the White House, his muscles straining his suit. His predator instinct was triggered at Baxter the dog sniffing his pants, and his Beast of Ahriman claws accidentally appeared, tearing his lapel.

The Senator looked at me with imposing blue eyes. "And Carole, my favorite girl, how did you meet Ari?"

I faked ingenue mannerisms, attempting to blush demurely. The Senator liked shallow, one-bit innocent girls. Unimaginative man. "Oh, us? Hah! A jazz bar." The sound of my overly feminine voice grated my mind, just as my patent leather pink pumps dug into my heels.

Performative femininity? UGH.

"Oh?" The Senator watched Ahriman crouch on the floor with Baxter the baptized dog, stalking him. Ahriman let out a lion's roar: Baxter whimpered and peed. "Well, Gen Z is very interesting. At least this Ari fellow is spirited."

"Yes," I smiled. "I'd like to see where this relationship goes."

Ahriman, triggered by the animal's whimper, ate Baxter.

The Senator whistled low, impressed: "Say, Carole: you think we could hire your boyfriend to do opps?"

I winked at the Senator, twirling a bang – *eugh.* He was gazing at my cleavage. "I'll see, sir, I'll see."

Ahriman stalked, bloody, to the lavender lemonade punch bowl, dunked his Beast of Ahriman head in – half-transformed

– and gulped the contents down into his flaming gullet. The crystal container shattered.

The First Lady laughed. "Why, Carole, he's delightful! Just like Brad."

"Hmm, yes, ma'am. You always *did* like Brad."

"A toast!" The First Lady said. "To the young, handsome staffer that put Baxter out of his misery! Now that Baxter's baptized – I never got around to it, you know, for sixteen years, the President said my dog was going to Irish Catholic Limbo – I feel my dear old Baxter can pass on properly to Heaven with Catholic Rites."

Ahriman froze. "Cheers? For me? People... really... like me...?"

He sobbed, then bowed.

"Take that you BITCH, Jahi!"

The staffers cheered.

#

Ahriman and I excused ourselves later that evening to Ben's Chili Bowl.

"That party was nice." Ahriman scarfed down a chili-covered hot dog. "Not as good as your cooking, Carole, but it does hit the spot."

"I just don't understand men, Ari," I sighed, blue. "You charm everyone. I can't even keep a man faithful. I'm old, Ari. Too old for love."

Ahriman's eyes grew tender. "Carole, I'm as ancient as Gog and Magog and the Space Antipodeans. To me, you are not even capable of mitochondrial digestion."

"You have such a way with words, Ari. I wish Earth had true romantics like you." I took his hand in mine. "Say, how is Jahi?"

Ahriman began to sob. "Gone."

"Oh, dear, I'm sorry."

"It's done. I got the divorce from Jahi the Space Whore. Amesha Spenta – my evil twin brother – can have the bitch."

"Welcome to the divorcee club, Ari." I said kindly. "You're a good man, Ari. You'll find someone kind, someone faithful."

He smiled through his tears. "And Carole, so will you."

We walked hand in hand through the autumn spiced rain, and went to go

hear

jazz.

Realizing, finally, that we had found each other, happily ever after.

QUIRKLAR
187

CRITICAL BLAST
PUBLISHING
20¢
APPROVED BY THE READING CODE AUTHORITY
CRITICAL BLAST PUBLISHING
THE HOUSE THAT CRAWLED AWAY
Paul Lonardo
A TERRIFYING KIND OF MOBILE HOME

COCAINE FOR PETS When your pets become too excited during mating season and you don't want additional burden of feeding more pets, shot them up with some fine liquid snow and chill them out.

STILL ONLY
35¢

RENT AN ANGRY MIDGET! When you need to stop a Bully from harassing, or when you need to look like a decent human concerned for poor ugly monsters.

BOX OF LIVE BATS When you feel like a millionaire crime fighting hero and need to dress up your special cave, to give it that extra touch of atmosphere... a box of live bats is perfect for you. Food not included.

SUPER SHARP PIRATE SWORD When you want to capture the hearts and minds of the people around you, this sword will cut through the muscle and bone to get to the vital organs you need to sustain your hunger.

MONSTER VALUE STAMP THIS IS IT! CLIP THEM & COLLECT THEM ALL!

EXPLODING DRINK Sit back and enjoy the highjinks as people unscrew their drink activating the chemical reaction, causing a foamy mess.

LEARN TO PLAY THE GUITAR! When you can't get a date for the weekend, rent a sexy Guitar Teacher to impress your friends and maybe you just might learn something too.

LIFE IS A BIG CHALLENGE, SO LET IT GO!

HEAD KNIVES 100% stainless steal daggers that launch from the top of your head and kill any conversation you find boring.

WELCOME MAT TRAP When you don't want people annoying you, a simple press of the button and the trap door will dispose of anyone who stands on it, while waiting for you to answer the door.

HYPNO-ROBOT use the special mind control eye harmonics to subdue the minds of your unwilling subjects. You'll never have to take out the trash and everyone will worship you as if their life depends on it.

FISH BOWL FULL OF WORMS Are you tired of eating meat? Get yourself a bowl full of yummy worms and feel you are saving the planet.

BOW AND ARROW KIT! When you need to go into battle on Tuesdays and don't know what weapon to take with you.

Paul Lonardo is a freelance writer and author with numerous titles, both fiction and nonfiction books. Paul has placed short stories and nonfiction pieces in various magazines and ezines. He is a contributing writer for several publications, including Tales from the Moonlit Path. Paul is an HWA member.

I know the exact moment that the monster invaded the house next door. I remember because school was over and summer camp was starting in the morning. It was almost two o'clock in the morning when the strange noises started. Dylan and I got out of our beds and went over to the window to see what it was.

"Maybe Oscar came back," Dylan said.

"I don't think so," I told him.

"If it's not Oscar, who is it, Devan?"

I didn't know who might be living there, but it couldn't be Oscar. He was a nice old man who lived in the house alone after his wife died. I don't remember her, but I liked Oscar. He always threw our baseballs back into our yard when they went over the shrub wall. About a year ago, Dad told us that Oscar took a bad fall down the stairs in his house and he had to go into a nursing home so someone could look after him. His house had been empty ever since. Although somebody was there now.

I looked at Dylan and he knew exactly what I had in mind. I didn't have to say anything. It wasn't unusual for one of us to know what the other was thinking without saying a word. He smiled and ran to get our crocs out of the closet. He silently dropped mine at my feet and I went to the door, opening it slowly to prevent the hinges from squeaking, just in case our parents were awakened by what was going on next door.

Creeping past their bedroom, Dad's deep, rattling snoring almost drowned out the racket coming from the neighbor's house.

"How can Dad sleep through all that noise?" I asked my brother.

"How can Mom sleep with Dad snoring like that?" he wanted to know.

"He's a sweaty elephant," I said, and we both laughed quietly.

Mom once told us that Dad snores like an elephant in heat. Thinking about a sweaty elephant snoring was funny and we joked about it all the time.

When we got downstairs, I realized that not only was Harvey not barking at the sounds coming from next door, but he wasn't waiting for us at the bottom of the stairs.

"Where's Harvey?" Dylan asked.

When we reached the kitchen, his white, shaggy tail was sticking out from under one of the chairs.

"Harvey, what are you doing under there?" I reached down to pull him out, and although he resisted, he was small enough for me to retrieve without much effort. He was trembling, pressing his head into the crook of my arm.

"What's the matter, boy?" Dylan asked, rubbing the dog's muzzle.

"He's scared."

"Harvey's never backed down from anything," Dylan said. "He even squared off against a fox that time, remember?"

"Something's got him spooked," I said.

I went to the cupboard to get a dog biscuit and placed it on his bed by the back door. When I set Harvey down, he left the treat and slunk back under the chair. I'd never seen him snub a treat before.

We went outside through the kitchen door, and the noise was even louder. It was clear that some kind of demolition was going on.

"There must be a hundred guys in there swinging sledgehammers," Dylan said.

Our street was a cul-de-sac, and Oscar's house was the last one before the dead end transitioned to dense forestland. Besides us, Oscar had no other neighbors, either on the opposite side, in front, or behind. I motioned for my brother to follow me as I led the way over to a stand of arborvitae that acted as a living wall between our properties. We found a gap between the twenty-foot trees and peeked our heads through the soft, scale-like leaves. It was an overcast night with no moon and there wasn't a single light on in Oscar's house. It was difficult to see much but there were piles of debris scattered across the yard. Splintered wood and clouds of pulverized ceramic tiles and drywall were being expelled from the busted-out windows on the first and second floors.

"Whoa!" Dylan screeched. "They're really ripping the place apart."

As soon as he said this, all the noise in the house ceased at once. We looked at each other, cringing, thinking that our presence had been detected, prompting the work stoppage. I put a finger to my lips to keep Dylan from saying anything else. We remained quiet, and a moment later a blue jay flew off from one of the trees beside us. It was gliding past Oscar's house when a long, flexible, blunt-ended arm extended out from a damaged second-floor window. It plucked the bird out of the air and pulled it inside the house as feathers fluttered to the ground.

I looked at Dylan, who stared back at me with his eyes bugging. "That was a *tentacle*," he said.

"It sure *looked* like a tentacle," I confirmed, disbelieving I was even saying that.

We watched and waited to see if the tentacle would appear again, but it didn't. All remained quiet, and after a couple of minutes we went back home, but there was no way we were going to get any sleep that night. We talked about what we'd seen and what it could be. While I believed a scientist like Doc Ock with mechanical arms had moved in next door to us, Dylan thought that the family might have a pet octopus.

"It can't be an octopus," I told him. "An octopus lives in water."

"An octopus that's been genetically designed to live on land and in the sea," he amended. "What do they call that? A hybrid."

I couldn't help but laugh. "That's stupid."

"No, it's not!" Dylan grumbled, his eyes narrowed in anger. "You're the one who's stupid. Those weren't even mechanical arms that grabbed that bird."

I tried to tell him that with today's technology, they could make mechanical arms that looked exactly like real skin, but he wouldn't listen. We argued about it until our eyes got heavy and we could no longer keep them open. No more sounds came from Oscar's house.

I was tired when I got up in the morning. Dylan was dragging, too. We had packed for camp the day before, so all we had to do was eat our breakfast.

"You both look exhausted," Mom said when she saw Dylan holding his head up at the table and me yawning. "You boys must have been so excited about camp you couldn't get to sleep last night."

"You'd feel like us if you were kept awake by what was going on at Oscar's house," Dylan said.

"Oscar's?" She frowned, looking down her nose at Dylan. "I didn't know that the house had been sold." She turned to Dad, who was filling his travel mug with coffee. "Fred, the boys think someone may have moved into the house next door."

"Oscar's?" Dad began with the same skepticism. "I haven't heard anything to that affect. But then again, I don't stick my nose into places it doesn't belong."

"You must have been hearing things," Mom said. "What kind of people would move into a house in the middle of the night?"

"Maybe they're not people?" Dylan suggested.

I elbowed him in the ribs.

"Ouch!" he cried out.

"Not people?" Dad scoffed. "What do you think they are, elephants?"

We both started giggling, and Dad laughed with us, as if he was in on the joke.

"Have a good time at camp," he told us and grabbed his briefcase off the kitchen table. "But behave yourselves. See you in six weeks."

"Why'd you hit me?" Dylan complained after Dad went off to work.

"What do you think will happen," I hissed, "if we tell Mom and Dad what we saw? Mom would overreact and Dad wouldn't believe us. He'd try to convince her that whatever was going on there was none of our business and they'd have a big fight. We'd miss camp registration and be stuck here all summer."

"You're probably right," Dylan said. "I didn't think of that."

"So don't mention another thing about Oscar's house to Mom," I warned him. "After a few days at camp, once we get settled in, we'll call and tell them what we saw. Okay?"

Dylan nodded.

"All right, boys," Mom called out to us. "Time to shove off. Make sure you have everything."

She shuffled us off to the campground in the Stygian Mountains, and during the two-hour drive my brother talked a lot but avoided the subject of Oscar's house altogether, most importantly the noises and the tentacle.

After the first couple of days at camp, there was so much to do we put what we saw at Oscar's house in the back of our minds, never mentioning it to our parents when we talked to them. There was kayaking, badminton, water balloon dodgeball, archery, scavenger hunts, and best of all, camp Olympics. Me and Dylan finally beat the Perotti brothers, Billy and Richie, winning five gold medals to their four. It was sweet revenge for the previous three years they'd won and bragged how easy it had been.

The six weeks flew by, and before we knew it the summer was over. During the final days of camp, Dylan and I were both anxious to get home to find out about our new neighbors. When Dad picked us up from camp, the first thing I asked him on the ride home was who our new neighbors were.

"I don't believe anyone is living in the house," Dad said. "I haven't seen a soul come in or out of there all summer. The remodeling project that was started has since been abandoned. Everything is still sitting out in the yard."

"You mean they made that mess on the lawn and just left it there?"

"Maybe the people who are renovating the house ran out of money," Dad said. "After gutting the place, the funds to rebuild must have hit a snag. That happens sometimes. That's why I don't think anyone is living there. Your mother wanted to go over and bring them some homemade muffins, but I talked her out of it. If anyone *is* living there, they're probably people who like their privacy. So, I want you boys to stay away from there, you hear me?"

We both agreed and that seemed to be the end of the conversation about the house, at least as far as our father was concerned. His only interest was the remnants of a hurricane that was headed our way. Mom was even more stressed out by the impending storm. That's why she had Dad pick us up from camp. She didn't want to get caught in the heavy rain and winds that were expected to come later that day.

"Where's Harvey?" I asked when we got home, surprised that he hadn't come around to greet us.

"He's in the kitchen under a chair," Mom said. "He's been acting strange all summer. I think he really missed you boys."

"We'll take him for a walk," I said, knowing that this would be the only chance we'd have of getting outside to see Oscar's house for ourselves. "I bet that'll make him feel better."

"Well, be quick about it," Mom said. "You have all that unpacking to do and there's a big storm expected to arrive any time now. It's supposed to be a whopper. Soaking rain and heavy winds that could produce tornadoes capable of lifting a house into the sky, like in *The Wizard of Oz*."

Dylan grinned with enthusiasm. "Awesome!"

"Your mother might be exaggerating a little, but there's nothing *awesome* about sustained winds of up to seventy-miles-an-hour," Dad told us. "It can be extremely dangerous. So, do as your mother said and come right back. You can help me take the patio furniture inside so it doesn't end up blowing halfway across the state of Virginia."

Harvey came out from under the chair when I called him, but when I put his collar on and attached the leash, he tried to go back under. I practically had to drag him out the front door.

Mom handed Dylan the poop bags and his shoulders drooped. "Why do I always get poop duty?" he complained.

The closer we got to the street, the harder Harvey fought me. When we reached the sidewalk in front of Oscar's property, the dog stopped and lay down, pressing his belly against the ground, refusing to go any further.

"He doesn't want to go near Oscar's house," I said.

Oscar's house was set back several hundred feet from the street and the wildly overgrown bushes and shrubs blocked the entire front porch. The discarded furnishings were still outside on the lawn, just like Dad said, only now tall grass and weeds sprouted so high they almost concealed the heaps of scrap material.

The wall of black clouds that had been rolling in from the south all morning finally succeeded in blotting out the sun. It became as dark as night, and I felt a chill as the temperature plummeted. The first drops of rain began falling and the wind started gusting.

"Look," I called out as a flock of birds coming from behind our house made a sudden sharp turn in the sky. "They're flying *toward* the storm to avoid Oscar's house."

Just then a low rumbling from the house caused Harvey to jump to his feet. He started snarling and baring his teeth like a vicious dog. As the sound intensified, Harvey grew stiff, his body straining to run into the yard, my grip on the leash stopping him.

"What's gotten into him?" I asked.

Harvey started to bark aggressively and, all at once, he shot forward. Before I could tighten my hold on the leash, the dog's momentum pulled it from my hand. He charged straight for the house, the tether line dragging behind him through the tall grass like he was being pursued by a snake.

"Harvey, come back here!" I screamed. Then I saw my brother running after him. "Dylan, what are you doing?"

"We can't let him go over there by himself. Remember what happened to that bird."

I knew he was right. I didn't want any harm to come to Harvey, or to my brother, so I gave chase.

Harvey rushed up the steps onto the porch, slipping easily between a narrow gap in the bushes. Dylan forced his way through, and I went in behind him. Harvey was barking frantically at something, but it was too dark to see much of anything. When I got to the door, I saw what had Harvey so worked up. There was actually no door to speak of. It was gone. However, the entrance was blocked by several pearl-white objects that tapered down to hooked tips, which looked like massive claws. They were moving ever so slightly.

Dylan was standing beside me. "Something's alive in there!" he said, his voice trembling. "It's blocking the entrance."

Harvey continued barking.

"We have to get out of here," I said.

The rumbling inside the house reached a deafening level, and Harvey went crazy. The monster-size claws at the front door began moving rapidly, making sharp clicking sounds as they rubbed against one another.

Harvey angled his body toward Dylan and began barking at him. When I looked around, I realized that he wasn't barking *at* my brother but trying to warn him as a tentacle came through the bushes behind Dylan and wrapped around his waist, immobilizing him. He groaned as its grip tightened.

I grabbed the thing and tried to pry my brother loose, but the appendage was too strong. The arm was thick and muscular, like an anaconda with no scales.

"Get it off!" Dylan shrieked.

"I'm trying," I screamed back.

"You're not trying hard enough!" he said as the tentacles swept him up off his feet, twirling him all around in the confined space. He was upside down and looking a little green, like he might be sick. Suddenly Harvey leapt, springing up higher than I ever thought possible for a dog with such short legs, and sank his teeth into the creature, which pulsed and flexed, trying to shake the animal off. But Harvey held on tight.

Another tentacle appeared and tried to grab me, but I was able to avoid it, ducking around and under it when it came at me.

Harvey was suspended two feet off the ground, growling fiercely as he clung to the monstrous appendage. Somewhere inside the house, a low, agonized moan could be heard. As the flexible limb tried more vigorously to dislodge Harvey, the dog snarled, grinding his teeth deeper into the alien flesh. Finally, it released Dylan, who fell to the porch floor with a thud, followed by Harvey.

"Let's go!" I yelled and scooped up the dog, pushing Dylan toward the porch steps, clogged with branches, ahead of me.

Out in the open on the front lawn, with the full force of the storm raging, the wind almost knocked me off my feet. The intense movement of air, and everything that it was propelling along with it, made it sound like I was on the tracks as a high-speed train was roaring by. The driving rain was stinging my eyes, but I could feel the presence of a pursuing tentacle as it thrashed the air all around me.

"Don't stop!" I shouted as loud as I could. "And *don't* look back!"

Although we were identical twins, Dylan was a little smaller than me and he could run faster. Carrying the dog slowed me down further. Dylan reached the arborvitaes at the edge of our property before me and crawled through.

Before I made it, a slimy, wet tentacle swiped at my feet. I tried to jump over it, but it was too big to hurdle, and I went flying. I landed on my butt and managed to hold onto Harvey, who snapped at the tentacle when it tried to get near us. I could see the teeth marks on the appendage, and it wanted no part of Harvey.

Although my visibility was severely impaired by the storm and limited by darkness, when I looked back at Oscar's house I could see tentacles extending from every window, their tips rooting into the wet ground outside like a jumble of boneless legs. They pushed and strained, making deep impressions in the soggy soil, all of which was accompanied by the sound of wood under great stress, creaking and explosively snapping. The old house shuddered and shimmied as it was slowly pulled from its foundation. It rose several stories off the ground, supported by the massive tentacles, then it slowly started to shamble away, like a nightmarish insect. It headed into the woods beyond the cul-de-sac, cutting a haphazard swath through the trees before disappearing, swallowed by the storm.

I stared at the empty spot where Oscar's house had been, unsure what I had just seen. I don't know how long I sat there before I was grabbed from behind.

"Come on, Devan," Dylan said. He helped me to my feet, and I followed him through the wall of trees that were twisting and turning in the wind.

Dad was calling our names from outside our house, clinging to the iron handrail along the sides of the front stairs. We were almost upon him when he saw us. He opened the door and we were practically shoved inside by the might of the wind. Mom was waiting with large towels that she wrapped around me and my brother. I put Harvey down and he vigorously shook the water off his back. Dad had to lean hard against the door to force it closed behind him.

"Jumpin' Jehoshaphat!" Dad exclaimed. "It's ferocious out there. You boys could've been swept away forever. Where were you all this time?"

"We were walking Harvey and all of sudden it started pouring," I began. "The storm came out of nowhere. With the wind blowing like it is, we got lost in the storm."

"I told you not to go out in this," Mom said. "Thank goodness you're both all right. Now get out of those wet clothes before you catch a death of a cold. You too, Fred."

We didn't say anything to them about Oscar's house just getting up and crawling away because I knew they wouldn't believe me. But when I was alone with Dylan in our room as we were putting on dry clothes, I told him what he'd missed.

"Wow!" he said. "That's unbelievable."

"I know. We had a real monster living next door to us all summer."

"What do you suppose it wanted with Oscar's house?" Dylan asked.

"I've been thinking about that," I began. "Remember in Mrs. Thompson's second grade homeroom, she had that hermit crab."

"Yeah, it was in that glass case and it had all those empty shells inside everywhere."

"That's right," I said. "Mrs. Thompson told the class that hermit crabs crawl inside empty shells to protect their soft bodies. And when they grow too big for their shell, or when they get really stressed out about something, she said that they leave their shell and find another one that they can fit into."

"You think there was a giant hermit grab living in Oscar's house?"

"I don't know if it was a hermit crab exactly," I began. "Maybe it was some kind of alien lifeform from another planet. Whatever it was, it must have gotten into Oscar's house the night before we left for camp. We heard it clearing out the place so it could fit inside."

"Where do you suppose it went?"

"Probably to find a bigger house," I said.

"Good thing our house is about the same size as Oscar's!" Dylan said with a sense of relief.

"Take those wet clothes off the floor," Mom said as she came into to our room. "Put them in the hamper."

Harvey ran in behind her and stood up on his hind legs, wanting to be picked up. Dylan reached down and scooped the dog up in his arms and it began licking his face.

"I think he did miss you," Mom said with a cheerful grin. "Maybe things will get back to normal around here."

I looked at Dylan and said, "I think they will."

"You can count on it," Dylan added.

The next day, we went outside with Dad to survey the damage from the storm. There were a lot of leaves and tree branches scattered around, and Dad was the only one among us to be shocked that Oscar's house was gone.

"What the fluffernutter!" he blared. "A tornado must have touched down right here. Look what it did to Oscar's house. We were lucky it didn't do the same thing to our house."

Over the next few days, pieces of Oscar's house were discovered scattered in the surrounding woods. According to the authorities, nobody had been living there. And they were right. Whatever had been living next door to us all summer, it was no person.

And it certainly wasn't human.

3¢
195
HAHABRIDE

CRITICAL BLAST PUBLISHING
20¢
APPROVED BY THE READING CODE AUTHORITY
NO ONE WOULD EVEN CARE
LCW Allingham
CRUEL SECRET IN THE CLOSET!

STICK IT TO YOUR ENEMIES!

Real Voodoo Doll! Guaranteed Quality checked by the finest Witch Doctors! Send lock of hair and a SASE to DUDAT VOODOO, Box 9, Haiti.

BATS, RATS AND CATS!

DEFEAT BLACK MYSTIC ARTS KUNG-FU Tired of getting your ass kicked every Tuesday by Black Mystic Arts Kung-Fu fighters? CALL 666-HELP to enroll in self-defense training every Hellspawn should know to survive any dark alley encounter. Become a Ninth Circle Master of Judante!

HELIUM GAS & BALLOON SET

Get away from the day to day grind of your boring life and steal a whole house while the owners are away.

MONSTER VALUE STAMP

THIS IS IT! CLIP THEM & COLLECT THEM ALL!

HUMAN MASK When you need to walk among the humans, without being singled out as a monster. Get this mask in black, white or polka-dot, to blend right in!

EXPLODING DRINK Sit back and enjoy the highjinks as people unscrew their drink activating the chemical reaction, causing a foamy mess.

HOBO IN A BOX When your street is getting over-runned by homeless people and you need someone to speak their language and run them off to the next street down the block.

LCW Allingham is a Philadelphia area author, artist, and editor. Her short fiction has appeared in numerous anthologies and publications and her short story "Cellar Door" won second place in the 2023 Bucks County Short Fiction contest. She is the co-founder and executive editor of Speculation Publications and a member of the HWA. Her horror novella Muse was released last year, and her debut novel, Lady, won a Critters Reader Award.

First the heart chill, soaking across her body like an ice bath, then the temperature of the whole room would drop. Raleigh would watch the clouds of her breath catch beams of yellow street light filtering through the chipped window blinds. The row of antique dolls on her dresser would seem to huddle together. She would tell herself to hide.

But she never did.

They'd moved into this house, into Northeast Philly, a few months ago, and on her first night in her new room, Raleigh had screamed her throat raw.

She didn't do that anymore. Screaming woke up Karl and Mom. Karl and Mom were always angry when they got woken up.

It didn't matter that there was a man in Raleigh's closet. Mom didn't believe her about that, or about the furniture that moved while she was at school, or that she didn't take Karl's keys or break Mom's stupid fancy vase and that she definitely didn't hide all the Christmas lights.

They didn't believe her about anything.

"For God's Sake, Raleigh, you're fifteen years old, will you act like it for a change?" Mom would huff while Karl pouted like a big-bellied toddler.

Raleigh didn't scream anymore.

Not when the closet door opened. Not when the wire hangers holding her school uniforms screeched against the steel hanging rod, and not when the eyes, impossibly big with impossibly bright whites peered out at her, the big black irises catching the glint of streetlight as they stared.

Raleigh could not look away. She would try to think of good things—Arizona, mac and cheese, Christmas at Gran's house—as she stared silently at the man in her closet.

He would eventually fade to a shadow. Sometimes he disappeared back into the closet. Sometimes the shadow drifted out and through the wall of her bedroom. No one else ever saw him, floating through the 1962 red brick split-level. She never saw him anywhere but her room, nor did she ever see him return to the closet. She would stay awake, vigilant every night, until she'd collapse from sheer exhaustion.

#

When Mom transferred hospitals during Covid, they'd moved from Mt. Airy to the Northeast and enrolled Raleigh at Blessed Mother. At first Raleigh had welcomed the change. She wasn't exactly popular at St. John's.

On Raleigh's first day, Sophia Plank had met her with open arms.

For weeks she'd invited Raleigh everywhere and texted until late at night. Raleigh had been bestie-smitten that beautiful, tough, confident Sophia wanted to talk to her. She'd confided everything to Sophia in a gush of optimistic trust.

Including her little crush on DeSean Whaley, the cutest boy in their class. Everyone loved him. Everything about him was absolutely perfect.

Sophia had told Raleigh he liked her back. She'd given Raleigh a makeover. She'd convinced her to ask him out.

One month after starting at Blessed Mother, Raleigh had nuked her entire life by approaching DeSean at lunch and saying exactly what Sophia had coached her to say.

"Is this happening, or what?"

DeSean had looked confused. "What's happening?"

Raleigh had realized everyone was looking at them, at her, and they were whispering. Someone was laughing. Her face got hot and she stammered, "Um, you know, hanging out."

DeSean didn't laugh. "Hey, it's cool, but I got a girlfriend." Pity had washed over his handsome face.

"Oh yeah, cool," Raleigh had sputtered.

Sophia had stepped in, and Raleigh had a moment of relief where she thought her new bestie was saving her from humiliation.

Then Sophia slid right into DeSean's arms. "Why would you ask out my boyfriend? I thought we were friends."

When they moved from Torresdale to Bustleton after the landlord sold their old house out from under them, she hadn't even considered that her luck could get worse.

A year after she'd made herself the biggest loser in school, Raleigh's day still started with jeers as soon as she got on the bus.

Except now, she got on the bus right after Sophia, who lived across the street from the new house. When Raleigh had realized this, she'd begged her mother to find anywhere else. She begged to transfer schools. To go to public school. Charter school. Anywhere.

"You live, you learn, RaRa," Mom had said. "Keep your head down and ignore her if she gives you trouble."

Sophia rarely had to give Raleigh trouble. Everyone did it for her.

Keeping her head down just made it easier for them to throw candy in her hair and dump their water bottles in the hood of her jacket.

She sat alone at lunch. No one dared the wrath of Sophia Plank by making room at their table for Raleigh.

Sophia sat with DeSean and spent half of lunch glaring at Raleigh.

Sophia had set her up and Raleigh had failed her test, sure, but it wasn't like she'd known. Why couldn't Sophia just let it go? Was it really that bad?

Just before Thanksgiving, Raleigh had confided in the guidance counselor who decided to call her and Sophia's mothers. Mom had been too busy with double shifts at the hospital. Sophia's mother had some sob story about Raleigh bullying Sophia.

The next day, Sophia and her friends had surrounded Raleigh when she got off the bus and grabbed the hem of her skirt, pulling until it ripped. Then they'd taken her backpack, with her keys and her phone inside, and run down the street, daring her to come for it.

It was one of those Novembers that felt like winter was gnawing on the neck of season. Raleigh ducked through the rusted chain-link gate into the brown patch of yard they shared with their elderly neighbor and crouched next to the old trash cans Karl kept by the back door. She hid there, holding her skirt over her underwear as her hands and legs blotched purple, until Karl got home from the shop.

He didn't say much when she explained. Just ambled across the street and knocked on Sophia's door. Mrs. Plank handed him Raleigh's coat and bag without a fuss. Sophia and her friends hadn't cared enough to hide their stolen goods. Karl sighed heavily as he came back inside to see her shivering in the kitchen, wrapped in the big crocheted blanket Grandma had made her.

"You gotta learn how to stick up for yourself RaRa," Karl said as hung her stuff up on the coat rack. "It's just gonna get worse if you don't."

All she took from that was that it was going to get worse. She could never defend herself against Sophia and her army of minions.

#

Grandma always told Raleigh that when things felt terrible it was because she needed to adjust her mind frame. Think about things that made her happy until she felt happy.

When the closet opened, two weeks before Christmas break, Raleigh tried to run through her happy thoughts, but could only think of Sophia, smirking at her from DeSean's lap. Maybe Sophia could be reasoned with. Maybe it was just a misunderstanding. Raleigh *had* asked out Sophia's boyfriend. Maybe she just needed to apologize.

It terrified her, so much more than the eyes, impossibly big with impossibly bright whites, peering at her from the dark closet. Sophia Plank was more frightening than the monster in her closet. She had to do something before Sophia destroyed her.

The following morning, she followed Sophia from the bus to the second-floor bathroom, where, once upon a time, they'd done their makeup together.

A few girls waited for Sophia, so Raleigh hid behind the gawdy, plastic nativity set up in the hallway. When Sophia was alone, Raleigh slipped in. Sophia's eyes immediately found her in the mirror where she leaned in with a brow brush.

"Are you stalking me?" A cruel smile curled on her lips.

"I just want t—t—to talk," Raleigh stuttered.

"I just want t—t—to t—t—talk." Sophia's exaggerated imitation caused to her jerk, messing up her brows. She cursed, tossing her brush into the stained porcelain sink. "You're a freaking disease who tried to steal my boyfriend."

"You *told* me to ask him out. I didn't want to."

"Are you saying he's ugly? God, do you have to pick on me, constantly?"

"I just want you to leave me alone!" Raleigh's traitorous tears burst out. "I'll do anything!"

Sophia's eyes, sparkling in the florescent light, found hers again in the mirror. "Anything?"

"I just want you to leave me alone."

Sophia turned around and raised her phone. "Say it on camera."

"Say what?"

"Say 'I am obsessed with Sophia Plank.'"

Raleigh balked.

"Say it!" Sophia's pupils were sharp points, aimed at Raleigh. "Maybe I'll call my dogs off."

"I'm obsessed with you," Raleigh sobbed, conceding.

Sophia played the video back, giggling. "Oh my God, you're so pathetic."

"You'll leave me alone now?"

Sophia shrugged. "It's a start."

By lunch everyone was calling Raleigh a stalker. By last period, boys were enacting her tearful statement in the halls.

"The crying stalker," they taunted.

"Sophia, you better lock your doors," they shouted on the bus. "She'll break into your house and cry at you while you're sleeping."

Sophia just smirked.

#

Mom was sleeping. Karl was out. Raleigh needed to scream.

She ran upstairs to her room and buried her face into her pillow. She punched the bed, she sobbed and she tried, desperately, to scream out the pain before it consumed her.

The closet door creaked open and she sat up, gasping for air.

She couldn't see him there, not in the daylight, but she felt those horrible, too-big eyes on her.

She felt his judgement.

"I don't like you either!" she shouted. "You're a freaking creep! *You're* like a disease!"

There was a stillness in the room, a dense cloud of energy, hanging, coiling, like a spring, tighter and tighter, the tension growing, and just when Raleigh was sure it was about to erupt, she exploded.

A cry burst from some dark part of her and she sprang from her bed, swinging her arms, sweeping Gran's antique dolls off her dresser, books, candles and makeup flung across the room. Screaming, she shoved the heavy dresser into the closet door, shutting and blocking it.

"Leave me alone!" Her voice was wrecked and completely unfamiliar to her.

"RaRa, what's going on?" Mom, bleary eyed, at the door interrupted her outburst.

Raleigh deflated, her rage shriveling back into humiliation. "Nothing. Sorry."

"Honey, tell me what's wrong."

But Mom didn't want to know.

If Raleigh really opened up, spilled her heart, Mom might spew some platitudes about how it gets better and everyone goes through these hard times, but she would do nothing. And Raleigh would have to accept that her mom didn't care enough to try.

"Nothing," she said again.

Mom left it at that. Raleigh dragged her dresser back, depleted. As she set the dolls back on top, she noticed a porcelain hand had broken off her favorite. That's what she got for freaking out. Gran would be so disappointed when she told her at Christmas.

"Hey, look what I found!" Karl cried when Raleigh came down for dinner.

He held up a box with "X-mas lights" scrawled on the side. "It was buried under a pile of scrap in the basement!"

"You wanna put up lights tomorrow when you get home from school, RaRa?" Mom asked from the kitchen where she was cutting cheesesteaks.

"I don't think so," Raleigh mumbled.

"Well, there ought to be some cheer around here," Mom said. "It's already gonna be rough working doubles on Christmas."

"Doubles?" Raleigh asked. "I thought we were going to Grandma's?"

"Not this year," Karl said. "Your Gran is in Florida. Your mom's on doubles, and I put in for overtime at the shop."

"We'll celebrate a few days after with all your favorite stuff. Will Ferrell, chocolate, the works." Mom's voice was too cheerful. She was trying too hard. "We can't pass this up, Ra. We get paid time-and-a-half for holidays."

"But..."

What about me?

The words trembled on her lips, unspoken. She didn't want to hear the answer.

That night she lay in bed and waited for the chill to seep over her chest, for the air to show her breath and for the man in the closet to come.

She fell asleep waiting.

#

Karl and Mom were both at work when she got home from school, so Raleigh was able to cry undisturbed as she washed fruit punch out of her hair in the shower.

But in her room, as she was about to change, the closet door creaked open.

"No!" she shouted. "Ew! Don't be a creep!"

The closet door slammed shut again. Raleigh changed in Mom's room, and crept back into her room afterwards to sit on the bed. She took the doll with the broken hand off the dresser. She wouldn't have to tell Gran about it now.

"Today Sophia promised me she would leave me alone if I dumped a juice box over my head in the middle of lunch. Everyone videoed it. Father O'Brien made me spend the last three periods saying Hail Marys. On the bus, everyone was calling me the praying stalker. Sophia didn't stop them. She's just going to keep making me humiliate myself until I die."

The closet door popped open a crack, but no more. For once, Raleigh didn't feel like it was judging her. She just felt sad. Sadness so heavy it was like weight around her shoulders, her neck, pulling her down into the bed, the floor, the earth, but never far enough that she could just disappear.

"Maybe I should die," she muttered. "Gran is the only person who cares about me and she's in Florida. Christmas used to be my favorite holiday. The one day that everything was okay, but now it's just another day in the nightmare."

There was only silence. Raleigh shook her head and snorted. Why was she telling the closet anyway? "No one would even care if I was gone."

#

On the last day of school before winter break, everyone had been too excited to notice the latest mortifying video of Raleigh that Sophia had demanded in penance.

Sophia had a nasty fight with DeSean during lunch that everyone had been talking about on the bus. Raleigh had been able to avoid being noticed. Sophia had shouted something at her at their stop, but Raleigh hadn't turned back.

When she saw Christmas lights twinkling from her house's dingy gutters, her heavy heart had lifted, just a little.

She had a full week before she had to face her classmates again. Christmas would be lonely, but being lonely alone was better than being lonely in a crowd.

The house smelled like pine and cranberries. Candles Mom must had been burning before she went to work, but still, Christmas.

Raleigh trudged upstairs to her room and was surprised to find a small gift, wrapped in a yellowing foiled paper on her pillow. She opened it carefully, just a little afraid that it was some kind of prank. Under the paper was an aged satin clamshell box with a big brown stain across the padded top. She struggled to pry it open until she realized the little brass knob in the front was a release.

The ring inside was so big and bright Raleigh actually dropped the box with shock.

She dove for it, plucking the ring from the old box and holding it up to the light.

A big opal, glittering with a rainbow of colors, surrounded by teardrop diamonds, each of them big enough to please Mom, if it was in an engagement ring from Karl. The band was thick gold, stamped with a 60's style pattern and engraved on the inside with the words *Sandra and Robert, forever*.

Raleigh's eyes welled up.

This ring was fine antique jewelry, very special to someone once, and no doubt very expensive now.

Who would have given it to her?

It was out of Mom's budget and Karl wouldn't give her something like this.

Gran must had sent it in the mail, feeling bad about missing Christmas. It was exactly the kind of thing Gran would give her, with the old paper and clamshell box. An heirloom, like her dolls.

Raleigh slid it onto her pointer finger and held it up to the light. It was a perfect fit and it made her pasty, freckled hand look fair and delicate. She'd have to keep it a secret, or Mom might get upset with Gran.

#

Mom went out Christmas eve for groceries. Raleigh stayed in her room, admiring her ring.

It caught the soft gold glow of the Christmas lights coming in through the chipped blinds, and she thought about wearing it someday in another place, at a better time of her life. She would graduate. She would live in Arizona and sell antiques. She would wear this ring with peasant dresses, her hair up in a messy bun. She'd have a boyfriend or girlfriend who loved her.

When Mom called, she'd let it go to voicemail.

Someone rapped on the front door and Raleigh groaned, broken from her happy fantasy. Mom must have forgotten her key. Raleigh slipped off the ring and put it on her nightstand before running down the stairs to let her in.

Sophia stood at the door, her eyes red and wet. "DeSean broke up with me."

"Oh, sorry." Raleigh felt that creeping cold feeling across her chest.

"Can I come in?" She didn't wait, just pushed in and looked around the house. "I always wondered what it was like in here. My Uncle Pete says some guy offed himself upstairs when he was a little kid."

"Sophia, I don't—"

"Can I go look?" Sophia's tears were replaced by a hungry, searching look. She dashed up the stairs.

Raleigh followed behind her, fear coiling in her chest.

"Oh my God, your room is ridiculous." Sophia glared around the bedroom with a feral glint in her eyes. "Are those dolls?"

"They're vintage."

"They're ridiculous."

Raleigh felt the hair on her arms rise as Sophia's gaze slid to the ring on the nightstand. Raleigh ran for it, but too late. Sophia snatched it up and held it to the window. "This is the most pretentious thing I've ever seen."

"Give it back," Raleigh gasped.

Sophia slipped it onto her finger.

It felt like she scraped a blade across Raleigh's nerves. "Give it back, Sophia!"

"Ew!" She jerked away from Raleigh's grasp. "I'm a guest."

"Give it to me!" The desperate tears came again.

Sophia smirked. "If you want it so bad, beg me for it."

She pulled out her phone and pointed it at Raleigh. "Go ahead."

Something hot popped in Raleigh's chest. She lunged. Sophia only had a second of surprise before Raleigh knocked the phone away and swung at her stupid perfect face.

But Raleigh's fury was no match for Sophia's savagery. She caught Raleigh's fist and shoved her back onto her bed. "I was trying to be nice to you!" She tackled her, pinning Raleigh's arms down with her knees.

"Do you think DeSean will notice you with one eye?" Sophia pushed the ring to the first joint of her finger and pointed its sharp tines at Raleigh's face.

Raleigh screamed, thrashing beneath her. Sophia's vicious grin spread up her rosy cheeks, her eyes sparkling with glee.

Raleigh barely heard the closet door creak open, the screech of wire hangers.

She barely saw the eyes, too big, too white, too dark, glaring down from over Sophia's shoulder.

She barely saw the bone-white hand reaching toward the ring Sophia held inches from Raleigh's eye.

As soon as Sophia released her, Raleigh scrambled off the bed and ran out of the room. She ran down the steps, and out of the house, off the porch and to the sidewalk.

It wasn't until she was there, standing on the big crack in the concrete that she realized the screaming she heard was not her own.

She turned to run back into save Sophia, but she only took one step toward the porch before she stopped herself. Why? Why save someone so intent on destroying her? But it was the right thing to do, right? Mom would tell her it was. Mom was a nurse. She said everyone deserved to be taken care of. The sisters at Blessed Mother would tell her it was the right thing to do. Christ had taught them to turn the other cheek.

But Raleigh wasn't a nurse. Or a nun. Or Christ. Didn't she get to decide not to sacrifice herself anymore?

Before she could really make up her mind, the screaming stopped. A moment later, Sophia stumbled out of the house. Her face was ashen and her eyes were too big, dull and staring blindly ahead. She staggered down the porch steps, past Raleigh and across the street. A car slammed to a stop a few feet from her, and honked loudly as she lumbered up the concrete steps to her own house. Sophia didn't flinch. She walked inside, leaving the door open to the December chill.

Raleigh sat on her porch, looking at Sophia's house. She wasn't sure what she was waiting for. Eventually someone shut the front door. Eventually Mom came home.

"The store was mobbed." She got out of the car with her arms full of groceries. "What are you doing out here? Scared again? Help me carry in bags."

She didn't wait for Raleigh to answer, just started loading bags into her arms. Raleigh followed her inside. The house was still and silent.

Mom had gotten all of Raleigh's favorite Christmas things, including a DVD pack of holiday movies. She would spend Christmas with Will Ferrell and Pop Tarts. Maybe it wasn't the worst ever.

After helping Mom start dinner, Raleigh crept up stairs. Her room was empty, undisturbed except for the ring sitting on top of Sophia's cell phone on the bed.

She slipped the ring onto her finger and picked up the cell phone. It turned right on as if it didn't have a lock code and Raleigh saw that it hadn't stopped videoing after Sophia dropped it.

Raleigh watched Sophia shove her onto the bed, hold the ring over her eye and threaten to take it out. She could use this to prove that Sophia was the bully.

Then he wavered onto the screen—a tall pillar of darkness, moving like light through water—toward Sophia. His eyes, too big, too white, too black, glanced toward the phone and he winked.

He picked Sophia up by the throat. He lifted her in the air.

Raleigh watched herself scramble from the room like a frightened baby.

He pried the ring from Sophia's fingers. He was not the full shape of a man, but there was enough to see his head lean to her ear. Even over Sophia's screaming, Raleigh heard his whispering, a low hissing gurgle that made the hair on Raleigh's arm stand up straight. He put Sophia down and she staggered back, her pupils filling her irises, her knees wobbling like a rag dolls.

He turned her around and pushed her toward the door and she staggered off. He looked back at the phone and the video shut off.

Raleigh gasped and looked up to the closet.

There he was. A man, sort of. His eyes too big, too white, too black and watching her.

"This ring was from you." Raleigh's voice was barely audible. He nodded his gaunt head. His dark hair fell against his face.

"Why did you give it to me?"

He whispered. Raleigh didn't understand his words, but she saw a vision of herself from a new angle, crying on her bed, saying no one cared. Then she saw another vision, a woman, pretty but sad-faced staring out Raleigh's window. "No one would even care if I was gone," she said and Raleigh's heart ached. Another vision. A casket in a cemetery. No one there except the man with wild dark hair and eyes too big.

"Robert?" Raleigh asked.

He nodded.

He didn't show her the details but Raleigh understood. He hadn't been there for Sandra. He hadn't listened to her when she asked to be loved.

And he had never forgiven himself for it.

"Thank you for saving me," Raleigh said.

He nodded again and turned back to the closet.

"Um, tomorrow... it's Christmas," Raleigh said. He looked back at her. He wasn't so scary.

He smiled a little bit and faded back behind her uniforms.

#

Raleigh woke up Christmas morning to find Mom had left presents under the Christmas tree. Karl left a tower of chocolates on the kitchen table.

She went through Sophia's phone, sending herself a bunch of content before deleting it. Sophia had blackmail videos of half the school. Now Raleigh had them. Insurance. Raleigh ran across the street.

Sophia's mom answered the door, looking pale and tired. "Sophia can't come out," she said. "She's not feeling well."

"I'm just returning her phone," Raleigh said. "Is she okay?"

Mrs. Plank scratched at her throat. "She isn't talking. Do you know what happened?"

"She told me her boyfriend broke up with her."

"That's probably it," Mrs. Plank said.

An hour later an ambulance pulled up in front of the house. Raleigh watched from her bedroom window as they took Sophia out on a stretcher, her eyes staring blankly at the sky.

Raleigh realized Robert was watching beside her. All the judgement was gone. He seemed just as glad as she was that Sophia was being taken away. Something in her body uncoiled and relaxed as she realized she'd never see that gleeful sparkle in Sophia's eyes again.

"Sophia really likes hurting people." It was a relief. A year of mining her own flaws, to realize it had never been her fault.

Robert nodded. He already knew.

Raleigh popped a piece of chocolate into her mouth.

"Have you ever watched *Elf?*"

3¢
241
LAFFWITCH

CRITICAL BLAST PUBLISHING
20¢
APPROVED BY THE READING CODE AUTHORITY
SPLIT DECISION: A SAM HELLER INVESTIGATION
Jacob Seinemeier
SOME CASES BITE BACK

RENT AN ANGRY MIDGET! When you need to stop a Bully from harassing, or when you need to look like a decent human concerned for poor ugly monsters.

RADIOACTIVE CANDY When you want to level up your personality and appear extra sweet to the people around you... and want to have a superpower over sugar... this candy's for you!

HEAD KNIVES 100% stainless steal daggers that launch from the top of your head and kill any conversation you find boring.

SNAKES IN A MAIL BOX Get these total mother-f$%Ken poisonous snakes and mail them with your get well gift cards.

YOU ARE NOT THE THING!

FISH BOWL FULL OF WORMS Are you tired of eating meat? Get yourself a bowl full of yummy worms and feel you are saving the planet.

HOBO IN A BOX When your street is getting over-runned by homeless people and you need someone to speak their language and run them off to the next street down the block.

BOX OF LIVE BATS When you feel like a millionaire crime fighting hero and need to dress up your special cave, to give it that extra touch of atmosphere... a box of live bats is perfect for you. Food not included.

WELCOME MAT TRAP When you don't want people annoying you, a simple press of the button and the trap door will dispose of anyone who stands on it, while waiting for you to answer the door.

COCAINE FOR PETS When your pets become too excited during mating season and you don't want additional burden of feeding more pets, shot them up with some fine liquid snow and chill them out.

Jacob Seinemeier is a speculative fiction writer based in Perth, Western Australia. You can continue his adventures with supernatural PI Sam Heller by reading stories in the upcoming anthology Fire and Ash by Dragon Soul Press; as well as in the final,100th issue of Andromeda Spaceways Magazine. Find Jacob online at www.instagram.com/jacobseinemeierauthor

I'm only about ten centimetres off the ground, *but it may as well be a thousand- it makes no difference to the whipcord wrapped around my neck choking the life out of me. I stretch my toes towards the floor, reaching for any kind of purchase or leverage- and I'm yanked even further upwards. The pressure on my throat squeezes tighter and I'm starting to see little blue spots on the corners of my vision.*

I dig my fingernails in, but the cord is slick, and my nails slip away before they can hook into anything. The room I'm in stinks like sweat and fear. Most of it's mine.

It's dark and getting darker.

Just one night, I think, *my lungs screaming for air as I flail helplessly in midair.* Just one normal fucking night. Poker, lukewarm pizza, a few beers. Was that too much to ask?

Above me, in the shadows, something laughs.

#

TWO HOURS EARLIER

There are three keys to a good poker night. Good pizza is number one.

I already had four of them keeping warm in the oven- picked up from Tommasino's in Mt Lawley this afternoon, best pizza in Perth- when the first of my quartet of potential suckers knocked on my front door.

That's number two- make sure you invite people that you know well enough to read their tells. Taking their money helps defray the cost of the pizza.

I opened the door and let Harriet in.

"Heller," she greeted me, flouncing inside. Harriet was blonde, with an olive complexion that suggested the colour probably wasn't entirely natural. Tonight she'd ditched the green smock and white scrubs that were her usual uniform from Cernunnos Celestial Contours, the cosmetic surgery where she worked- which was also owned by my employer, The Bard Group. She spent most of her day helping Hiders- monsters- to blend in with a world that didn't know they existed. Now she was in a big blue fluffy skirt that reached down to the soles of her feet and a leather jacket over a tight T-shirt with a penguin on it. She carried a small bowl covered in foil and had a sling bag over one shoulder.

"Sorry we're late," Harriet said, swinging the heavy bag up and onto my kitchen counter and dropping the bowl next to it. She shrugged off the jacket and hung it on a chair. "Somebody doesn't know how to read a clock."

The bag bulged and twitched, and a small hairy figure pushed the bag down around its ankles and stepped onto the counter.

He was thirty centimetres tall, covered in wiry red hair from head to toe. Two goggling, golf-ball sized eyes and a bulbous nose emerged from the tangle of hair at one end.

He stretched. "At least I am knowing how to park," Dmitri said. His voice was surprisingly deep, with a strong Eastern European accent.

"Excuse me?" Harriet said, offended.

"You hear me," Dmitri said. He perched himself on the counter, his callused feet with their yellowed nails dangling over the edge. "I swear by Putin's wrinkly nutsack Heller, it is painful to watch. She drives around the block three times before she finds place. Three!"

"Really?" I said, smiling.

"I don't parallel park," Harriet declared. "It's not in my skill set. Anyway Dmitri, how would you know how to park? What are you driving around in, the Barbie Dream Car?"

"Grand Theft Auto." Dmitri grinned. His teeth were huge, and as yellow as his toenails.

"Well, thanks for coming," I said, setting out bowls of chips on the kitchen table. "Been meaning to have folk over since I moved in, but I kept putting it off."

"You live here, what? A year?" Dmitri asked. The furry little humanoid hopped off the counter with surprising agility and landed on the floor like a cat. He strolled into the living room, craned his neck up and regarded the books on the shelves curiously. He looked back at me. "No, wait." He sniffed at the air. "Year and one week."

"Yeah, exactly. How do you-" Oh, wait. He would know. Dmitri was a kind of Hider called a domovoi- a house spirit. His people had been displaced from Europe during World War Two, coming to Australia with the rest of the flood of refugees. Before that, they had lived in the walls of family homes- mostly in Poland, parts of Russia, places like that- and taken care of their inhabitants for generations- fixing shows, scaring off intruders, that sort of thing. These days, they worked for The Bard Group, just like I did. They were tech support. My job description was a little more fluid. Fewer spreadsheets, more picking locks and punching things. "Never mind."

"It's nice," Harriet said, peeling the foil off the bowl and unpacking a stack of small toast pieces from the bag. She looked around at my place; the bare walls, the bookshelf with a half-dozen books and mostly empty shelves. "A little sparse."

"I don't have much stuff," I admitted. "It's a habit. When I was growing up, we moved around a lot. Always got used to travelling light." The pungent smell of the stuff in the bowl struck my sinuses and I blinked, my eyes watering. "Wow. That's...aromatic."

"*Patê de Atum*," Harriet said proudly. "Brazilian tuna dip. My grandmother- it's her recipe. She's famous for it."

"Had to breathe that all the way over in the car," Dmitri

said, wandering back into the kitchen. He hopped up onto a chair, then onto the table, and began inspecting the stacks of poker chips. "Smells like my feet."

"Hey!" Harriet said, gesturing threateningly with a toast point. "You giving shit to my *vovó?*"

"Hell no," Dmitri said. "Everybody know the worse food smell the better it taste. So that-" he pointed at the bowl, "is going to be fucking amazing."

My intercom buzzed. I walked over to the door and leaned on the button. "Yeah?"

"Delivery from Liquor Locals," rasped the bored voice on the other end.

"Booze?" Dmitri perked up. He was spreading the cards out onto the table and shuffling them with his feet.

"Booze," I confirmed to him. "I'll be right down," I told the delivery guy, and released the button. "You guys okay to hold down the fort here?"

"Sure," Harriet said. "I'll keep an eye on Dmitri, make sure he isn't stacking the deck."

"Please." Dmitri scoffed, and kept shuffling the cards, sliding them around with his prehensile toes. "Like I am needing to cheat to beat you lightweights. You are all about to become very, very poor."

#

Downstairs, I buzzed in the delivery guy and took possession of a carton of Little Creatures Pale Ale and two bottles of wine. As he left and the door was closing on him, in the late afternoon sunlight, I caught a glimpse outside of a small figure laden with bags, hobbling for the rapidly closing automatic door.

"Waitwaitwait!"

I hit the button and let him in.

"Thanks, Sam." Ernesto puffed, lifting the stuffed bags of groceries and shuffling inside. The ten-year old was short for his age, with dark eyes that always seemed shadowed, like he'd been punched even when he wasn't. "I forgot my key and I didn't want to bother Mum."

"No hassle, Ernesto. How is Luz doing?"

He shrugged. "She's okay. The baby keeps waking her up at night. Doing backflips, she says. And she's sick a lot."

"That's pretty standard pregnancy stuff, I think."

"Yeah," he said, dragging the bags towards the elevator. "I suppose. But she's tired all the time, and she can't sleep. Says she has nightmares. And she doesn't want to eat. Says everything tastes funny, like metal."

I frowned. "Has she seen anybody?"

"No. But Mrs Collins, the old lady on the top floor? She's been giving her some herbal tea and checking in on her. Says when she was younger she was a...dougle?" Ernesto squinted. "A drooler?"

"A doula?"

"Yeah. One of those. So she knows about babies and stuff."

"Okay- that's good, I guess," I said doubtfully. "But you tell Luz to call me if she needs a ride to the doctor."

"I will, I- *Madre de Dios!*" He cried out, staring over my shoulder.

I turned. Looming before the closed sliding door, fringed by the orange waning light from the afternoon sun, was a massive dark figure. At least seven feet tall, with long, lanky arms, dressed in black leather, wearing a tinted motorcycle helmet. They carried a heavy canvas bag in one hand.

I smiled. "All good, 'Nesto. He's a friend of mine."

"Seriously?" Ernesto's gaze darted between the terrifying black figure and me.

"Sure," I said, and buzzed him in. The leather-clad figure ducked his head under the doorframe as he entered. He wore heavy-soled workboots that were ludicrously, ridiculously oversized. His feet were practically the size of small canoes. He held up a hand. I slapped his palm. He wore leather gloves... and if one were paying close attention, one might notice that each hand had only three fingers and a thumb.

Ernesto was not paying close attention. He was gazing up at this man-mountain and trying not to stare.

"Ernesto," I said, "meet Tavric D'Aubigny."

Tavric bowed slightly, the bag he carried clanking as he did so. Ducking down did nothing to make him look less intimidating. When he spoke, the voice held a slight lisp and a pronounced French accent. It echoed inside the oversized helmet. "*Bonjour, mes ami.* Thutch a pleasure to meet you. How do you know our Detective Heller here?"

"Sam? H-h...he's a friend of my *mami.*"

"Ah, I thee." Tavric gestured with one hand at the groceries that Ernesto was struggling with. "Can we help you with your bagth?"

"No...no, I'm good." Ernesto lifted the sacks and nudged the elevator button with his elbow. "Anyhow Sam, I gotta get back to my Mum. I'll tell her you said hi."

"You do that," I said. "And don't forget about what I said about the doctor. You guys need anything, I'm just a few floors up."

He nodded.

"You are taking care of your mother, little one?" Tavric asked him.

"I'm not that little," Ernesto protested weakly. "But yeah. It's just the two of us, but I'm looking after her. The baby too, when it's born."

"*Très bon*," Tavric nodded approvingly. He raised his hand to his helmet in a strange, archaic-looking salute. "That's good. A boy should take care of hith mother. You are a fine young man. She ith lucky to have you."

Ernesto's chin went up, and he stood a little straighter under the weight of the shopping bags. When the doors opened, he stepped inside, nodded to Tavric and me, and they closed again.

Tavric turned to me. The fluorescent overhead lights glinted off the visor of the motorcycle helmet. "Nice kid."

"You scared the crap out of him," I laughed. "Materialising out of the darkness like that. You look like the Terminator in that getup."

Tavric shrugged. "Imagine how he'd react if I took the helmet off. Anyway, your jealouthy is tho unfortunate. You know you couldn't pull off thith look if you tried." He leaned down and scooped the carton of Little Creatures off the floor with one gloved hand and raised it to his shoulder, seemingly without effort.

"So, you ready to play some cards?" I asked as we waited for the lift.

Tavric snorted. "That little reprobate Dmitri'th been bragging all week how he'th going to bankrupt me. I'm looking forward to taking him to thchool."

"I'd like to see that."

#

A few minutes later we were back in the apartment.

"Hey Tav!" Harriet called out from her place at the table where she and Dmitri had just finished dividing up the poker chips.

"Hey yourthelf, *chérie!*" Tavric dropped the beer on the counter and leaned his canvas bag carefully against one wall. He reached up and began undoing the strap of the motorcycle helmet. I took four beers out of the carton, popped the tops and started passing them out.

"Tavric," Dmitri said, eyeing the canvas bag. He was wearing a green translucent visor he had produced from somewhere and was setting up a card holder in front of himself. "Please be telling me you are not bringing your fucking weapon to poker night."

Tavric pulled off the helmet and unfurled his ears. He shook them out. Long, furred and rabbitlike, they added almost a foot and a half to his height and brushed against the ceiling. His face was also covered in brown and white fur, except for his pink nose, which twitched. His eyes were a vivid violet.

He grinned. Two prominent square upper teeth protruded over his bifurcated upper lip, but the rest of his teeth were white, straight and very human. "Come on man," he admonished the domovoi, taking off his gloves and accepting a beer from me. "You don't expect me to leave my baby at home? Yvette ith the love of my life." He took a swig and dropped into a chair at the table, which creaked under his weight.

He wasn't kidding. The way Tavric had explained it to me, the Cuniculari were a group of Hiders with a martial culture, and they were expected to always be ready for battle. In the margins of old illuminated manuscripts from the Middle Ages, there are drawings- considered fanciful embellishments by most serious historians-of rabbits carrying spears, pikes, swords, and charging into battle alongside Medieval knights. Tavric told me that was because sometimes their helmets came off and word got around. Fortunately most of the monks who illustrated those scrolls were drunk off their arses, so nobody took them seriously.

"I can't believe you gave your glaive a girl's name," I said.

"I didn't," he said, placing a three fingered furry hand over his heart. "Yvette named herthelf."

"Boys," Harriet said. Her green eyes flashed and she smiled at me, dealing out the cards, her hands moving almost too fast to see. "We gonna talk all night? Or are we gonna gamble?"

#

"Ha!" Dmitri crowed, throwing down his cards. He did a little jig as we all realised that he'd pulled another straight out of his fuzzy behind. "Read 'em and weep, you fuckers of mothers!"

"Christ," I said in disgust. "How do you keep doing this?" I reached for another slice of pizza. The meatlovers was all gone, but there were a couple of slices of vegetarian left; Tavric had polished off the rest of that one.

"Is just numbers," Dmitri said, scooping his winnings over to his side of the table, adding to his already towering stack of chips. He buffed his knuckles against his hairy chest. "I am good with numbers."

"You mean you're counting cards? That's not exactly cheating, but it's close."

Dmitri shrugged, his gigantic eyes wide and innocent-looking. "You say potato, I say vodka."

I threw up my hands and turned to the other gamblers for consolation. They weren't listening; Harriet was talking to Tavric. "So there's how many of you left?"

"Only fifty or so," Tavric lamented, draining his beer

and reaching behind him for another. "The Cuniculari are not tho good at staying off the radar as other Hiderth. The Spanish Inquithition wathn't kind to us. My people tend to fight when cornered. Motht of us went down in a blaze of glory. Took a lot of the bastards with us though." He gave another one of those ritualistic salutes. "Thtill, makes it hard. We're thpread out all over."

"You couldn't get your numbers up over the years? I thought you guys would be all...y'know." She gestured to him with her glass.

"Copulating like rabbits?" Tavric laughed. "Hell, if only. Our birthrate ith a lot lower." He grinned and sat back in his chair, stroking his whiskers. "Thtill, it isn't for lack of trying, *chérie*."

There was a pounding at the door. Loud and frantic.

"You expecting somebody?" Harriet asked. I shook my head. Without a word, Dmitri leaped off the table and scurried behind the kitchen counter. Tavric stood up and stepped to one side of the door. I opened it.

It was Ernesto. He was standing in the hallway, his dark eyes wide and terrified and brimming with tears.

"Sam," he said, "You have to come. There's something wrong with Mum." He was shaking, almost vibrating in place.

"What is it?" I said, alarmed. I stepped out into the hall with him.

"I don't know!" Ernesto cried. "She took a nap, and she won't wake up."

"She's breathing?" Harriet said, joining us.

"Yeah- but she sounds really sick. You have to help her, Sam, I don't know what to do-"

"Hey," I said grabbing him by both shoulders. "It's okay.

She'll be okay. My friend here's a nurse. We'll come right now."

"Okay, but hurry. I didn't want to leave her alone, but-"

"I get it. You did the right thing. Let's go." I called back into the apartment. "We won't be long."

From his place next to the door Tavric nodded. I shut the door and Harriet and I followed Ernesto, who ran ahead of us, hopping in place, waiting impatiently for us to catch up.

"Heller," Harriet said quietly to me as we made our way to the elevator, Ernesto in the lead, "If she's really non-responsive, we'll need an ambulance. We should call one now, just in case."

"Wait a bit," I replied. "Check her out first. Then only if we have to."

"Why on Earth not? Is she a Hider?" I shook my head. "Not exactly."

"What do you mean 'not exactly?'"

I looked at her. Her mouth was set in a hard line. She didn't appreciate me holding things back. I didn't blame her. Not that it mattered. I sighed. "She's pregnant. And she has a restraining order against her ex-husband."

She raised an eyebrow. "Okay, but I don't see-"

"Her ex is a cop. He doesn't know where she is."

Ernesto was standing by the elevator jabbing at the button. He was listening to us, but barely. His attention was on the floor above, and his mother, waiting for him.

Harriet frowned. "I see."

"Yeah. So if she goes to the hospital, there's a record. He may not know where she is now, but if I call an ambulance the asshole definitely will."

"I get it," Harriet said. "I do. But I won't risk her life."

I looked her in the eye. "Neither will I."

The three of us stepped into the elevator, and she took my arm. "Sam, who is she to you?"

"A friend," I said.

"And what else?" Harriet asked. Her green eyes bored into mine. I looked away, shook my head again, and the doors closed on us.

#

Ernesto and Luz's apartment was lightless when he let us inside. A chill wind blew through the hallway. He hesitated, and flipped the light switch. The hallway lit up, and he hurried us inside. " 'Nesto, what is it?" I said, sensing his nervousness.

"I thought I left all the lights on," he said.

We followed him through the flat, flicking on light switches as we went. We passed through to Luz's bedroom. Like the rest of the house, the lights were out.

This room was the source of the cold air. The window next to the bed was wide open, and the freezing wind rippling the curtains.

I turned on the light. Luz was lying in bed, dressed in a thick robe and fluffy blue pyjamas. Her dark hair was sweaty and stuck to her forehead; her delicate features were pinched and pale. She was sprawled on top of the covers, her arms wrapped around her pregnant belly, and she was motionless.

"Mum?" Ernesto called to her, racing to her side and taking her hand. It sat limply in his own. "I brought Mr Heller, and a nurse. You're going to be okay now."

"Luz?" I reached her side. "Luz, you awake?" She didn't move. Her breathing was rapid, but shallow.

Harriet approached the bed and placed a hand on Luz's forehead. "She's freezing." She looked at the window. "Why's this open?"

"Mrs Collins," Ernesto said absently, rubbing the back of his mother's hand.

Harriet looked at me.

"The doula, apparently," I told her.

"She told us cold, fresh air is good for Mum, and the baby," Ernesto explained. "Said we should always keep it open."

"Well, she's wrong," Harriet said firmly. "Your mother is going to catch a chill this way." She felt under Luz's jawline. "Heller, get that shut, will you?"

I reached up and yanked. It didn't move. I tried again, pushing until my muscles were straining and sweat broke out on my cold skin.

"You okay there, champ?" Harriet said. She lifted Luz's pyjama top, exposing the brown expanse of her pregnant stomach. She pressed gently, moving her hands back and forth. Luz moaned slightly. Harriet stopped, then peered closer.

"It's stuck," I explained. I examined the jamb. What I saw chilled me worse than the freezing air drifting through the open window. There were nails driven into the runner of the window frame, hammered in inexpertly in clusters, and bent over so that the window couldn't be closed.

"Fuck," I muttered.

"What?" Harriet looked up.

"Somebody jammed this window open. Permanently."

"That's not good. But that's not the worst thing," Harriet said.

"What's the worst thing?"

"This." Harriet pointed. I looked down. The flesh of Luz's stomach was pockmarked by tiny wounds. Dozens of them. Some were clearly fresh, some were red and inflamed and nearly closed over, but each one consisted of three small incisions in the rough shape of a triangle, with a small puncture in the centre.

"What are those?" cried Ernesto. "What did that to her?"

"Ernesto," Harriet said to him, calmly. "I'm going to need you to go to the kitchen. Find three or four clean dish cloths. It's important that they're clean. Soak them in hot water, not boiling, and put them in a bowl and bring them to me. Can you do that?"

"But-"

"Ernesto, I'm a nurse. I'm going to take good care of your mother, I promise. Can you get those cloths for me?"

He nodded, swallowing hard, and ran out of the room.

"Heller," she whispered to me, running a shaking hand through her short blonde hair. "I don't know exactly what did this, but these are injection sites. Or bite marks. Something has been feeding on this woman, maybe for weeks. Probably the baby too. Blood or amniotic fluid, or both."

I looked at Luz's pale face. She shivered once, all over, and I looked out at the darkness. "The window." I said. "That's how it gets in." I moved over to the open window, grabbed hold of the sill, and turned myself around. I stuck my head out the gap and looked skyward along the side of the apartment block.

The staring thing that was clinging to the side of the building shrieked, and my scream echoed its own.

Its eyes were wide and bloodshot, its mouth distended into a grotesque snarl. It was hanging upside down, lank, stringy hair dangling over its face. Leathery wings buffeted at my eyes and enveloped me in a stink like rotting, flyblown rancid meat. I caught a glimpse of something like long ropy tendrils flailing the air as it spun in place, then it was gone- and I dived inside, retching, dropping to all fours.

"Heller!" Harriet ran to my side and helped me up. "Jesus, you're shaking. What was it?"

I swallowed my gorge and leaned against the wall. "I don't know," I said. "But it was waiting. It was outside the window, waiting for us to leave so it could get to Luz again."

"Where did it go?"

"It went up."

Harriet looked to the nailed-open window, then back to Luz- then to me. "That doula, Mrs Collins. What do you know about her?"

"Not much." My eyes kept going to the blackness outside the window. "She's been in the building a month. I never met her."

"Where does she live?"

I looked at Harriet. "Top floor."

She nodded. "I think we need to pay her a visit."

"What about Luz?"

She shook her head. "Her pupils are dilated and her pulse is weak. The baby's too. I can't wake her. If I'm right, then nothing will- not until we find what did this. Hospital won't help. They can't even diagnose something like this. They might even kill her trying to help her."

"Okay," I said. I leaned down and scooped up Luz. Despite her condition, she seemed to weigh nothing at all. Her sweat was cold against my neck. She cried out softly, but her eyes stayed shut. "But we need to get her out of this room."

#

We left Ernesto with his mother in the living room, locking the bedroom door behind us. Luz was wrapped in a thick blanket on the couch, with Ernesto laying the warm cloths across her belly and whispering to his comatose mother in Spanish. The cloths wouldn't help, but then- nothing would. Not until we found the thing from the window.

Before I left the apartment, I borrowed a couple of things from the kitchen.

Presents. For the creature that hurt Luz.

#

The top floor was kind of a weird situation.

The place where Mrs Collins lived had originally been the building Super's apartment before superintendents stopped being a thing and the owners subcontracted the job out to a company that serviced twenty different blocks of flats. Now it was just a regular apartment half the size of the rest. It was located at the end of a long, dusty hallway and surrounded by storage rooms that lay open and empty and festooned with spiderwebs and rat-droppings. Across the hall, just past Collins' apartment, was a stairway to the roof that had been chained up years ago after one of the tenants had taken a swan dive off the top of the building. Good times.

The tiny size and general disarray of the place had put off a lot of potential renters, but apparently this Collins woman had been fine with both the cramped quarters...and the isolation.

A better detective than me would have found this suspicious. Harriet stood beside me while I pounded on the door.

"Mrs Collins!" I called out. "Are you there?"

There was no answer.

I thumped the door, harder this time. "Mrs Collins, it's about Luz, the woman downstairs you were helping. She's in a bad way and I wanted to talk to about it."

Still silence from beyond the door.

I turned to Harriet. "You might want to step back. One of two things are about to happen; either I'm busting into a weird monstrous Hider's lair- or I'm about to give a little old lady a heart attack." She stepped aside.

I took a few steps back and drove my boot into the door, near the lock. It splintered, but held. A second kick and the door flew open, crashing into the opposite wall and swinging drunkenly.

It was pitch-dark inside; however the familiar repellent stench that wafted from the lightless space stung at my eyes and made my stomach turn over unpleasantly- from both nausea...and fear.

"Answers that question," Harriet muttered, wrinkling her nose.

I moved into the space. Like Luz's apartment, it was freezing. I could hear the wind whistling from somewhere on the other side of the room.

I flicked the light switch. Nothing happened. "Well, that's unsettling," I said.

Harriet took out her phone and switched on the torch. The narrow beam revealed a drab one-room apartment. A Murphy bed lay folded against one wall. A small kitchenette was squeezed into one corner. A reclining armchair sat by the open window. It was occupied.

Someone sat, cross legged, in the recliner. The shadowy profile of their knees was outlined by the open window behind them.

"Mrs Collins?" I said. "That you?" I stepped closer.

No answer.

"There's a young lady downstairs who's in a bad way," Harriet said behind me. "We think you might have something do with that."

Still nothing.

I reached the chair. Something about the outline of the dimly lit figure looked- wrong. I pointed, and Harriet shone her phone-light onto the chair.

It was occupied...but only halfway. Sitting in the chair were a pair of severed legs, torn off at the waist, one denim-clad knee casually hanging over the other, sneakered feet dangling. Above them was a bloody, red stump where the torso should be.

"Jesus-fucking-Christ!" I cried out.

Behind me, Harriet muttered something in Portugese. It was either a prayer or a curse.

So much for Collins, I thought numbly. *Whatever was outside the window must have gotten her too. But why prop her up like this? And where's the other hal-*

The pair of legs uncrossed itself—and recrossed the other way. One toe bounced slightly in mid-air.

I didn't scream. I was pretty proud of myself. I opened my mouth to say something, but nothing came out. I turned to Harriet, who had closed the gap between us and was now pressed against my back. She was trembling, but had not lowered her phone light. "Oh no. Oh nononono," she whispered.

"What?" I said finally. I couldn't take my eyes off the severed legs, waiting for them to move again.

"This is very bad," Harriet said.

"You think?"

"I've heard of this," she said. She leaned closer and shone the light onto the place where the body's torso should have been. I suddenly realised that no blood seeped from the wound. There was not a drop spilled on the purple velvet armchair on which the legs sat. "But I genuinely thought they were extinct. Nobody's seen one in...fuck, centuries."

"Seen what?"

"A Manananggal."

"Say that again?"

"A....kind of vampire. They're from the Philippines. Except nobody ever saw one anywhere else. I mean ever. This is...this is impossible."

"There's a lot of things that are impossible about this, Harry. Geography's pretty far down the list for me. I need more from you than just how this shouldn't be here."

I resisted the urge to run screaming from the room and peered closer at Mrs Collins' bottom half. The veins, arteries weren't gushing blood...but they did have blood in them. They pulsed rhythmically with a heart that was simply *gone*, but the blood as it left the severed blood vessels just...vanished. It should have been spurting over the armchair, the floor. I should have been wading through gore right now. But it was like it was disappearing into somewhere else.

"The way I heard it, during the day, a Manananggal looks human." Harriet whispered. "Then at night, the top half separates from the rest. Its torso grows wings and flies around looking for victims to feed on. Specifically pregnant women, Heller. Like Luz."

I nodded. "Figures. Any idea how do you kill one?"

"Are you kidding?" Harriet shook her head, staring at Mrs Collin's severed legs. "I have no idea."

"But you know about Hider biology, right?"

"This isn't fucking biology!" Harriet's voice was pitched higher than normal. She jabbed a fingernail at the horror in the chair. "Nothing about...about that thing makes sense. We need to get out of here. This is outside our pay grade. We need to call it in to Bard before the thing gets back."

"*The thing gets back*," echoed a mocking voice from the darkness of the apartment. It was accompanied by a low, liquid laugh.

We fell silent.

Somewhere in the shadows around us that Harriet's phone-light stubbornly refused to illuminate, something slithered. There was a dry rustling, perhaps of leathery wings.

I slowly reached out my hand and slid the nearby window closed. I flicked the latch shut.

"What are you doing!" Harriet hissed.

I started backing towards the front door, Harriet still behind me. I watched the shadows for movement. My two presents, purloined from Luz's apartment, felt woefully inadequate in my pockets.

When we reached the door, I turned and pushed Harriet into the hallway. She clutched at my shirt. "Heller, this is crazy, let's just go, we can call it in, Evelyn can send a team-"

I ignored her. "Go downstairs," I whispered. "Get Tavric and tell him to come up here. Tell him..." I paused, grinned, aware that I probably looked insane. "Tell him to bring Yvette."

Harriet took one look at my face and the next objection died behind her lips before she uttered it. "Why are you doing this?" she asked instead.

"Hurry," I said without answering.

Harriet nodded, stepped closer, and kissed me once, hard, on the mouth, hands pressed against the side of my face. She kept her eyes open, big green pools staring into mine. Even with the creature's stink still wafting from the open doorway, she smelled like lemon soap and fear.

"What was that for?" I asked, once I could breathe again.

"For good luck," she said. She pressed her phone into my hand and fled down the hallway.

"*Good luck,*" hissed the mocking voice from the rank emptiness behind me.

I stepped inside and closed the door behind me.

"Alone at last," I said to the dark. I propped Harriet's phone against the wall where the beam could stream across to the opposite wall. I wanted both hands free. "Why don't you come out here and we can have a chat about what you did to Luz?"

From the space above the fridge, just to my right, something crawled into view. My eyes had started to adjust slightly, and that- along with the glimmer from the phone light- allowed me to watch the thing as it squeezed itself from its hiding place, crawling across the ceiling and into the centre of the room. Two large leathery wings spread outwards, almost meeting the opposite walls. It hung from an exposed beam in the ceiling, and I saw it properly for the first time.

The Manananggal was a horrorshow. From its torso, pointed towards the ceiling, hung ropes of severed entrails- loops of intestine, the jagged stump of a broken spinal column, ropy clusters of arteries and wormlike veins that writhed and contorted, seemingly with a mind of their own. The creature, regarding me from upside down, had stringy black hair that was thin, lank and looked like it would come free of the grey skin of its scalp if you pulled on it. The eyes were wide and staring, lidless, the whites shot through with broken capillaries, its pupils tiny black dots. Its mouth hung open in a wide gaping jaw filled with broken, jagged teeth. From its maw lolled a long thin tongue that curled and twisted, tasting the air. Its wings flexed slowly.

I swallowed. "I gotta say, lady," I said. "You're only half as ugly as I thought you'd be."

The face of the thing that masqueraded as Mrs Collins split into a snaggle-toothed grin. "*Funny*," it rumbled. Long-fingered clawed hands, jointed oddly, rubbed together as it regarded me.

"Even so," I went on, "that still makes you one hideous fucking broad."

The tongue struck.

I had no idea it could stretch so far- more than ten feet covered in a moment, and it was wrapped around my throat before I could blink. I grabbed the end of it, and just in time, because it was going for my eyes. Three sharp tooth-like profusions emerged from one end, which snapped together with a hideous clicking noise, desperately trying to reach me. The creature's tongue squeezed- and I was pulled into the air.

I struggled to breathe, feet dangling, but my windpipe was clamped shut by the pressure of the Manananggal's prehensile tongue. I kicked, thrashed and fought, but every movement just burned away precious energy and oxygen, and I was lifted even closer to the creature hanging from the rafters.

"What were you going to tell me about the woman?" the creature hissed, speaking from the side of its mouth. The teeth at the end of her tongue clicked rapidly. They sounded like laughter. *"Luz, yes? So sweet. Weeks I have fed on her.*

Weeks. Every day she grows weaker. How did you not know, little hunter? Why did you not check on her?" It shook its head, white staring eyes regarding me with mock sympathy. *"So sad. She trusted you."* The black wings curled inwards, enveloping us in a stinking embrace.

Rage filled me. I took the end of the creature's tongue which hovered in front of my face, seeking my eyes- and jammed it into my shoulder. The fangs bit deep, slicing through my flesh, but with my now free hand I dug in my back pocket, coming up with a can of insect repellent. I pointed the nozzle upwards and sprayed it straight into the thing's eyes.

The Manananggal uttered a squeal so high-pitched I thought my skull would crack in half. The creature dropped from the ceiling, the tongue relaxed, I hit the ground and I thrashed free of the nauseating organ. The creature was on the floor, its hands digging into its awful face to clear its eyes of the poison.

I stepped up to it and dropkicked it straight in the throat.

It gagged, turned away and dragged itself with one hand across the room, towards the window and the chair with its hideous contents. With the other hand it scooped white toxic foam from its eyes, flinging it away as it continued its mewling cries. Its wings had retracted close to its body. The ropes of its guts dragged across the floor.

"What were you saying?" I told it, coming up behind it. I aimed a second kick at the protrusion of its exposed spinal column, and the thing skidded forward a foot on the slick floor.

"What was that? I can't hear you." I kicked it again, knocking it down, and pulled the kitchen knife I had borrowed from Luz's place from the back of my belt. "You were saying something funny. About how you hurt my friend. I was kind of distracted by your gross fuckin' tongue, so I might have missed something."

I leaned forward, grabbed a handful of its scabrous scalp from behind. "The hell with it," I said in its ear. "Wasn't funny anyway." I jammed the knife into the side of its head, all the way down to the handle.

I shoved it forward, and its face bounced off the floor. It lay still.

But only for a moment...then the creature began shaking uncontrollably, its head jerking forward as it struggled to lift itself off the floor with its skinny arms. The wings rattled. The sound....oh god. The sound it made.

It was fucking laughing.

I stepped back as it spun, balanced on its hands, and spread its wings wide again. The insect poison was dripping from its chin, its eyes now more bloodshot than ever. It had my knife jutting from one temple. Its mouth grinned even wider. With hallucinatory clarity, I saw that from the corner of one eye, the tip of the knife protruded, sharp steel winking in the faint light from Harriet's phone.

Its tongue re-emerged as I stood, frozen. The prehensile organ reached up, wrapped around the handle of the kitchen knife, and pulled it free. There wasn't a drop of blood on the blade...and nothing emerged from the hole it made.

I'd stabbed it through the brain- and it was like I'd done nothing at all.

In an instant, the Manananggal leapt forward, using its powerful tongue to drive the knife through my left foot, into the floor, where it stuck.

I screamed, blood welling up through the top of my shoe and spilling into a widening pool on the floor. I clutched at my ankle, cursing.

The Manananggal laughed again.

"*Alors!*" The shout came from the doorway. The creature and I both turned at once. As I did so a flash of agony ran up my leg like an electric shock.

The door had been flung wide. Standing in the the hallway was a massive figure, two long ears silhouetted against the dim light. "Move away from *Monthieur* Heller, *madame.* I have yet to take all hith money."

Leather-clad, Tavric stalked into the room. Balanced in one hand he carried an intimidating weapon, resembling two short spears joined at the hilts. The centre of the glaive was bound in sweat-stained red cloth. It was here that Tavric held the instrument of mayhem, spinning it in place like a helicopter blade, twin points flashing. He fell into a martial stance in the middle of the room, knees crouched, shoulders braced.

The rabbitman grinned, beckoning with one paw in a *come-hither* gesture. "Come to us, *madame.* Yvette would very much like to meet you."

The Manananggal shrieked, flapped its powerful wings and catapulted across the room. Tavric met the creature's charge by flipping backwards, landing with one leg splayed behind him, with the blade of the glaive pointed outward. The Manananggal, unable to stop its momentum, was skewered on the point of the spear.

Tavric roared something French in triumph. Only to have his voice trail off as the monstrosity, unfazed by the lance through its midsection, dragged itself forward with its hands, moving determinedly along the shaft of the weapon that transfixed it. Its tongue lashed out and scored a long vicious wound across the warrior's face, narrowly missing an eye.

"Heller!" Tavric shouted in alarm. "Is there thomething you forgot to tell me?"

"A little busy here, Tav!" I grunted through gritted teeth. I reached down and took the handle of the knife in my hand. I tried to pull it out, but the hilt was too slick with blood; I couldn't keep hold of it. Instead, I started rocking it back and forth, jolts of nauseating pain pulsing through my entire body with every movement. Blood continued to gush from my foot, the trickle becoming a torrent. It was a little alarming how much there was.

Tavric leapt into the air, taking the Manananggal with him, and drove two powerful legs outward into the thing, pushing it away before it could reach him. The horror slid off the spear shaft, but took to the air again before it struck the ground, seemingly unhurt. It swept out a long back-jointed arm and narrowly missed taking Tav in the throat with its sharply crooked nails. His glaive, now freed from the monster, spun in the air again and he slashed out at it, striking once, twice- but it just kept coming, diving and swiping at him. He ducked and weaved with blinding speed-but the Manananggal was faster.

Finally the knife in my foot- snapped. The point stayed in the floor, but the blade came free. I yanked it out and looked at Tavric. He was fending off the creature, but had sustained multiple slashes from its claws. He couldn't keep this up. I tore off one of my sleeves and wrapped it around my bleeding foot. The cloth turned scarlet immediately.

There had to be a way to hurt it. It didn't seem to bleed, no matter how many holes Tavric put in it. Although....I looked over at the pair of legs that sat in the armchair. They seemed to have *plenty* of blood pumping around, didn't they? It just... .disappeared where it left the body. Maybe there was a reason the thing left its lower half behind.

I limped over to the pair of legs, took the broken knife in both hands and drove it into the discorporated limb's left thigh.

The legs kicked out spasmodically. Blood welled up around the blade. There was an answering shriek behind me.

Gotcha, I thought, and went for another strike. Before I could, I was knocked to the ground by an outstretched bat wing. The knife flew from my hand and skittered into the darkness. I was driven to the ground by a stinking, fetid weight, cold flesh bearing me down. The beast slammed a fist into the back of my head. I tried to flip over, but the thing had hold of me.

"*When I'm finished with you*," the Manananggal hissed, claws digging into my shoulders, "*I'm going to eat that little bitch and her baby. I'm going to hollow her out. I'll make Ernesto watch while I rip her open-*"

"*Dégénéré*! You'll do nothing of the thort!" Tavric cried. He lunged out of the darkness, bleeding from a dozen different wounds, wrapped his arms around the beast and drove his powerful legs into the floor, leapfrogging the two of them backwards, covering the entire length of the kitchen in one bound. They struck the fridge with a crash.

I struggled to my feet. I had to finish her quickly. No time to look for the knife. I needed to do a lot of damage, fast. I looked at the window next to the chair. I darted over, unlocked it, pushed it open.

Tav cried out in pain, but the beast screamed in frustration. He had it in a Full Nelson and wasn't letting go, despite the damage it was doing to him with its teeth and tongue and claws. The two of them writhed on the floor in a hideous embrace.

I took hold of the denim-clad legs. They kicked out at me with their sneakers, as if sensing what I was about to do. I ducked down and slung them over my shoulders, taking a heel in the chin for my trouble that probably cracked a tooth, but I ignored it. The legs bucked back and forth, I leaned forward- and shoved them out the window. The disembodied limbs disappeared into the night...and dropped straight down.

"No!" the Manananggal howled.

"Oh yes, madame!" Tav crowed, clutching it tighter.

Seconds later, from far below, outside the window, eight floors down- there was a crash, as of a heavy weight hitting something in the street. Glass shattered and metal shrieked.

In the apartment, there was a horrible cracking sound- like a series of dry twigs breaking; like uncooked pasta snapping...I looked back into the room.

Tavric had released the thing and stood over it, holding Yvette at the ready. He didn't need it; the Manananggal was a twisted wreck, its breath coming in a high, keening whistle. Its wings were shattered like broken umbrellas, white bone poking through leathery flesh. Its multi-jointed arms jutted out from its hideous torso in different directions and its long clawed fingers looked as if it had stuck them in a ceiling fan on high power.

In short- it looked as if it had fallen eight stories from a high window.

The beast flopped once on the floor, then fell still.

I hobbled over to where it lay, leaving bloody footprints as I went. The creature that had masqueraded as Mrs Collins stared up at me. Its skull was misshapen, pushed in on one side, its jaw shattered. Its blood-filled eyes rolled slowly towards me, tongue unfurling limply onto the floor. The three teeth clicked once.

I spat in its face.

"Just so you know," I said to it, my voice seeming to come from very far away. My pulse pounded in my ears. I wanted to throw the thing out the window all over again. "Luz has been dealing with scarier things than you her whole fucking life. You're not even a distant second."

The Manananggal took another long, whistling breath through punctured lungs....and didn't take another.

Tavric, leaning on Yvette like a cane, limped over to the window, the blade making divots in the floorboards as he walked. "That was good thinking, Heller," he said. He looked out and gazed down into the street. He didn't speak for a good ten seconds. "Merde."

"What?" I asked, concerned.

He dragged his eyes from the window with a pained expression. His long ears twitched. His whiskers drooped. "They landed on my motorthycle."

#

By the time I got back to Luz and Ernesto's apartment, Luz was awake. Pale and confused and terrified- but awake. Ernesto was pressed against her, his head nestled between her neck and jaw, arms wrapped around her. He stayed that way the whole time. Luz was wrapped in a thick knitted shawl. Her eyes were deeply shadowed- but clear.

"So she was...what? A human trafficker?" Luz said. "Secuestrador? She was going to take the nina when they are born?"

"We think so," I told her. "She was taking samples from you for some reason. Maybe to pass on details to her buyers. And keeping you drugged with the tea she was giving you, so you wouldn't realise until it was too late."

"I can't believe it," Luz said, stroking her stomach. "She seemed so sweet." "According to the documents I found in the apartment, and online," I said to Harriet. "She wasn't even living in the building. Officially. The apartment is still listed as unoccupied."

"So who was she? Really?" Ernesto asked.

"We'll never know," I said. "But she's gone. I turned her in to some people I know who deal with this kind of thing. She's never coming back."

"Never?" Ernesto asked. He was looking at me carefully, watching my expression. "You promise?"

"Never," I told him. He nodded, and held his mother tighter.

"Oh, careful papi," she laughed, shifting awkwardly on the couch to accommodate the two of them. "You're going to squeeze your sister too hard."

"It's a girl?" Harriet smiled.

"Of course," Luz said gravely. "She has been through terrible things and is still alive and kicking and wanting to see the world. Of course, she is a girl."

"Luz," Harriet said, "her vitals- heartbeat and such- seem okay from a quick examination- yours too- but I'll leave a prescription for some iron supplements, and a topical antibacterial for the wounds. And you should make an appointment with your obstetrician as soon as you can."

"I didn't know you could write prescriptions," I said, interested.

"Don't get any ideas," Harriet warned me.

"Wouldn't think of it."

Luz turned to me. Her eyes were wide and her mouth a tight line. "And these people you know, who took Senora Collins...they will not tell-"

"No," I cut her off. "No, you're safe. He'll never find you. Ever."

Luz reached out her arms and grabbed my jacket, pulling me close. She kissed me on both cheeks. "Thank you, Sam," she whispered. "You are a good man."

I extricated myself from her embrace as carefully as possible, given her delicate condition. "Most would disagree, but I appreciate the thought. Look, Harriet and I have to sort out some things back at my place, but I'll be back in a little while. I'll bring a hammer to pull those nails out of the window frame"

"I can do it!" Ernesto said confidently.

"Kid," I assured him, "If you told me you could pull 'em out with your teeth, I'd believe you. You're tough enough."

#

By the time I got back to my place, my foot felt like it had been set on fire, and I could barely stumble the last few feet to my front door.

"You know," Harriet said, helping me fish my key out of my pocket, while I leaned against the door. "That superglue I used to seal the entry and exit wounds is a temporary fix. You've lost a lot of blood. And you're going to tear it open again if we don't get you stitched up."

"You're just looking forward to poking me with a sharp object," I said. "You're a sadist, masquerading as a nurse."

Inside, Tavric, having cleaned his blades, was packing them back into the canvas bag. He was wearing his motorcycle helmet again.

"And where are you going?" Harriet asked, visibly frustrated. "You're as bad as this guy."

"Chérie," Tavric declared, "The night is young. I have a victory to celebrate and a thlain motorcycle to mourn. I am going to a bar where I can find some ladieth to regale with my heroic deedth and who might be willing to offer thuccor for my wounds....and other thingth." His face was hidden, but his voice held a self-satified smirk behind the visor.

"Yeah!" Dmitri smirked. He stuck his head out of the interior pocket of Tavric jacket, giving a thumbs up. His hairy face was smiling widely. "Tav says there is being some lady gnomes there who'd appreciate the ah, hirsute types like me."

"That ith the rumour," Tavric pronounced gravely.

"Well," I said. "Have a drink for me. Or ten."

"Will do," Tavric said, clapping me on the shoulder. I staggered but managed to stay upright. "You really know how to throw a party, Heller. I look forward to the next one."

I let them out, and collapsed into a kitchen chair. I lifted my injured foot and rested it on a second chair.

Without a word, Harriet cracked open two beers and passed one to me. She sat across from me. I drained the entire beer, belched politely, and levered myself out of my chair for another.

"Let me, you idiot." She fetched a second beer.

"Thanks." I sipped this one more slowly.

The silence that followed stretched into the empty apartment and seemed to fill the space. Harriet was looking at me with an expression that was unfamiliar to me. I realised it was expectation.

I cleared my throat. "You know," I said, "it's not my kid. In case you were wondering."

"I wasn't," Harriet said mildlly.

"Most would."

"Most people would be wrong."

Her green-eyed gaze was unflinching. I put the beer down.

"She was abused," I said. "By her husband. I worked with him, while I was still a cop."

Harriet nodded. "Go on."

"Alan met her online while Luz was still living in El Salvador. The place she lived was controlled by gangs. Crime, drugs. Her boyfriend was a low level runner for one of the MS13 gangs. When he got killed, Luz was targeted. They wanted her to work for them, smuggling. Other...stuff. Ernesto was four years old, and she was desperate. Alan offered her a better life. So she came here.

"They were married three months when he hit her for the first time. It just got worse after that. She was beaten regularly. He put her in hospital twice." I tore at the label of the beer I was holding, shredding it. "Ernesto saw a lot of it. Too much."

Harriet didn't say anything at first. Then she asked the question I had been dreading, the question I knew she would have to ask: "Did you know?"

I didn't meet her eyes. I knew what I would see in them. "Yeah. Yeah, I knew. We all did."

Harriet was very still. Her beer sat on the table undrunk. "I see."

I kept shredding the beer label. "He was pretty careful. But we all recognised the signs. You don't get to be a cop without knowing what a battered woman looks like. Sunglasses on a cloudy day to hide a black eye. Wearing long sleeved shirts in summer to cover up the bruises. We all knew. And not one of us said or did a goddamn thing. No-one wanted to be the one to speak out against another cop. So we let it happen."

"What changed?"

"I got fired," I said. "Then about a year ago, Luz came looking for me for help. She'd left Allan and had a restraining order, but he didn't care, kept showing up and threatening her at her work, at home. She wanted to disappear. I knew about a guy in my building that was looking to sublet. I convinced him to keep her name off the lease, so she moved in here."

"Why did she come to you?"

"Because I wasn't a cop any more," I said. "Nobody on the force was speaking to me, Alan included. So she was pretty certain I wouldn't tell her husband. But mostly... .she was desperate."

The silence stretched again.

"You know," I said to the quiet, "When you're a boy growing up, you're always imagining yourself as the knight in shining armour, you know? You tell yourself that if you ever saw a girl getting hurt, or threatened, that you'd step in to save her, be the hero. When I joined the police force, I thought that was what I'd be doing. Then when I had the chance to actually be the hero-" I swallowed hard. My eyes unfocused, swimming, and I took another pull on my beer. My chest was tight. "I was just a fucking coward like the rest of them. All I had to do is speak up. And I didn't."

Harriet didn't move. She just looked at me. When she finally talked, it was with a careful voice, without inflection. "If you're hoping that I'll tell you that it's okay...that's it wasn't your fault...I can't do that. Because it isn't. It was."

"If you did tell me that," I said shakily, "I'd say you were full of shit. Because I fucked up. Nothing I ever do can change what I did."

"Do you think you should die for it?"

"What?" I blinked.

"Heller," Harriet said patiently, "you threw yourself at that thing upstairs with a can of flyspray and a fucking kitchen knife. It should have killed you. You got lucky. And it's not the first time. Eventually your luck is going to run out. So I ask you again- do you think you should die for your mistakes? Because I know a lot of people who would miss you if you did. Luz. Ernesto." A smile quirked at the corner of her lips. "Me."

I drank some more beer. "I don't know," I said. "I genuinely don't know."

Harriet moved her chair to sit beside me. She leaned a head on my shoulder. "No-one," she said quietly, "should be judged based on the worst thing they ever did. Anymore than they should be judged for the best thing they ever did. It doesn't define you. What defines you is the next thing. And the thing after that. The next choice. That's what makes you a good person."

"The next choice," I said. "And what if that one's wrong too?"

"You get to find that out when it happens," Harriet said. Her spiky blonde hair tickled the underside of my chin. I kind of liked it. "That's life."

The next silence was better. Quiet, rather than tense. I put the beer down and put my arm around her shoulder.

"Don't get any ideas," Harriet said, her head against my chest. "How did Tav put it? I'm just offering succor."

"Is that what it's called? What about that kiss?"

"I told you. It was for luck. I thought you were going to die."

"On a purely existential level," I said, "Aren't we all going to die?" She shook her head. I felt her smile against my shirt.

We sat at my kitchen table for a little while longer. My muscles ached, but I didn't want to move and ruin it. Somewhere on the top floor, the corpse of a dead Manananggal was decomposing and needed to be disposed of. In the city, a seven-foot tall warrior rabbit and a hairy house-spirit were trying to pick up ladies and drink themselves into a coma. Luz and her baby and Ernesto were waiting for me to come fix their window. Harriet still smelled like lemon soap and was very warm against my side.

I was alive.

That would have to be enough for now.

Jacob Seinemeier

Jacob Seinemeier

CRITICAL BLAST PUBLISHING
20¢
CRITICAL BLAST PUBLISHING
LET THEM REST
Eric Avedissian
APPROVED BY THE READING CODE AUTHORITY
OLD MONSTERS NEVER DIE... DO THEY?

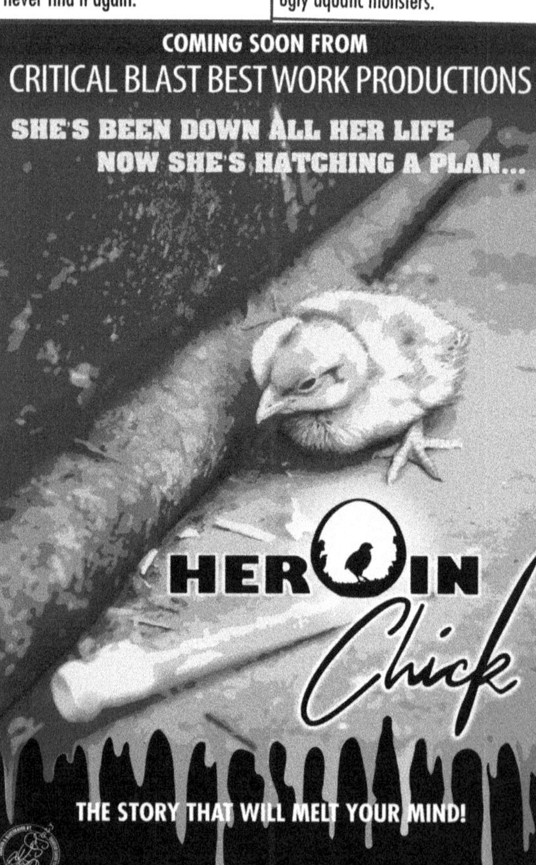

Eric Avedissian is an adjunct professor teaching English Composition. His published work includes the novels Accursed Son and The Ocean Hugs Hard. His short stories appear in various anthologies, including Across the Universe, Great Wars, and Rituals & Grimoires. He is a 2024 Fellowship in Prose from the New Jersey Council on the Arts, and a member of the Science Fiction & Fantasy Writers Association (SFWA) and the Horror Writers Association (HWA).

Lashley's Home for Geriatric Monsters sits atop a lonely bluff on the far side of town. A moldering house with askew pillars supporting a yawning portico, the building has always been there as far as the neighbors can recall.

An ancient sycamore, branches spreading like a hundred flagellating tentacles, grows at the center of the overgrown crabgrass lawn.

Lashley's might not be pretty, but to the residents and staff, it's home.

The townsfolk give the mansion a wide berth and gossip about the monsters who dwell within. They've petitioned local officials several times to have us removed and even write letters to the newspapers advocating for the home's destruction.

They call us an eyesore, a menace, and say that we're enabling a delusion that monsters and humans can co-exist. Yet we're still here behind the wrought-iron gate adorned with gargoyles like we've always been.

Lashley's serves one important function in this closely-knit, close-minded town: We don't exist to keep the outside world safe from the monsters; we exist to keep the monsters safe from the outside world.

#

When the Hulking Horror is admitted, he's absolutely terrified. The giant monster is all gray hair, massive shoulders, and shaky muscles. One of his fangs is chipped, and the other is missing. Dark circles haunt his eyes, and his drawn, pallid face reveals a life of untold anguish. In other words, he looks perfectly fine, a monster showing all of his beastly qualities with notable exceptions.

He is old.

Ancient.

And he's scared.

Like most of our residents, he doesn't want to be admitted. Maybe a loved one can't handle caring for their monster, or a monster relief organization finds it before the angry townsfolk do.

Hulking Horror is no different. His brood can't sustain him, so they admit him to Lashley's.

I guide him through the orientation. His eyes dart around the room, like a panicked animal unsure of its surroundings.

"I'm Marybeth," I tell the skittish beast. "What's your name?"

"They … Uh, people call me the Hulking Horror," the monster replies.

"What do you call yourself?" I ask.

The thing's eyes grow wide, like nobody ever asked him that before.

"I... I call myself... Larry," the monster says. "Is that okay?"

"That's perfect, Larry." I open the door to the activities room. "Let me show you around. I think you'll enjoy your time with us." My voice is honeyed, pleasing.

Larry smiles, his one intact fang showing gloriously.

He's a fearsome, beautiful thing. Rugged and ragged, a towering behemoth brimming with fearsome hunger.

He's also fragile and needs care.

So I show him around.

#

Lashley's has an activities area with tall Gothic windows that flood the room with daylight. Monsters don't really like too much light, so we pull the drapes shut during the day. Our vampire residents especially appreciate this.

There are a dozen tables, each with an activity: arts and crafts, chess and checkers, coloring books and crayons. Every day at 3 p.m. we have a Bingo game where residents clamor for prizes of handmade trinkets and charms.

Sometimes we give away fresh, raw steaks. We usually have to grind the steaks in a blender because many of the residents can't chew anymore.

Larry lumbers around, the other monsters keeping a watchful eye on him.

The Countess, a disheveled vampire with long black hair and a dressing gown, pulls me aside.

"Marybeth, dear. Who's the new creature?" she asks with reeking breath.

"He's Larry," I tell her.

"Ooh! Larry! What's his deal?" The Countess's denture-fangs nearly pop out.

"He'll be staying with us."

The Countess preens for a moment like a glamorous movie star. "Another man, eh? Let the games begin."

"I don't think Larry is here for that, Countess," I say.

She rolls her eyes. "Ah, you're no fun, darling."

A withered zombie sits on his overstuffed chair, his desiccated eyeballs glued to daytime television. Another soap opera, game show, court drama, or infomercial. He doesn't mind.

Every so often he spits up a black tarry substance and the orderlies clean it from the carpet. He looks around sheepishly, as if embarrassed. We tell him it's not a problem. A little smile creases his face.

I can tell Larry doesn't know what to make of this. His eyes turned downward, like he's going to cry.

"Come on, Larry. There's someone I want you to meet." I guide the shambling thing to a deeper part of the house.

#

Some monsters are confused.

They have dementia and forget who they once ate, or what tiny hamlets they tormented. There are monsters who don't even know they're monsters and think they are accountants, or salesmen, or corporate executives. They ask about their jobs and pretend to collate papers in an office.

A few of them know they're monsters and try recreating their past glories. They try torturing the nurses thinking they are past victims. In these cases, we have to talk them down.

A slimy swamp creature bares its webbed claws at me. He puffs his gills aggressively, viscous drool dribbling down his large mouth.

Larry shudders at this.

"It's only Nigel," I say to Larry. "He thinks he's back at the swamp fifty years ago. Nigel would eat divers and haunt the coast. Isn't that right, Nigel?"

The swamp creature hisses and gnashes his needle-like teeth, the stench of fish a sickening miasma.

"Come on, Nigel. Tell me all about your favorite swampy haunts," I prod.

Nigel blinks. His enormous mouth closes and he sits in his favorite chair. For an hour he regales me with tales of his exploits driving fishermen mad and harassing passing boats.

Distracting a resident is easy; you just have to divert them to another topic. These de-escalations take many forms but usually end up with the monsters calmed down and chatty.

"Is that... normal?" Larry asks when we leave the activities room.

"Not only is that normal, but it's encouraged. Our residents can't help who they are or what time does to them. They can't help that they're monsters. They shouldn't apologize or feel ashamed. We don't judge you here, Larry."

"That's... good," Larry replies.

Not everyone takes that advice to heart; we have plenty of complaints from neighbors upset over our nursing home for monsters. Some of these complaints are in writing. Others are less subtle.

#

A group of protestors loiter around the front gate, brandishing hand-painted signs. I squint and read them: *FREAKS GO HOME*, *DEATH TO MONSTERS*, and *MONSTERS ARE EVIL*.

Usually, we ignore these disgruntled neighbors and they leave, but this rabble isn't budging. I stride down the path and confront them.

"This is a care facility. What do you want?" I ask. "What do you expect to accomplish by harassing these elderly folks?"

One prune-faced woman, nose pinched, retorts, "Elderly folks? They ain't elderly folks in there. They're monsters."

"Yes, they are," I say firmly. "Please leave them alone. They don't leave the home and wander the night anymore."

"We don't care," a man brandishing a *DEATH TO MONSTERS* sign tells me. "We want those horrible things out of here. This is a wholesome community."

"Aren't they entitled to grow old with dignity, with security?" I ask. "Let them rest."

He curses at me, calls me all sorts of names, and threatens my job. When I flee towards the house, the monsters watch my retreat from the windows.

I wash my face in the bathroom and exhale. I won't let them see me upset. I won't cry in front of them. I can't. You can't let the monsters see your emotions; it's not professional.

But in the activity room, my face betrays me. Residents surround me with burning eyes. A few gnash their teeth in anger.

"Disgusting," one withered vampire says. "Disgusting what they did to you, hon."

"I oughta feast upon their bones, sup upon their flesh, devour them while they still live," a feisty old werewolf howls.

"I think she was admirable," says a shambling terror, all white fur and skeletal face.

"Yes, Marybeth," the Countess replies, looking up from her chess board. She pulls her tattered gown tightly around her emaciated body. "You deserve our gratitude. And perhaps revenge? Who wants to stick it to those townies?"

A chorus of grunts, howls, and unearthly bellows erupts.

"No," I tell them. "Nobody is doing any revenge."

"Oh, but we'd *like* to do something diabolical," the rotting zombie in the corner pleads.

"Yes, a little bloodshed never hurt anyone. Well, it hurts *them*, but not us," the vampire adds, smacking his parched lips.

"No! No revenge. You're better than that. Those people out there hate you because they don't understand you. They don't *want* to understand you. You probably haunted their childhood nightmares and they never forgave you. They never saw you as anything other than wicked creatures," I say.

"Not even a little revenge?" the Countess persists.

"No," I snap.

"Oh, you're no fun," the Countess pouts and continues her chess game with the shambling terror, who eats half the chess pieces. He does this when he's losing, and he loses a lot.

The orderlies spend the better part of the morning chasing the shambling terror with a plastic bag until they recover all the pieces.

#

To the monsters, I'm "Mother."

Some think I raised them when they were little as their minds regress. They snuggle close and regard me with wonder, like they're my children.

"Clean your room," I tell them.

"Yes, Mother," they growl, and head off, skipping down the hallway.

"Mother, I love you," a gigantic troll tells me with sweetness in his voice.

"I love you, too, Gargar." I say and give him an orange sherbet.

Not all nurses are this considerate. I've seen nurses ridicule monsters when they regress. They sit in the break room, talking shit about the residents, calling them "soft-headed" or "senile."

I confront them when we're out of earshot and tell them off.

"Listen, you're new here. If you don't want this job to be your last, you'll treat these residents with respect. Time doesn't treat all things with the same grace or tenderness. Entropy wears us all down, including monsters," I say.

The nurses usually roll their eyes or smirk.

"But these things... these creatures... they don't know that they're monsters anymore," they'd say.

"Even more important that we treat them with dignity," I reply.

"Dignity? Marybeth, they're vicious monsters. These aren't people. It's like they're animals and we're zookeepers."

I grind my teeth and narrow my eyes.

The new ones don't treat this job with the sensitivity it deserves. They giggle at the residents' misfortunes and mock them on their smoke breaks when they think nobody is listening.

But I'm listening. I'm the eyes and ears in this house.

"If you think you're here to grab a paycheck and leave, you're in the wrong field," I tell them. "Elder monster care demands you be present and empathetic every day. If you can't see these creatures as entities worthy of respect and understanding, then maybe you'd be better off somewhere else."

They refer to me as "Crazy Marybeth."

So be it.

Unlike them, I'm present for these creatures, no matter how grotesque or horrible. Any Mother would be.

#

When the werewolf soils the carpet, I'm there to clean him up.

When the shape-shifter is paranoid and changes form to its past incarnation, I'm there to talk her back to reality.

When the soul-munching fiend asks, "Is my castle ready? I want to go back to my castle," even though the castle was destroyed 200 years ago, I don't tell it that. Instead, I smile and say, "This is just as good as your castle, plus there's TV here."

The fiend's eyebrows furrow and it appears lost.

"You like TV, right? Let's watch your favorite program," I say, and we watch a mind-rotting game show. The residents cheer the contestants and forget about the crumbling palace that's in ruins, villages they terrorized, or spouses slain by monster hunters.

"Oh, Mother, you should find someone. Why haven't you settled down?" the monsters ask me.

"I just haven't had the chance. I'm too busy here," I reply.

The truth is, I could've married. Could've had the house with the white picket fence in suburbia. Could've had the minivan, the kids, the Pilates classes. I could've been the ideal housewife.

Instead, I chose the monsters.

The men my sister tries fixing me up with all ask the same questions: "Why spend all your time with monsters," or "What do the monsters offer that a man can't?" Or if they're incredibly ballsy, "Why don't you let a real man take care of you?"

My answer is always a variation of, "The monsters truly need me, and men don't."

Monsters too feeble to care for themselves wouldn't be safe without me.

Besides, monsters are better company than most men I've met.

Case in point: A shambling creature with two jutting tusks and sharp claws falls out of her chair and hurts herself. She bellows in agony, her green blood seeping onto the floor.

On any given day this beast could've taken my head off with those sharp talons, but now she lies helpless, bleeding and whimpering. I apply a cold compress and an orderly helps me get her on the sofa where I hand her a butterscotch pudding.

"Take it easy, Shirley," I say.

The monster slurps her pudding and looks at me with big aquamarine eyes. "Thank you. I will," she sniffles.

Larry, thick eyebrows raised, pulls me aside. "You… helped that monster?" Larry asks.

"It's what we do here at Lashley's."

"I guess I'm getting used to this place. What I remember about humans is they don't like us much."

"It's not like that here, Larry," I say with a smile. "We're not like any humans you've met."

#

Exercise is important at Lashley's; residents here participate in regular physical activities. Many of the monsters haven't moved in centuries, so keeping them fit and in shape is one of our priorities.

We do calisthenics, with several zombies moving their pale limbs (cautiously), and ghouls bending their nimble spines backwards. A few vampires transform into bats and fly around the courtyard, while the werewolves rip up the furniture with their yellowed teeth.

Larry enjoys exercising with the others. They complement him on his size and agility. Then they start trading stories about past feats of strength.

After lunch, when the rest of the residents sit around the day room or head to their Bingo game, Larry lingers behind. He regards me through innocent eyes, two yellow spheres robbed of memory, dimmed by age. Larry tells me he misses who he used to be.

"My previous life, before everything slowed down and people labeled me the Hulking Horror, I found a strange tranquility in the mundane." Larry scratches his hairy arms. "I had love once. Bernice. Yes. My Bernice. She was a beastly thing, a grotesque monstrosity with hideous jaws and bat-like wings. I adored her and she adored me."

"You miss her?" I ask.

"Every day. That is, when I remember who she was. She died about six years ago. That time... hasn't been kind," Larry murmurs.

"Larry, you don't have to talk about this if you don't want to, but if you do, I'll listen."

"Thank you," Larry smiles feebly. "Me and Bernice were in love. You ever love someone so intensely, that when they're gone, it feels like you died, too? Have you known grief that strong?"

I say I haven't, but I really have.

In high school I dated a boy who I thought would be with me forever. Clancy Simmons. Quarterback for the varsity football team. A real heartthrob. I thought he was my soulmate, that we'd get married and... But that didn't happen. He was killed by a drunk driver at 18 while walking home from work. I found out two days later. Clancy had been dead for two whole days and I didn't know. I continued living in blissful ignorance for two days while he was on a slab in the morgue. I was so upset I didn't date anyone for years. I couldn't. My heart still hasn't healed. There's a dark void inside of me where the part of me that allowed me to be vulnerable was.

But I don't get emotional at work. Instead, I hold my sorrow in. This job isn't about me. It's about them.

"Bernice sounds like a wonderful monster," I tell Larry.

"She was." Larry polishes his bifocals on his fur and slips them on, where they drift down the bridge of his nose. "She crossed a monster hunter one night and he got the drop on her." Larry shudders. His thousand-yard stare peers into his tumultuous past. "Fortunately, she didn't suffer," Larry adds softly. "No. She didn't suffer."

I reach out to him. Larry's huge claws find my dainty hand.

"What happened, Larry?" I ask.

Larry's head slumps. "I tracked the monster hunter to his house and cornered him. He was settling down to dinner with his family when I smashed through the door. His wife and kids screamed as I towered over them. The monster hunter sank down on his knees and begged for his life. He pleaded that I spare his family. Everyone was so scared. Wife in tears, kids clutching her legs, monster hunter's hands clasped in front of him. And I didn't know what to do."

I tighten my grip on Larry's claws. "What did you do?"

"I thought of my Bernice. Would my beloved recognize me, teeth bared, claws out, snarling at these terrified humans?"

I open my mouth to speak, but before I do, Larry interrupts.

"This little man robbed me of my Bernice," Larry says, fighting back tears. "He took her life without hesitation. He didn't question it. Why should he have everything I didn't? So I slaughtered him while his family watched. I wanted his suffering, his anguish. Hearing him scream was the sweetest music. Knowing I made him suffer, made him helpless..."

Larry sighs. He lets my hand fall and turns away.

"And his family?" I prod.

"I... don't remember." Larry's gaze darts from me to the floor. "What came after I ate the monster hunter is a blur."

Larry describes the crunching bones, the fresh burst of blood, and the toothsome flavor of raw meat. He says as he ate the monster hunter, he locked eyes with the man's terrified wife and kids. Larry says they quaked as he smacked his lips and growled, a feral invader that happily devoured the most important man in their lives.

"You were grieving your wife, Larry," I say.

The monster grunts.

"That's no excuse for what I did, Marybeth."

"I know, but grief can make us do things we wouldn't normally do."

Larry laughs dismissively, quietly.

"I traumatized his wife and kids. The last image for those children of their father is one of his screaming as I bit him in half. I'm no better than the monster hunter I devoured."

Usually I'd comfort a resident having a violent flashback, but I can't. I've run out of words and anything I can say would sound condescending and petty. I simply pat Larry's arm and check on the others, disturbed in the knowledge that most of Lashley's residents are horrid ogres who tortured people and ate the innocent.

#

When the weather is nice, the residents skulk in the courtyard. They creep on the grass, sniff the flowers, or climb the trees. A few make meals of the squirrels until I put an end to that.

Larry suns himself in the garden. He tells me how being an old monster is bad. How his muscles and arthritis hurt. How he has flashbacks of past bloodlust, the brutal slayings and bellowing in the night.

Larry says he feels guilty about the lives he took. He plays with the tulips, his sharp talons gently caressing the petals.

"Do you believe monsters can change?" Larry asks, eyes half shut.

"It doesn't matter what I believe, Larry. *Do you think monsters can change?*" I reply.

Larry thinks for a moment and grins.

"I sure hope so, Mother. I really do. All the pain and misery I inflicted upon others. Sometimes I lie awake at night and think about them. I feel their pain wash over me. I hear their tortured screams. What I wouldn't give to wash it all from my memory."

I put my hand on Larry's hairy shoulder. His fur feels like an old shag carpet.

Larry flinches and adjusts his position so we're not too close. He's uncomfortable with another human being nearby, like he doesn't trust himself with me.

"You don't have to be afraid of me, Larry."

"I'm not afraid of you. I'm afraid of myself and what I am," the monster tells me. "I'm the Hulking Horror."

"Have you forgotten already?" I respect Larry's boundaries and don't touch him. "You're Larry, a monster who loved someone and who has friends."

Larry's eyes bulge and he opens his mouth wide.

"I am?" he asks with a lilt in his voice.

I remind Larry about the other monsters here at Lashley's and how much fun they have together. The large creature groans, like his own dwindling memories embarrass him. He moves on tiptoes around the yard, careful he doesn't tread on a flower.

Larry plucks a tulip and hands it to me with a graceful bow.

"This reminded me of you," Larry tells me with a shy grin. "I like the talks we can have here. Before I came here, I hadn't talked to a human in a long time. It's nice to hear from someone who isn't screaming in terror."

I thank Larry and accept the tulip, even though the residents aren't supposed to pick the flowers.

I pin the pilfered tulip to my lapel and wear it until it browns and withers. The other nurses ask me about it, and I concoct some bullshit story about the flower being for some social cause. Satisfied with my answer, they leave me alone, but I can't help but stare at the dried tulip for several weeks until it falls off.

Things die all the time at Lashley's, but they still add beauty to my life before they go.

#

A bat-headed monster takes his medication, lapping up the pills with a long black tongue. When I enter, he squeals with glee and straightens his frayed cardigan.

"How are we today, George?" I ask.

The bat-headed monster emits a series of shrill chirps and scratches his pointy ears with a shaky hand.

In his heyday, that same monster frightened villagers for miles. Now all he can do is take his medication and stare at the ceiling, possibly remembering a time when he hung upside down with his family.

A once-frightening banshee sits in the day room, her emaciated frame sinking into an overstuffed chair. Her voice paralyzed anyone who heard her; now she rarely wails, preferring hushed whispers.

She cut off her long tresses, and sits bald and forgotten.

"You're looking terrifying today, Maeve," I reassure her with a smile.

The banshee smiles back, half her teeth missing.

"Give us a wail, then," I plead.

The banshee inhales and breathes out the most nerve-piercing keening I've ever heard. When Maeve finishes, her eyes go wide, like it's the first time she's ever heard herself.

"Mercy. What a racket," Maeve says, still smiling.

Time is not kind.

It wears you down and makes you realize your best days are behind you.

Monsters come to us, broken and wrecked.

Larry feels all of the changes to his body at once. He's grunting every time he adjusts himself in his chair while watching TV. He takes a longer time to come to breakfast with the others. On Saturdays, he skips the dancing lessons and heads straight to the library, where he nods off with an open paperback on his chest.

Larry wakes up and rubs his eyes. He sees me and says, "I remember what happened with the monster hunter's wife and children."

"What happened, Larry?" I kneel down beside his chair.

"I spared them. They visited the monster hunter's grave every year. I know because I lurked in the bushes, watching them. They seemed so distraught. After a while, I stopped going." Larry's attention drifts for a bit, then he blinks. "Mother, what do you think happens when we die?"

When I honestly reply that I don't know, he lowers his head and sighs, like he's disappointed.

"Is there a Heaven for monsters, or do we all go straight to the other place?" Larry asks like an innocent child.

"Maybe, if there is a Heaven, it's for everyone, even monsters," I tell him, trying to be as diplomatic as I can.

Larry looks downward. "Uh-huh. That would be nice."

"Larry, why are you talking this way?"

I know monsters get the morbs, but Larry has been especially quiet and pensive. He looks at me with his dark eyes, eyes that have beheld too much sorrow and suffering for one lifetime.

"I hope when I do go, you're with me, Mother," Larry tells me. "I hope you're right there with me until the end."

"I will be," I say.

Larry wraps his long arms around me. His embrace hurts at first, and his claws scrape my arms, but I don't mind.

Larry needs this.

We both do.

"I appreciate you, Marybeth," Larry says, choking back tears.

#

Death happens here.

I've watched fearsome creatures, monsters with sharp fangs and claws, scales and fur, horns and bat wings, slip away and die. We make them as comfortable as we can, on fluffy pillows and down mattresses, their hideousness covered with silk sheets.

Monsters, as cruel and as horrid as they were in their youths, are really harmless in the end. It's like they understand a reckoning has come for them, and make peace with their past selves.

Larry is afraid of dying alone.

He wraps the blanket around his massive frame and slumps down in his chair.

"I'm a monster. I should be killed by the townsfolk, run through with a pitchfork or set aflame," Larry laments.

"You'll never die alone while you're with us," I reassure him.

"But I'm a monster." Larry's chest heaves. His yellow eyes get all misty. "I'm nothing but a monster."

"You're more than a monster," I tell him. "You're a friend."

Larry's one fang protrudes when he bites his lip.

"I am?"

"Yes," I say. "Now you can rest. No zealots, monster slayers and bloodthirsty townsfolk will bother you here. Here all you'll find is peace."

Larry sighs heavily. He closes his eyes and a placid grin washes over him.

"Peace would be nice, Marybeth," Larry grips the blanket tighter. "I would like peace very much."

That night, as the others sleep soundly, Larry slips away.

I hold his hand when he goes. As the last breath escapes him, his face appears serene, as if he's ready to move on.

There isn't a death rattle or the ghastly rictus you see with humans. Larry exhales once and is gone.

I don't think he even knew I was there with him, but I gave my word.

It's all about trust at Lashley's. We need to trust one another or this place falls apart.

Bringing contentment to elderly monsters grants me a sense of purpose. Showing these creatures that not all humans will murder them with an enchanted dagger or bind them with eldritch magic brings me joy.

After we bury Larry, I continue my work, my demeanor sober and emotionless.

In the morning, I assist a werewolf with finding his dentures. That afternoon I listen to a vampire drone on about his life over the last 500 years. We share a cup of tea. Well, I drink the tea. He sticks to warm blood (from the butcher). But there are still biscuits and he relaxes.

Larry creeps into my mind throughout the day in tiny bursts: our conversations, his solo-fanged smile, his gentle self-reflection. Sadness flutters through me, but I stop myself and attend to the residents.

If Lashley's taught me anything, it's that even monsters crave sympathy and kindness.

Isn't that what everyone wants?

A tentacled leviathan starts breaking down over his children not visiting. I reassure the gibbering thing that he's valued and loved and that his spawn might be too busy terrorizing the ocean depths to check on him. One by one, the creature's tentacles wrap around me in a tender embrace.

"Thank you," he burbles, before sobbing. "Thank you."

A tear rolls down my cheek. The monster notices, makes a deep guttural noise older than the ocean, and wipes it away with a tentacle.

I'll be all right.

So will they.

Let them rest.

Let them rest.

CRITICAL BLAST PUBLISHING
20¢
A NIGHT AT WOLFE'S LAKE
Damascus Mincemeyer
APPROVED BY THE READING CODE AUTHORITY
MORE THAN THE FISH ARE BITING

HEAD KNIVES 100% stainless steal daggers that launch from the top of your head and kill any conversation you find boring.

HELIUM GAS & BALLOON SET Get away from the day to day grind of your boring life and steal a whole house while the owners are away.

WELCOME MAT TRAP When you don't want people annoying you, a simple press of the button and the trap door will dispose of anyone who stands on it, while waiting for you to answer the door.

DIGITAL PUZZLE T-SHIRT Get people's undivided attention when they get engrossed trying to solve the constantly changing puzzles.

MAKE MINE MONSTERS!

COCAINE FOR PETS When your pets become too excited during mating season and you don't want additional burden of feeding more pets, shot them up with some fine liquid snow and chill them out.

LEARN BLACK MYSTIC ARTS KUNG-FU When you find yourself cornered by Jive Turkey Demons and alternate versions of your bad self, you can always rely on your skills as a High-Kicking, Ass-Kicking Sorcerer of the Black Mystic Arts. CASH ONLY. 6 MONTHS TUITION UP FRONT. NO REFUNDS.

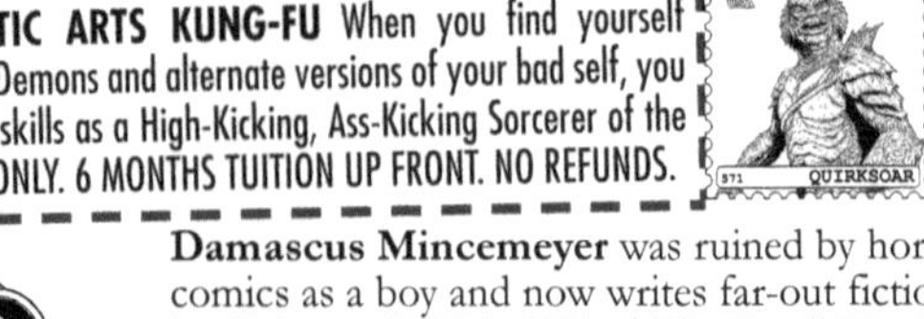

Damascus Mincemeyer was ruined by horror, sci-fi and comics as a boy and now writes far-out fiction that's appeared in all three of Critical Blast's The Devil You Know collections, The Monsters Next Door, The Fables Next Door, Gods and Services: New Location, Fire: Demons, Dragons and Djinn, Earth: Giants, Golems and Gargoyles, Air: Slyphs, Spirits and Swan Maidens, No Anesthetic, Appalachian Horror, Dragons Legends, A Tree Lighting In Deathlehem, and many more anthologies. Hailing from St. Louis, Missouri, U.S.A, he spends his spare time writing book and movie reviews and posting horror trivia games on Instagram and Threads @damascusundead666

"Ahhh, nothing like the great outdoors,
is there, Stu?" Bruce said as he trudged up the trail. "Nature in
its pristine state. The forest primeval. No aggravations of
modern society. No petty technological distractions. No
insidious fiends trying to suck your blood."

Stuart slapped a mosquito on his arm. "Except this one."
He paused in the tall grass between the lake's dock and the
edge of the Michigan woods and sighed. "Can we slow it down?
I'm getting tired."

"*Already*?" Bruce turned around. "Geez, if I knew you were
this big a wuss I never would've brought you out here. It's only
a quarter mile back to the cabin. You didn't have a problem
this morning."

Stuart put down his fishing pole and tackle box. "No, but
all we've had to eat since then is stale beef jerky." He rubbed
his spine. "And being cramped in that row boat nine hours
didn't do wonders for my back, either."

"Fine, you old fart. We'll stop. I need to take a leak
anyway." Bruce set the cooler filled with captured trout he'd
been carrying on the ground. "But don't rest too long. It's
almost sunset, and I really don't want to get caught outside
after dark."

Neither do I, Stuart reasoned. The tangled timberland on
the eastern edge of Wolfe's Lake State Park wasn't anywhere
one wanted to become lost, day or night. The nearest town was
almost twenty miles off, and a world away from the Kalamazoo
suburbs both men called home.

Stuart swatted more mosquitoes. *Seventy-two years old, and
after everything we've been through I still let Bruce talk me into
stuff like some dumb teenager.* Of course, at seventy-four, Bruce
was no spring chicken, either. *But try telling him that.*

When his lifelong buddy initially proposed a wilderness retreat, Stuart humored him, thinking the idea, like many of Bruce's schemes, wouldn't bear fruit. It probably wouldn't have, either, if their senior rec center pal, Hoppy, hadn't told them about the Upper Peninsula cabin he'd rented.

There's a lake for boating, a hammock for lounging, and a grill for cooking, Hoppy promised when he'd handed Bruce the cabin's keys the next time they'd met. *You two go up Friday and get the place ready, and I'll be there Saturday morning with some steaks and beer. We'll make an Old Boys weekend out of it. Just the three of us.*

Stuart's wife Deborah wasn't keen on his going ("When's the last time *anything* Bruce suggested turned out okay?" she'd questioned), but he'd eventually managed to persuade her, and Stuart spent the ensuing week excavating long-unused camping equipment from the attic.

The drive upstate in Bruce's lumbering 1970 Buick Riviera had been long yet largely uneventful. They'd only gotten turned around once, when Bruce took a wrong turn in Manistique and had to double back to a gas station that proved the last bastion of civilization. An SUV full of rowdy college-age kids were making a nuisance of themselves in the parking lot, drinking and blasting their music too loud; one of them, a broad-shouldered youth wearing an **ELON ROCKS** t-shirt, was hassling a family of three who'd arrived in their minivan, whistling catcalls at the mother as she passed by. When Stuart had attempted to intervene, the youth's eyes narrowed to contemptuous slits.

Mind your own business, Grandpa, he'd snarled. *And don't forget to take your Alzheimer's meds.*

Stuart wondered if there'd be more to it, but then Bruce returned carrying armfuls of that awful expired jerky and they were off.

Don't let it bug you, Stu, Bruce advised him as they'd reached the cabin. *We were obnoxious little shits just like them once upon a time.*

Maybe you *were,* Stuart had replied. *I don't remember being like that.*

A shrill cry yanked Stuart's attention back to the woods. Bruce stumbled from the bushes, his cargo shorts unfastened, anger crimping his face.

"You aren't gonna be*lieve* this. Some pervert's got video cameras in the trees." Bruce hastily zipped his fly. "I feel so *violated.*"

Stuart couldn't suppress a chuckle. "Right, because peeping Toms everywhere are hot to record unsuspecting retirees whipping it out for a piss in the middle of nowhere."

"You don't believe me?" Bruce tugged Stuart's flannel sleeve; fifteen feet off the trail a bracket-mounted camera was nailed to a pine.

"I'm sure it's just for security," Stuart deduced. "Hop rents this whole lot."

Bruce stomped towards the tree. "Maybe. Or maybe we don't know good ol' Hoppy like we *think* we do. I can hear the breaking news now: SENIOR CITIZEN SERIAL KILLER BURIES BODIES NEAR LAKESIDE CABIN. SPORTS AFTER THE BREAK."

Stuart almost laughed again until Bruce stood on his tiptoes and began twisting the camera side-to-side. "What are you *doing*?" he asked.

"Upholding my reputation," Bruce grunted. "Nobody's ogling Lil' Brucie unless I get *paid*."

The camera finally disconnected, and a self-satisfied smile spread across Bruce's chin that immediately melted when a stranger's husky voice roared from behind him: *"HEY! GET AWAY FROM THERE!"*

A man stalked from the clearing opposite the pines. Up close he looked probably forty, bespectacled, bearded and thick-set, with a bulging military-surplus backpack draped over one shoulder. By the camouflage the fellow wore Stuart would've judged him a deer hunter, but June was far out of season for scoring bucks.

"The hell you doing to my equipment, Pops?" The man snatched the camera, then scowled. "Perfect. Juuuust perfect. You *broke* it."

"Serves you right, pal," Bruce seethed. "You get off spying on innocent urinators or something?"

"*Spying*? I'm conducting field research," the man insisted. "Name's Lehner. G.W. Lehner. Lenny. Me and my business partner Kyle co-host a weekly podcast, *SasqWatchers*. These woods are a *major* hot spot and we're prepping a three square-mile chunk for surveillance in advance of tonight's show."

"A hot spot?" Stuart cocked an eyebrow. "For *what*?"

"*Cryptids*," Lenny explained. "Assumed mythic creatures that are actually undiscovered animal species. Chupacabras. Abominable Swamp Slobs. Lizard Men. Yetis."

"Giant mutant spiders?" Bruce cracked. Lenny's scowl reappeared.

"Poke fun all you want, Pops. But this is a serious scientific inquiry. We got a dozen 1080 high-res night-vision cameras with built-in zero lux filming and Zoom audio parabolic mics."

Lenny surveyed the woods. "Trust me, if there's a 'squatch out here, we'll find it."

"*Squatch?*" Stuart repeated. "You mean… *Sasquatch*? As in… Bigfoot?"

"The bigger the feet, the bigger the meat," Lenny joked. When that failed to elicit a laugh, he said, "Sorry. Little 'squatch humor. On the podcast we try to avoid using the word *Bigfoot*. It erodes any respect cryptozoology has gained by reinforcing negative, media-manufactured stereotypes. Plus, it sounds fuckin' stupid."

"Look, G.W., Lenny, whoever you are, this is private property," Stuart reminded him. "You're *trespassing*."

"Yeah, no worries. Me and Kyle broadcast from an Airstream trailer about a mile down the road so we can monitor our equipment in real time. Except *this* one, I guess." Lenny slid the damaged camera inside his backpack. "But here's a word to the wise: nighttime's prime time for cryptid activity. Wherever you're gettin' to, I'd get there fast."

Lenny waved, retreated across the clearing, then vanished into the brush. Stuart and Bruce quietly retrieved their fishing gear, and only just returned to the trail when a coyote's faraway howling made Bruce stiffen.

"What's the matter?" Stuart asked.

Bruce shrugged. "Oh, nothing."

"You're worried about Bigfoot now, aren't you?"

"*Hell no.*" Bruce laughed the suggestion off. "Are *you?*"

"Of course not."

"It's *absurd.*"

"Ridiculous."

A second distant howl caused Bruce to stop altogether. Looking at Stuart, he said nervously, "Race you back to the cabin?"

"Last one there has to get a Pacemaker," Stuart replied, and both men shuffled up the path as quickly as they could.

#

Before seeing Hoppy's cabin, Stuart had entertained fearful visions it was some dirt-floored, backwoods hovel and was relieved to find a weathered-yet-cozy two-story Western Red Cedar cottage with a peaked A-frame roof and covered porch.

Inside, the cabin's open-concept layout merged a living room, dining area and kitchen into a single space. A large bay window and floor-to-ceiling fireplace were situated near the entrance, and a set of French doors in the kitchen faced the rear patio; a short hallway led to the bathroom, master bedroom, and den, while upstairs was an ample sleeping loft. Hoppy's cluttered decorative sense skewed towards the rustic, timber-frame furniture, pastoral paintings, mounted hunting trophies, and an honest-to-God bearskin rug.

Soon after arriving, Stuart set about pan-frying the trout. One of the kitchen's perks was an impressive walk-in pantry Hoppy kept stocked with canned goods and pickled vegetables that Stuart used to prepare a pepper sauce before starting some rice.

Bruce kept vigil near the bay window the entire time Stuart was cooking. Every few minutes he'd peek through the shutters, suspiciously survey the nighttime landscape, then close them again.

"Will you *stop* doing that?" Stuart moaned. "You're making me paranoid."

"We *need* to be paranoid after all the shit we've seen." Bruce secured the shutters once more. "I don't know about you, but *I'm* not going to end up King Kong's plaything if I can help it."

Stuart chuckled, checked the food, then flipped off the gas stove. "Bruce, if Bigfoot *is* out there, I seriously doubt it's going to waltz up and knock on our door."

He brought the hot skillet to the dining table when something actually *did* hit the front door, loud, fast, and hard. Startled, Stuart swore, lost his grip on the skillet and the trout slid to the floor.

"*HELP ME!*" someone on the porch shouted. *"For fuck's sake, help me!"*

Bruce parted the shutters again; when he glanced back to Stuart, his mouth drooped.

"It's a girl, Stu."

There was more pounding. Another plea. Stuart set aside the empty skillet, unlocked the deadbolt, then opened the door.

A blonde in a pink tank top and cut-offs leaned on the threshold. She was twenty-ish and chubby with round, sweet features that belied the terror in her expression. She panted like she'd been running; one sandal was missing and her bare sole was caked with mud. Scratches covered her arms and legs. Blood splotched her clothes.

"*My God...*" Stuart guided the girl to the sofa while Bruce slammed the door shut.

"What was that you said about paranoia?" Bruce whispered to Stu.

"Go get the First Aid kit," Stuart told him. "I spotted one in the bathroom earlier."

Bruce nodded and hurried down the hall. Stuart filled a glass with water and passed it to the girl. Her hands shook so badly she could barely drink. When Stuart asked her name, it took a long minute to hear an answer.

"J– Julie…" she eventually said. "Julie Mueller."

"Okay, Julie. I'm Stuart. My friend's Bruce. You're safe now, all right?"

The girl's eyes widened. "We're not. We're *not* safe *any*where!"

Bruce returned with the First Aid kit and started applying antiseptic to some of Julie's nastier cuts. "I'm guessing these aren't mosquito bites."

Julie hissed from the disinfectant's sting. "M– my friend Trent invited us to his dad's cabin this weekend. To celebrate the end of school. Me, my other friend Nicki, and Owen. We… we were partying, you know? Just having fun. Everything was fine until Nicki said she saw someone outside. S– she likes to play jokes, and we…we thought she was just messing with us. B– but then it smashed the sliding glass doors and got inside…"

"*It*?" Bruce balked. "What do you mean, *it*?"

Julie tensed up. "I don't *know*. I've never seen anything like it. The fucking thing was *huge*, and *hairy*, and *strong*. It got hold of Nicki and… God, there was so much *blood*. And the screams…" Fresh tears streaked her mascara. "Owen clubbed the thing with a fireplace poker, but that barely slowed it down. If Trent hadn't gotten his dad's shotgun from the bedroom, we'd *all* be dead. It sounds crazy, b–but it's *true*. I *swear*."

"Huge, hairy, and strong, huh?" Bruce mouthed the words *I told you so* to Stuart, then looked back to the trembling girl. "Don't worry, we believe you. We've seen some crazy in our day. *Crazy* crazy. *Trust* me."

Stuart stood. "Listen, Julie. We'll take you to town. We'll get the police, an ambulance, get you som—"

"*No!*" Julie grabbed Stuart's arm. "We *have* to go back! Trent only *wounded* that thing. We trapped it in the pantry, but it's *still* alive. And it hurt Owen *really* bad. He could *die* by the time we go to town. There's no phones or cell service up here, and we couldn't drive out because that thing trashed Trent's Cherokee. That's why I ran. When I saw your lights on, I was kinda hoping somebody, you know, *younger* lived here. Somebody with lots of guns, but... You're our only hope." Her lips quivered. "*Please.*"

"*Shit.*" Stuart ran a hand through his thinning silver hair. "What do you think, Bruce?"

"I think the great outdoors isn't so great after all." Bruce pulled the Buick's keys from a pocket. "You up for this, geezer?"

"I am if you are." Stuart glanced to Julie. "Where did all this happen?"

The girl shivered, then told them, "The next cabin down the lane."

#

A newly-risen full moon cast jagged shadows on the windshield as Bruce's Riviera jounced along the gravel road. It was well past ten o'clock and a howling breeze unraveled Stuart's already frayed nerves. Bruce perched in the driver's seat, knuckles white on the steering wheel; in the back, Julie huddled among the unpacked camping equipment.

"This car smells funny, like my grandparent's house," she said, scrunching her nose.

"That's the aroma of *experience*, kiddo." Bruce affectionately stroked the dashboard. "I was making out in The Love Boat before your parents were even born."

"*Ew*," Julie's lip curled distastefully. "That's just...*ew*."

"How far is the neighboring cabin?" Stuart asked her. He vaguely recalled Hoppy mentioning other lakeside properties, but didn't know how many there were. Julie only shook her head.

"I– I'm not sure. It felt like a long way. A mile, maybe?" She pointed to an approaching curve. "*There*. Around that bend."

The Riviera had just negotiated the turn when something darted from the trees into the lane. "Bruce, look out!" Stuart yelled.

"*SHIT*!" Bruce slammed on the brakes and swerved. The heavy Buick fishtailed, then skidded to a halt in the opposite ditch. Bruce gunned the engine, shifted gears, but the tires only dug themselves a deeper grave. "*Damn* it," he grumbled. "We're *stuck*."

Stuart looked up and saw Lenny standing in the road, excitedly waving both arms and shouting: *"We've got video! We've got video!"*

"It's that G.W. guy," Stuart snarled, opening his door.

"Who's G.W.?" Julie asked.

"Someone with a freaky Bigfoot fetish," Bruce replied before getting out of the car and poking a finger in Lenny's chest. "What's the big idea, wise guy? You trying to get us killed?"

Lenny was almost out of breath, but still couldn't stop smiling. "Forget dying, Pops. Me and Kyle, we got *confirmed video evidence*. Twenty minutes ago. One of our cameras captured a clear image. Big. Fast. Definitely bipedal. We triangulated the position and followed it here."

There was a rustling nearby, and a stocky, sandy-haired man with a scruffy goatee and camouflage identical to Lenny's trooped from the brush, strapped with a canvas satchel and a head-mounted camera and carrying a GPS device.

"G.W., we've got movement in quadrant four," he announced. Noticing Stuart and Bruce, the newcomer asked Lenny, "These the fuddy-duddies you were talking about?"

"Kyle, I presume?" Stuart said.

"The one, the only, the legend." Kyle unzipped his satchel and removed a sleek black tranquilizer pistol that he passed to Lenny. "Here. Fully loaded to fuck all."

Bruce eyed the pistol. "Nice squirt gun you got there."

Lenny smirked. "Pneu-Dart X-2. Top of the line. Green Beam laser. Holographic sight. One load can ejaculate enough ketamine to drop Dumbo."

"From the sound of things, you might need it to," Stuart informed him. "Just don't poke your eye out. Or *mine*."

Julie had exited the car by then. Studying Lenny and Kyle, she cautiously asked, "A— Are you two after that thing in the pantry?"

"What's she going on about?" Lenny asked Bruce.

"Your 'squatch committed a little home invasion tonight. Among other crimes against humanity." Bruce gestured up the hill. "That's where we're headed."

"Not fast *enough*," Julie fumed. "You know what? *Screw* this! My friends are in *danger*. I'm not *waiting* anymore."

She took off then, bounding around the bend. Stuart started after her, but Bruce pulled him back.

"Wait." He popped the Buick's trunk, rummaged around, and returned toting a Maglite and a tire iron. Handing the flashlight to Stuart, Bruce glanced to Lenny and Kyle. "You two bumblebutts coming or not?"

"Hell *yeah* we are." Lenny tapped Kyle's shoulder. "Tell 'em our podcast's slogan."

"SasqWatchers are always on the hunt!" Resolve chiseled Kyle's chin. "Let's *do* it."

The four of them marched along the lane. Once away from the car, the Maglite and the moon's glow provided the only illumination. The breeze grew sharper with every step. Somewhere, those far-off coyotes were howling again.

The cabin was atop a hill, its every window lit up, the Jeep Grand Cherokee Julie mentioned parked near the porch. *What's left of it, anyway,* Stuart noted. The vehicle was smashed, one door sheared off, the driveway strewn with twisted metal and automotive fluids. The cabin's interior wasn't much better; its layout was identical to Hoppy's, though the décor and appliances were more upscale, but the open space resembled a battlefield. Broken glass littered the hardwood floor, the French doors were demolished, the dining table was overturned. The refrigerator had been moved in front of the pantry as an impromptu barricade, reinforced by a recliner and some chairs.

Inside the pantry, something growled.

"I don't like the sound of *that*," Stuart worried.

"Me, neither." Bruce's nose crinkled. "I like that smell even less."

He was right: the cabin stank, a swampy combination of filthy hair and mildew. *Like a wet dog on steroids,* Stuart thought.

A young man in a sleeveless shirt and blue jeans slouched on the couch, moaning, both hands clamped over a crimson-soaked towel covering his torso. Julie knelt beside him, gently stroking his perspiration-dampened hair. "Y– you're gonna be okay, Owen," she promised. "We're gonna get you out of here."

"Not if we don't get The Love Boat afloat, we aren't," Bruce huffed.

"*What?*" Frustration seeped into Julie's tone. "Owen needs a doctor *now*."

"Hey, don't get mad at me." Bruce jerked a thumb towards Lenny. "If Kolchak over there hadn't jumped in front of us, we wouldn't have gotten stuck in the first place."

"I heard that, Pops," Lenny chided as he and Kyle approached the kitchen. Suddenly Lenny stopped, cried out, and moving up behind him Stuart realized why. A grisly smear of blood trailed through the French doors; a woman's slender leg lay severed on the patio, beyond which was an incomprehensible mess of pulpy viscera, bone shards and shredded clothes.

Lenny staggered to the sink and promptly threw up. Wiping his mouth on his sleeve, he said, "W– what... What could've *done* that?"

The pantry captive pounded on the door, hard enough to rock the refrigerator. Stuart tightened his grip on the Maglite. "Your cryptid cousin ranks high on the suspect list."

"No *way*," Lenny argued. "There's zero evidence Sasquatches exhibit aggressive behavior towards humans."

"Ape Canyon incident, 1924," Kyle corrected.

"That was a *hoax*." Lenny pointed out the French doors. "And *that... had* to be a bear."

"It *wasn't* a fuckin' bear," someone from the hall declared. A sweaty brute with a linebacker's build and a buzzcut appeared, a Remington 870 pump-action shotgun slung over one massive shoulder, carrying another chair that he added to the barricade. Once the furniture was in place, he pointed to Stuart and Bruce.

"These the codgers you told us about?" he asked Julie.

"Don't be an ass, Trent," she answered. "They came to help."

Trent grabbed Julie's forearm so tightly she yelped. "Who you callin' *ass*? If it weren't for me, you'd be *dead*, Jules. Just like *Nicki*."

Stuart stepped forward. "Get your hands off her, you little punk."

Disbelief carved Trent's brow; when he turned around, Stuart saw his ELON ROCKS t-shirt and the memory from the gas station resurfaced: the SUV and the college students.

Recognition flared with Trent, too. "Bit past your bedtime, ain't it, Grandpa?" He relinquished Julie's arm and faced Stuart. "This is *my* daddy's cabin and *I'm* the one with the boomstick, which makes *me* the Alpha Male here, not you. Shove your nose where it don't belong again and it might just get blown off. We clear about that?"

"Cold-blooded murder's probably not the best idea right now," Kyle announced, tapping his head-mounted camera. "Livestream, douchebag."

"You're *recording* this?" Trent's leer shifted from threatening to annoyed. "The fuck are *you*, anyway?"

"Kyle Hoffstetter," he motioned to Lenny. "That's G.W. Lehner. Cryptozoologists and hosts of *SasqWatchers*."

"Sasquatch?" Trent soured. "*Bigfoot*? You tellin' me we're dealin' with Bigfoot?"

"*Not* Bigfoot," Kyle asserted. "We think that word erodes any respect crypto—"

"Man, *fuck* what you think." Trent pointed to the blockaded pantry. "I've *seen* that thing, and it ain't Bigfoot, or a bear, *or* a fuckin' unicorn, either. So take your Ghostbusters bullshit and the Grumpy Old Men act and get lost."

"Trent, *stop* it!" Julie yelled. "We *need* them. Owen's gonna *die* if we don't get him to a hospital."

A shouting match erupted then, Trent, Julie, Kyle, Lenny, Bruce, arguing over each other, all at once. The noise agitated the pantry-dweller; the growling and pounding intensified, and when the door nudged open ever-so-slightly, Stuart experienced a surge of dread.

"*Oh, hell*," he whispered. "It's not going to hold."

Lenny was closest to the pantry. Stuart reached out to pull him away, but it was too late: a thick, woolly, clawed arm sprang from the narrow opening, fastened around Lenny's head and yanked him backwards. Caught between the refrigerator and the door, blood streamed from Lenny's scalp; his legs flailed uselessly, and when he attempted to raise the tranquilizer pistol it clattered to the floor.

Kyle stood frozen beside Stuart, watching as Lenny was pulled further into the pantry. His head had almost completely disappeared through the gap before Stuart dropped the Maglite and seized one of Lenny's thighs.

"*Grab his other leg!*" Stuart cried. The command snapped Kyle from his stupor; he grasped Lenny's right calf and a tug-of-war began.

The creature in the pantry was strong; even against two men it was unyielding. Only when Bruce bashed the tire iron onto that clawed limb could Stuart and Kyle finally wrest Lenny free.

The pantry-dweller roared and pushed against the door, splitting the wood with a body so wide and thick and muscly it seemed too large for the opening. Behind the splintering door Stuart saw a snout and two incandescent eyes, but it was that toothsome maw that scared him most, open and ready to devour him whole.

The creature pushed the refrigerator over, scattered the barricade, and barreled straight ahead. With one vicious swing the beast knocked Stuart aside, yanked Lenny from Kyle's grasp and bit deep into his shoulder. It'd swallowed the meat and was readying for a second bite when Trent unloaded three shots into the creature's flank.

The beast went down, but wasn't dead. It writhed and yowled, scraping furrows into the floor with its claws. When Trent delivered another bullet into its head, blood spattered Stuart's shirt.

"You idiots still think it's fuckin' Bigfoot?" Trent admonished Kyle.

Kyle stared at the body, bewildered. "I... I don't know *what* it is..."

Stuart examined the creature, too. Though it was covered in coarse, blood-thickened, gray-black fur, the overall shape resembled a man, deep-chested with bulky shoulders, slender forearms and powerful legs, but the rest was decidedly bestial: claws, paws, a bushy tail, a large heavy head, triangular ears, and a long, blunt muzzle with sharp, sharp teeth.

In the kitchen Lenny was still screaming. The mauling had flayed his scalp and shredded his face, but when Kyle attempted to hoist him up, Lenny flinched.

"*Don't*... don't *touch* me..." he spit. "Something's... something's wrong..."

"No shit. You're in shock." Kyle reached out again. "Come on."

"*Get away from me!*" Saliva foamed around Lenny's mouth. His breathing quickened, then he clutched his midsection and doubled over. "*It hurts!* Christ, it fuckin' *hurts!*"

Lenny's neck swelled; when he tried speaking his voice came out a growl.

"*Oh my God!*" Julie yelled. "What's *happening* to him?"

Nothing good, Stuart thought. When Lenny looked up, his eyes reflected the cabin's light like an animal's. *Just like that thing in the pantry.*

Lenny's clothes tore as his muscles bulged to twice their normal size. His limbs contorted at impossible angles, bones and joints cracking as his body rearranged itself. Skin rippled and hair sprouted needle-like from beneath the flesh; a tail wriggled from his rump, his hands curled into paws. Lenny's jaw split, distended into a snout, and a second, sharper set of teeth punctured through his gums. Once Lenny dropped to his haunches to sniff the air, Trent raised the Remington.

"*NO!*" Kyle bumped Trent's arm, and the errant shotgun blast blew out the kitchen window. Trent pushed Kyle back, but before he could aim again the thing Lenny had become bounded towards them, knocking Stuart down and flipping Bruce clear across the cabin.

Stuart rolled over and saw the tranquilizer gun four feet away amid some debris. Snatching the pistol, he sat up and aimed the laser at the creature's massive chest.

Lenny bellowed as the dart struck, but kept charging. Stuart backpedaled, tripped, then braced for impact. *At least I won't have to worry about developing Alzheimer's.*

Suddenly Lenny stumbled and skidded head-first to the floorboards, mere inches from Stuart's shoes. His muscles twitched, his eyelids sagged, his breathing slowed.

And just that fast: silence.

Stuart dropped the tranquilizer pistol and rushed to where Bruce lay crumpled beneath the raised hearth. Bruce's bifocals were broken, his nose was bloodied and his Hawaiian shirt ragged, but he still managed a weak smile once Stuart pulled him to his feet.

"King Kong really packs a wallop." Bruce rubbed his head. "So much for a peaceful fishing trip."

Nearby, Kyle shrank against the wall, hyperventilating. Trent stormed across the room and shoved him again.

"What's your *problem*, asshole? I had that motherfucker dead to rights," he aimed the shotgun at the unconscious creature Lenny had transformed into. "'Course, I can fix *that*."

"*Don't!*" Kyle pleaded. "That's... That's G.W."

"Not *anymore* it ain't," Trent grunted. "You said so yourself. We don't know *what* it is."

"It's a werewolf," Julie blurted out.

"*What?*" Trent's expression curdled. "First it's a bear. Then Bigfoot. Now a *werewolf*? Are you *nuts*?"

"There's a full moon tonight." Julie pointed out the bay window. "*Think* about it. The thing that killed Nicki bit this guy, and since the moon's full, he became just like it. Haven't you ever seen *An American Werewolf in London? The Wolf Man? Ginger Snaps?* It's how this *works*."

Stuart remembered the howling he'd heard. *Maybe that wasn't coyotes after all.* "She might be right."

"That so, Grandpa? Well, *fine*, if *that's* how it works—" Trent leveled the Remington at Owen. "*He* could be one, too."

"Dude, what the hell?" Owen recoiled. "Get that out of my face!"

Julie stepped in front of the shotgun. "No, Trent! That thing only clawed Owen. If he'd been bitten, he would've already *turned* by now."

Trent ground his teeth, then reluctantly lowered the Remington. "You're *crazy*, Jules. But okay. Let's discuss *werewolves*. What do we know about werewolves?"

Bruce looked at Kyle. "You're the Monster Man. Got any pointers?"

Kyle shook his head. "Not many. There are definite reports of Canid cryptids. The Beast of Bray Road comes to mind. The Michigan Dog Man. And belief in shapeshifters exists in cultures worldwide. But as far as what *stops* them, wolfsbane and silver bullets... that's just hearsay and Hollywood."

"We don't need silver bullets," Trent bragged. "Regular ones did the trick just *fine*."

Something groaned behind them then, and the werewolf Trent shot slowly stirred. Even from where he stood Stuart could see the beast's injuries, so grievous minutes earlier, mending themselves, cartilage and sinew and ligaments restitching like knitter's yarn into solid tissue. The creature edged upright, its bristling flesh expelling buckshot onto the blood-smeared floorboards.

Bruce glanced to Trent. "You were saying?"

"No *way*." Trent's bravado faltered. "No *fuckin'* way."

The resuscitating wolf loosed a sickly howl that reverberated throughout the cabin, but more troubling to Stuart were the similar cries answering from outside, growing louder and closer with each passing heartbeat.

"Sounds like Big Bad's brothers are coming to blow the house down," he said to Bruce.

"Pack hunters. *Damn.* And here I thought the night couldn't get any worse."

"That was foolish of you." Stuart secured one of Owen's arms over his shoulder. "Help me with this kid. If we can reach your car, maybe we can rock it free and get the *hell* out of Dodge."

Bruce lifted Owen up, but they didn't complete three paces before the bay window exploded. What crawled through the obliterated frame was larger than the pantry wolf, taller and heavier, its claws longer, its stench muskier. A bulbous erect cock swung from the groin, and its snout glistened above a carnivorous mouth so wide it seemed to dominate the entire head.

"S– something tells me Trent's not the Alpha Male anymore," Kyle stammered.

Trent had backed into the kitchen, and fearfully popped off a misjudged shot that struck the larger wolf's shoulder. The Alpha yowled, reeled, but didn't fall. When Trent pulled the trigger again, nothing happened.

Panic filled his voice. *"I'm out of ammo!"*

The wolf lunged, and Trent desperately clubbed the oncoming beast with the shotgun's stock. The Alpha battered the weapon aside, upended Trent by an ankle and violently twisted his legs apart at the groin like a wishbone. Trent's hips dislocated, his waist split, and he shrieked as he was cleaved in half straight to the sternum, his uncoiling innards spilling from the ever-widening gash.

The Alpha dropped Trent and buried its muzzle deep into the steaming carcass, savoring the kill. Soon the smaller pantry wolf joined the feast. The sloppy noise of their gnashing jaws as they crunched marrow and chewed organs turned Stuart's stomach.

"*Stu!*" Bruce hissed. "Out the master bedroom window. While they're distracted."

Together they slunk towards the hall with Owen between them. When Stuart glanced back, he saw Kyle and Julie close on their heels wearing the same shell-shocked expression. Scared as he might've been, though, Kyle abruptly stopped partway to the bedroom.

"We have to take Lenny with us," he proclaimed.

"What? *Hell* no," Bruce objected. "I'm sorry your buddy was turned into Jojo the Dog-Faced Boy, but I've got a strict rule: *No* pets in The Love Boat."

"I don't *care.*" Kyle was resolute. "You wouldn't abandon *your* friend, and I'm not abandoning mine. No matter *what* he's become."

Stuart raised an eyebrow at Bruce. "Boy's got a point."

"*Crap.*" Bruce relented. "*Fine.* But you're vacuuming the fur off the upholstery."

They pivoted to double-back, but the Alpha noted their presence, spat a length of Trent's trachea on the hardwood and stampeded across the cabin, too fast to outrun. The creature rammed headlong into Kyle and they crashed to the floorboards, a thrashing windmill of limbs and fangs. The wolf pinned Kyle down and disemboweled him before ripping open his ribcage. For a few anguished moments Kyle still moved, but soon there was the sickening egg-crack of his snapping neck. And that was that.

Stuart didn't wait to see what happened next. He ducked with Bruce into the master bedroom, then bolted the lock. Julie already had the window open and was helping Owen through when the Alpha struck the door so furiously the hinges twisted.

Bruce scuttled out the window, then poked his head back inside. "Hurry up!"

Stuart's backbone protested as he climbed over the windowsill. Outside, the air chilled his sweat-soaked body; in the fading moonlight the four of them waded into the tall grass towards the gravel lane. Stuart's lungs burned, his thighs wobbled, his chest ached. From the way Bruce wheezed, he was having difficulty keeping up, too.

"God, I think I'm going to have a stroke," he rasped.

Stuart almost laughed. "And you call *me* a wuss."

The Buick was where they'd left it, mired in the mud. Once Owen was nestled into the passenger's seat, Bruce tossed Julie his keys.

"You steer. We'll push. Be gentle with my baby, okay?"

Julie slipped behind the steering wheel and the Riviera's V8 thundered to life. Stuart and Bruce placed their hands on the hood, but the initial push did little beyond spatter sludge onto Stuart's pants. A second attempt from the rear wasn't more productive, no matter how much Julie revved the engine. Only on the third try, again at the front, did the tire finally budge.

Stuart and Bruce were both wheezing then, but hope for rest fled when another howl echoed from the forest.

"*That's* not good." Bruce forced all his weight against the car. "*Push*, Stu!"

Stuart obeyed, telling Julie: "*Floor* it!"

This time the Riviera gained traction and spun ten feet back. Rolling the window down, Julie shouted, "*Get in!*"

Stuart and Bruce scrambled into the back seat when a shadow fell across the Buick's hood. Owen screamed, and glancing up Stuart saw a third werewolf looming in the headlights, smaller than the Alpha but still taller than a man, its eyes glistening, its claws bloody from a half-eaten doe it held. By the exposed teats running along the abdomen, he guessed this wolf was female. By its snarling, crimson-coated fangs, he also guessed it wasn't happy.

"Momma wolf's angry." Stuart looked at Bruce. "We're going to need a bigger boat."

The wolf threw the deer aside, unleashed a guttural bellow and charged just as Julie stomped on the gas and met the beast at forty miles an hour.

The impact rattled the entire car as the wolf tumbled onto the hood and over the roof. Julie cranked the wheel so sharply Stuart and Bruce slid around amid the camping supplies before she straightened the car and gunned it up the lane.

"Slick moves, Evel Knievel," Bruce said to her.

"I was a go-kart champion in middle school," Julie admitted proudly. Glancing in the rearview mirror, her smile dissolved. *"SHIT! IT'S STILL BEHIND US!"*

The car accelerated, but when Stuart looked, Momma Wolf was five yards back and gaining. Julie accelerated, but the creature leapt, landed squarely on the Buick's trunk, then smashed in the rear window. Glass flew across the back seat as the wolf's head wedged inside, its jaws clacking mere inches from Stuart's face. The smell of rancid meat rankled his nostrils. *This gives dog breath a whole new meaning.*

A can of mosquito repellent rolled off the seat onto the floor by Stuart's shoe. As the wolf snapped at him again, he fumbled for the can and sprayed a poisonous stream directly into its eyes.

The creature's pained bawl was deafening in the enclosed space. It withdrew through the broken window, then crawled atop the Buick's roof.

"What's it *doing*?" Owen hissed. An instant later, claws punctured the Riviera's ceiling, the metal crumpling like cardboard as a hole opened. The wolf's muzzle appeared, then its shoulder, its arm.

What happened after was almost a blur. The she-wolf pulled Owen through the opening to his shoulders, wrenching his head to one side ferociously enough it severed from the neck. Owen's spinal column slithered loose as his decapitated body plopped into the seat, spraying scarlet geyser-squirts across the dashboard.

Julie screamed. Her grip on the steering wheel loosened and the car veered across the lane, hit the ditch and flipped.

Stuart felt weightless as the Riviera rolled. When the vehicle came to rest it was upside down. Stuart's head swam. Blood dripped into his eyes. When someone touched his shoulder, he winced.

"*Hey*." Bruce's voice shook. "You alive, old man?"

"I hope so," Stuart groaned. "Deborah would kill me if I wasn't."

The passenger's window had shattered in the rollover. Both men crawled out onto the grass. The scent of gasoline tainted the air. Through the leafy canopy the sky was gray with the first hint of pre-dawn.

Bruce stared at the Riviera, his lower lip quaking. "Damn... The Love Boat. At least the Titanic had the dignity of hitting an iceberg."

"Where's Julie?" Stuart asked.

"*Here*," the girl limped from the Buick's front, cradling her right elbow. "M— my arm's messed up."

Stuart looked at Bruce. "How far you figure it is to Hop's cabin?"

In the woods, another howl.

"Too far!" Bruce answered.

The three of them maneuvered around the wrecked car. On the opposite side, Momma Wolf lay twenty feet away, hurled by the accident into the base of an oak. A low-hanging branch had impaled her abdomen, one of her front forelimbs was broken, and several fangs were missing. Hearing the creature's whimpers somehow stirred sympathy in Stuart, yet the wolf's wretched shape was already repairing itself, ejecting the branch from her belly. *How long until she's at us again?*

Stuart picked up a nearby stone, heavy and round like a bowling ball.

"What are you doing?" Bruce asked.

"This has to end." Stuart heaved the stone above his head.

"Stu, that's not gonna work... *Bullets* won't even finish these things off."

"Then she'll get one hell of a headache while I try."

Stuart was about to swing the stone down when the she-wolf convulsed. The tremors began in the creature's arms, and then suddenly her entire anatomy was in flux, a shimmer of shriveling muscles, cracking joints, realigning bones. The wolf's pelt became mangy; fur fell out in clumps. When she moved again, Stuart saw pale skin beneath the hair. Its next howl evolved halfway through into a person's agonized scream.

Once the metamorphosis was complete, the beast was gone; a nude brunette woman lay in its stead, curled into a shaking fetal ball, coated in a newborn's bloody ichor. Her eyes, though, still gleamed like an animal's.

Bruce gawked at the woman. "Well, well. The sheep in wolf's clothing."

Julie glanced to the sky. "The moon's gone down."

Stuart had lowered the stone once the change began, but hadn't dropped it. The woman was disoriented, unsteady. When she sat up, Stuart gasped.

"You were at the gas station," he muttered, astonished to recognize the mother Trent had whistled catcalls at, the one he'd risked a confrontation to defend. The revelation burned like fire. "Who *are* you?"

The woman's voice was hoarse. "*Kate*. M– my name's Kate. My husband's family owns the cabin across the lake. E– every month Chris and I drive up here with our son. During the full moon. All of us are..." She hesitated. "We have cages in the cellar. So we can't escape. So we don't *hurt* anyone. But Robbie... he's a teenager now... getting too strong for his cage. Chris and I couldn't stop him... breaking out. We tried finding him before we transformed, but that didn't happen."

Until then Stuart only considered the wolves driven by mindless appetite, but now understanding took root. *They're a family*. He thought of Deborah, of his own grown children, his grandkids, and the evening's mayhem assumed new perspectives: Robbie, the lost pantry-dweller; Chris, the Alpha, a dad searching for his wayward pup; Kate, the protective mother. Yet bloodshed remained bloodshed. And they had shed plenty.

He looked again at the stone in his hands. Kate did, too.

"*Do it...*" she begged. "We can only be killed when... when we're *human*. But I *deserve* it. We *all* do."

Stuart weighed the stone. It would easily crush her skull. One blow and it'd be over.

Beside him, Bruce appeared unusually solemn. Resting a gentle palm on Stuart's shoulder, he said, simply, "*Don't, Stu*."

Stuart looked at his buddy. After a long pause he dropped the stone to the ground.

Julie was livid: "That's *it*? You're gonna let her *go*? My friends are *dead* because of her and her fucking monster family!"

"There's been enough death for one night," Stuart lamented.

Outrage poured from Julie; she seemed primed to argue, but instead sank into Stuart's chest, sobbing, "This isn't *fair*. They killed my friends…"

Stuart wrapped a comforting arm around the girl. Peering at Kate, his tone hardened. "Take your husband and son and *leave*. Before we change our minds."

Astonishment settled onto Kate's face; she waited another moment, then bolted into the brush without looking back.

Peace enveloped the forest. Morning birds trilled. An owl hooted. Still hugging Julie, Stuart said to Bruce, "Let's go. We've got quite a walk."

Sunrise daubed the horizon by the time they reached Hoppy's cabin. To Stuart's astonishment, Lenny sat glumly on the porch wearing only a pair of Bruce's cargo shorts, his skin coated in the same viscous grime as Kate's, his beard matted with blood. The wounds to Lenny's face and scalp were healed, though the bite mark on his shoulder had left an unseemly scar.

"Well I'll be," Stuart marveled. "Didn't expect to see *you*."

Lenny seemed surprised, too. "And *I* didn't know this was your cabin. Front door was unlocked. Went in and stole some pants. Hope you don't mind."

"Are you… okay?"

"All things considered. Woke up buck-ass naked with one motherfucker of a hangover." Lenny coughed, then spit a gooey hairball on the ground. "And I think I ate a raccoon."

"The cryptid hunter turns cryptid. Poetic," Bruce joked.

"Poetic my ass, Pops." Lenny's expression sank. "I found what was left of Kyle. Telling his folks isn't gonna be easy."

"He wouldn't leave you," Stuart revealed somberly. "Even at the end. He refused to abandon his friend."

A small smirk lit Lenny's jaw. "That's Kyle. Too dumb to know when to quit." The smirk faded. "*Fuck*, I'm gonna need time to process all this."

"Yeah, well, you might want to finish processing by the next full moon," Bruce advised him. "You might want to invest in more tranquilizers, too. A bank vault wouldn't hurt."

"And *we* might want to get our stories straight," Stuart noted. "'Assaulted by Werewolves' won't look kosher on the police report."

"We could blame Bigfoot," Bruce quipped.

Lenny winced. "Funny, Pops."

"I vote bear attack," Stuart suggested.

A distant engine broke the morning tranquility, and soon Hoppy's mud-spattered Wrangler rumbled up the gravel road. The vehicle stopped in front of the cabin and Hoppy clambered out, clad in fishing waders over his dungarees. He gave a cordial wave, but his smile waned approaching the porch. Leaning on his cane, Hoppy studied Stuart and Bruce, adjusted his ever-present Al Capone cap and grimaced.

"Dear *God*. What shenanigans did you goons get into *this* time?"

Stuart, Bruce, Julie and Lenny quietly exchanged glances before replying in unison: "Bear attack."

"A bear?" Hoppy sounded skeptical. "That's *all?*"

"No, but that's what we're sticking with." Stuart led Julie to the Wrangler. "Can you take us to town, Hop?"

Hoppy frowned. "Now? What about our Old Boys weekend? We were gonna barbecue, remember?"

"*No.* No meat. Ever again," Bruce insisted. "After last night I'm going vegetarian."

"You and me both, Pops," Lenny agreed.

Once everyone was situated inside the Wrangler, Hoppy backed away from the cabin, made a U-turn, and soon they were heading towards the highway. Stuart's body finally relaxed, and as the serene scenery sped by, he chuckled.

"What is it?" Bruce asked.

"I just realized why this is called Wolfe's Lake State Park," Stuart answered before settling in for the long journey home.

CRITICAL BLAST PUBLISHING

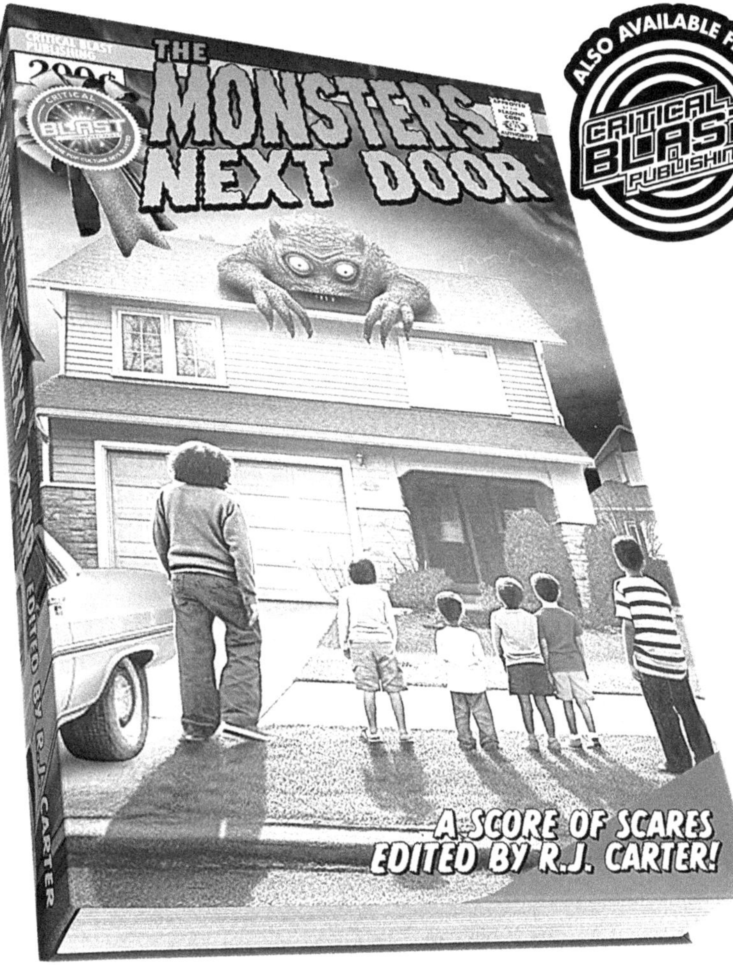

20¢

THE MONSTERS NEXT DOOR

EDITED BY R.J. CARTER

A SCORE OF SCARES
EDITED BY R.J. CARTER!

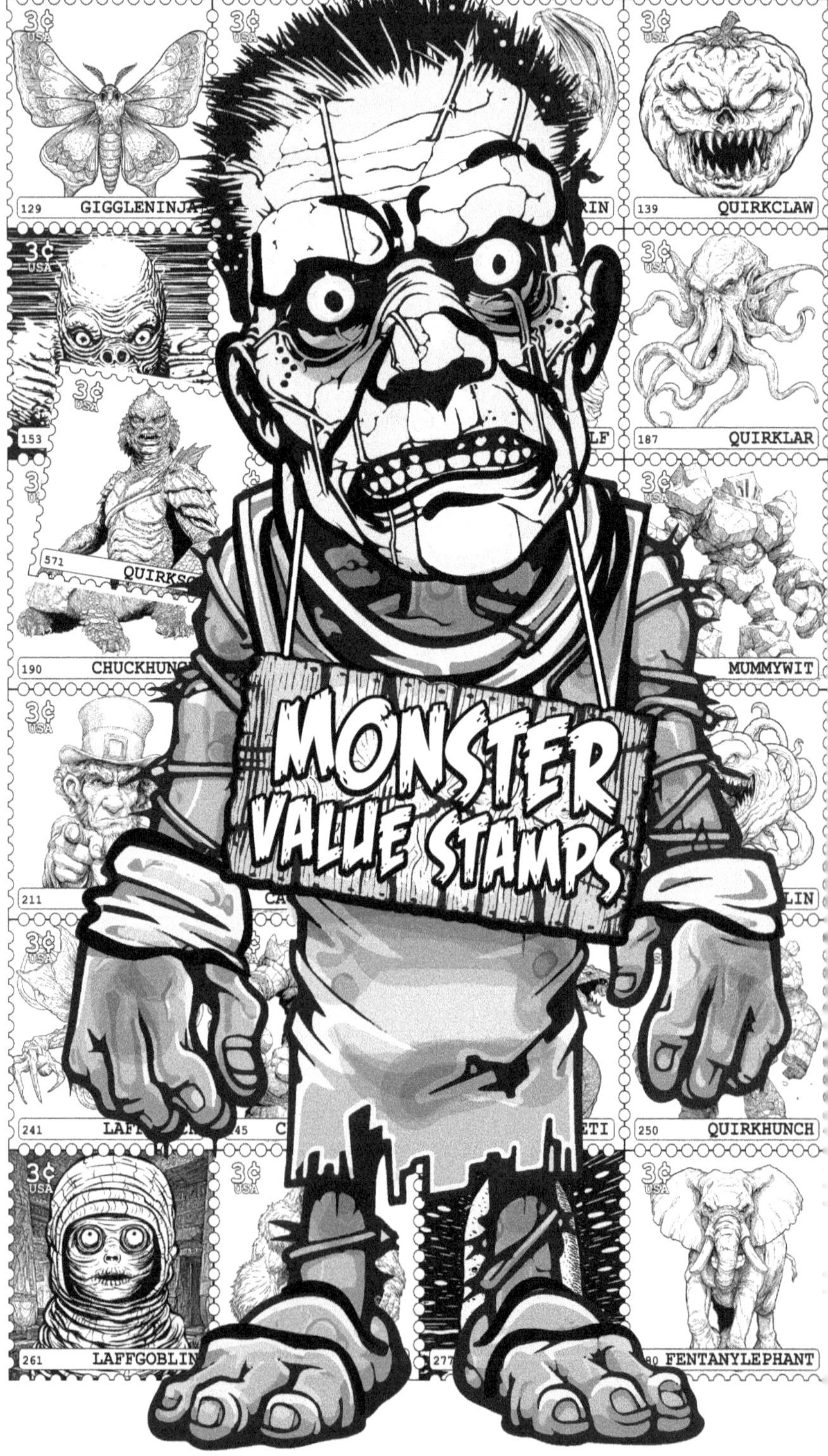
3¢ USA
129   GIGGLENINJA
139   QUIRKCLAW
3¢ USA
3¢ USA
153
187   QUIRKLAR
3¢ USA
571   QUIRKSO
MUMMYWIT
190   CHUCKHUNG
3¢ USA
211
LIN
3¢ USA
241   LAFF
45   C
ETI
250   QUIRKHUNCH
3¢ USA
3¢ USA
261   LAFFGOBLIN
277
80   FENTANYLEPHANT
MONSTER
VALUE STAMPS

THE MONSTER VALUE STAMP CHECKLIST! (-1-)

☐001 BOUNCER	☐057 TIN FOIL CON	☐113 WITTYWISP	☐169 CHUCKLESTEIN	☐225 GROUCHYSHADE	☐281 JOKEMONSTER
☐002 GHOST WHALE	☐058 SMIRKLORD	☐114 SNICKERCLAW	☐170 DRACUCHUCK	☐226 CACKLEWHIRL	☐282 QUIRKZILLA
☐003 BEAR GOBLIN	☐059 GROUCHYFANG	☐115 LAFFTANGLE	☐171 GIGGLESMUMMY	☐227 POTATOE JOE	☐283 CACKLINA
☐004 SPIDER OCTOPUS	☐060 CHUCKLEBOP	☐116 HAHAWHIZ	☐172 WOLFIEWIT	☐228 GIGGLESHUNCH	☐284 CHUCKLEBYTE
☐005 BEETLE BILLY BOB	☐061 GIGGLESWAMP	☐117 GRINWHISPER	☐173 QUIRKENSTEIN	☐229 JOKVAMPIRE	☐285 QUIRKSHADE
☐006 NO HEAD MAN	☐062 SNICKERWICK	☐118 QUIRKLING	☐174 JOKULA	☐230 QUIRKGOBLIN	☐286 GIGGLESNACK
☐007 CRAB NAB JAB	☐063 LAFFNINJA	☐119 GIGGLESCRANK	☐175 GROUCHYPHANTOM	☐231 CACKMERMAN	☐287 SNICKERTHUD
☐008 BAT-GOD BUNJABIE	☐064 QUIRKLING	☐120 CHUCKLEQUILL	☐176 CACKLEBLOB	☐232 SMIRKULA	☐288 MIRTHQUAKE
☐009 MAD MAC MANLEY	☐065 GROUCHFIZZLE	☐121 SMIRKPAW	☐177 SNICKERELLA	☐233 LAFFGHOUL	☐289 DRACUFIZZ
☐010 VAMPI VETALA	☐066 WITTYWHIRL	☐122 LAFFLING	☐178 LAFFZILLA	☐234 CHUCKLEGHOST	☐290 LAFFNUDGE
☐011 ABAGALE VIPER	☐067 CACKLEHOP	☐123 WATER GIRAFFE	☐179 HAHASWAMP	☐235 QUIRKWITCH	☐291 GROUCHGLEE
☐012 SPIKE VALARION	☐068 HAHAGLOOP	☐124 GROUCHFLAME	☐180 QUIRKULA	☐236 GROUCHYWOLF	☐292 WITTYZAP
☐013 CRY BABY	☐069 JOKULITE	☐125 QUIRKCLAW	☐181 GROUCHHUNCH	☐237 MIRTHBATS	☐293 HAHACHOMP
☐014 AQUA-SANDY	☐070 CHUCKLEWHIZ	☐126 SNICKERSNARL	☐182 SMIRKFISHMAN	☐238 CHUCKRAT	☐294 JOKUBUZZ
☐015 CRYPTO-DILLY DALI	☐071 GIGGLESKULL	☐127 HAHABUZZ	☐183 CHUCKHYDE	☐239 QUIRKBLOB	☐295 QUIRKZILLA
☐016 HANGOVER HARPY	☐072 QUIRKBEAST	☐128 CHUCKLEJESTER	☐184 MIRTHWOLF	☐240 JOKBOLT	☐296 CACKLEBUMP
☐017 JINGWEI SLASHER	☐073 SNICKERFLARE	☐129 GIGGLENINJA	☐185 SNARKULA	☐241 LAFFWITCH	☐297 SMIRKLASH
☐018 MRS. PLACED	☐074 MIRTHPAW	☐130 LAFFPHANTOM	☐186 GIGGLESBRIDE	☐242 SNICKERHUNCH	☐298 GROUCHYJOLT
☐019 HOARIS	☐075 DRACUGRIN	☐131 WITTYHOWLER	☐187 QUIRKLAR	☐243 CACKLEPHANTOM	☐299 CHUCKLEFLUFF
☐020 KALAVINKALI	☐076 CANDY HEAD	☐132 QUIRKQUAKE	☐188 CACKVAMPIRE	☐244 GROUCHOWIT	☐300 GIGGLESWIRL
☐021 SIREN SALLY	☐077 GROUCHSHADE	☐133 GROUCHBOP	☐189 GROUCHOBOLT	☐245 CHUCKLEMUMMY	☐301 SNICKERTHUNK
☐022 ACHELOIS THE PAIN	☐078 CHUCKLEQUILL	☐134 SMIRKWHISPER	☐190 CHUCKHUNCH	☐246 HAHAYETI	☐302 LAFFFLICK
☐023 LADY SIL LAMBENT	☐079 QUIRKHOWLER	☐135 JOKUBAT	☐191 LAFFLOCK	☐247 SNARKWITCH	☐303 QUIRKBOUNCE
☐024 TERP SICHOARE	☐080 HAHAJESTER	☐136 SNICKERWISP	☐192 WITTYMUMMY	☐248 GRINBLOB	☐304 GROUCHFROLIC
☐025 SWAN KNEE SAM	☐081 JOKUBAT	☐137 HAHAGRIN	☐193 MIRTHRA	☐249 JOKULA	☐305 WITTYWHAM
☐026 CINNAMON KILLER	☐082 SNICKERSPOOK	☐138 CHUCKLESNARL	☐194 CACKLEWORM	☐250 QUIRKHUNCH	☐306 CACKLEPLOP
☐027 DEVIL BOY BOB	☐083 GIGGLESCRANK	☐139 QUIRKCLAW	☐195 HAHABRIDE	☐251 CHUCKLEPHANTOM	☐307 HAHASQUISH
☐028 MIRACULOUS MAMA	☐084 CACKLEJINX	☐140 GROUCHYJINX	☐196 SCREAMHAHA	☐252 LAFFBOLT	☐308 JOKULUXE
☐029 COPPER CLAWS LOU	☐085 LAFFSHADE	☐141 LAFFWHIRL	☐197 GRINPHANTOM	☐253 GROUCHMERMAN	☐309 CHUCKLEZOOM
☐030 THE SLAVIC COOK	☐086 CIY CLOPSIE	☐142 WITTYSHADOW	☐198 CHUCKLEFLY	☐254 HAHAGHOUL	☐310 GIGGLESCRUNCH
☐031 PRIMORDIAL OOZE	☐087 WITTYFLAME	☐143 SNICKERHOWL	☐199 LAFFINVISIBLE	☐255 SNICKERGHOST	☐311 QUIRKROAR
☐032 VISHNU NOODLE TIM	☐088 GRINWHISPER	☐144 GRINFLARE	☐200 GROUCHYBLOB	☐256 CHUCKFISHMAN	☐312 SNICKERBEAM
☐033 HABA-HABA HILGA	☐089 QUIRKCLAW	☐145 LAFFSPARK	☐201 QUIRKYETI	☐257 QUIRKOOP	☐313 MIRTHPOUNCE
☐034 HUCK-CHU SNEAZY	☐090 GROUCHYWHIRL	☐146 CACKLEBOUNCE	☐202 CHUCKWRAITH	☐258 SMIRKWIT	☐314 DRACUGIGGLE
☐035 SNUGGLE PORKY	☐091 CHUCKLEJOLT	☐147 JOKUPOP	☐203 LAFFBOLT	☐259 GIGGLESRAT	☐315 LAFFTWIST
☐036 FLUFFY MCTOE	☐092 SNICKERGRIN	☐148 GROUCHYFLUFF	☐204 SMIRKENSTEIN	☐260 CACKLEFLY	☐316 GROUCHYZEST
☐037 WOLFDOG MAN	☐093 GROUCHOSTEIN	☐149 CHUCKLEGLIDE	☐205 QUIRKBRIDE	☐261 LAFFGOBLIN	☐317 CHUCKLEGLIDE
☐038 MORTIMER VORTEX	☐094 QUIRKNINJA	☐150 SMIRKROAR	☐206 GROUCHOBATS	☐262 CHUCKLEYETI	☐318 QUIRKSOAR
☐039 XANDER DAYSHADE	☐095 GIGGLESSNARL	☐151 WITTYFLICK	☐207 MUMMYWIT	☐263 GRINBRIDE	☐319 HAHACHUCKLE
☐040 LUCIUS GRIMRIDER	☐096 MUMMY MCQUIRK	☐152 QUIRKCRUNCH	☐208 HAHAMERMAN	☐264 GROUCHOWITCH	☐320 JOKUPOP
☐041 SELENE BLACKHEAD	☐097 GIGGLESWORTH	☐153 FISHWOMAN	☐209 GIGGLESFLY	☐265 QUIRKULA	☐321 SNICKERBOUNCE
☐042 KAEL GRIMSHADOW	☐098 SNICKERELLA	☐154 LAFFQUAKE	☐210 CHUCKCYCLOPS	☐266 SNARKENSTEIN	☐322 GIGGLESWHIZ
☐043 LILITH BLOODMOON	☐099 JIMMY COFFEE	☐155 CACKLEBUZZ	☐211 GRINZILLA	☐267 HAHAPHANTOM	☐323 CACKLEZAP
☐044 VAL ABSISSY CLAW	☐100 CHUCKLES DRAC	☐156 JOKUSHADOW	☐212 JOKSTEIN	☐268 CACKLESWAMP	☐324 LAFFSPROUT
☐045 SELENE DOOMCLAW	☐101 LAFFULA	☐157 GROUCHCLAW	☐213 QUIRKOOP	☐269 CHUCKHUNCH	☐325 SMIRKPOP
☐046 BUMIE VON GOBBLE	☐102 QUIRKULA	☐158 CHUCKLENOODLE	☐214 SNICKERBLOB	☐270 GIGGLESBLOB	☐326 WITTYZOOM
☐047 GIGGLES MCGLOOP	☐103 FRANKENFUNNY	☐159 SMIRKWISP	☐215 CHUCKLEWORM	☐271 CHUCKIE	☐327 GRINBOUNCE
☐048 FIZZLE FUZZYPAWS	☐104 ASENA THE BILLION	☐160 WITTYBEAST	☐216 DRACUWIT	☐272 QUIRKSTER	☐328 QUIRKCHOMP
☐049 SNICKER DOODLKINS	☐105 AMAROKIE	☐161 QUIRKHOWL	☐217 LAFFULA	☐273 GIGGLESNARL	☐329 GROUCHZOOM
☐050 GIGGLES WOBLEWAG	☐106 BUGBEAR	☐162 SNICKERFIZZLE	☐218 QUIRKRAT	☐274 SNICKERCLAW	☐330 CHUCKLEZIP
☐051 FUZZZILLA	☐107 FAT LOUIE	☐163 LAFFQUAKE	☐219 WITTYMERMAN	☐275 MIRTHQUAKE	☐331 SNICKERSNORT
☐052 JIGGLYPUFF SALLY	☐108 POUKAI	☐164 GIGGLESBOP	☐220 GROUCHFISHMAN	☐276 DRACUCHUCKLE	☐332 HAHARUMBLE
☐053 HUMA BIRD	☐109 EAGLE EYE ERNIE	☐165 HAHAFLAME	☐221 CACKLEPHANTOM	☐277 LAFFTANGLE	☐333 QUIRKTWIRL
☐054 QUEEN MOTHER	☐110 GARLIC ROOSTER	☐166 CHUCKLEPHANTOM	☐222 HAHAGOBLIN	☐278 GROUCHETTE	☐334 GIGGLESWHAM
☐055 HENRY	☐111 BASAN	☐167 JOKUKNIGHT	☐223 SNARKFLY	☐279 WITTYWISP	☐335 LENNY THE FIG
☐056 SIMURGHA	☐112 THUNDER THIGHS	☐168 QUIRKNOODLE	☐224 CHUCKLEYETI	☐280 FENTANYLEPHANT	☐336 GRINSWAMP

WHY WAIT FOR THE LARGE HADRON COLLIDER TO OPEN THE DOOR TO HELL... WHEN YOU
CAN COLLECT ALL 666 CARDS AND OPEN THE DOOR YOURSELF! GOULISH HUNTING!

THE MONSTER VALUE STAMP CHECKLIST! (-2-)

- ☐ 337 CHUCKLEFIZZ
- ☐ 338 QUIRKGLEAM
- ☐ 339 GIGGLESNAP
- ☐ 340 SNICKERDUNK
- ☐ 341 MIRTHQUAKE
- ☐ 342 DRACUSIZZLE
- ☐ 343 LAFFJOLT
- ☐ 344 GROUCHGLIMP
- ☐ 345 WITTYZEST
- ☐ 346 HAHACHOMP
- ☐ 347 JOKUSHINE
- ☐ 348 QUIRKZILLA
- ☐ 349 CACKLEDAZZ
- ☐ 350 SMIRKFLASH
- ☐ 351 GROUCHYJOLT
- ☐ 352 CHUCKLEFLUFF
- ☐ 353 GIGGLESPREE
- ☐ 354 SNICKERDAZZ
- ☐ 355 LAFFTWIRL
- ☐ 356 QUIRKBOUNCE
- ☐ 357 GROUCHFROLIC
- ☐ 358 WITTYWHAM
- ☐ 359 CACKLEBOP
- ☐ 360 HAHASQUISH
- ☐ 361 JOKULUXE
- ☐ 362 CHUCKLEZOOM
- ☐ 363 GIGGLESCRUNCH
- ☐ 364 QUIRKROAR
- ☐ 365 SNICKERBEAM
- ☐ 366 MIRTHPOUNCE
- ☐ 367 DRACUGIGGLE
- ☐ 368 LAFFTWIST
- ☐ 369 GROUCHYZEST
- ☐ 370 CHUCKLEGLIDE
- ☐ 371 QUIRKSOAR
- ☐ 372 HAHACHUCKLE
- ☐ 373 JOKUPOP
- ☐ 374 SNICKERBOUNCE
- ☐ 375 GIGGLESWHIZ
- ☐ 376 CACKLEZAP
- ☐ 377 LAFFSPROUT
- ☐ 378 SMIRKPOP
- ☐ 379 WITTYZOOM
- ☐ 380 GRINBOUNCE
- ☐ 381 QUIRKCHOMP
- ☐ 382 GROUCHZOOM
- ☐ 383 CHUCKLEZIP
- ☐ 384 SNICKERSNORT
- ☐ 385 HAHARUMBLE
- ☐ 386 THE WARP
- ☐ 387 GIGGLESWHAM
- ☐ 388 LAFFSPARK
- ☐ 389 CACKLEBOUNCE
- ☐ 390 JOKUPOP
- ☐ 391 GROUCHYFLUFF
- ☐ 392 CHUCKLEGLIDE
- ☐ 393 SMIRKROAR
- ☐ 394 WITTYFLICK
- ☐ 395 QUIRKCRUNCH
- ☐ 396 SNICKERSWOOP
- ☐ 397 JERRY THE NAIL
- ☐ 398 GIGGLESWHIZ
- ☐ 399 HAHACHUCKLE
- ☐ 400 CHUCKLECRUNCH
- ☐ 401 JOKUZIP
- ☐ 402 QUIRKBOUNCE
- ☐ 403 GROUCHZOOM
- ☐ 404 SNICKERSWIRL
- ☐ 405 WITTYWHAM
- ☐ 406 LAFFCHOMP
- ☐ 407 SMIRKPOP
- ☐ 408 QUIRKZOOM
- ☐ 409 GROUCHYZIP
- ☐ 410 HAHAPOUNCE
- ☐ 411 CHUCKLECHUCKLE
- ☐ 412 GIGGLESFLICK
- ☐ 413 SNICKERBOUNCE
- ☐ 414 LAFFSPROUT
- ☐ 415 WITTYWHIZ
- ☐ 416 GRINCHOMP
- ☐ 417 QUIRKTWIRL
- ☐ 418 GROUCHYWHAM
- ☐ 419 CHUCKLEZOOM
- ☐ 420 JOKUZIP
- ☐ 421 SNICKERSNORT
- ☐ 422 HAHARUMBLE
- ☐ 423 GIGGLERUMBLE
- ☐ 424 QUIRKBOUNCE
- ☐ 425 LAFFTWIST
- ☐ 426 SMIRKWHAM
- ☐ 427 CHUCKLEWHIZ
- ☐ 428 SNICKERSWOOP
- ☐ 429 QUIRKFLICK
- ☐ 430 GROUCHPOP
- ☐ 431 HAHAWOOSH
- ☐ 432 LAFFWHIZ
- ☐ 433 CHUCKLEFLUFF
- ☐ 434 GIGGLESNORT
- ☐ 435 QUIRKBOUNCE
- ☐ 436 JOKUPOP
- ☐ 437 CHUCKLEFIZZ
- ☐ 438 QUIRKGLEAM
- ☐ 439 GIGGLESNAP
- ☐ 440 SNICKERDUNK
- ☐ 441 MIRTHQUAKE
- ☐ 442 DRACUSIZZLE
- ☐ 443 VLAD CHAD
- ☐ 444 GROUCHGLIMP
- ☐ 445 WITTYZEST
- ☐ 446 HAHACHOMP
- ☐ 447 JOKUSHINE
- ☐ 448 QUIRKZILLA
- ☐ 449 CACKLEDAZZ
- ☐ 450 SMIRKFLASH
- ☐ 451 GROUCHYJOLT
- ☐ 452 CHUCKLEFLUFF
- ☐ 453 GIGGLESPREE
- ☐ 454 SNICKERDAZZ
- ☐ 455 LAFFTWIRL
- ☐ 456 QUIRKBOUNCE
- ☐ 457 GROUCHFROLIC
- ☐ 458 WITTYWHAM
- ☐ 459 CACKLEBOP
- ☐ 460 HAHASQUISH
- ☐ 461 JOKULUXE
- ☐ 462 CHUCKLEZOOM
- ☐ 463 GIGGLESCRUNCH
- ☐ 464 QUIRKROAR
- ☐ 465 SNICKERBEAM
- ☐ 466 MIRTHPOUNCE
- ☐ 467 DRACUGIGGLE
- ☐ 468 LAFFTWIST
- ☐ 469 GROUCHYZEST
- ☐ 470 CHUCKLEGLIDE
- ☐ 471 QUIRKSOAR
- ☐ 472 HAHACHUCKLE
- ☐ 473 JOKUPOP
- ☐ 474 SNICKERBOUNCE
- ☐ 475 GIGGLESWHIZ
- ☐ 476 CACKLEZAP
- ☐ 477 LAFFSPROUT
- ☐ 478 SMIRKPOP
- ☐ 479 WITTYZOOM
- ☐ 480 GRINBOUNCE
- ☐ 481 QUIRKCHOMP
- ☐ 482 GROUCHZOOM
- ☐ 483 CHUCKLEZIP
- ☐ 484 SNICKERSNORT
- ☐ 485 HAHARUMBLE
- ☐ 486 QUIRKTWIRL
- ☐ 487 GIGGLESWHAM
- ☐ 488 LAFFSPARK
- ☐ 489 CACKLEBOUNCE
- ☐ 490 JOKUPOP
- ☐ 491 GROUCHYFLUFF
- ☐ 492 CHUCKLEGLIDE
- ☐ 493 SMIRKROAR
- ☐ 494 WITTYFLICK
- ☐ 495 QUIRKCRUNCH
- ☐ 496 SNICKERSWOOP
- ☐ 497 LAFFTWIST
- ☐ 498 GIGGLESWHIZ
- ☐ 499 HAHACHUCKLE
- ☐ 500 CHUCKLECRUNCH
- ☐ 501 SLICK VINCE
- ☐ 502 QUIRKBOUNCE
- ☐ 503 GROUCHZOOM
- ☐ 504 SNICKERSWIRL
- ☐ 505 WITTYWHAM
- ☐ 506 LAFFCHOMP
- ☐ 507 SMIRKPOP
- ☐ 508 QUIRKZOOM
- ☐ 509 GROUCHYZIP
- ☐ 510 HAHAPOUNCE
- ☐ 511 CHUCKLECHUCKLE
- ☐ 512 GIGGLESFLICK
- ☐ 513 SNICKERBOUNCE
- ☐ 514 LAFFSPROUT
- ☐ 515 WITTYWHIZ
- ☐ 516 GRINCHOMP
- ☐ 517 QUIRKTWIRL
- ☐ 518 GROUCHYWHAM
- ☐ 519 CHUCKLEZOOM
- ☐ 520 JOKUZIP
- ☐ 521 SNICKERSNORT
- ☐ 522 HAHARUMBLE
- ☐ 523 GIGGLERUMBLE
- ☐ 524 QUIRKBOUNCE
- ☐ 525 LAFFTWIST
- ☐ 526 SMIRKWHAM
- ☐ 527 ALI EAN
- ☐ 528 SNICKERSWOOP
- ☐ 529 QUIRKFLICK
- ☐ 530 GROUCHPOP
- ☐ 531 HAHAWOOSH
- ☐ 532 LAFFWHIZ
- ☐ 533 CHUCKLEFLUFF
- ☐ 534 GIGGLESNORT
- ☐ 535 QUIRKBOUNCE
- ☐ 536 JOKUPOP
- ☐ 537 CHUCKLEFIZZ
- ☐ 538 QUIRKGLEAM
- ☐ 539 GIGGLESNAP
- ☐ 540 SNICKERDUNK
- ☐ 541 MIRTHQUAKE
- ☐ 542 DRACUSIZZLE
- ☐ 543 LAFFJOLT
- ☐ 544 GROUCHGLIMP
- ☐ 545 WITTYZEST
- ☐ 546 HAHACHOMP
- ☐ 547 JOKUSHINE
- ☐ 548 QUIRKZILLA
- ☐ 549 CACKLEDAZZ
- ☐ 550 SMIRKFLASH
- ☐ 551 GROUCHYJOLT
- ☐ 552 CHUCKLEFLUFF
- ☐ 553 GIGGLESPREE
- ☐ 554 SNICKERDAZZ
- ☐ 555 PRETTY BOY LENI
- ☐ 556 QUIRKBOUNCE
- ☐ 557 GROUCHFROLIC
- ☐ 558 WITTYWHAM
- ☐ 559 CACKLEBOP
- ☐ 560 HAHASQUISH
- ☐ 561 JOKULUXE
- ☐ 562 CHUCKLEZOOM
- ☐ 563 GIGGLESCRUNCH
- ☐ 564 QUIRKROAR
- ☐ 565 SNICKERBEAM
- ☐ 566 MIRTHPOUNCE
- ☐ 567 DRACUGIGGLE
- ☐ 568 LAFFTWIST
- ☐ 569 GROUCHYZEST
- ☐ 570 CHUCKLEGLIDE
- ☐ 571 QUIRKSOAR
- ☐ 572 HAHACHUCKLE
- ☐ 573 JOKUPOP
- ☐ 574 SNICKERBOUNCE
- ☐ 575 GIGGLESWHIZ
- ☐ 576 CACKLEZAP
- ☐ 577 LAFFSPROUT
- ☐ 578 SMIRKPOP
- ☐ 579 WITTYZOOM
- ☐ 580 GRINBOUNCE
- ☐ 581 QUIRKCHOMP
- ☐ 582 GROUCHZOOM
- ☐ 583 CHUCKLEZIP
- ☐ 584 SNICKERSNORT
- ☐ 585 HAHARUMBLE
- ☐ 586 QUIRKTWIRL
- ☐ 587 GIGGLESWHAM
- ☐ 588 LAFFSPARK
- ☐ 589 CACKLEBOUNCE
- ☐ 590 JOKUPOP
- ☐ 591 GROUCHYFLUFF
- ☐ 592 CHUCKLEGLIDE
- ☐ 593 SMIRKROAR
- ☐ 594 WITTYFLICK
- ☐ 595 QUIRKCRUNCH
- ☐ 596 SNICKERSWOOP
- ☐ 597 LAFFTWIST
- ☐ 598 GIGGLESWHIZ
- ☐ 599 HAHACHUCKLE
- ☐ 600 CHUCKLECRUNCH
- ☐ 601 JOKUZIP
- ☐ 602 QUIRKBOUNCE
- ☐ 603 GROUCHZOOM
- ☐ 604 SNICKERSWIRL
- ☐ 605 WITTYWHAM
- ☐ 606 LAFFCHOMP
- ☐ 607 SMIRKPOP
- ☐ 608 QUIRKZOOM
- ☐ 609 GROUCHYZIP
- ☐ 610 HAHAPOUNCE
- ☐ 611 CHUCKLECHUCKLE
- ☐ 612 GIGGLESFLICK
- ☐ 613 MOUNTAIN CINDY
- ☐ 614 LAFFSPROUT
- ☐ 615 WITTYWHIZ
- ☐ 616 GRINCHOMP
- ☐ 617 QUIRKTWIRL
- ☐ 618 GROUCHYWHAM
- ☐ 619 CHUCKLEZOOM
- ☐ 620 JOKUZIP
- ☐ 621 SNICKERSNORT
- ☐ 622 HAHARUMBLE
- ☐ 623 GIGGLERUMBLE
- ☐ 624 QUIRKBOUNCE
- ☐ 625 LAFFTWIST
- ☐ 626 SMIRKWHAM
- ☐ 627 CHUCKLEWHIZ
- ☐ 628 SNICKERSWOOP
- ☐ 629 QUIRKFLICK
- ☐ 630 GROUCHPOP
- ☐ 631 HAHAWOOSH
- ☐ 632 LAFFWHIZ
- ☐ 633 CHUCKLEFLUFF
- ☐ 634 GIGGLESNORT
- ☐ 635 QUIRKBOUNCE
- ☐ 636 JOKUPOP
- ☐ 637 CHUCKLEFIZZ
- ☐ 638 QUIRKGLEAM
- ☐ 639 GIGGLESNAP
- ☐ 640 SNICKERDUNK
- ☐ 641 MIRTHQUAKE
- ☐ 642 DRACUSIZZLE
- ☐ 643 LAFFJOLT
- ☐ 644 GROUCHGLIMP
- ☐ 645 WITTYZEST
- ☐ 646 HAHACHOMP
- ☐ 647 JOKUSHINE
- ☐ 648 QUIRKZILLA
- ☐ 649 CACKLEDAZZ
- ☐ 650 SMIRKFLASH
- ☐ 651 GROUCHYJOLT
- ☐ 652 CHUCKLEFLUFF
- ☐ 653 GIGGLESPREE
- ☐ 654 SNICKERDAZZ
- ☐ 655 LAFFTWIRL
- ☐ 656 QUIRKBOUNCE
- ☐ 657 GROUCHFROLIC
- ☐ 658 WITTYWHAM
- ☐ 659 CACKLEBOP
- ☐ 660 HAHASQUISH
- ☐ 661 JOKULUXE
- ☐ 662 CHUCKLEZOOM
- ☐ 663 GIGGLESCRUNCH
- ☐ 664 QUIRKROAR
- ☐ 665 MAD MANDY
- ☐ 666 SNICKERBOUNCE

WHY WAIT FOR THE LARGE HADRON COLLIDER TO OPEN THE DOOR TO HELL... WHEN YOU CAN COLLECT ALL 666 CARDS AND OPEN THE DOOR YOURSELF! GOULISH HUNTING!

CRITICAL BLAST PUBLISHING
20¢
APPROVED BY THE READING CODE AUTHORITY
SENSEI NOSFERATUPAC vs FEMALE ELEPHANT
WEIRD FANTASTIC WORLDS
CRITICAL BLAST PUBLISHING
WHERE POP CULTURE GETS BLASTED
INCREDIBLE STRANGE STORIES
YO, DEMON! YOU AIN'T GOT NO PLACE IN THIS CRAZY CREATURE'S GROOVE!
WITH THE POWER OF THE COSMOS AND THE FUNK OF THE UNIVERSE, I CAST YOU OUT! BREAK THOSE CHAINS, AND SET THIS ELEPHANT SPIRIT FREE!
AN EPIC TALE OF THE HIGH-KICKIN ASS-KICKIN' WITH IT MAN OF MYSTERY.
A SORCERY-SUMMONED DEMON AND A DRUGGED UP PACHYDERM SPELL CURTAINS FOR
THE MASTER OF BLACK MYSTIC ARTS KUNG-FU!

CRITICAL BLAST
PUBLISHING

9 781967 199662